# REJECTS PARADISE

Cover Design: Covers by Aura
Photographer: Valua Vitaly
Proofreading: Danielle Stansbury
Editing: Heather Fox
Editing & Formatting: Sheridan Anne

BARBIE
B*tch

*Dedication? Oh, umm ... okay....*


*Blah... Blah... Blah....*

# CHAPTER 1

The sharp edge of the broken wine bottle slices through Jude's flesh and that very first scream of agony is enough to send satisfaction pumping through my veins. The heavy metal door slowly closes and rebounds off the lock with a loud, sharp bang, leaving it propped open with a sliver of light shining through Jude's cold, dungeon.

If I was smart, I'd open the door wide and leave a way out, somewhere to run and make a quick getaway, but not today. All senses of right and wrong left me the second I saw his face.

I won't be walking out of here until this is done. Revenge is a dish served ice-fucking-cold.

No one gets away with putting their hands on me. I've allowed Nic to walk all over me for too long and I won't stand for it anymore.

From now on, I walk on my own two feet and I do it with pride. I deal with my problems, and I will be the one to right the wrongs made against me. I've always seen myself as strong, but I was anything but. I was weak. Defeated. Scared.

Never again. I don't care how sick this makes me. I don't care if it puts me on the same level as Nic. I'm ending this and I'm ending it now. I'm tired of looking over my shoulder and seeing his face in every shadow. I'm sick of remembering the way his hands felt against my body or the way he tore my dress and left me completely defenseless to take what he wanted.

I'm done letting him win.

"Fuck, you little bitch," Jude growls low, his teeth clenching as he pulls hard against the chains keeping him hostage. Blood pours from his thigh and a maniacal grin spreads across my face.

Damn. That felt good.

I tilt my head and let my eyes sparkle with excitement, showing him just how fucked up I can be. "What's wrong, Jude? You don't like that? You don't like me taking whatever the fuck I want?"

"You're fucking insane," he spits at me as I spin the broken wine bottle in my hand and step closer to him, watching as he desperately tries to pull away, scrambling across the cold concrete floor.

A laugh bubbles up my throat. "You know what's fucking insane?" I taunt, brushing the broken glass over his skin, teasing him with the power I hold and loving the way his eyes follow my every little movement. "Thinking you can drug and rape me then walk away without punishment." I lean in, pressing the jagged glass a little harder into his skin and grinning as I pierce it. My voice lowers to a sadistic, twisted whisper. "That's not how this little game is going to play out."

"You won't get away with this," Jude says, his eyes wide and terrified. "My father is going to find out and he's going to have you committed. You'll never walk this town again. You're going to wish you were dead."

Ha. What a joke.

"What's that I hear?" I laugh, tearing my hand back and watching the glass slice through his delicate skin like a warm knife through butter. He cries out and the satisfaction pulsing through my body intensifies. "Hiding behind Daddy's power, money, and sick morals again? But guess what? He can't hear you scream down here."

"You're fucking sick."

"I'm fucking sick?" I grab his shoulders and slam my knee up into his junk, then step back to watch as he falls to the ground, doubling over in agony. He lands in the puddle of blood at his feet and for a slight second, I'm thrown back to the Black Widow's warehouse, watching as two murderers died by the hands of my so-called best friend. They too collapsed into pools of their own blood, right before Nic introduced me to his dark side.

Looking at Jude's pathetic self laying in agony at my feet, I finally get it. Without hesitation, I'm going to end him just like Nic had done to those who had wronged him and I won't stop until the job is done. I deserve peace. I've only been living with this for a few weeks, but what about the other girl he hurt? She's been living with this for who knows how long? She deserves justice just as much as I do, if not more. They laughed at her and claimed she was a liar. They disregarded her pain, embarrassment, and shame.

I won't let him get away with it any longer. People like Jude need to realize that their money won't always speak louder than their crimes. If justice won't get served in a courtroom, then it sure as hell will be served in this old, secret room in the back of Charles' private wine cellar.

I kneel, watching him writhe in pain. "You're scum, Jude Carter. I'm going to enjoy ending you."

A twisted laugh tears out of Jude as he tips his head back to meet my eyes. "I fucking dare you," he taunts.

I narrow my eyes and really take him in. He's skinny and malnourished. It's clear he's been down here since the masquerade party, and it's damn near clear that Colton was the one who put him here. Who else would know about this fucked up little dungeon back here?

Jude has bruises covering his body, both old and new. There are cuts, grazes, burns. All sorts of shit covering him and it's clear that Colton has been taking his frustrations out on him. But why? Is this Colton's way of trying to protect me? All I know is that Colton has known exactly where this asshole has been for the past three weeks and didn't say a fucking word.

He lied to me and that's inexcusable. Unforgivable.

Unforgettable.

As I watch Jude, I see the desperation in his eyes. He wants me to end him. He wants me to slice this jagged glass deep across his throat and end his suffering, and for once, I'm inclined to give him exactly what he wants. But he should know, I won't be doing it without taking what I want first.

He's going to remember me when he's gone. He's going to rot in hell and he's going to know for all of eternity that I was the one who put him there. I'm going to make him wish he never touched me, never even fucking saw me.

"Is that what you want?" I question, leaning toward him. "You want me to kill you? Do you a fucking favor and take away all of your pain?"

"Just do it," he spits with desperation.

"Don't you worry about that," I tease, spinning the wine bottle in my hand again, feeling a piece of my soul darkening to the point of no return. A laugh bubbles up my throat, making me sound like a psychotic serial killer. "I have big plans for that, but the show is only just starting. Do you really think I'm about to skip ahead to the big finale when I haven't had a chance to make you hurt, just like you did to me?"

Jude pulls himself back to his feet and I don't miss the way his knees shake beneath his weight. "You don't have the fucking guts," he says as I straighten myself out to meet him face to face. "Just turn around and fuck off. We both know Colton is going to keep me down here as his little chew toy, so unless you're here to let me finish what I started, then I suggest you go."

I see fucking red.

The jagged edge of the wine bottle slams up into Jude's stomach, the broken glass plunging deep inside of him. "The fuck did you just say to me?" I demand, tearing the bloodied wine bottle out of him.

Jude instantly falls to his knees, his hands clutching at his stomach. They turn red within seconds and his dirty shirt becomes drenched in his own blood. "What's your fucking problem, bitch?" he says, staring down at his hands in shock. "You fucking stabbed me."

"AND YOU FUCKING RAPED ME." The light from the door shines against his shimmering red hands and happiness sparks within my dead soul. I didn't realize how badly I needed that. "But about fucking time, right?" I laugh, wondering what parts of my soul will still be intact when I walk out of here. Maybe I'll lose it all and spend the rest of my days suffering, or maybe I'll sleep like a fucking baby knowing that he'll never be able to touch me again.

For good measure, I swing my hand around and the remains of the wine bottle smash against Jude's temple and he falls to the ground with a heavy thud.

He groans on the ground, clenching his eyes as the pain rocks through him, but I'm not nearly done with him. I've barely even gotten started. "Get up," I demand, kicking my foot out against his ribs. "Be a fucking man and face me." Jude's glare snaps up to mine and it's as though those words hurt more than anything I've done to him like it's some kind of trigger to something much, much deeper, but in the end, all I can do is grin down at him. His issues aren't mine to deal with but I sure as hell will use them against him. "That's your thing, right? You like being the man. You like fucking women and being the big boss in charge. Dominating, overpowering. Forceful. Do you think that's sexy? Do you like being the man?"

"Fuck you."

"I've got news for you," I say, my eyes shimmering with a sick enjoyment. "I'm the fucking man now."

"Really?" he laughs, struggling to push back up to his knees. "You're so much of the man around here that you didn't even know I was down here, did you?"

My eyes narrow and he laughs a little harder as he spits a mouthful of blood onto the concrete. "Oh, I struck a nerve, didn't I? He lied to you. Your precious little guy lied. I wonder what else he hasn't told you. Just imagine all the things I could tell you."

Anger pulses through me and I clench my jaw, momentarily lost for words. Jude shakily gets back to his feet while still clutching his stomach. The side of his lips lift into a sick grin and within the blink of an eye, he grabs me, his heavy chains rattling against the concrete. He pulls me against his body and his bloodied hands mar my skin.

I fight against his hold, but he has me too tight. "Where's your boyfriend now?" Jude questions right in my ear. "I don't hear him coming." He spins me in his arms, wrapping his chains around my neck and holding me still. His hand drops and he cups my pussy, squeezing tight. "There's no one here to stop me now," he taunts. "Colton's going to kill me anyway. I might as well take what I want."

Panic surges through me as the memories of his hands on my body flash through my mind—the sound of my dress tearing, his evil laughter knowing nothing could stop him. My mind was foggy, but I'll never forget the fear. I will never allow that to happen again. I don't give a shit how hard I have to fight. My body is mine to do with as I please and no one will ever take that right away from me again.

My elbow slams back into Jude's stomach and we both go crashing down. I scramble out from under the chains, scraping my knees against the broken glass littering the cold floor. Blood soaks my clothes, but I put it to the back of my mind. I can't think about that yet. I have to end this. That was too close.

My fingers curl around a stray piece of glass and I struggle to hold it as it slips against my bloodied hands.

My pulse thumps loudly in my ears, and my eyes are wide and frantic. I'm losing control.

I rush around him and he keeps his eyes on me, always on me, only now just realizing how far I'll go. I grab a fistful of his hair and tear him up with a strength I didn't realize I was capable of, yanking him back to his knees.

I don't let go. Instead, I yank his head back, exposing his neck the same way I'd watched Nic do. "Are you kidding me? You don't get to touch me."

"Just fucking do it," Jude roars. "Kill me."

I slam my knee into the center of his spine, delighting in the sound that comes tearing out of him. "YOU DON'T THINK I WILL?" I demand. "YOU FUCKING RAPED ME. YOU TOOK MY INNOCENCE. YOU TOOK MY ABILITY TO FIGHT. YOU TORE MY FUCKING DRESS OFF MY BODY AND TOOK

WHAT WASN'T YOURS. I will not allow you to get away with it. You destroyed me, but I can guarantee that I'll be the last woman you will ever touch. You will never hurt anyone ever again, and I don't care if I have to turn into a monster to make that happen. You took the light in my soul, but you will pay for it with your life."

"Fucking chicken shit. JUST DO IT."

I suck in a breath, clenching my jaw as I bring my hand to his neck. The sharp edge presses against his throat, and I watch as it digs into his skin. A trickle of blood runs down his throat and I smile, knowing it will finally be over. "Any last words?"

His blood soaks into the top of his shirt and just as he goes to say whatever the fuck he needs to say, a loud bang in the adjoining wine cellar has my eyes snapping up to the heavy metal door.

I hold my breath, my eyes widening with fear.

"JADE? WHERE THE FUCK ARE YOU?"

Fuck.

Colton.

"Jade? Are you in here?" His voice grows closer and I know it's only a matter of seconds before he finds me. I hear his footfalls. He's moving fast and something tells me he knows exactly where I am. "Ocean?"

My hand shakes against the glass at Jude's throat. Should I do it? Do I just slit his throat and have it over with? What would he think of me if he walks in here and sees me? I'm a fucking monster—just like Jude, just like Nic.

There's a loud creak, and the small sliver of light around the door grows wider. As light floods the room I see Colton standing in the doorway, looking horrified by the stranger he sees before him.

"Ocean," he says slowly, not making any sudden movements as his hazel eyes flick between me and Jude. "What are you doing, baby?"

"I ... I ..." As I meet his eyes, I feel my own filling with tears. The emotions are overwhelming. "I have to end this."

He shakes his head. "No, Jade. You don't."

My brows furrow as I watch him while Jude remains absolutely motionless, hardly even breathing as my shard of glass presses against his throat. "What do you mean?" I cry. "Of course, I do. He raped me. I have to end this. Don't you want that too?"

"Trust me, I do, Jade. I want that more than anybody, but not like this. Not at the risk of you losing yourself. I can't have this on your shoulders. The guilt ..."

"I ..."

"Look at yourself, Ocean. I mean really look at yourself. Look at what you're doing, who you're becoming."

My eyes drop to the shard of glass still clutched tightly between my fingers. Blood covers me from head to toe, drenching my clothes. My heart races like never before, feeling the burn of the cuts and scrapes along my knees and hands for the first time.

I'm a stranger. I don't even recognize myself right now.

Am I seriously about to kill a man? I was terrified after watching Nic do just the same only a week ago. His ruthlessness was enough to make me run and vow to never go back there again. How can I stand here prepared to do the exact same thing? What is wrong with me?

I glance back up and meet Colton's loving gaze, so full of concern. A gasp travels up my throat and the tears continue to stream down my face. My hand shakes and I pull it away from Jude's neck, releasing him into a clump of pain on the floor.

I did that. I tortured him. I cut, stabbed, kicked, and hit him. Who am I? This isn't how I deal with things, this isn't me. I'm not a cold-blooded murderer.

The glass drops from my hand and clatters against the ground, the sound louder than anything I've ever heard.

I run.

I run and I don't look back.

I barge past Colton in the doorway and run through the wine cellar. I all but throw myself back up the stairs in a race for distance. I don't dare stop until I'm as far away from the horrors of Charles' wine cellar as I can possibly get.

# CHAPTER 2

I crash through one of the many bathrooms of the Carrington mansion, hearing the door slam shut behind me with a loud thud. I race to the sink and fall into it, my hands coming down on either side of the white porcelain and leaving bloodied smears on either side.

Tears stream down my face. What have I done?

I look up and meet my reflection in the room-length mirror and see nothing but fear. My eyes are wide and frantic, not the eyes I've gotten so used to over the past seventeen years. I'm a stranger to myself.

If Colton hadn't walked in ... I can't even think about that. What I would have done ... I would have been just like Nic. I would have slit his throat and walked out of there as though nothing had ever happened. I would have cleaned my hands of Jude and wiped him from my memory. I would have been a cold-blooded murderer. I would have killed him and in the process, I would have killed what little of myself still exists.

I turn on the tap and frantically scrub the blood from my hands. The water runs red, splashing up over the sink and onto the vanity, only making me panic that much more. If someone was to walk in and see this mess ... If mom was to walk in ... Fuck. I'd be ruined.

What have I done?

Blood stains under my nails and I struggle to get it out, squirting soap into my hand and scrubbing at my nails over and over again until the blood finally disappears. I wash up my arms and then try to clean my face but the water never runs clean. It's red. Always red.

I step away from the sink and find it covered in Jude's blood from my clothes. Panic surges through me. What am I going to do? It won't go away. It's like a constant reminder of what I nearly did. Who am I?

I tear my shirt over my head and dump it into the bathtub before following it up with my jeans and underwear. I have to get rid of it. If there's anything I've learned from spending the last however many years with the Widows on my doorstep was to always get rid of the evidence. No. Matter. What.

I frantically search through the cupboards and after finding a small box of matches, I turn back to the bathtub. Is this shit even going to light after being soaked in blood? The flames will probably just sizzle out, but I have to try.

I climb up onto the edge of the bathtub and reach the window above. I slide it wide—not wanting to smoke out the bathroom—and drop back onto the marble floor. I look down at the destroyed clothes that hold my darkest secret and lean over it.

I let out a shaky breath and light them up as I struggle to hold back my sobs. I grab a few of the small white hand towels from the cupboard and throw them onto the fire, encouraging it to burn quicker, then stand back and watch as the sobs threaten to suffocate me.

Keeping my eye on the fire, I step into the shower and turn on the taps as hard as they will go. I stand under the scalding water and scrub myself. Once. Twice. Three times.

I do it again and again until the water at the bottom of the shower finally runs clean and all physical traces of what I did to Jude are gone.

How did I become this? I've said for weeks that if I was to find Jude that I'd end him, but never in a million years did I think I had the ability to take it that far.

What is Colton going to think of me now? What he walked in on ... that couldn't have been easy. It would have been the same as me standing back in that warehouse and watching as Nic ended those men's lives. They deserved it completely, just as Jude did, but it doesn't make it any less wrong.

I lowered myself to their standards. I should have fought like a hero, but instead, I fought like a villain. I tortured him; I stabbed him with a broken wine bottle. I kicked him while he was already down. Where's the honor in that? Where's the courage? Where's the fucking humanity?

I should have called the police. I should have had him arrested and taken away. Fuck, what good would that have done? Colton would have ended up in trouble and I refuse to allow that to happen. Colton deserves the chance to explain himself just as Nic and the boys had, and fuck, I'm hoping that what he has to say isn't going to kill me the way the boys did. I can't lose Colton too.

I fall back against the cold tiles of the shower and sink down to the ground. My arms wrap around my knees and I hold myself in a tight ball, wishing I could somehow go back and walk out of the wine cellar without laying a hand on him.

I've always thought that having the courage to deal with your problems meant being ready to end someone. But there is no strength in murder. I was wrong ... Nic is wrong. The fucking boys are wrong. Ending someone like that, that's weak. That's taking the easy way out. An eye for an eye.

I allowed my emotions to run the show instead of playing it smart.

I could have taken him out of there and hand-delivered him to the cops. I could have recorded a confession and had him locked up. There are so many things I could have done. I failed myself, and now I don't know if I'll ever get justice.

My head falls against my knees as the water sprays down over my hair and runs down my back. I wonder what Colton is doing. Is he staying behind to cleanup my mess or is he finishing off Jude himself? Hell, maybe he's out there somewhere trying to work out what the fuck he's going to tell me, how he's going to explain himself. Though, maybe I should be the one thinking about an explanation.

What's he going to think of me? The concern in his eyes was

astronomical. How could he look at me the same after witnessing that? I turned into the one thing I hate. I turned into a monster with no self-control.

I should be in prison. I should be somewhere far, far away from the people I love. I should be suffering. I should be the one lying on the ground in pools of my own blood.

The bathroom door opens and my head snaps up, my eyes wide and frantic, terrified of who's about to walk in here and what they're about to see, but when I find Colton looking back at me, my fears settle.

He walks straight to the shower and opens the glass door, not bothering to strip off his clothes before he steps under the hot water and sinks down beside me. He ignores the shitty fire in the bathtub and pulls me into his arms, but I don't miss how the water runs red again.

My sobs reach their peak and I cry into Colton's neck, neither of us saying a damn word until I'm finally able to calm myself. He pulls me up onto his lap and I hold him closer, needing his comfort, but most of all, needing him. "It's going to be okay," he whispers, his voice barely audible over the sound of the water crashing down against the shower tiles.

"How do you know that?" I question. "I nearly killed a man and not out of self-defense, out of revenge. What does that make me?"

"It makes you human, Jade. It makes you flawed just like the rest of us, but the fact that you were able to stop and pull yourself away, baby, that makes you so fucking strong."

I shake my head, not even close to agreeing with him. "I'm a monster. I did horrible things just to make myself feel better. I wanted revenge. I wanted to make him hurt like he did to me, but it doesn't change anything. The memories are still there, the feel of his hands on my body is still there, the sound of my dress tearing, the fogginess. It doesn't change anything."

"Time," he tells me. "Nothing is going to take it away but time, but until that happens, you can't stop living your life. You can't allow what he did to keep you from moving forward. What he did does not define you, only you can do that, Jade."

"I already know what I am, Colton. What I did ... that's the kind of thing that deserves to have me locked up for the rest of time. I'm just glad you came when you did. If I had ..." I glance away, unable to meet his eyes, letting that thought trail off. "You would have been right, I would have lost myself. I don't think I would have been able to come back from that."

Colton peels the wet hair off my face and forces my eyes back to his. "Don't be afraid of yourself. He hurt you and you did what you had to do to make it easier to get through it. That doesn't make you a monster. You're fucking perfect."

"I'm capable of awful things, Colton. I'm not someone you should be with. I wouldn't blame you if you wanted me to get out of here."

"That's never going to happen. I told you, I'm in this. You're my girl, Jade, and I'm not about to leave you, especially when you're going through this. You are not a monster. You're Oceania Munroe and you're a fucking warrior. You got that?"

My eyes drop and I lean back into him, resting my cheek against his wide chest. "I hate that you saw that."

"I hate that you had to go through any of that at all."

We both fall silent and I listen to his soft breathing as he holds me. "Were you ever going to tell me?" I question, my voice shaky and terrified as I anticipate his answer.

Colton lets out a heavy breath. "I thought about telling you every single day, but the longer it went on, the harder it was. I kept tossing up my options. If I told you, I didn't want you scared that he was so close and I didn't want you to feel as though you had to take matters into your own hands like you did today. I wanted to protect you from that. But not telling you, I ran that risk that you were going to be pissed at me, but also terrified that he could come back for you. It was a lose/lose situation, Jade, so I went with the one that kept you protected. I can live with you hating me for keeping it from you, but I can't live with you hating yourself for something I could have prevented."

I consider every last word before looking up and meeting his eyes. "I wanted to be so mad at you for keeping that from me. I wanted to put you in the same box as Nic and the boys, but it's not the same."

Colton shakes his head. "No, it's not. Yes, I lied to you. I kept the truth from you and that makes me sick. I hate that I've had to keep something so big from you, but I needed to protect you. The Widows ... they lied to protect themselves."

I nod, knowing all too well that he's right. The boys lied to me to protect their stupid gang. They didn't want any of the bullshit coming down on their shoulders. Kian didn't want the truth coming out about my connection to the Wolves, while Nic just wanted to keep me around for his own selfish needs. How am I ever supposed to trust them again? They didn't just lie about what happened, but they lied to me about who I am, and that's not something I can live with. They should have been upfront with me from the start and allowed me the option to make my own damn decisions.

Not wanting to linger on the boys, I stare at the wall over Colton's shoulder. "The clothes Jude was wearing ... they were the same ones he was wearing at the masquerade ball. You've had him down there for three weeks and that fact alone should scare the hell out of me, but after what I just did ... I can't find it in me to pull away from you."

Colton holds me a little tighter. "I don't want you to, Jade. I want you right here. Please don't be afraid of me. I would never hurt you."

"What happened ... after I left. Did you ...?"

"Kill him?" he questions, letting out a heavy breath. "No. I didn't kill him. As much as I wanted to and as much as he begged for it, I didn't. He'll live but he'll be living in a lot of pain for the next few days."

"Why'd you do it?"

"Why'd I not kill him?"

"Why did you lock him down there? You could have handed him over to the police or to Nic."

Colton shakes his head. "I've spent years with Jude by my side and I've watched him get away with atrocious things time and time again. He has no morals, no decent understanding of right and wrong. I watched as he stood back and tried to place blame on other people for things he's done. I've watched as he got out of rape charges and

I've watched as his parents stood back and allowed him to destroy the poor girl who he hurt. His father is powerful and has many of the Bellevue Springs cops in his back pocket. Had Jude been taken to the police, he would have gotten away with it again and I wasn't about to let that happen to you. Nic would have shot him between the eyes and he wouldn't have suffered for what he did. I have stood by far too long. I know every awful thing he's ever done and I wasn't going to hand him over to Nic until I made sure that he paid for every little thing he did."

"I'm assuming that what I did kinda tops this list?"

Colton presses his lips into a light line and nods before taking my face gently in both hands and tilting my head down to press a kiss to my forehead. "What can I say?" he says with a small shrug. "You've always been one for the dramatics."

A tear rolls down my cheek and he instantly wipes it away. "You're going to be okay, Ocean. Just stay away from the wine cellar and you won't have to think about it. Just go about your day pretending he's not down there. There's no reason for you to beat yourself up over this."

"He was defenseless, Colton. In heavy chains and already skin and bones, bruised, and beat up. I'm not going to be able to forget what I did any time soon."

"In that case, revel in it. You kicked his ass while he was down. You took away his will just as he did to you. He drugged and raped you and took what he wanted. It's called karma and when karma comes around with a face like yours, she's a fucking bitch."

I smile even though I shouldn't. "I can get on board with that," I murmur.

"Good."

His hands slip around me again, pulling me into his chest, pulling me home, and I let out a soft sigh. "So, what now?"

Colton shrugs his shoulders. "I don't know," he tells me. "I can't say that I've ever held someone hostage before. I guess we wait and see if he lives through to morning and then take it day by day. I can't let him go, Ocean. I can't risk him doing it again and I can't risk him talking to the police."

"He won't go to the police. *He* can't risk that."

"True. What do you think?"

"I think we have no choice but to do what I've always wanted to do. We hand him over to Nic."

"Nic will end it. Are you okay with that?"

I bite down on my lip, really thinking about it. I wasn't okay with being the one to end it, I wasn't strong enough, but am I okay with still being responsible for his death? I don't know. "Can I let you know?"

"Of course, Jade," he whispers, leaning in and pressing a soft kiss to my lips. "Are you going to be alright?"

I shrug. "Can I let you know about that too?"

Colton nods. "Do you want to stay with me tonight?"

I look up and meet his deep, loving eyes. "Is that alright?"

"I wouldn't have it any other way."

I fall back into his chest and smile against his warm skin. "Uh, Jade?" he questions. "I know you're sort of going through something here, but did you want to put that fire out? You're kinda burning the ceiling and my bedroom is above this."

Oh, fuck.

I get up off the shower floor and Colton raises behind me, reaching for a massive white towel that he wraps around me. I turn off the shower as he peels off his wet clothes and as I dry myself off, he deals with the fire in his bathtub, knowing damn well that he's going to have to have someone come in to replace the ceiling.

"Sorry," I murmur, looking up at the damage I've caused. "I was trying to get rid of the evidence."

"It's alright, Jade. It's nothing I can't fix."

I find a silk robe and pull it on, dropping the towel in the hamper. "How did you know I was down there?" I question as Colton grabs a towel of his own and quickly dries off before wrapping the towel around his narrow waist.

"My mom," he admits with a cringe. "She came to tell me about your little … run in. She mentioned that she'd sent you down to Dad's personal wine cellar and the second the words came out of her mouth, I ran."

I cringe. "I forgot about that bitch," I say, not in the mood to mask my opinion of his mother, though, from his carefree response, I'd dare say his opinion isn't too far from mine.

"I don't blame you," he says. "But don't worry, knowing her, she'll be gone in no time."

I nod and let out a breath, trying my hardest to file all this bullshit away in my brain and not allow it to continue eating me up. "So, Spencer?" I ask as Colton reaches for the door handle and opens it for me. "He knew about this the whole time?"

Colton nods and I stop in the middle of the open doorway to look up at him. "That phone call you made after Jude … in your room. You called Spencer just before I passed out."

He nods again. "He helped me move him."

"And Charlie?" I question. "I'm assuming he doesn't know seeing as though he keeps trying to find him?"

"Yeah, Charlie … he's too good. He has a kind heart. This shit would destroy him."

"And when he finds out?"

Colton sighs and slips his arm around my waist before leading me out of the bathroom and up the hall, both of us desperately ignoring the drops of blood that lead the whole way back to the wine cellar. "I guess we'll cross that bridge when we get to it."

# CHAPTER 3

The early morning sun beams through Colton's bedroom window as I stare up at the ceiling, just as I've been doing for the past twelve hours. Neither of us has slept as the heaviness of yesterday afternoon weighs on our hearts, bodies, and minds.

The emotions, the fear, the unknown—they're all so real and I have no idea how to handle it. One part of me wants to run through this stupid mansion screaming at the top of my lungs, tearing my hair out, and searching for the goodness that I lost while the other part wants to go down to the wine cellar dungeon and finish the job. At least that way I know it would be over, but I'll be condemning myself to a lifetime of guilt that's bound to have me turning myself in and spending my days behind bars.

I can't do that to myself. I can't allow Jude to win. It seems that no matter what decision I make, he's always going to get the better of me. Just like he did the night he raped me, just like every time I'm alone in a dark room and the fear cripples me when I see his face, and just like he did yesterday. No matter what I do, Jude is always going to win.

How am I supposed to get through every day knowing that my rapist is in the same house, breathing the same air and getting to live? I should have ended him, made it easier for myself to breathe. Fuck the guilt. I would have found a way to live with it. I should have slit his … fuck.

Who am I?

I don't even recognize myself anymore. I guess Nic and the boys will be proud. I've finally come to the dark side. There's no need for them to keep their dirty little secrets anymore because now there's no goodness left to protect. I'm just like them.

Colton held me all night just as I knew he would but I don't deserve it. I don't deserve the happily ever after that he wants to offer me. How could he even want that after what he saw? I don't doubt that he's been processing it all night and soon enough, he's going to start pulling away. It only makes sense.

What kind of man wants to be with a woman who's going to murder him when he fucks up? Burnt the dinner? Get an ass-whooping. Forget to do the dishes? How about a puncture wound? Look at another woman? Would you like a side of slit throat with your pasta?

Fuck this. I couldn't really be capable of being such a monster, could I? If Colton hadn't walked in … yeah, I would have done it and I would have paid for it for the rest of my life. Colton may have saved me from myself yesterday, but exactly how much did I lose in the process?

Colton's arm pulls tighter around me as he draws me closer into his warm side. "Did you get any sleep?"

I shake my head. "No, I just … I couldn't stop thinking about it."

"Which part? What actually happened or if he made it through the night?"

I let out a heavy sigh and nuzzle my face into his chest. "Does it make me a bad person that over the past twelve hours, I haven't even considered the possibility that he might not make it through the night?" I groan as the guilt triples in size. "I'm such a selfish bitch. I nearly killed a guy and all I can think about is how it affects me. Fuccck."

"Jade, come on. We talked about this. You have nothing to worry about. You're beautiful inside and out. He deserved what was coming for him and I'm not about to let you start hating on yourself because of it. If you think you're bad then the shit I've done to him over the past three weeks … shit, babe. You don't even want to know just how dark it can get. To me, you're still fucking perfect and there's nothing you could do to Jude Fucking Carter that's going to change that."

I lift my face from his chest and meet his eyes. "You mean that?"

"So fucking much."

I scramble up onto him, straddling his waist and meeting his warm, inviting gaze. "So, you're telling me that you're even more fucked-up than I am?"

A grin tears across his face and he pulls me down to him. "You've got no fucking idea," he murmurs just moments before his lips crush against mine.

He kisses me deeply, giving me exactly what I need to get my mind off Jude even if it's only for a second. His large hand slides down my waist until he's firmly gripping my ass, squeezing it tight and sending a thrilling warmth through my body.

I pull away, not exactly in the mood to fuck around. "I should probably go and get ready for school."

"Are you sure?" he questions, sitting up and pulling me up with him. "You don't have to go. I can take the day off and we can stay right here until your mom comes and busts my balls for being a bad example and keeping you from your education."

I shake my head, so clearly able to picture Mom doing just that. "No, it's fine," I tell him, raising my hand to his cheek and feeling his warm skin brush beneath my fingers. "The past few weeks have been so insane. I just want everything to go back to normal … or at least, whatever normal is now. Besides, you have so much to do. I'm not going to be responsible for putting you behind."

"Hey, I'm the CEO, remember? The man in charge, the fucking boss. I make the rules around here and if I want a day off with my girl, then I can take a fucking day with my girl. The work can wait."

I lean into him and brush my lips over his, so fucking thankful to have him in my life. "Thank you," I whisper. "You have no idea how much that means to me, but I'm fine. I can manage a day at school without causing issues or trying to kill anyone. You don't need to babysit me." Colton raises a brow and I roll my eyes at his silent lack of faith. "Really. I'll be okay. What's the worst that's going to happen? I fall asleep during my classes and get detention?"

Colton sighs and gets out of bed before striding across the room and peeling his shirt off. "Okay," he calls, stepping into the bathroom. "But don't say that I didn't warn you. You're going to have a better day with me, but if you insist on suffering through calculus then that's on you."

I roll my eyes and follow him to the bathroom. I stand in the doorway, watching as he drops his pants to take a shower. "I'm going to go."

"Okay," he says, walking over to me in his six-foot whatever deliciously naked glory. A somber expression filters over his handsome face as his hazel eyes zone in on mine. "I'm going to run down and check on Jude. I'll let you know how he's doing." I nod and he continues. "You know you can call me, right? If your day sucks or anything. I'll come and get you."

My hands fall to his strong chest as I push up onto my tippy-toes and gently kiss him. "A girl could really get used to this sweet version of Colton Carrington."

"Sweet?" he laughs. "Jade, you've got it all wrong. I'm just reeling you in. Getting you exactly where I want you and then when you're too invested to walk away, the real me will come out."

"Ugh," I groan, stepping out of his arms and turning away. Just as I go to start walking, a delicious sting hits my ass followed by the sound of his joyful laughter. I walk to his bedroom door, trying my hardest not to allow him to pull me back in. "You killed the moment."

I look back over my shoulder to find him watching me with a sparkle in his eyes. He winks and everything south of the border clenches, making me walk faster because if I stay here a second longer, I won't be emerging from his room until we're both utterly exhausted and raw.

"What can I say?" Colton grins, leaning against the doorframe of the bathroom. "That'll teach you to call me sweet."

I roll my eyes and push out of his room before I decide to show him just how sweet I can be, but as I step out into the hallway, I instantly regret my decision not to spend a little longer with Colton.

One of his bratty twin sisters strides down the hallway and her glare instantly settles on me, but more importantly, the room I just stepped out of. "What do you think you're doing in there?" she snaps, her eyes dropping to my hands to make sure I wasn't trying to steal something.

I resist rolling my eyes and push out in front of her, ignoring her lethal stare that tears into my back like a deadly laser beam. My hands pump in fists by my sides as I take three slow, calming breaths. I had completely forgotten about the bitch twins and their fearless leader, Momma Carrington. Colton briefly reminded me of their existence last night, but they're just so forgettable. It was like going in one ear and straight out the other.

Maybe it'll be better to stay home with Colton after all. I can only imagine how his sisters are going to make life for me at school. Though unluckily for them, I have the girls at school tied around my little finger and unlike the bitch twins, they like me for me, not for what I can offer.

I practically race down the stairs, determined to get as far away from Colton's little sister as possible. That's probably going to be my life now. They're going to be everywhere that I go so I'm either going to have to learn to keep my mouth shut or avoid them at all costs. Seeing as though biting my tongue is like asking for world peace, the avoiding thing is going to be my best option.

I hear her ridiculous heels on the marble stairs behind me and I roll my eyes. She's dressed for school, but does she seriously think those heels are going to get her far? She looks even more stuck up than ever before. She just needs to pair it with a Birkin bag and she'll be all set to head to school in her over-the-top McLaren 720S.

Geez, how simple would life be to be one of the rich and famous? Imagine never having to worry about paying bills or getting through every day knowing you'll be coming home to a hot meal, warm water, and electricity.

Damn. How do I get myself there without selling my soul?

Ignoring the frustrating heels clicking against the marble floor, I make my way through the mansion then have to physically restrain myself when I hear her high-pitched wail coming from the kitchen. "Where's my breakfast? Maryne always had it ready for me. You'll never be as good as her."

I clench my jaw. That better not be my mother she's talking to.

I pause, my feet coming to an abrupt stop as I listen, waiting for a response. "I'm sorry, Miss Cora," one of the maids hurries out. "I will get it for you right away."

Cora's scoff is audible even from two rooms away, but knowing it's not my mom has the fire easing within me. Though don't get me wrong, that shit still isn't acceptable, but it's not my fight. I have a feeling I'll be having plenty of rounds with the twins so the more I can put it off, the better. Besides, those maids have had to learn to have the Carrington's comments bounce off them, though it's been a while since they've actually had to deal with them.

Keeping myself moving, I head out to the pool house and although I spent a good hour sitting in the shower yesterday, I find myself desperate for another. I dump my clothes in the doorway of the bathroom and hurry through a quick shower, washing my hair and scrubbing at my body as though I can still feel his blood all over my skin.

Twenty minutes later, I sit on the edge of my bed, staring at my reflection in the floor to ceiling mirror, and feeling like a stranger in my own skin. So much has been going on, so much change that I hardly even recognize myself anymore. I've had to grow up a lot since coming here just over a month ago, but the person I'm becoming? I don't think I know her.

Today is a chance for a fresh start. I'm going back to school now knowing everything there is to know and I can finally start to put it all behind me and focus on my future. You know, apart from the whole 'who killed my father and Charles' thing, not to mention that I still don't know why the Widows' mark was on the front of that folder.

I showed up at the warehouse demanding answers—though so many were revealed—one massive question still burns the back of my mind despite all that's happened to distract from it.

Why was that mark on the folder? Nic confirmed that my dad was a Wolf, and a fucking bad one at that. He told me how my father had sold me to pay a debt with Charles Carrington but none of that actually explains why their mark was on the folder.

Hell, I even asked Kian if he was responsible for killing my father and he was adamant that he and his Widows didn't lay a finger on him, and for some reason, I trust that. The look in Kian's eyes told me that he would have loved to be the one to do it. He would have taken pleasure in ending Louis Munroe's life, and hell, he even looked a little pissed that he didn't get to be the one to do it. Kian was the kind of man to boast, he would have sung it from the rooftops, and had my father been as important as Nic and Kian made him out to be, he would have made sure that every last person knew it was him. He would have worn my father's murder like a trophy.

I let out a frustrated sigh, unanswered questions only mean one thing—there's a trip to Breakers Flats in my near future, but I can assure anyone who asks, that it will be done far, far away from Nic.

I don't know what's gotten into him lately, he's so ... possessive. It's borderline obsessive and I don't think I have room for that shit in my life. I don't understand it. Nic has been so chill since we broke up six months ago. There have been plenty of random hookups at parties and he's never said a word, never really cared. He would always pop in to remind me that he was my end game and I'd smile and nod which would satisfy that wildness within him, but things are changing. I think he can sense that whatever this thing is with Colton is something real and now that it's suddenly official, he sees me slipping further away and he's aiming all that frustration at me.

I wonder if he even realizes just how crazy he sounds when he comes over here and demands that I go home with him? Does he realize that he's losing it? Losing me?

As for my boys, they're just as much a mystery to me. Not only have they been lying to me about who I really am, but they're allowing Nic to get away with that behavior. If anything, they're encouraging it. It was only a short time ago that had Nic even thought about leaving a bruise on my skin, the boys would have annihilated him. It doesn't make sense to me anymore. Do they not care about me like they once did? Hell, did they even care about me at all?

I don't get it. Everything is changing and right now, we're in this place of unknown and I hate it. I hate not knowing what's going through their minds. I've always been so in sync with the four of them but right now, I've never felt so far away.

I promised myself that after that night, I'd never go back there again. I said that I was done with them, but now that the anger has worn off, I really don't know where I stand. One thing is sure, things between me and Nic will never be the same. Hell, maybe after last night's dungeon activities, I have a deeper understanding of their darkness and I'll slip right back into where I've always belonged. After all, I'm just like them now, just like my father. They should be so proud.

"Ocean?" My mother's concerned tone tears through my bedroom and my eyes snap up to realize that I've just been sitting here for who the hell knows how long, completely lost to the torture of my own mind. Mom steps into my room, her eyes narrowed in suspicion. "What's wrong, honey? Something seems … off?"

I can't help the scoff that travels up my throat and sounds loudly through my room, an instant confirmation that something has been going on. "It's nothing, Mom. You don't need to worry."

She steps further into my room and it's almost as though some kind of possessed spirit enters her body. "Oceania Elaine Munroe, you tell me what's been happening with you this very minute before I force it out of you."

I swallow back the hint of fear that arises every time my mother takes this tone with me. It used to work like a lucky charm when I was a kid but as I got older, it lost its magic. Though it never ceases to take me back to my childhood, being the scared kid who was about to get an ass whooping for coming home with three detention slips from the same class in third grade. This tone used to have my every last confession slipping from between my lips but as I look up and meet her eyes, I realize that I can't tell her this.

My mother is sweet and innocent, she has a kind heart and is the most generous woman I've ever met. I can't darken her soul by telling her what Jude did to me, I can't tell her about dad and crush her heart, and I sure as hell can't tell her what I did to Jude last night. I won't do that to her. I'd prefer to carry the burden on my own.

I stand up and grab my school bag off the floor. It gets pulled over my shoulder before I step into Mom and wrap my arms around her.

"Honestly, I'm fine," I tell her. "There's really no need to worry. I'm just nervous about the trouble that Casey and Cora are going to cause today at school."

"Oh," Mom says, drawing back to meet my eyes. "Are you sure that's it? It seemed like something was really bothering you. Bitchy high-school girls have never been something to get you down before."

I shrug my shoulders and give her a tight smile. "What can I say?" I tell her, grinning as I used Colton's exact words that he'd said to me this morning. "These are Colton's little sisters. I have to play this smart. Now, unless you're ready to tell me all about how Hendrix's father was trying to sweep you off your feet on Saturday night, then I better go. Milo should be here any minute and I don't want to be late."

Mom's lips press into a tight line as she steps back, giving me room to walk past her. "For the record," she says. "He wasn't trying to sweep me off my feet. We were just two people having a nice time together."

I raise my brow and together we walk through the pool house. "Uh-huh."

Mom shakes her head, not ready to get into this with me. "Get out of here, trouble maker. I'll see you after school."

With that, I walk out towards the main house, looking back over my shoulder and blowing my mother a kiss. "Love you," I tell her with a cheesy grin. "Try not to fall for any other rich eligible bachelors while I'm gone."

# CHAPTER 4

I'm halfway down the massive front steps of the Carrington mansion when Milo's shiny Aston Martin comes to a stop at the bottom. He looks up at me through his tinted window and I give him a beaming smile that feels more than fake on my lips.

I continue down to him and as his window slides down, a familiar voice sounds from behind me. "Jade."

I stop halfway down the stairs and turn back to look up at Colton, having to shade my eyes from the bright early morning sun that stares directly into my eyes. "Yeah?"

Colton's gaze flashes down to Milo, and he lifts his chin in greeting before glancing back at me with a strange wariness in his eyes. "I, uh

… checked on that thing," he says discreetly.

I raise a brow, my interest more than piqued. "Yeah?" I question slowly, feeling my heart beginning to race in my chest. I hold my breath, anxious to hear what he has to say. His response could change it all. It's one thing beating a man to near death but actually killing him? Fuck, I know I've dreamt about taking his life over and over again but actually doing it? That's a dark road, one I'll never come back from.

"It's wounded," he says. "But it's going to be okay."

A weight lifts off my shoulders and for the first time since running out of that stupid little dungeon, I feel myself able to take a deep breath. Is what I did okay? No, not by a long shot but can I live with the fact that all I did was hurt him? Hell yes, I can.

I let out a shaky breath, not really knowing what to say but as I glance back up at Colton to find his lips pulling into an encouraging smile, my world finally begins to fall back into place. "There's my girl," he murmurs from the top of the stairs. "I'd thought I'd lost you for a while."

His eyes are warm and fuck, I've never seen them so full of love. Just like that I know that no matter the outcome of what happened to Jude, Colton wouldn't have looked at me any differently, and honestly, I don't know whether that's a good thing or not. But for now, it's so much more than I could have asked for.

I smile up at him. "Is it wrong that I kinda want to celebrate? I mean, that's kinda twisted, right?"

"So fucking twisted," he laughs before spreading his arms wide. "My offer still stands though. If you want to stay here, I'm more than happy to spend the day helping you celebrate."

I roll my eyes and walk down a few more stairs before glancing back over my shoulder. "I told your stubborn ass already, I'm going to school to play damage control from your sisters and there's no changing my mind."

"Have it your way," he says darkly. "But just know, my offer won't last all day."

"Bullshit," I grumble, skimming over the fact that he didn't call me out on my comment about his sisters, and didn't even try to deny it. We both know it's going to happen so there's no point pretending that it won't. Though, the fact that he also didn't warn me to play fair also speaks volumes. "You and I both know that you're going to spend your day thinking of all the ways you can torture me for turning you down and when I finally get home from school this afternoon, you're going to be more than ready to go."

Colton scoffs and takes a step back toward the open front door. "Get your ass to school, Jade."

His lips pull into an affectionate smile and for the first time since that stupid dungeon, I feel myself actually giving a real smile, not the fake one I've offered everyone else, but a full-on, beaming one that comes straight from my heart. "I'll see you later."

Colton winks and with that, turns on his heel and stalks back inside his overgrown mansion. I look down at Milo and find my pace picking up, suddenly feeling a million times better. I have a renewed energy to help me through the day and I'm sure as hell going to need it.

"What the hell was that about?" Milo asks through his now open window when I finally reach the bottom step.

I skip around to the passenger's seat and pull open the door. "Oh, nothing," I say, glancing away and refusing to meet his eyes. Knowing he's too curious for his own good, I give him a shitty explanation, one that I hope he won't question. "I went for a drive last night and accidentally hit a stray. Colton checked in with the vet this morning and it looks like the dog is going to make it."

"Oh, that's a relief," he says, putting his Aston Martin in gear and hitting the gas just as my door slams behind me. I hardly click my seatbelt into place before we're halfway down the drive and my back is crashing into the soft leather of the passenger seat.

"You've got no idea," I tell him.

He reaches down between us and hits a few buttons, rolling the windows down and blasting music through the car. "You're in a good mood this morning," I comment, finding his steering wheel drum solo and carefree attitude refreshing after the bullshit weekend I've suffered through.

Milo shrugs his shoulders and glances over at me for the shortest second but it's enough to see the sparkle hitting his eyes. "Out with it," I tell him. "What happened?"

His lips press into a tight line and I watch his inner battle to keep his mouth shut over the excruciating need to tell someone what's been going on. "Fuck. Okay," he finally says after the shortest pause. "I fucked around with Jess again last night."

"WHAT?" I screech, slamming my hand down between us and adjusting the volume. I need to hear every little word of this and I need to make sure I hear it right. "What do you mean you fucked around with Jess? What happened to your big declaration of eating dicks for breakfast, lunch, and dinner?"

Milo's hands flap around on the steering wheel, the frustration in his actions loud and clear. "I don't fucking know. I do love that. I love it so hard, but Jess …" A dreamy look appears in his eyes before his lips twist into an odd smirk. "You know she does this thing with her tongue that—"

"Okaaaay," I cut him off before he can get too descriptive. "That's more than enough information out of you."

He lets out a heavy sigh, and I glance back at him. "I think you're right," he tells me, almost sounding disappointed. "I think I'm bi. All this time I've been so certain that I was just into dudes. I didn't stop to consider that chicks could do it for me too. Though … I don't know. It's not quite the same thrill that I get from being with a guy. I definitely prefer dick to a tight vag."

I stare across at him, wondering how my day can go from talking about murdering a rapist with Colton to going over a pros and cons list with Milo and trying to work out his sexual preferences all before 9 am. "Well then, maybe it's just Jess that has a little something special. I mean, she kinda walks like a dude and has oddly broad shoulders for a girl."

Milo rolls his eyes. "I don't know," he says, seriously confused about what's going on with himself. "No, I … I don't know. Maybe I am just gay but like to fuck around with her for fun."

"Maybe," I say. "Do you get hard at the thought of fucking me?"

His eyes bug out of his head and he gapes at me in horror. "No," I snap, cutting off his bullshit response before it can come streaming from between his lips. "Just think about it before jumping to your go-to horrified rejections. Really think about it."

Milo's lips bunch up and he glances out through the windshield, watching the traffic as he drives. "I, um …" he starts, really thinking about his response. He shakes his head. "No, don't take this the wrong way, you're fucking bomb. I've never met a sexier chick with the hottest fucking body. I'm sure guys all over the world are dreaming about giving you a cream pie, but no … just no. I couldn't. I can't. Vaginas are just so … ugh. They're fucking weird. I mean, they're not remotely sexy."

I roll my eyes, skipping over that last comment because fuck him, my vagina is so fucking sexy that I'd turn lez for it if I could. After all, I've fucked it more than anyone else has, but I'm not about to tell him that. Though after Colton walked in on me in my bedroom that one time, I'm pretty sure that's not such a big secret. I look back up at Milo and raise a brow. "So, they're not sexy but you'll fuck Jess?"

Milo groans low, his emotions all over the place. "What the fuck is wrong with me? Am I fucking sick?"

"No," I laugh. "There's nothing wrong with you. You're just confused. Why do you even need to define it? Who cares what you are. You like dicks but every now and then, the right pussy comes along and you don't mind fucking that too. Who cares? Just go with it."

"Just go with it?" he questions, dumbfounded.

I roll my hand out like a wave. "Just go with."

"That easy, huh?"

"So fucking easy."

"Fine," he finally agrees, relaxing heavily against his seat as he steers his Aston Martin toward my fancy new private school for girls. "I'll just go with it. From now on, I dip my fingers into both pies."

"That's the spirit."

"But I'm not going crazy," he warns. "I'm not about to do a Charlie and start fucking everything with a pulse. I'll stick to the blueberry pie but occasionally take a bite of a cherry pie. You know, if it's on offer."

I shake my head, wondering if he used blueberry and cherry as metaphors but realize that this is Milo I'm talking to and of course, it was intentional. "You know, sometimes I wonder what it'd be like living inside your mind. It'd be an interesting place."

"Oh, you don't know the half of it, babe. I've learned to filter everything that comes out of my mouth so I stop scaring people away. It can get a lot worse."

"You're telling me that pie shit was filtered?"

His lips pull up into a sly grin and as he looks over at me with a sparkle in his eye. I realize that I probably don't want to know the unfiltered version. I can only imagine how bad it gets.

Milo pulls up to the front gates of Bellevue Springs Private school and within seconds, I spy the devil twins being welcomed in by their long lost bitch friends. Girls crowd around the famous Carrington twins and a scowl instantly settles onto my face.

Milo turns in his seat, raising a brow as he shoots daggers at me. "You mean to tell me that the fucking wicked witches of the west are back and you just forgot to mention it?"

"I …" I cringe. "I mean, I had a lot going on with the whole running over that stray dog thing last night …"

"Not even a quick text to say 'Hey Milo, guess what? Bitch one and bitch two are home to destroy my life.' Jesus, Ocean. Where's your head at?"

"Sorry," I say, scrunching my face. "They showed up yesterday afternoon and declared that they're going to ruin me and after Momma Carrington basically said that she was going to take Colton away from me, I kinda forgot they existed."

"Dammmmn," he grumbles, leaning back in his seat and watching out the window at the over-the-top display playing out before us. "I have a feeling shit is about to get interesting."

"I can guarantee it. I don't doubt that they've already started spreading whatever awful rumors they've cooked up."

"I can only imagine. They would have sat up all night with notepads and pens working out some ridiculous little plan to humiliate you, and I can assure you, it's going to be epic. These girls don't come to play, they come to win."

I raise my brow and give Milo a silent reminder of who the hell he's talking to. "You're right," he continues. "They can't touch you. I mean, they can. They can say a million kinds of awful things but it's going to take a fucking army to take you down."

"And what don't they have?"

"An army."

"Exactly. I have the school at my back. They've been gone for too long, so let them say what they need to say because, in the end, their little games aren't going to work. They can't touch me."

"God, I wish I had your balls."

A knock sounds at Milo's window and both our heads whip around to find Jess bending down, trying to peer through the dark tint of the window. "Argh," Milo grunts, looking back at her smiling face in horror. "What do I do? Make it go away."

"Hell no. This is far too entertaining," I laugh, crawling over Milo's lap and finding the button for the window. "Hell, why don't you take the morning off and get your dick sucked instead."

"Ocean," he snaps.

"Too late." The window goes down and I grin up at Jess who gives me a strange look for being sprawled out all over her little chew toy's lap. "Hey girl," I smile, grabbing the door handle and swinging it open. "Come around. Take my place."

I climb over Milo as Jess happily squeals and hurries around to the passenger side. "I'm going to fucking kill you," he grumbles before groaning when I accidentally knee him in the balls. "Get the fuck out of here."

"I'm trying," I laugh, getting stuck and having to swan dive through the open door, landing on the pavement, then scrambling to my feet and fixing my skirt. I get all of one second to grin widely at Milo before my school bag comes hurtling towards my chest. I catch it with a grunt and don't even get a chance to laugh at Milo before the Aston Martin is peeling away from the curb with Jess' high-pitched squeal telling me she'll see me later.

With Milo and Jess out of the way, I focus my energy on getting through the school gates without getting mauled by bitchy comments and nasty glares. Putting one foot in front of another, I make it through the gates, but not without the stares of my fellow peers, but they're not the stares that Casey and Cora were hoping I'd get.

Just as I'd suspected, the devil twins have gotten here early to spread the word that there's a war brewing. But the girls at BSP aren't looking at me as though I'm the enemy, they're watching me with excitement, with power, knowing damn well that if anyone was going to take them down, it's going to be me. If they aren't looking at me like that, then they're sitting back to watch the show, because I can guarantee that the Carrington twins going up against their brother's girlfriend will be the talk of the town.

This is the kind of shit that reality TV shows are made of. I should be checking out all these girls and figuring out which one has a daddy in entertainment law. I bet this could make me as big as a Kardashian. I wonder what kind of paycheck goes along with that?

The locker beside mine closes with a loud bang and I jump, whipping my head around to find Hendrix staring back at me with a wide grin. "Oh, girl. What kind of shit have you gone and got yourself involved in now? The rumors going around about you … dammmmn."

I close my locker and let out a frustrated sigh. "Let's hear it," I tell her, falling against the cool metal of my locker. "What are the devil spawns saying about me?"

# CHAPTER 5

By the time lunch rolls around, I've created a mental list of all the things being said about me and I have to give it to the devil twins, they're creative. But so far, their little lies aren't enough to have the student body believing a word they say. They're at least twenty different rumors going around, and every single one of them is just a little too dramatic. Eyes seem to roll when a new rumor pops up, everyone knows it's just a little more fuel on the fire.

There's the usual 'she's pregnant' rumors, the 'she's transexual' ones that come from being enrolled in BSA for my first few weeks in Bellevue Springs, then of course, the obvious 'she's fucking Colton to get ahead in life' rumors.

None of them hold any merit and as the girls at this school have gotten to know me over the past few weeks, they've come to learn this shit isn't enough to faze me. All of it is too obvious, too much too soon.

The bitches only just arrived back at the school and within seconds, rumors are flying like announcements being made. If they wanted to make it believable, they should have waited a few days and then spread it like Chinese whispers so the gossipy girls would take their word for it. Instead, they just look like a bunch of bitches, annoyed that their big brother's attention is somewhere else. Besides, the girls of this school would rather hang onto me with my connection to Colton than be on the side that's so clearly against him.

I drop into my seat in the cafeteria and take a bite of my sandwich as Drix drops down beside me. "Girl," she laughs. "Have you heard the latest rumor?"

I groan and roll my eyes before glancing over at her. "Is this one actually worth mentioning or is it some stupid shit about being abused as a child?"

"Oh no, nothing like that," she tells me. "They're starting to get a little more creative."

"Oh, yeah?" I question, actually intrigued for once.

Drix nods. "Yeah, so the word is that you were booted out of BSA because you were having an affair with that PE teacher that got arrested."

"Hmm," I say, thoughtful, trying not to gag at the thought of getting with that predator. "That one's got a little bit of merit. It's certainly more entertaining than the pregnant one and would leave someone wondering. I give it a solid six out of ten. Though, they would have earned extra points if they combined the pregnant rumor with that one. Now that's a scandal that would have got the student body talking, but in reality, they're only doing me a favor by highlighting the very real issues within that school."

"Right?" she laughs. "They really haven't thought this one through. But I'm not done yet. It gets a little juicier."

I wave my hand out, inviting her to continue. "Then what are you waiting for? Hit me with it."

Hendrix laughs, knowing all too well that these rumors have been bouncing straight off me. I mean, after spending my night fretting that I was maybe a murderer and having Nic and the boys tear my life apart with the truth of who I am, a little scandalous rumor isn't going to hurt me.

"So, you were screwing the old PE teacher and then dobbed him in when you thought you were going to get caught, but instead of having the Dean kick you out back then, you started screwing him too and that's why he allowed you to stay there for so long."

"Ewwwww. Dean Simmons? He's balding, fat, and has a sweaty, body odor issue."

"I know," she laughs. "but don't worry, that one won't stick either. As if anyone is going to believe you were dropping your panties for them when you were screwing around with guys like Milo, Charlie, and Colton."

"You know I never actually screwed Milo, right? We're just friends."

A knowing grin spreads across her face and she gently nudges me with her elbow. "Uh-huh. Really, *really* good friends."

I roll my eyes. Clearly, she thinks I'm holding back on that one but whatever, it really doesn't matter. The more girls that people think Milo's been with, the better for his whole 'hiding out in his closet' thing he's got going on.

Realizing I'm not about to give her anymore to go off, she moves the conversation along but the excited sparkle in her eyes instantly puts my nerves on edge. "You know, I think our parents really hit it off at the Gatsby party. Who knows, we could be sisters one day."

"Oh, geez," I laugh. "Don't get ahead of yourself. They danced for a little while and had dinner together. It's not as though they were planning their wedding."

"I don't know," she says with a shrug, looking down at her lunch. "You don't know my dad like I do. He was so into her. To him, that's pretty much a done deal."

I raise my brow as I look back at Hendrix with a million thoughts roaming through my mind, every single one of them wondering if Mom is even ready for something like this. "Are you sure? Because I haven't seen my mom like that for ages. She was practically shining with him. My dad only died eight months ago, and that's still really fresh for her, for both of us, but at the same time, I want her to be happy. If your dad could make her happy …"

A seriousness comes over her and she looks at me as though she's diving right into the bottom of her heart to find the right words. "You know, my dad is a real genuine guy and if your mom isn't ready and whatever they felt on Saturday night is real, then I really think he'd wait. He's not the kind to screw a woman around and to be really honest with you, I haven't seen him happy like that in a really long time."

"Really?"

"Yeah," she whispers. "As long as your mom feels the same too, then I think this could actually turn into something."

"All this from just one night together?"

"Just think about how romantic it would be. It's literally a *Cinderella* story. They met at the ball and everything."

"I'd hardly call the Gatsby party a ball."

"True, but around here, it's probably the closest we'd ever get."

"Bullshit," I laugh. "If I even hinted to Colton that I wanted to go to some fancy ball, he'd have the party planners and caterers there within minutes."

"Good point," she laughs. "That guy has got it bad for you."

I can't help the warm, fond smile that stretches across my face. "Yeah, he kinda does, doesn't he?"

"Understatement of the year," she tells me. "We might not have really known each other during that masquerade ball but I was there, and I saw the way he danced with you, everyone did. And then that kiss … fuck me, if only I was that lucky. Everyone here knows what you mean to each other. There's no denying it. At every party and even on that boat right at the beginning, he watches you. He's so aware of everything that you do. You two are like a real-life *Romeo and Juliet*."

I gape at her. "*Romeo and Juliet* died at the end of the story."

"Yeah, well, take out that part and the whole families at war thing and then …wait. I'm pretty sure there was an arranged marriage in there somewhere too. You know what, screw it, you guys aren't *Romeo and Juliet*. That was a bad example. You can be a modern-day telling of *Cinderella*."

"How did this conversation go from trying to set up our parents to figuring out what me and Colton are supposed to be? Can't we just be us?"

Drix shrugs, looking less than impressed by the idea. "I mean, I guess you could just be you two, but that's so boring."

"Forgive me, I didn't realize my life was supposed to be here for your sole entertainment. However shall I make it up to you?"

Her eyes bug out of her head. "WAIT. *Cinderella* had an evil stepmom and bitch twin sisters. Colton has that."

I let out a heavy sigh. Here I thought the whole *Cinderella* comparison was over but it sounds like she's only just getting started. Either way, it's better than talking about rumors and somehow, it's gotten my mind off my shitty weekend, so for now, I'll play along. "True," I tell her. "But then wouldn't that make Colton *Cinderella* and me *Prince Eric?* I don't know how he's really going to feel about that."

Hendrix gives me a blank stare. "First of all *Prince Eric* is from 'The Little Mermaid.' If you're going to try and keep up with me, then at least get your stories straight. The prince you're looking for is *Prince Charming*. And secondly, who gives a shit if he has to play the role of Cinderella? I'm sure deep down, Colton will get a thrill out of putting on a gown and acting like a princess for a day."

"You know," I say, thoughtful. "You're not wrong, but if we really have to get into this, can't we be *Rapunzel* and *Flynn Ryder?* Now that's a guy I could get down with. He's got that whole smoldering thing going on."

Hendrix lets out a deep groan. "You're ruining my whole point here."

I give her a cheesy grin. "Sorry, but where I come from, we didn't exactly grow up memorizing every Disney movie on the market. It was more like trying to figure out the easiest way to hit the concrete that'll cause the least damage during a drive-by shooting."

Drix's eyes bug out of her head and I regret the words the second they come out of my mouth as I'm thrown back to standing outside the Widow's clubhouse, only to have to face that exact situation. Kian didn't stand a chance.

"Are you serious?"

"Unfortunately," I say, glancing around the cafeteria and trying to shake off the fear that the memory invokes in me. Having bullets zooming past my face isn't exactly something I'll be forgetting any time soon. "Trust me, the people in Bellevue Springs wouldn't last a few hours in Breakers Flats."

"You're telling me," she scoffs. "Just the thought of a drive-by shooting is making me sweat. I wouldn't even know how to respond to something like that. I'd probably panic and start running down the street screaming."

I nod, knowing just the type. I've seen it before and believe me when I say, it's not the response you want to have in a situation like that. When in doubt, always get down.

I'm just about to tell her that when the wicked witches of the west walk through the door with their adoring fans at their back. Hendrix and I instantly look their way along with every other girl in the school.

Cora and Casey are the new shiny toys at BSP and they're soaking up every last ounce of attention. They freaking love it and honestly, it's nauseating, but at the same time, they're kinda old news. They already went to school here for a year before their mother divorced Charles and dragged them away and I'd put what little money I have on the fact they weren't well-liked back then either.

They're bitches. It's as simple as that and everyone knows it, but they also know that they just got all their inheritance from their father, making them the wealthiest sixteen-year-old twitches on earth and who could resist that?

They walk in like they own the place and I really wouldn't be surprised if they did, though what I am surprised about is the way their sharp gazes seek out mine and they instantly start making their way toward me.

"Oh, shit," Hendrix groans as I sit straight in my chair. "This is going to be interesting."

All eyes start shooting our way, knowing damn well about the shit that's been going down since they first arrived at school this morning. Drix isn't wrong, this is going to be interesting and how the rest of the school responds to whatever is about to go down here, is going to set the standard for the rest of the school year. So, whatever this is, I need to bring my A-game and at the risk of sounding like a cocky fuck, it won't be a hard task—I always bring my A-game.

Cora and Casey step up in front of our table and within the blink of an eye, Jess comes bounding toward us from the other side of the cafeteria, desperate not to miss a showdown. She stumbles down into the space beside me, putting on a show of her own and silently declaring whose side she's on.

Cora and Casey watch the three of us closely. Hendrix and Jess are the two most popular seniors at Bellevue Springs Private and the fact that they haven't moved from my side speaks volumes. The twins weren't expecting this when they threw down their bullshit taunts yesterday, claiming they were going to ruin me. It's thrown them, and for that, I'll always be grateful.

The twins are juniors and around here, that's really nothing special. Unless you're at the top, you're a nobody. It was like that back home and I have a feeling it's like that in every school, so the fact that they have some sort of following should be impressive but I just can't find it within me to like them.

*They're Colton's sisters. They're Colton's sisters. They're Colton's sisters. You need to try, for him.*

Hendrix leans back in her seat and smiles up at the girls as the room seems to fall silent around us. "Is there something you need?"

The twin on the right scoffs and I mentally reprimand myself for not taking a moment to figure out who is who. I mean, that's kinda stupid on my part. If I'm going to go to war with them then I should at least know who I'm up against. She turns her icy glare on me and a smirk pulls at her lips. "What's this, Oceania? You need your *friends* to fight your battles for you?"

Fuck it. Screw being nice for Colton. I need to end this and I need to do it now.

I laugh and enjoy the way both of their gazes narrow. They don't take their eyes off me and it's clear that without saying a word, I'm already so far under their skin. I slowly stand, enjoying every last moment of this. My hands press down against the table and I lean forward, feeling the tension in the room rising. "You two are adorable. It's sweet that you think you have any chance of winning this. I already have your brother wrapped around my finger. I have your home, your school, and now your friends. All you have are a few shitty rumors to spread around and I have to admit, I'm kinda disappointed. I thought you could come up with something a little more … exciting." I look around at the crowd gathered. "You guys thought so too, right?"

They chuckle and the few who are too afraid to join in desperately try to smother their smirks. The twins silence them with one nasty glare but it's clear whose side they're on.

Cora and Casey don't stand a chance.

The twin on the left fixes me with a hard stare that would have any weaker girl shrinking back in fear, but not me. I've never been so ready. "We're only just getting started. You're nothing—trash. Do you really think these bitches are going to stand by you for much longer? Hell, I sure know Colton won't. You're just a toy, something new to play with until something better comes along, and you bet your fat ass that we're going to remind him of that every fucking day."

"What's your deal? Are you jealous? I'd understand one of these other girls trying to get rid of me so they can take my place by Colton's side, but you two? What's up with that? Are you hoping to suck his dick too, maybe be the ones to slip into his bed at night? I mean, I'm all for everyone having their own little kinks, but that's just a little fucked up if you ask me."

The disgusted look they share is nothing short of priceless. "You're fucking gross. He's our brother," The twin on the right spits.

"I know, it's crazy, right? Super gross if you ask me, but what other explanation is there for trying to take down the girl who's currently making their brother happy? You couldn't be that low, could you? Geez, only jealous bitches would sink like that."

"You don't know what the fuck you're talking about."

"Really? I know you and your skank mother took off and left him behind. Tell me, how often did you call? How many trips home did you make over the past few years? I can guarantee it's zero. Then you show up out of the blue, right when his pockets get heavily lined. Who're the real fakes around here? It's damn clear what you two and your mother are after and Colton won't fall for that."

"You're a fucking bitch."

I shrug my shoulders. "That may be true but at least I'm not fake like you two. How about instead of trying to get at me, you spend your time trying to build a relationship with your brother?"

They both pull a face and it's almost as though the idea of mending the bridge between them and Colton is something they've never even considered. "Our relationship with our brother is none of your damn business," the one on the right says.

I lean in just a little closer, making sure I have both of their undivided attention. "Then stop getting in my face and making it my business."

Uptight barbie twin on the right rolls her eyes before looking down at Jess and Hendrix. "I'm so done with this. You whores better watch your backs. You're fucking stupid for siding with this bitch and we're going to make sure you know it."

Drix laughs beside me as though their threat is the funniest thing she's ever heard. "Okay, babe. Whatever you say. I look forward to it."

The twins glance at each other and I watch in fascination as their jaws clench in unison and their eyes swivel back to mine. "I expect my bathroom scrubbed tonight."

I bow my head and wave my hand out in a sarcastic gesture. "It would be my pleasure, my queen. However, I saw the skid marks you left all over it this morning, and unfortunately, I don't clean up after other people's shit. So, you can go right ahead and clean that bowl yourself. Now, I can direct you to the cleaning supplies if you need. I know you've never cleaned up after yourself a day in your life."

Her face goes bright red and they glance back at each other again, both lost for words and unsure how to fight back. I find a wide grin stretching across my face. All morning, they've been spreading shitty rumors about me, trying to humiliate me and bring me down, and in a matter of seconds, I've thrown it right back in their faces.

They turn with a huff and start taking off but if they're going to give me their backs, then they should know that I'm more than capable of stabbing them in them. "Oh, hey twinnies," I call in a singsong voice, watching as they both look back over their shoulders. "It was a nice try, but next time, you're going to have to work harder than that."

The twins storm away and just like that, I drop back into my seat and look across at Jess while picking up an apple and taking a nice juicy bite. "Now, tell me what went down with Milo this morning."

# CHAPTER 6

I walk through the front door of the Carrington mansion, being extra loud and making a point of not coming in through the service entrance, because why the hell not? It hasn't even been 24 hours since the three long-lost Carringtons came home but I'm determined to do absolutely everything in my power to get under their skin. With that in mind, I dump my school bag right at the front door for the twins to trip over. Hell, maybe I'll move back into the spare room that I was in when I first got here, but on second thought, that's also the room Jude attacked me in, so I might give that one a miss.

I make my way through the house until I'm pushing through to the staff quarters. It's a mess of people busy cleaning up and it leaves me wondering if Colton had people here again today. The poor guy. He's so freaking busy, he hardly gets a chance to be an eighteen-year-old kid. He has the weight of a billion-dollar company resting on his shoulders. I don't even want to imagine the kind of stress that comes along with that.

As I glance around, I find myself looking for Maryne until the ugly reminder settles into my heart. She's not here. She'll never be here again.

She's gone.

I let out a heavy sigh and struggle against the tears forming in my eyes. I don't think I'll ever get used to not seeing her face in here again. She was everything. Her presence was known no matter where you were in the mansion and now without her, it just seems so empty, so lonely.

I could always count on Maryne for a smile. She was there to lift me up after a shitty day. I never actually sat down and talked with her about everything that was going on at the beginning but she could sense something was wrong. She was very maternal, especially for a woman who never got the chance to actually be a mom.

My phone dings from deep in my bra and I fish it out of there. This stupid private school uniform is trying to kill me. What uniform doesn't have pockets for us to hide things in? It's ridiculous.

I glance down at my phone and everything inside of me shatters.

Sebastian.

No, I'm not ready for this.

It's only a text, but I know exactly what it's going to say and reading those words is going to kill me.

I don't know what it is about Sebastian but out of all of my Widows, he's the one I always bonded with the most. He was my best friend—not in the way that I was friends with Nic. This was something different, something deeper. He was a brother to me, a protector, the guy that I always knew would be there.

What a joke that was. Out of all the guys, Nic and Sebastian's betrayal hurts the most. Those two were supposed to be the ones I trusted the most, they were supposed to be my world, but they lied. Just like my father did.

I look down at the notification on my phone, trying to find the strength to read Sebastian's message. I've heard from them all over the past week … in fact, I've probably heard from them a little too much, especially Nic, but after the weekend and the bruise he left on my arm, it's going to take a little more than some shitty apology to reel me back in. Nic is sick. He's obsessed and it's becoming unhealthy, but out of the four of them, if one of them was capable of reeling me back in with shitty words, it's Sebastian, and deep down, we both know it.

Taking a breath, I press on his message and mentally prepare myself.

**Sebastian – Can we talk? I miss you, O.**

I find myself staring at the message. One minute passes and it turns into two. Before I know it, I've been staring down at my phone for at least five minutes and I still have no idea what to do. Do I message back? Do I tell him that I miss him so freaking bad that it hurts? Do I ignore it? Why does it have to hurt like this?

I want them back in my life so desperately, but they betrayed me. They lied, they did the one thing I never thought they'd do. Sure, they've kept things from me before but it was never an outright lie. They've been deep in the Black Widows since before I knew them and I always knew that there were some things that they weren't going to share with me. They kept that part of their lives concealed in an attempt to protect me from it, but this was *my* father, *my* life. How am I supposed to forgive and forget that?

I quickly realize that I'm going to have to do something unless I'd prefer to stand here awkwardly in the middle of the staff quarters staring at my phone. But what?

Sucking up the courage, I allow my finger to move over the keyboard

**Ocean – I miss you too.**

Delete.

**Ocean – Talk? How am I ever supposed to talk to you again? You lied to me.**

Delete.

Fuck. I need to be real with him.

**Ocean – I want to forgive you, Sebastian. I want to forgive you so freaking bad, but I can't. It hurts too much. I don't trust you anymore...**

Taking a breath, I read over the message four times before I remember that my balls are supposedly made of steel and hit send. The text sends and I find myself staring again, looking down at the phone and anxiously waiting for his reply, knowing damn well that my words would have cut deep.

After ten minutes of waiting, I realize that no reply is coming and for some reason, it kills me just a little bit more. I hate knowing when my boys are hurting. Shit, I really need to stop calling them that. They're not *my* boys anymore. They belong whole-heartedly to the Widows. The four boys I thought I knew don't exist anymore.

I take myself out to the pool house and quickly change into a comfortable pair of sweats and a white tank, but as I'm rummaging through my clothes drawer, my hand curls around the red Widows bandana that I'd stolen from Nic.

Everything crushes inside of me.

Fuck, I miss them.

I can't keep breaking down every time I find something that reminds me of them, otherwise, I'll never survive this. I need to be stronger.

For some reason, the bandana gets tied over my hair and I make a quick knot in the back. Who knows? Maybe this is my way of being close to them without actually seeing them.

Trying to keep my mind off all my problems, I dive deep into my homework, and as much as I'd prefer to be doing anything but this, I don't emerge from the pool house until every last bit of it is complete.

I head back into the Carrington mansion with a plan to work all night, as long as it takes until my brain stops circling around the boys. And to think this all started because my father sold me to a billionaire.

What was his fucking problem? Who sells their child like that? No wonder he ended up dead. I can only imagine the other shady things he would have done over the years.

The reminder of my father's wrongdoings has me moving through the mansion with a mission. I can't be owned by someone. Hell, I doubt I'll ever get married just for the sake of not having myself tied to someone else so permanently. What's the point of marriage anyway? It's just some piece of paper stating that you're officially together with a no return policy.

Fuck that. I like my freedom. Don't get me wrong, I have no aversion to commitment. Hell, I plan on being as committed as I can to Colton as long as he does the same for me, but this bitch won't be signing on a dotted line. At the same time, the idea of being his wife … that hits differently.

I find myself standing in the doorway of Colton's office. It's after seven at night and he sits at his desk with a single lamp, the only light in the room. It's almost as though he's been so busy working away that he didn't even notice when the sun went down and certainly had no time to get up and flip the light switch.

Leaning against the door frame, I silently watch him do what he does best. "Are you going to come in or are you just going to stand there and stare at me all night?"

"I don't mind staring," I tell him, my lips lifting into an amused smirk.

Colton finally glances up and I watch as he leans back in his desk chair and puts his hands behind his back. His muscles bulge in his shirt and everything south of the border clenches. How it is possible for one man to have so much sex appeal? It shouldn't be legal.

"What do you need, Jade?"

I raise a brow as I continue studying him. God, there's so much I need from him right now and from the cocky smirk spreading across his face, he's well aware of it. "Do you have a few minutes? There's something I wanted to talk to you about, but I can wait until you're finished if you're busy."

His brows drop in suspicion. "It's fine," he says with a small nod, indicating for me to come in.

I stride through his office and instead of dropping myself down into one of the expensive chairs opposite his desk, I walk right around to his side and slide my ass back onto his desk.

His hand instantly curls around my leg as he looks up at me. "How was school?" I scrunch my face, really thinking about how I should answer that when he lets out a heavy sigh. "Fuck, what did they do?"

I bite down on my lips, still a little lost for words. "I mean, they might have said a few things suggesting that I was with you just to get ahead in life and they may or may not have told everyone that I was pregnant. Oh, and there was also something about me having an affair with Dean Simmons after I screwed the pervy PE teacher and had him fired for it."

Colton's head falls back against his seat and he closes his eyes, letting out a frustrated groan. "I'm sorry, babe. I told them to back off but the twins are … a little difficult. They do things their way and when you try to intervene, it only gets worse."

I slide my hand down my leg until my fingers find his. "It's okay, I don't need you to fight my battles. I handled it and now they're fully aware that it'll take a little more than a few immature rumors to take me down."

Colton's eyes narrow and he watches me for a silent second. "Do I even want to know what you did?"

I shrug my shoulders and fight the smile that attempts to spread across my face. I scrunch up my face and shake my head. "Yeah, maybe it's best I keep that one to myself."

Colton laughs and adjusts himself in his seat to see me better. "Why do I get the feeling that my sisters aren't exactly the reasons you wanted to talk to me?"

"Because they're not," I tell him. "I wanted to ask you about my dad."

His brows shoot up. "Your dad?"

"Yeah, more specifically about what he stole from your father."

Understanding flashes in his warm eyes and within seconds, he yanks me down off his desk until I fall down onto his lap. "I was wondering when this was going to be brought up."

"Yeah, I'm sorry. I know it's a bit of an awkward topic."

"No, Jade. Awkward is when you accidentally walk in on your parents fucking. This is just entertaining."

"Entertaining?" I shriek. "I'm so glad my pain amuses you."

"It doesn't," he soothes, "but watching you fight with yourself over which are the right words to use does. It happened. Your father stole from mine, and while that might be embarrassing or shameful for you, theft isn't exactly something new for me. It happens all the time. They're both gone now. It's in the past."

I shake my head. "But it's not. My father sold me to your dad. I'm Carrington property. I can't …" I let out a heavy sigh, unable to find the right words.

"I get it," he tells me, "and I already told you, I'll do whatever you need to make it go away. I don't look at you as a possession. As far as I'm concerned, the deal ended when my father was killed. You're a free woman, Ocean."

"You see, that's just the thing. I don't see it like that. There's still a debt, still a deal that didn't get seen through."

"But it did, you were sold and you came here."

"I … I don't know. I can't describe it. It's like this feeling in my gut that this isn't over. I don't even know what my father stole or how much he owed your dad. How could me being here for a month make up for it?"

Colton's lips press together and the way that his eyes briefly flick away from mine has me narrowing my gaze at him. "You know, don't you? You know what my father stole?"

Colton sighs and meets my gaze once again. "Yeah," he says softly. "I looked into it after you first told me about it."

I suck in a breath, feeling my heart begin to race the same way it does every time my father is brought up in conversation. "Like a band-aid," I tell him. "Just tell me how freaking bad it is. How much is the debt?"

"3.7 million dollars."

"WHAT?" I throw myself off Colton's lap and stare at him in horror, my eyes wide and my heart beating so damn fast that it threatens to beat right out of my chest. "3.7 million dollars? How is that even possible?"

"It was a small velvet bag that was hidden inside my father's car. It was filled with uncut diamonds that my father hadn't exactly bought the legal way. He'd parked at a restaurant to meet with some business associates and caught the whole thing on security footage. Your father smashed the window, rummaged through the car, and took off with a whole lot of shit, but the diamonds were the most valuable."

"3.7 million?" I confirm.

Colton nods and I fall back against his desk, hardly able to hold myself up. "How am I supposed to pay that back?"

"Jade," he whispers.

"No," I cut him off before he can give me the bullshit about wiping the debt. That's a lot of money. Too much to just wipe away and forget. I know his businesses make more than that in the blink of an eye, but that's not the point. It was stolen from his father, from him by my own flesh and blood and it's now my responsibility to make it right. "I have to pay it back," I tell him. "I don't know how, but I will."

"Jade, I can't accept that. Your father sold you to mine and they both agreed that the debt was settled and now I'm letting you go. My family no longer owns you. I'll do whatever you want, Jade. I'll sign a fucking release if that will make it better. I'm not going to accept money from you."

"Why did your father agree to this? What could he possibly have gotten out of having me here with him?"

Colton shakes his head. "I don't know," he tells me, just as lost as

I am. "It doesn't make sense to me. Had the diamonds been bought legally, I don't doubt my father would have had yours arrested and sent to prison. I guess he just wanted to take something from your dad like he'd done to mine."

"So, that's it then. That's the value of my life. 3.7 million dollars."

"Well," Colton says, reaching for me and dragging me back into his lap. "If you ask me, my father got a bargain. I'd say you're worth at least 4 million."

A smile cracks across my face and I shove my hand against his chest, playfully pushing him away. "You're an ass, you know that right?"

"An irresistible one though." I roll my eyes and let out a heavy breath and he instantly catches my hands in his. "We're agreed, right? There is no debt and you're a free woman? I don't own you, nor do I want to. I want you here as my girlfriend because you have a tight ass and a nice set of tits, not because some dickhead wanted to settle a debt. Got it?"

I look over his shoulder and press my lips into a hard line. "I'll think about it."

Colton raises his chin and his lips brush against my jaw before moving up to my ear and sending shivers through my body. "Is there anything I can do to convince you?"

I squirm on his lap and enjoy the low groan that pulls from deep within him. "I don't know," I whisper. "What did you have in mind?"

I feel his smile against my skin and just as his hand slips inside of my sweatpants, I hear the door swing open so hard that it bangs against the drywall. "Yuck," one of his sister's grunt of disapproval comes flying through the room. "What the fuck do you think you're doing, Colton? Stop letting the whore play tricks with your mind. She's trash and you're allowing her to seduce you. You're better than this."

I look back over my shoulder as Colton lets out a heavy sigh and pulls his hand out from between my legs. "Get the fuck out of here, Casey. Go and fuck with someone else's day. Ocean is a shitload more welcome here than you are."

"This is my house too," she screeches.

Colton raises a brow and fixes her with a hard stare. "How much do you want to bet?"

Casey's face drops and I take a quick moment to try and notice the small differences on her face that set her apart from her sister and all I can come up with is a small freckle by her jaw. I just hope Cora doesn't have the same otherwise I'll never be able to tell them apart. "You're such an asshole," she spits at her brother. "And to think I was coming in here to mend bridges."

Colton laughs and Casey turns on her heel, stalking away quicker than she came. "Mending bridges?" Colton asks. "What the fuck is that about?"

I can't tear the smile off my face. "Trust me, you don't want to know," I tell him, pleasantly surprised that Casey was willing to make an effort with her brother.

He shakes his head and leans back in his seat, but I'm not nearly done with him. Hell, I haven't even started. "Now, where were we?" I question, leaning into him and brushing my lips over his.

"I think you were about to show me that you're worth a hell of a lot more than 4 million dollars."

"Is that a challenge?"

"Only if you want it to be."

"Well, damn," I laugh, grinding against him and feeling his hardness through his pants. "Maybe we should take this upstairs instead. I'm going to need room to move."

Colton's brow raises and just like that, I'm thrown over his shoulder. He races out of his office and with a hard slap on my ass, he takes me up to his room and neither of us emerges until the sun is beaming through his bedroom window, our worlds have thoroughly been rocked, and we're both utterly exhausted.

# CHAPTER 7

I sit on the kitchen counter with my legs crossed under me, staring out at the ridiculously awesome pool that Charles was so proud of. It's a Saturday morning and for the first time in my life, I don't know what to do with myself.

My Saturdays used to consist of waking up hungover on one of the boys' couches before spending the next hour regretting my decisions as I became way too familiar with the toilet bowl, and honestly, the boys' toilet bowls are not something any woman should ever get that close to.

Colton woke up early, probably to work out and get a few hours logged in the office. Milo was out with someone last night who wasn't me and is spending the morning in bed. Mom is busy putting together the employee schedule for this coming week, and the girls, I have no idea. Hendrix said something about some guy's yacht and Jess practically drooled at the chance so I'm assuming that's what they're doing.

Maybe it's time to broaden my horizons, maybe make a few friends so shit like this doesn't happen.

Eh, fuck it. More friends equal more drama. I'm all good. I should probably go and grab a vacuum and spend the next few hours vacuuming every single room that surrounds Laurelle's just to drive that bitch insane. Hell, maybe I'll just turn it on and walk away.

I dip my spoon down into the tub of ice cream and slip it into my mouth, dying of satisfaction as my taste buds burst in excitement. There's nothing better than oreo ice cream. It's simply the best thing that was ever created and I will fight to the death against anyone who even attempts to challenge that. It's a fact. Just like the earth is round, the sun rises in the east, *Massimo Torricelli* is going to be my baby daddy, and oreo ice cream is the best.

Hearing footsteps out in the hall, I dump the tub down beside me on the counter and jump off, landing wobbly on my feet after sitting cross-legged for way too long.

I hurry out into the hall and look out, expecting to see Colton striding toward me, only the noise is coming from behind.

My heart rate kicks up as I spin around and come face to face with Spencer.

There are only two rooms down that end of the hall—Colton's

home gym and Charles' wine cellar, and judging by the grim look on his face, there's only one place that he's coming from.

He knows.

He knows what I did to Jude. He saw the cuts, the stab wound, the dried blood that sits beneath his nails. He knows what I did and from the dark flare in his eyes, he knows that I'm more than aware of where he's just been, yet neither of us says a damn word.

It's like a secret that sits heavily between us but neither of us is willing to admit it out loud despite knowing exactly where each other sits in this fucked-up situation, and I have a feeling that's how it's going to stay. Once something gets said out loud, it makes it real even though we've both seen things and done things that should never have had to be done.

Spencer silently steps around me and enters the massive kitchen and I find myself following, feeling a strange camaraderie floating between us. It's a feeling that I've never really gotten with Spencer before. It's as though all of a sudden, we're in this exclusive, dark club together, one that's hosted by Colton. I mean, should we all get matching tattoos now? Get branded and make a vow to take this secret to the grave?

Spencer scoops my tub of ice cream off the counter and leans back against it while helping himself to what's mine. "So, Laurelle and the twins haven't run you out of here yet?"

Oh, okay. So we're literally going to pretend that the Jude situation doesn't exist. I can get on board with that. I jump back up onto the counter and get comfortable before snatching the tub out of his unsuspecting hands. "They're not smart enough to know how to run me out of here," I inform him, looking at him pointedly with a smug grin. "None of you were."

"Ain't that the truth," he says with a scoff. "I have to admit, I didn't like you much at first but your annoying little screechy whine has grown on me."

"My screechy whine?" I gasp. "You and I both know that you're the only one with a screechy whine around here."

"Mooooooooom," comes a drawn-out squeal from upstairs by one of the twins.

"I stand corrected," I grumble.

"They'll come around," Spencer promises me, but the lie is all too obvious in his tone. We both know that Cora and Casey are not the type to 'come around.' They're the fight till the death type just like me, only unfortunately for them, they're now playing in a whole new league, one they're not strong enough to win, not even with their combined twin power.

I give Spencer a blank stare and he bursts into laughter. "Yeah, that didn't even feel convincing coming out of my mouth," he admits. "You're going to be up against those girls for as long as you live. Even if you and Colton break up. They'll never stop tearing you down until they win and when it comes to you, I have a feeling those girls will never win."

"Never."

"Though, to be fair," he continues. "I didn't think you were ever going to come around."

"Me?" I laugh. "I didn't come around, Spencer. You idiots just realized that if you can't beat me, it's best to join me."

"Bullshit. You're the one who realized that if you wanted to live peacefully here that you were going to need to reel in your attitude."

"Dude, my attitude is still shining bright. It didn't get reeled in at all. Besides, I think it's more like you realized that if you didn't climb aboard the Ocean train that you were going to get left behind. I had Charlie wrapped around my finger in a matter of days and Colton … well, he was mine the second I walked through the door. And as much as I'd rather not admit it, Jude wanted me too. You had no choice but to accept me or be left out in the dark. Just face it, I'm a force to be reckoned with."

Spencer looks back at me, playfully narrowing his eyes. "Keep your friends close and your enemies closer."

I roll my eyes and dig my spoon deep into my ice cream again. "You're an idiot," I tell him around my full mouth. "You know that, right?"

"Ughhhh. Anyone can tell that you didn't grow up around here," he says, scrunching his face in disgust. "Where are your manners? Don't you chicks take etiquette classes or some shit like that? Ice cream is going everywhere. Close your damn mouth."

I roll my tongue around my mouth, making a point of not giving a shit. "This is as good as it's gonna get," I laugh. "Loosen up, Spence. Trust me, it'll look good on you. Who knows, people might even start to like you then."

"Ha. Ha."

A noise sounds outside the kitchen before Colton's deep voice is hollered through the impeccable mansion. "Jade, where are you?"

I look over at Spencer as a wide grin spreads across my face. "Kitchen," I call back and rise to my feet on the counter.

"What the fuck are you doing?" Spencer questions, looking up at me with a fearful suspicion.

I glance up at the cupboard above the massive fridge. "Lift me up there."

His brows dip as his face crunches in distaste. "What? No."

I throw myself at him, leaving him no choice but to either catch me or let my stubborn ass fall to the floor. And just as I knew they would, his survival instincts kick in, and he catches me with ease. "Get off me," he grunts as I try to claw my way up his body to reach the top cupboard.

"Shut up and shove me in the cupboard. The more you complain, the longer it's going to take."

Spencer groans low and giving up his fight, hauls me up as high as he can go. I laugh to myself as I get my feet up on his shoulders and do my best to open the cupboard. "Fuck me," he grunts. "You're not as light as you look."

I scoff under my breath. "Maybe you just don't log enough hours in the gym like Colton does. That man can throw me around with one hand and you're here struggling while I do all the hard work."

Spencer ignores my jab and shoves his hands up against my ass before giving me a hard shove and sending me soaring into the back of the cupboard. A sharp laugh tears out of me as I slam into the back wall and try to adjust myself into a little ball so the cupboard doors can be closed. "Holy shit, dude. I think I just put a hole in the wall with my head."

"Hope it hurt."

"I hope your face hurts."

"I hope your brain hurts."

I scoff. "I know yours does."

Spencer sneers at me before reaching up and closing me into the cupboard. "I wonder if there's a padlock around here somewhere. It would be nice not having to see your ratchet face every day."

"Lock me in here, Spencer, and I swear, I'm going to fuck your dad and become your new stepmom then change the wifi password and send you to your room."

He chuckles under his breath before going a little too quiet. "Yo," I hear Colton saying while listening as his footsteps grow deeper into the kitchen. "Where's Ocean? I could have sworn she just said she was in here?"

"Don't know, man," Spencer says. "I just walked in. You must have just missed her."

There's a soft sigh before I hear the sound of my ice cream tub being scooped off the counter and I curse myself for not bringing it with me. "Did you check on Jude?" Colton asks, his voice becoming louder as he moves closer to the fridge.

"Yeah, the fucker will be fine, but he ain't eating. I think he's going to try and starve himself."

"Fine by me," Colton grumbles. "That'd be one less thing to worry about.”

“You’re telling me. I heard starvation is a painful way to go. If that’s what he wants to do, then he can be my guest. But it might not have to get that far, not if your girl gets her hands on him again.”

“Yeah,” Colton says, his voice thick with emotion. “She did a fucking number on him.”

“‘She did more than just a number on him. She’s a fucking savage.”

“You should have seen it, bro. She was fucking going for it. Had I not walked in … I don’t know. I don’t want that for her but if it comes down to it and we have to finish him, it’ll be me. I don’t want that shit on either of your shoulders. She’s too fucking good for that.”

Well, shit. This just got heavy.

Spencer laughs. “I mean, she’s not bad, but she’s nothing special.”

“Dude, you told me just last night that you think she’s fucking awesome.”

Spencer coughs and I roll my eyes. “Nah, you must have been hearing shit. I definitely didn’t say that.”

Colton groans and I hear him walking through the kitchen, tearing open the cupboard doors. “She’s in here, isn’t she?”

I can’t help the snicker that comes bubbling up my throat and just as he steps in front of the fridge, I throw the cupboard doors open. “SURPRISE, BITCHES!”

Not having expected me to be up so high, Colton’s eyes bug out of his head and as I laugh and go to reach for him, I underestimate the momentum I had from throwing the doors open and topple right out.

A loud screech comes tearing out of me as I fall face first, panicking as the marble floor rapidly comes closer and closer to my face. My arms and legs flail about but Colton's quick reflexes have his arms snapping around my waist and catching me just mere moments before my face becomes a jumbled mess and I'm left with no choice but to beg Laurelle for her plastic surgeon's phone number.

"Fuck, Jade. What the hell are you doing?" Colton gasps, looking down at me with wide eyes.

I glance up at him and give him a pathetic smile. "Whoops," I say, swallowing back the fear and doing my best to recover from the sheer panic that tore through my chest.

Colton shakes his head, far too amused by my idiocy to remember to help me to my feet until I start squirming around in his arms. He gets me safely back on my feet and as soon as a soft kiss has brushed over my lips, I look over at Spencer with a cheesy as fuck grin. "You think I'm awesome?" I question. "Are we supposed to braid each other's hair now?"

He rolls his eyes and just as he goes to start denying that he ever said it, we hear Laurelle's chirpy tone welcoming someone into Colton's house. "Ah, Melissa. How lovely it is to see you again. Please, come on in."

There's a short silence before Laurelle's guest replies in a warm tone. "You too, it's been far too long. How are the girls?"

The boys go stiff at my sides and I glance up at them to find them staring at each other, both locked in some sort of silent conversation. "Who the fuck is Melissa?" I ask when they don't give anything away. Though I don't think I need them too, there's something familiar in her voice, something off-putting.

Their sharp stares drop down to mine and I see their dismissal before anything's even been said.

"Colton," I demand in a no-bullshit tone. "Who is Melissa?"

He presses his lips into a tight line before letting out a soft sigh. "Melissa Carter. Jude's mom."

"Fuck," I grunt. "What is she doing here? Why would your mom invite her over here?"

Colton shakes his head. "I don't know, but she's not welcome. You stay here with Spence and I'll get rid of her. The last thing we need is her getting too comfortable here."

"Excuse me?" I snap as he turns and starts for the kitchen door. "Like hell I'm staying back here. I have a few things to say to that woman."

Colton whips back to me but I'm already passing him and now he's the one trying to keep up. "You're not going to say a damn word," he hisses, trying to keep his voice low as we get closer and closer to the foyer with Spencer right on our heels.

"Just try and stop me, Colton," I snap at him. "You weren't the one he drugged and attacked. You didn't have your clothes torn off. You weren't the one that lost every bit of happiness when he slammed himself deep inside you. You lost nothing, so you sure as hell don't get the option to silence me. I'll say whatever the hell I need to say and I'll do it without feeling bullshit pressure from you two dickheads. If I feel the need to tear that woman to pieces, you two are going to take one hell of a step back and keep out of my way. Hell, have a little fun with it. Maybe you can score my performance out of ten."

The boys share a glance and a million messages pass between them before Colton pulls me into his chest and presses his lip to my temple. "Okay," he finally says. "You do whatever the fuck you need to do, but you don't let on that you know where he is otherwise, we're fucked."

"This ain't my first rodeo, Colton."

I step out of his arms and with the boys at my back, we storm toward the foyer.

Within seconds we find both Laurelle and Melissa crowding the foyer, and the second I see them together, all I can do is rage. The last time I had a conversation with Laurelle, she was sending me down to the wine cellar after telling me that I was worthless and not good enough for her son. The last time I saw Melissa, she was doting over her poor lost son, acting as though he wasn't a monster.

A sound of disgust comes tearing from my throat and the women both snap their gazes toward me. They look over me as though I'm trash before focusing on the boys at my back, and it's almost as though they're acting like I'm not even here.

"Colton," Momma Carrington says. "What have I told you about spending time with the help? She is here to work, not to socialize."

Colton steps into my back and although I'm not facing him, I feel the tension coming off him in waves. "And what have I told you about addressing my girl? She's not working today. This is just as much her home as it is mine. Hell, she's more welcome here than you are."

Laurelle sucks in a loud gasp. "Colton," she shrieks as I mentally high five him. "We have company. How can you be so rude? You weren't brought up that way. It's this … girl that you're spending your time with. She's a bad influence on you. I forbid you from seeing her anymore. I thought I instructed you to cease her employment."

Colton laughs at my back and I feel the rumble right through to my chest. "Careful, Mom," Colton says in a low, chilling tone. "Ocean bites a lot harder than you can."

Pride surges through me. There's nothing quite like the feeling of having your boyfriend stand up to his toxic mother to defend you, and not just in the 'leave her alone, she's important' kind of way, but the real 'come at us and we'll fucking destroy you' way.

Laurelle's eyes drop to mine and her lips pull up in a disgusted sneer. "Go and fetch my guest some refreshments and while you're at it, you can find yourself a uniform. What have I told you about showing respect for your employers? My home is not yours to holiday in. If you must be here, then I expect you to work."

Melissa looks over me in the same way and I quickly realize that these two are exactly the same. "Your home?" I question. "That's funny. You divorced Charles nearly three years ago. This home is Colton's. I've seen the deed, Lauren, and you aint on it."

She sucks in a horrified breath, quickly realizing that I've gotten her name wrong on purpose and knowing damn well that it's a show of disrespect. "You have two seconds to get out of my sight before I …"

I take a step forward. "Before you what? Tell me, really, because I'm so damn interested to see what a classy lady like yourself is about to say. What is it that you think you can do to me that this town hasn't already done? Though I have to admit, I'm a little more curious to see if you're the kind to get your own hands dirty. But then, you'd never admit to that in front of your snotty country club friends, would you?"

Her jaw clenches and she snaps her gaze back to Colton's as I hear Spencer choking on a laugh and getting silently scolded by Melissa. "You need to handle this."

I feel Colton's eyes on my body, heated, hooded, and full of seduction. "Oh, believe me, I plan to." Gasps are heard from both the women but they don't get a chance to express their horror before Colton continues. "Actually, I wouldn't mind doing that now. So, unfortunately, I'm going to have to cut this little catch up short. As always, Melissa, it was such a treat seeing you again. I'm sure we'll see you again soon."

Colton walks to the front door and opens it wide for her and for a short moment, she starts to go until she realizes that she's being kicked out by her friend's eighteen-year-old son. Not to mention, her husband's new boss. "No," she snaps. "I will not be forced out by a bunch of children. I have come to discuss my son."

I take a step forward, forcing her gaze on me and making her uncomfortable with my proximity, but in comparison to how her son made me feel, I figure I still have a few levels of fucked-up to go before I cross a line. "What about him?"

"He ..." her eyes flick around to Colton's and then to Spencer's before coming back to mine. "He's missing."

"Your son is a fucking pig," I spit. "He's a rapist. I hope that wherever he is, he never comes back."

She sucks in a horrified gasp. "How can you say that? You don't even know my son. You've been here for two minutes. My Jude is a good boy."

"Oh really? I don't know him? I actually think I know him pretty damn well. I know him well enough to know that years ago, he raped a sixteen-year-old girl, and I know him so fucking well that only a few weeks ago, he raped me too."

Melissa's hand slaps hard across my face. "You're a liar," she shrieks as Spencer rushes into my back and grabs my wrists, restraining me from making a dog's breakfast out of her face.

"You know it's true," I tell her. "I heard all the fucking stories. I know how you and your husband paid her off to make that story disappear, but don't you think it's funny how no one has seen her since? Fucking suspicious if you ask me. I wonder what kind of damage a scandal like that would cause?"

Melissa glances around in a panic, staring at a horrified Laurelle though something tells me she's horrified at possibly having her name involved in a scandal and not because of the news she's hearing. "NO. SHE'S LYING. YOU CAN'T BELIEVE HER." Melissa looks back at me. "You're trash. I've heard stories about you, sleeping your way through Bellevue Springs. You're just after a payday, but guess what? You won't be getting one from me."

I step a little closer and watch as she takes a hesitant step back. "Did I mention anything about wanting your dirty money? You're a delusional bitch if you honestly think your precious little Jude is a good little momma's boy. He's a monster. A rapist."

She shakes her head so violently that I fear it will rock right off her shoulders. "You. Are. Lying."

"Really? Do you want me to tell you how he drugged me, how he forced me up the stairs, how he shushed me when I tried to scream for help? How about when he hit me? Tore my dress and forced himself inside of me while I cried, begging for him to stop? That's the piece of shit you're defending."

She watches me for a short second before her eyes begin to narrow. "You know where he is."

I grin, not daring to hold back despite knowing that the boys must be shitting themselves right now, terrified that I might just say a little too much. "If I knew where that fucker was, I can assure you, he'd be dead. You better hope that you find him before I do because I will end him. No one gets away with touching me. Unlike the poor girl before me, you can't buy my silence."

With that, I storm over to Colton and rest my hand against the door handle. "Now, if you don't mind, my boyfriend has already asked you nicely to fuck off. You don't want to wait around to see how I'm going to ask."

Melissa huffs while Laurelle stares on, shocked but also far too intrigued and I have a feeling that this news is going to spread like wildfire, but I don't need to be ashamed, I should be proud to fight back. No one takes from me and gets away with it.

I will not be silenced.

With no other options, Melissa takes her sorry ass out the door, and just before I get the chance to slam it in her face, she shoots one hell of a nasty glare at me. "This isn't over, Oceania Munroe," she says, letting on that she already knows exactly who I am.

I grin wide, knowing damn well that I have the upper hand here, after all, I have her son rotting in the wine cellar dungeon. "Try me, bitch. I dare you to come for me."

She huffs once again and just like that, she's gone. The door gets slammed and by the time I turn back around, Laurelle is nowhere to be seen.

# CHAPTER 8

My feet dangle in the warmth of the heated pool as the afternoon sun shines down on my face. It's so damn relaxing out here. Any other time, I'd be loving it, but the emotions welling inside of me from tearing open the fresh scars is all too much to deal with.

It's as though I was on some kind of emotional roller coaster ride. I went up and hit it hard when the adrenaline started pumping and now I'm coming down the other side, crashing and burning into a pile of nothingness.

I lean back against the polished concrete flooring and swirl my legs through the water. I've been sitting out here for nearly an hour. I was hoping that the peace and quiet in the fresh air would help me to store the memories away again, and lock the box, never to be looked at again, but it hasn't. If anything, it's only reminded me just how many fucked up issues I have right now, but what's worse, I miss Nic.

I miss all my boys and I hate being apart from them. I hate that I can't just call them and tell them to suck my dick. I hate that there's a dark cloud that hovers above my head every time I think of them. I hate the secrets. I hate the lies.

I want to hate them … but I can't.

"You look like you're thinking too much," Colton says from behind me. I crane my neck to look up at him and see nothing but concern etched across his handsome face.

He drops down behind me with a leg on either side of mine. My back rests against his chest as his arms circles my waist, holding me close. I don't know how it's possible to fit so perfectly with someone, but when it comes to me and Colton, it just works.

"Is it that obvious?"

Colton scoffs and spreads his fingers wide on my stomach, claiming as much of me as he possibly can. "Melissa hadn't even cleared the bottom step before you ran out of there like your ass was on fire. Spence and I figured you wanted to be alone, but I can't take it anymore. I tried to give you some space …"

I relax into his chest and close my eyes, soaking up every last bit of sunlight. "It's okay. It's actually better now that you're here. I was starting to work myself up yet somehow you show up and my brain goes to mush."

"Of course it does," he laughs. "Because I'm fucking awesome. Irri-fucking-sistable."

"And not at all cocky."

"Not at all," he agrees. "I don't know where you'd ever get that idea."

I can't help but laugh as I nudge my elbow back into his stomach. His lips come down on my forehead, so soft and gentle. "In all seriousness, Jade. How are you? Do you want me to go and leave you alone?"

I shake my head. "No, please don't go. I'm just … processing."

"Do I need to be worried?"

"No, I'm good," I tell him. "I guess I just wasn't expecting to have to talk about it today, especially in front of those two. I wasn't mentally prepared, but it's over and I think I feel better for letting it out."

"Think?"

"Think."

"Okay," he murmurs, running his fingers through my hair. "But you know now that they both know, word is going to spread and eventually the rumors will get twisted?"

"I know," I tell him. "I can handle rumors."

"Can you though? It's one thing when someone is spreading lies about you, but what about when it's the truth? What are you going to do when someone gets in your face and calls you a liar, saying exactly what Melissa just said to you?"

I shake my head and let out a heavy sigh. "I … I honestly don't know. Up until now, when shit like this has gone down, I've had the

Widows at my back and no one was brave enough to say a damn word. As much as I want to say that I'll be fine, I just … I don't know. This place is forcing me to stand on my own two feet. It's one thing acting tough when you have a wall of muscle at your back, but now it's just me."

"It's never just you," he whispers. "I'm right fucking here, Jade. I won't let them touch you."

I look up to meet his eyes and see the intense honesty staring back at me, it's nearly enough to cripple me. "I know," I tell him. "I like you there, but I don't want you having to fight my battles. I want to stand at your side, not cower behind you. I want to be your equal. Hell, if I'm going to be sticking around in this town, I'm going to have to learn how to protect myself."

"I don't think you need protection," he says with a soft smile. "After seeing you handle my mom and Melissa, you can take down a fucking army. You never needed the Widows to handle things for you, you handle shit perfectly on your own."

"You know," I say. "You didn't have to defend me like that to your mom. I don't want to be the reason shit goes south between you."

"Shit went south between us a long time ago," he explains. "Mom left and she took my sisters with her. She didn't care about fighting for me, she just gave me up to my dad so as far as I'm concerned, there's no relationship between us worth saving. I'm allowing them to stay because they're the only family I have left, and at the end of the day, that has to mean something. But my mother … she's a complicated one. She doesn't like to lose and she sure as hell doesn't like it when a seventeen-year-old nobody from the wrong side of the tracks is making a dent in her carefully sculptured world. If I didn't defend you and put a stop to her shit, she's going to keep coming for you, and each time, it'll get worse. She's like the twins on steroids, so despite knowing that you can handle her with ease, I had to say something and I'll say it again and again if I have to."

"You know, you're kinda amazing."

"And you're kinda sexy as hell. Watching you dominate that back there … fuck, babe. I was struggling to control myself. I could have fucked you right then and there. Fuck them all, they could have watched."

"Really?" I say, my tone dropping as my eyelids grow far too heavy for their own good. My hand falls to Colton's thigh at my side. "Just how bad did you want it?"

His hand at my stomach slides down and I suck in a breath filled with anticipation. His fingers flirt with the waistband of my sweatpants until they're slipping down beneath my panties, so strong, large, and calloused.

"Let me show you."

I bite down on my lip and sink further into him, feeling his growing hardness pressing against my back. "Did Spencer leave?"

"Uh-huh."

"Your mom? Sisters?"

"Gone."

"What about my mom and Harrison?"

"I gave them the afternoon off. We're alone."

My breath comes in short, needy pants. Holy shit, I need him so bad.

His long, thick fingers find my center and as they brush over my clit, I feel every single one of my troubles fading away. "We're really alone?"

"Uh-huh. I could fuck you right here by the pool and no one would ever know. Hell, I'll take that sweet pussy in the pool if that's what you want."

Shivers sweep over my skin at his soft tone in my ear. "Right here? Out in the open?"

Two thick fingers push up into me and I let out a low moan, hearing his soft breathy chuckle against my shoulder, getting off to the sound of my pleasure. "Mmhmm. I'll fuck you on every surface of this house if you want me too."

"This house is pretty fucking big," I remind him, grinding down against his hand. "That could take days."

"I'm down if you are."

"I'm down for everything you've got."

His fingers slam deeper within me just as his thumb presses down over my clit. I groan as my head falls back against his shoulder. Colton's free hand comes around my body, slipping up under my tank and grabbing hold of my tit, squeezing it tight and giving me exactly what I need.

He tortures me with his touch—rough, ruthless, and relentless and it's all I need to forget about the horrors of this morning.

I focus solely on him, on his touch, the feel of his hands so hypnotic on my body. He claims me. There's no other way to describe it. The way he takes me and makes it so that no one else exists is intoxicating. Colton Carrington is all I will ever need.

Colton's lips drop to my neck as he continues working my body, but it's not nearly enough. I need more, so much more. I need to feel his skin upon mine. I need his taste in my mouth, and I need his hard cock plunging deep inside me.

I peel my tank over my head and as I do, Colton moves out from behind me. I watch him eagerly as he drops down into the pool between my legs, putting him at just the right height. He grabs hold of my sweatpants and tears them down my legs, discarding them in the pool and letting them sink to the bottom.

I bite down on my lip as I watch him. His eyes heat with need and as he looks up and meets my gaze, everything inside of me clenches.

He licks his lips and I just about die.

The anticipation builds within me. I need him more than I need my next breath.

Colton takes my knees and slowly peels them apart. "Open up, Jade. Show me that pretty pussy."

Holy fuck. I'm definitely going to hell.

I keep my eyes on him, watching as I slowly open my legs wide, showing him exactly what he wants. His eyes flare with desire. He's like a kid in a candy store, too excited to wait.

He takes my legs and yanks me right to the edge before moving in closer and hooking both of my legs over his shoulders. "That's right, baby. Come to Daddy."

Damn. I never thought I'd get into the whole daddy thing but fuck me, I like it. In fact, I fucking love it. I need to hear it again and again.

I'm panting before he's even touched me, but he doesn't make me wait long before his lips are closing down over me with his tongue roaming freely over my clit. Up and down and around and around. It's like a torturous game.

His hair tickles my inner thighs and I tighten my fingers into it, feeling as though I can somehow control his wild pleasure, but there's just no way. No one controls Colton Carrington, not even me.

I groan loud, needing so much more and he doesn't hesitate slipping those two thick fingers back inside me, plunging deep and exploring every little bit of my pussy. His tongue presses down harder against my clit and I scream out, no longer capable of holding it in.

My free hand comes up and cups my tit, squeezing, pinching, playing. God, I'd do anything to feel him bite my nipples right now and suck them into his mouth but I won't dare distract him from what he's already doing.

He sucks hard on my clit as his fingers work away and his tongue rolls over it, my orgasm quickly building. How is it possible for a man to be this good? I've never met a guy who could get me off like this. It's incredible. He's opened me up to a whole new level of fuckery and I won't ever go back. Screw just fucking in a bed, there's something so thrilling about being out in the open.

Colton fucks me with his fingers and doesn't relent on my clit until I scream out his name, for once not caring about how fucking loud I can get. "FUCK, COLTON," I groan. "I'M GOING TO COME."

He plunges his fingers deeper and rolls his tongue over me one more time and it's all it takes for my orgasm to tear through me. My legs squeeze around his head as my fingers ball into a tight fist in his hair. "FUCK," I scream. "YESSSS."

I feel his smile against my pussy and just when I think he's done, he grabs my legs and pulls me into the pool. My arms fall around his neck and within seconds, my lips are on his, tasting myself as my legs lock around his waist.

Not once removing his lips from mine, he walks us toward the shallow end of the pool and puts me down. The water barely reaches my knees and he turns me until I'm facing the house with my back against his warm chest. "Get down on your knees."

A thrill sweeps through me and I don't hesitate to drop down. He comes down behind me and I feel his cock heavy against my back, but it's not the only thing there. "Spread your knees."

Well, damn.

I spread them as wide as they'll go and only then does his hand at my back start pushing me down. My tits brush against the floor of the pool with the shallow water hitting my shoulders. I have to put my arms under my face to keep my head out of the water but I don't give a fuck because the anticipation of having my ass up and every little piece of me exposed to Colton like this is the most thrilling thing I've ever done.

His hands roam over my ass and my pussy clenches with need. "Do it," I beg.

His hand slaps down hard over my ass and the sting makes me

groan. "Patience," he warns.

I all but wave my ass at him, enticing him, desperately needing him to give me whatever he's got while silently begging for him to spank me again, harder and harder.

His fingers trail between my ass cheeks and start heading south, teasing my hole as he goes. His fingers gently press into me and I push back against him, letting him know just how down I am. "You like this?" he questions.

The only response I'm physically capable of is a low groaned, "Mmhmm."

His other hand slips under me and starts teasing my clit all over again and I'm left completely dumbfounded by how he can get me so worked up so soon after just coming. "Please," I beg. "I need you."

Colton's hand falls away from my clit and before I get a chance to complain, his hard cock is there, slowly rubbing up and down, and without a doubt, if my hands weren't the only things keeping my head out of the water and drowning myself, they'd be down between my legs, grabbing hold of him and guiding his impressive length home.

He continues teasing my ass while finally taking pity on me and sliding his cock deep inside of me, the angle having him plunging deeper than ever before. "Holy fuck," I moan as he hits just the right spot.

"That's right, Jade. Take all of me."

He pushes harder against my ass and in return, I push back against him, taking him deeper as he slams into me over and over again.

Hell, there's no way I'm going to last long before I come, and I'm fucking positive that he won't either. This is too good, too tight, too fucking delicious.

Colton's other hand grabs my waist, his fingers digging deep into my hips, his only sign that he's about to lose control. "Fuck, Jade. You're so fucking perfect."

"I don't think," thrust, "I can hold," thrust, "on much longer."

"Then we'll make it quick."

True to his word, Colton's fingers squeeze on my hip and he fucks me like a fucking pornstar, hitting me in just the right spot, over and over again, showing my pussy the time of its life. My orgasm sneaks up on me and just as I come, Colton groans low.

His body stiffens but he keeps his hips moving as I ride it out, unable to catch my breath. "Holy shit," I pant as Colton finally relaxes behind me. His hand spanks down on my ass and I squeal out just as he comes crashing down in the shallow water beside me.

"Fuck, I'll never get tired of your sweet pussy."

"I'll hold you to that," I laugh before looking his strong body up and down. "So, you want me to start calling you 'daddy' now, huh? I didn't realize you were into that."

Colton's face splits into a beaming grin and he grabs my waist before hauling me onto his chest but instead of curling in like he's expecting, I splash water up over his somehow still dry face and dive deep into the water.

Within seconds he dives after me and I'm instantly reminded of the time I graffitied his back wall and then dumped the dirtied water all over him. I'd thrown myself into this same pool and while it was only a few weeks ago, I feel like so much has changed since then.

We fuck around in the pool for a while before the sun disappears behind a cloud and the heat is sucked away. "Come on," Colton says, grabbing my naked body and hauling me out of the pool. "Let's get you dried up so I can take you out for dinner."

I suck in a gasp as he throws me over his shoulder and starts heading for the pool house. "Is this your twisted way of asking me out on a date?"

My ass is spanked and with the chill running through my body, the sting hits just a little harder than before. Though, that could entirely be due to the fact that my boyfriend was in the middle of rocking my world. "Shut up. It's just dinner. If I was asking you on a date, you'd know."

I scoff. "Yeah right. That was it, wasn't it?"

"Do you want to go out for dinner or not?"

"I mean, I'm not going to say no."

"Good," he laughs, squeezing my ass cheek. "Wear something sexy so I can show you off."

"My sweatpants aren't sexy enough for you?"

"By all means, wear your sweatpants," he tells me, eyeing them as they sit heavily in the bottom of the pool, "But you're going to have to go and get them."

Without a second of warning, Colton tosses me through the sky and I go crashing down into the water with a high-pitched squeal, and just as my head goes under, I catch the back of Colton as he darts away, terrified of my version of revenge.

That's right fucker. You better run.

# CHAPTER 9

Light filters through the massive windows of the living room and I groan as it hits my face just as Colton's arm tightens around my waist. We'd spent the afternoon getting all too familiar with each other's bodies on as many surfaces of this house as possible and reluctantly put clothes back on when our stomachs started to grumble and we remembered that he'd promised dinner that was apparently not a date.

It was nice actually being alone for once. No staff members walking around, no friends popping by, no threat of my mom or Harrison accidentally walking in to find us. Just us.

I curled up with Colton on the couch and feeling somewhat

normal for the first time in weeks, we crashed in each other's arms with nothing but the throw blanket hanging over the back of the couch to keep us warm. It was the most perfect night … that is until the sun had to rise and ruin it.

It's way too early to be waking up, especially considering that we only fell asleep at four.

I peel Colton's arm off me and somehow detach his hand from my left tit. How is it that guys always manage to find their hands on a set of tits? Even in their sleep.

I slide across the couch, being careful not to wake him and adjust the throw blanket over him to keep him warm. He works so damn hard. He deserves to sleep in. Most days he's up at the crack of dawn getting a good workout in before spending the next ten hours locked in an office signing a shitload of paperwork and somehow making sense of it. Charles really was an ass, especially to his kids but I can't deny that he taught them well. The way Colton has been able to effortlessly slip straight into his role and not skip a beat is the most impressive thing that I've ever witnessed.

Leaving him to sleep, I push up from the couch and cringe at the deep ache within me. I guess that's what happens when you spend hours being well and truly fucked by a man like Colton Carrington. My pussy is fucking raw and I love it.

I creep across the living room and up the two steps into his massive kitchen, taking each step carefully and adjusting to the pain within. I've never been so glad for the weekend. If I was heading to school today and had to spend hours sitting on the stiff chairs, I'd be in trouble, but as it is, I have the whole day to recover. Unless Colton gets his hands on me again and I have a feeling that could be a very strong possibility. In fact, I'm willing to make bets on it.

I get busy making breakfast and coffee and by the time I have everything I need, I take it all back down to the couch and sit by Colton's head as he rests peacefully. I put his breakfast and coffee down on the table, knowing he's bound to be hungry when he wakes. After all, he used a lot of energy yesterday.

Getting comfortable beside him, I cut off a piece of my pancake, making sure to get a bit of cream and a strawberry on my fork before delivering to my mouth with a groan. I've never claimed to be a good cook, but damn, I'm the fucking queen of pancakes.

Grabbing the remote, I turn on the TV and after flicking through and deciding there's nothing holding my interest, I settle on the morning news. I watch a story on some guy who was held at gunpoint during a daylight robbery of his gas station in the town across from Breakers Flats followed immediately by a story of some big-time developer who is attempting to tear down the old mall and replace it with a new fancy one, complete with designer stores that the residents of that town won't be able to afford to shop in.

I find myself rolling my eyes and zone out, focusing on my pancakes and knowing damn well that if Colton doesn't wake up soon, I'm going to end up eating his as well. Hell, I'm just about finished with my coffee and was eyeing his plate the whole way through that last news story.

After finishing off my plate and waiting a whole five long,

impatient minutes, I reach forward and slip my plate onto the coffee table before switching it out for his. I'll make him a new batch when he wakes. I can't have him eating cold pancakes. He's Colton Fucking Carrington, he deserves the best. You know what, I'll go ahead and make him another coffee too.

I get halfway through his breakfast when an arm shoots out and grabs hold of my ankle. Colton starts dragging me down the couch and I laugh as the stack of pancakes topples from my lap. "What are you doing?" I screech as he pulls me towards him.

"Breakfast," he grumbles, his eyes blazing with need.

He doesn't stop pulling me until his head is right between my legs and without warning his other hand shoots out and he throws me down until my back is crashing against the soft cushions of the couch.

My sweatpants are ripped down my legs and my panties all but torn straight off my body. Colton props himself up on his elbows just as I do the same, intent on watching the show. His eyes meet mine and seeing the thrilling sparkle in his, everything clenches.

My legs are tossed over his shoulders. "You wanna watch, Jade?" he questions, his tone low and grumbly, still thick with sleep but it only makes it that much better.

I bite down on my lip and slowly nod and my pussy starts pulsing. It's as though his words have the ability to open the flood gates. I just can't help myself around him.

He grins and keeps his eyes locked on mine as his head dips closer to my promised land. I feel his hot breath against my skin and a shudder ripples through me. He licks his lips as his fingers softly tease my pussy, starting from the top and making their way down. I suck in a breath, watching as he brings his finger to his mouth, glistening with my arousal.

He sucks them dry, his eyes somehow darkening even further. "You ate without me," he accuses.

My tongue runs over my lips, mimicking his movements as his fingers drop back to my pussy, rubbing slow, teasing circles over my clit. "I might have eaten a little," I whisper. "But I left dessert for you."

"Good," he says, his voice raspy with need. "Because I'm fucking starving."

His head finally drops to my pussy and I squirm under his hold as his mouth closes over my clit. My eyes close and despite how badly I want to watch, my head drops down to the couch and I soak up every last ounce of pleasure until he's throwing me right over the edge.

I come on his fingers with his skilled tongue expertly rolling over my clit while I bite down on my lip to force myself not to scream out his name. His mom and ratty sisters are home and judging from the sound of the vacuum in the dining hall adjacent from the living room, I'd dare say my mom is also too close for comfort.

Colton grins and I feel it against my skin and then all too soon, his head pops back up from between my legs, his lips shimmering with my arousal. He crawls up between my legs until his lips are pressing down on mine and his heavy cock is resting against my pussy.

He reaches down between us and keeping his lips on mine, he guides himself inside of me, taking it slow as though he already knows that yesterday's wildness has left me sore.

His fingers tangle with mine, squeezing them tight as he leisurely slides in and out, taking me deeper with each thrust. He doesn't dare stop kissing me until we come together, keeping as quiet as we can.

Colton pulls back ever so slightly so he can look down and meet my eyes. "I hope you know what you're getting into," he tells me with confidence, a beaming smile tearing across his face. "I plan on waking up like that every fucking day of my life."

"With your lips on my pussy or cock deep inside of me?"

His eyes shimmer with elation. "Both," he grins.

"Promise that you'll make it that fucking good every single day and you'll have yourself a deal."

Colton grabs my waist and flips us so that I hover above him, my hair dancing down around us like a thick curtain concealing us from the rest of the world. "Interesting," he says, his eyes still shimmering and making everything inside of me swell with happiness. "I took you for the kind to drive a hard bargain."

"Good point," I laugh. "I should remember not to make deals with you while I'm in a post-orgasm fog."

"Sorry, Jade," he grins, pushing my hair back behind my ear to see me better. "It's a done deal, but it won't just be good, it'll be fucking incredible."

"Is that a promise?"

"When it comes to you and me, it's a guarantee."

My swollen lips drop back to his and just as the idea sparks to return the favor and I start crawling down his body towards his very hard dick, the massive TV screen steals the spotlight.

Both our heads whip toward it as the breaking news hits the screen with the too-pretty for her own good reporter standing outside a massive estate in the bright morning sun. "It was only minutes ago that the police raided the DeCarlo estate and son of Vincent DeCarlo, 28-year-old, Lorenzo DeCarlo was arrested. The details are still unclear but from what little information we've been able to gather, Lorenzo is being questioned as the mastermind behind one of the biggest crime syndicates the Northern Hemisphere has ever seen."

I suck in a gasp and climb off Colton as our attention becomes solely glued to the screen.

The reporter continues. "At this point in time, it is believed that Lorenzo DeCarlo was involved in gun-trafficking and illicit drug manufacturing. More details to come."

The camera pans to the estate to where cops are flooding through the doors of the property and bringing out boxes upon boxes of evidence while I sit here with my mouth hanging open.

An amused chuckle has my gaze flicking toward Colton. "Did you know he was involved in this shit?"

His eyes sparkle and the way his lips pull up into a devilish smirk tells me that he knows a shitload more than he'll ever let on. "I might have heard a few things along the grapevine."

I narrow my eyes at the man I'm very quickly falling in love with. "Did you have something to do with this?" I question, hooking my thumb toward the screen and recalling the exact moment Colton stood in this very room with Vincent DeCarlo and vowed to take down each of his sons and then leave the old man for last.

He shrugs his shoulders. "Don't know what you're talking about," he says, his smirk not budging one bit. "The cops have been looking into Lorenzo for years now, they just lacked a little … proof. What can I say? It's not my fault that video footage from their break in just happened to land on one of the only good cop's in Bellevue Springs' computer showing exactly what they needed to put him away for the rest of his life."

My mouth drops as I stare at him in awe. "Hmm, strange," I say, taking on the same devilish smirk. "I wonder how that could have happened."

"Like I said, it's a mystery to me."

I stare at him in awe. "You know you're kinda incredible?"

"Just kinda?"

"Yeah," I laugh. "Now, if you were the guy who actually handed that footage over and sealed his fate, then I'd be a little more impressed, but like you said, it's a mystery to you."

Colton grabs my arm and yanks me back to him. I go crashing down onto his wide chest and his hand spanks down on my ass as I fall. "Watch it, Jade. I won't hesitate to show you exactly how I feel about that."

I laugh and find myself staring down at him, the seriousness of it all instantly sobering our moods. "Maryne would be proud of you," I whisper. "You did good."

His eyes flare with love and he watches me for a long, drawn-out second and it's almost as though he needed to hear those very words, that my support has some kind of weight lifting from his shoulders.

"Including Vincent, there's still five more of those bastards to go," he tells me. "I promised Harrison that I'd take each and every one of those fuckers down and I intend to keep my word."

"I know you will," I tell him. "They won't get away with this. You're Colton Fucking Carrington, and they're going to learn the hard way that you can't be fucked with, and not only that, it's sending a message to every other douchebag who wants to take you down that you can't be beaten. Never have, never will."

Colton's hand slips up my back until it's wrapping around the back of my neck. He pulls me down to him and seals my words with a deep kiss, conveying everything that he's not ready to say out loud.

"Come on," I tell him when we finally break apart. "You must actually be hungry. What do you want? I can make pancakes or bacon and eggs."

"You know I have staff that does that for me."

"Ha," I scoff. "You're looking at her."

"Babe," he says with a low groan as I grab his hand and pull him up from the couch. "You know I don't actually look at you as one of my staff, right? You're my girlfriend who just happens to clean my place in the sexiest little outfits."

I raise my brow as I search around for my sweatpants. "The fuck are you talking about?" I question. "It's not like I'm getting around in those tiny little maid outfits with my ass showing and hooker heels. I've only ever worn sweatpants and whatever tank I can find that has the least stains on it."

"I know, but it's fucking sexy. The way you dance around with your earphones in, forgetting that everyone can see you. It's you and it's real. It's not like the others who wear those ridiculous uniforms. They look so robotic, but if you wanted to get one of those sexy maid outfits and wear it for me, I'm down for that ..."

"Careful," I tell him, dragging him into the kitchen and trying to ignore his last comment before I allow him to bend me over the kitchen counter and fuck me senseless. "You're drooling."

He rolls his eyes. "Is it that hard for you to just accept a compliment when you hear one?"

"Yeah," I laugh. "It really is."

He shakes his head as I go about the kitchen, grabbing all the things that I'd only just put away an hour ago. "Actually, I think I'll get rid of the uniforms. It's so formal—too fucking formal. That's not the vibe I want when walking around my home. That's one of those bullshit rules Dad brought in after he fucked one of his maids and she claimed sexual harassment in the workplace. It was probably his way of punishing her and enjoyed making everyone else suffer right along with her."

I stare at him with my mouth hanging wide. "Your dad really was a creep."

He laughs, coming to stand by me. "Trust me, you haven't heard the half of it."

"I can't wait," I tell him, reaching across him to grab the large mixing bowl and looking over everything I have before me, trying to figure out what I've forgotten. Eggs, butter, milk, baking powder ... "Ahh," I say, grabbing the eggs and cracking them against the side of the bowl. "Could you grab the flour and vanilla extract?"

He gives me a blank stare as I put the broken eggshells aside. "The what?"

I raise a brow and look back at him. "You don't know what flour is?"

He rolls his eyes. "I'm not fucking stupid. I know what flour is," he says, darting across to the pantry and quickly scanning the shelves before grabbing the packet. "What's the other shit you need?"

I roll my eyes and step across to the pantry to join him, realizing it's going to be a hell of a lot quicker to get it myself than have to explain it to a guy like Colton. He's so fucking smart and business-minded but shove him in a kitchen and he's a lost little boy.

I measure up all my ingredients from memory while ignoring the way Colton stares at me dumbfounded. "How do you know how to do this?"

"Make pancakes?" I question, dumping in all the ingredients and grabbing my whisk.

"Cook in general," he says. "Did your mom teach you?"

I press my lips together and look down at the mixing bowl, making sure to get all the lumps. "She taught me a little but truth be told, she was always out working and I was left at home to figure it out. It wasn't until Nic started hanging around that I really started to learn. He's a bit of a whiz in the kitchen," I say, feeling the heaviness of all the amazing memories come rushing in. "He didn't like the idea of me cooking the same three meals over and over again. He taught me that just because you have to eat cheap, doesn't mean you have to eat like shit. Best lesson I ever learned. All the boys kinda taught me a little something when it comes to cooking, except Kai. He can't cook to save his life which is why he's fucking around all the time, hoping the girl will feed him before he fucks her off in the morning. That kid has eaten way too much take out for his own good. If the grilled chicken place wasn't down the road from him, he'd probably starve."

Colton drops his elbow onto the counter and he brushes my hair back over my shoulder. "You really miss them, don't you?"

My whole world comes crashing down as the emotions begin to overwhelm me and I find myself unable to meet his eyes, afraid that my truth will hurt him in some sort of way.

Seeing the mess his question put me in, he steps into me and pulls me deep into his arms. "I hate that you're hurting, Jade," he whispers, resting his chin above my head. "I'm not going to lie to you and say that I love that they're such a big part of your life, because I don't. I don't like them, but I'll tolerate them for you. I hate the way Nic put his hands on you and left you bruised and I hate the way you're always so hurt every time you come back from seeing them, but if making things right with them and learning to forgive and forget is going to bring back your smile, then go to them and talk it out."

"I ..." A heavy breath escapes me and I force myself to hold back my tears. "I'm not ready to forgive them and I sure as hell will never forget."

"You don't have to forgive them, Ocean, not if they haven't done anything to earn it, but you can talk to them and make your pain go away. I hate seeing you so down about this."

I step out of his arms and meet his eyes. "You really think so?"

"Don't get me wrong, I'd prefer to spend my day buried deep inside of you, but you need to do this. You need those dickheads in your life. Just go and talk. You don't have to come to any conclusions, but let them know where you stand, and hell, maybe give Sebastian a fucking hug or something … anything to get that fucker to stop calling every phone in my fucking house."

I raise a brow. "He's been calling the house?"

Colton doesn't reply but his unimpressed scoff is answer enough. "Here," he says, stepping across the kitchen and pressing his hand against the small screen that's been built into the marble countertop. His hand is scanned and a second later, a small drawer pops out, displaying an impressive array of car keys. He picks up a small key and places it in my hand. "Take the Audi and go see them. Make it right or don't, it doesn't matter. Just go and see them and heal whatever part of your heart it is that's been aching for them."

I raise my chin and meet his eyes, curling my hand around the keys. "Are you sure?"

He dips his head and gently brushes his lips over mine. "I'm sure, but if I don't hear from you throughout the day, I'm coming down there and bringing your stubborn ass home."

Excitement begins filling me as well as fear. Am I really going to go back home and meet with my boys? The idea of seeing them again fills my heart with warmth, but the constant reminder of how we left things kills me.

I'm nowhere near ready to forgive them for all the secrets and lies, but to start mending the bridge between us … I don't know. The thought has a spark of electricity burning within me.

When I saw them last, I told them I never wanted to see them again, but at the same time, they're also my boys. They're my family. How could I turn my back on something like that?

I look down at the mixing bowl with the pancake batter. "What about your breakfast?" I question, glancing back up at him.

"I'll survive, Jade. Just go, I'll be here waiting when you get back."

A smile tears across my face and I press up onto my tippy-toes, crushing my lips against his. "I'll be back for dinner," I tell him before taking off like a bat out of hell and rushing toward the garage, not giving a damn about the fact that I haven't showered, haven't brushed my teeth, and haven't gotten a fresh pair of panties after Colton ripped them off me. All that matters is mending the divide between me and my Widows and this time, I won't be returning until things are right.

# CHAPTER 10

The Audi drives like a dream as I speed down the road, pushing it to its absolute limits in my need to get back home to Breakers Flats.

I get to see my boys.

I really shouldn't be so excited about that. I should be a ball of nerves. I should be carefully picking out the words that I'll say, and I should be reminding myself of the reason I ran in the first place. They're not good guys, they're gangsters, murderers … liars. But above all, they're my family. Always have been, always will be.

I love them without a doubt even when they force me to hate

them. Why is it so hard to hate them?

I get to Breakers Flats in record time, somehow managing it without being pulled over. I broke far too many traffic laws to get away with. Maybe luck is on my side today. At least, I hope it is. I couldn't possibly handle any more bad luck when it comes to my Widows.

I pull into the shitty underground parking of Nic's apartment complex and instantly notice that his mom's car is gone. It's just after nine on a Sunday morning. She would have gone to work and started her shift by now, but I don't understand why she bothers. With Nic being the big guy in charge, they certainly don't need the money. Hell, they could afford to move out of this shitty apartment and buy a proper home with a yard, but here they stay.

Nic could probably afford to buy his mom a place of her own but I know that will never happen. He likes her close. Being the leader of the Widows isn't exactly always sunshine and rainbows. There is a lot of shit that goes along with it too. Shit like having massive targets on the backs of the people you love. Something Nic has always been aware of.

After parking the Audi beside Nic's rundown piece of shit, I open the door and instantly feel the nerves come over me. These are the nerves that I should have felt the second Colton suggested that I come here.

Nic is a cold-blooded murderer.

I watched the darkness come over him and then I watched as the man that I once loved slit the throats of two men before shooting a third in the back. It wasn't even done with grace. He taunted them, teased them with the knife, he even broke off the trigger finger of the man who shot and killed his father. I've never seen anything like it and I'm damn sure that I never want to see it again.

I don't know what came over me when I was down in that wine cellar dungeon with Jude. Maybe I was channeling my inner Nic. Something came over me and I lost all control. I gave myself over to the darkness and now I can never go back. I'll never have that innocence I once had. I'll forever be the girl who almost killed a man—a very shitty man with no morals, but nonetheless, I almost killed him and that fact will always sit heavily on my heart.

I pump my hands at my side, trying to talk myself into moving one foot in front of the other. It's not that hard, I just have to keep moving, and eventually, I'll be standing at his door.

The last time I saw him was the night of the Gatsby party when he crashed and came storming through. He grabbed my arm and tore me down the steps. I was tumbling and falling, even slammed my chest against the hard front steps of the Carrington mansion. It wasn't exactly Nic's finest moment, but it wasn't mine either. I should have known he was going to show up and demand to see me, but pulling me down the stairs … I wasn't prepared for that. I don't know if he'd been drinking, or was just emotionally fucked-up, but something wasn't right. That crazed possessive man wasn't my Nic. I just hope that what I'm about to walk into isn't going to leave me with regrets.

I hope the old Nic is back. I miss that guy, not the monster he's quickly turning into.

I find myself at his door. It's too early for him to be up. He's usually awake until four in the morning and then sleeps till after midday. Usually, I'd just walk in, but it doesn't feel right, not anymore.

Too much has changed between us and I have no idea where we stand. Hopefully, we can clear the air and find that common ground again. Then once that mission is complete, I can do the rounds.

Dealing with Eli, Kai, and Sebastian won't be nearly as hard as dealing with Nic. Sebastian will just fall at my knees and wrap his arms around my waist, refusing to let go until I forgave him. Eli will stare at me from across the room, biting his lip as he struggles to find the right words while Kairo will sit me down and deliver the lengthy speech that's been circling his mind for the past two weeks, not giving me a chance to even get a word in.

My fist comes to the door and my knuckles bang against it before I can talk myself out of it.

What was Colton thinking sending me here? I know he wants to see me happy but what if I'm not ready for this? What if Nic hasn't had enough time to lick his wounds and is still being a possessive douche? Screw Colton and his obsessive need to see me happy. Why can't he be one of those jealous guys who refuses to let me see my boys? I can deal with that shit like a pro.

Groans of protest come from within Nic's apartment and the sound of a whiny girl instantly draws my attention. I should have known he would have had company in there. There's no way a guy like Nic would have gone to bed alone on a Saturday night. That's just who he is.

I hear soft murmurs and the sounds of the doors opening and

closing and then finally, the familiar rattle of the lock sliding out of place. The door handle twists and then Nic is there, standing before me in his bare-chested glory.

He stares at me as though he doesn't believe what he's seeing. "What are you doing here? Did he hurt you?"

My brows furrow and I shake my head while he holds every bit of my attention just as I hold his, that is until his little guest steps into view and everything crushes within me.

Carmen Fucking Saunders.

Fuck, that hurts.

I meet Nic's eyes and I see the instant regret and despite us not being together, he knows that this move has only managed to fuck things up between us just that little bit more.

His chances of ever getting me back were well and truly blown when he first slept with the whore while we were together, but doing it again has more than sealed our fate. It's a knife straight to the back and I want nothing more than to tear him apart.

"Really?" I whisper, keeping my voice low in fear of it breaking. "Out of all the girls you could be fucking around with, you pick her?"

His heart is on his sleeve and I see him desperately trying to figure out a way to make this all okay. He turns and looks back at the half-naked girl. "Get out," he demands, his voice a low warning that sends chills spiraling down my spine.

"What?" she snaps, looking back at me with distaste. "No. Tell that little slut to come back later. I'm not nearly done with you yet."

Nic moves like lightning. One second he's standing before me in the doorway and the next his arm is stretched out with the tip of his gun pressed firmly against her temple. "GET OUT," he roars, making my back stiffen with fear as he uses that same tone he used in the warehouse. "You're the fucking reason she's not with me in the first place. Just because you've got a tight fucking pussy doesn't mean I won't hesitate to end you, now get the fuck out of my house."

Her eyes are wide and she doesn't wait a goddamn second before darting through the open door, slamming her shoulder into mine in the process.

Nic lowers his gun as his dark gaze sweeps back to mine. "Was that really necessary?" I question, silently getting a thrill out of seeing her fear. In the end, she's the girl who knowingly seduced a taken man, but he's the one who cheated. So even though she's also at fault, the error is on Nic, but that doesn't change the fact that seeing her squirm felt like fucking victory.

Nic shrugs his shoulders as I hover awkwardly in the doorway. "I wasn't really going to kill her."

"Really? Could have fooled me."

"O, come on. That's not fair."

"You're shitting me, right? You just held a gun to the girl's head and told her that you wouldn't hesitate to kill her for what? Not barrelling out of your bedroom window before I could see her? Why her, Nic? You could literally have anyone you wanted, so why pick her?"

I see the answer in his eyes and he doesn't bother responding, knowing damn well what I see. He wanted to make me hurt just like I make him hurt.

I let out a heavy breath. I guess a congratulations is in order because it fucking worked. He walks back to the door and grips the hardwood. "Come on," he says, waving me in. "I suppose we have a few things to talk about."

No shit.

I meet his eyes and warily step through to his apartment, feeling a wave of heartache take over me. "Should I call the boys to come over?" he questions, watching every tiny step I take across his apartment until I sit down on his couch.

I meet his eyes and shake my head. "Not yet," I tell him. "You and I …"

"Yeah," he says, not needing me to finish my train of thought. He knows we need this moment to talk alone just as much as I know it. He lets out a heavy sigh and moves across the room. "Come here," he whispers, dropping down beside me and pulling me into his chest.

I curl into him as though this space was made solely for me and within moments, the raw emotions well up and overwhelm me. I try to hold the traitorous tears at bay but they spring from my eyes and slowly roll down my cheeks.

"Don't cry, baby. You have no idea how sorry I am that I hurt you. I hate that I allowed you to see that side of me and I hate that what you saw forced you further into his arms. I'm so sorry, O. I wish I could take that back. I wish I could go back and force myself to stay here instead of dragging you out of that party. I was fucking drunk and I've never felt jealousy like that before. I wasn't thinking … I fucking hurt you. Twice over the last two months I've left you fucking bruised and baby, it makes me so fucking sick to my stomach."

I wipe my tears across his shirt and take a deep breath, desperately trying to calm myself. I can't allow my emotions to get the best of me, otherwise, we're going to sit here on this stupid couch all day long and get nowhere. "I don't know who you are anymore," I admit. "This new version of you is terrifying. You've never put your hands on me before and all of a sudden, you're grabbing me every chance you get. The old Nic would have killed anyone who even thought about touching me like that, but you … I don't know. You're different now. I miss the old Nic. I miss my friend."

"I'm still that guy," he urges. "I swear to you, Ocean. I'm still him. I'm just going through some shit. Losing you to that world and then losing my father and taking over the Widows. It's a lot, and I know my excuses aren't going to validate how I treated you, but trust me, the boys have made sure that I've been paying for it. I know you're not speaking to them right now either, but we're all still in your fucking corner. They made sure I knew how fucking badly I fucked up."

I dry my eyes and pull out of his arms, hating the way he watches me with such need. It's as though my words hold the power to either make or break him and that power terrifies me. No one should hold that kind of power over another. "You really did fuck up, Nic," I tell him, not holding back. "You showed me the real you. The dark one that you always promised to protect me from. In that warehouse … those men were forced to their knees and you brutally slit their throats. You looked right at me, Nic. You knew I was there. You should have sent me away, but you didn't. You opened my world to your darkness, you brought me into that and when I look at you now, I see that man, I don't see the gentle loving guy that would whisper sweet nothings in my ear and protect me from the world. I see that cold-blooded killer, the one who lies and is surrounded by darkness and misery."

Nic lets out a heavy breath and leans forward onto his knees, staring ahead at the coffee table. "I don't know how to make it right, Ocean."

His confession slices straight through me and I fall back against the couch, both of us content to sit in complete silence. When the heaviness finally begins to fade between us, he leans back and pulls me into his arms again. "I tried to come and see you the other day," he tells me. "I've actually tried a few times but I talk myself out of it each time knowing you'll just send me away. I got as far as the outskirts of Bellevue Springs yesterday."

"Why didn't you just keep going?"

"You needed time, Ocean. The things I've done … they're not just going to go away. I've hurt you too much."

"You have."

"I'm glad you finally came around."

"I didn't," I admit. "I wasn't ready. I was content with letting you guys sweat it but Colton saw how much I was hurting and pushed me to come. He doesn't like seeing me like that, but he was right. I needed to be here and fix what's been broken."

Nic raises a brow. "He sent you here to talk?" I nod and Nic lets out a frustrated breath. "I guess I can't be mad at that, huh?" he grumbles. "I hate that you felt like you couldn't come here though."

"You lied about my dad, Nic. You murdered two guys in front of me and then became possessively jealous and hurt me. I needed time to breathe, but so did you."

His hand drops to rest on top of mine. "I did," he says. "I'm not going to lie to you anymore, O. I'm still insanely jealous. I hate that you're with him and I hate the light that shines in your eyes whenever he's around. You're falling for him and I'm terrified that when that happens, you're going to forget about us. I still stand by my word, O. You belong here with me."

"I'm not so sure about that anymore," I admit. "You are right though, I am falling for him, but where you're wrong—I'll never forget about you. You guys are my home, my family. Just because I'm away from you right now, doesn't mean that I'm not still here."

Nic makes a soft sound, clearly not agreeing with what I've just said. "He's going to take you away from me."

I shake my head against his warm chest as I listen to the sound of his beating heart. "No," I whisper. "He knows you guys make me happy, that's why he sent me here. Don't get me wrong, he hates you. He could kill you for the way you've treated me over the past few weeks but he'll never hold me back from you because he knows how much I love you."

He grumbles under his breath and I let out a sigh, more than ready to move along. "Why did you lie about my father for all those years?"

"It wasn't my decision," he tells me. "It was your father's and I respected it."

"What do you mean?"

"Look," he says, giving it to me straight. "I'm not going to sugarcoat it. Your dad wasn't a great man. He was fucking sick and twisted in the head. He got off on killing people and that made him un-fucking-stoppable. He was the best at what he did and everyone knew it and because of that, everyone wanted him on their side and they would go to great lengths to make that happen. Why do you think my dad put us in your life? He wanted us close to you in case we needed to make a move. None of us expected that you would become the fucking world to us. It was supposed to be a business deal but you became family, and no, before you ask, I don't regret it. I don't regret lying to you, because in the end, it kept you hidden from that darkness and allowed you to live in a world where you thought everything was perfect. You had the sweet doting father and friends who would die to protect you. I was never going to take that away from you."

"You're making it really hard for me to hate you right now," I warn him as my eyes begin filling with tears again.

"Good," he says. "I don't want you to hate me. I just want you to understand why. Surely you must know that none of us would ever hurt you purposely like that."

"You could have told me that he sold me to Charles, or at least given me a bit of warning before letting me go there."

"Believe me, Ocean. I did everything I could to keep you here with me. Fucking *everything*."

"I know," I murmur, recalling all the effort he put in to keep me at home, all the begging, the offers to move in, the desperation he felt. "Everything is so fucked up at the moment, but I feel like we're finally coming out the other end. Charles and my dad are both gone, as well as Maryne, but the dust is finally starting to settle. I have Colton and some new friends while you have the opportunity to turn things around for the Widows, hell, maybe even do something good with it."

Nic scoffs. "I don't think my men are really going to get on board with suddenly being upstanding members of the community."

I find myself laughing and while things are certainly still very strained between us, I feel that the broken pieces of our relationship have finally started to mend. Maybe there's a chance for us to find that same incredible friendship that we had before all of this shit went down.

"Come on," I tell him, getting up from the couch. "I'll call the boys and tell them to come over while you go and burn your sheets. I know you're technically allowed to sleep with whoever the fuck you want to sleep with, but if you bring that cow in here ever again, I'm going to castrate you."

"Alright," he laughs, while his eyes beam with relief. "You have yourself a deal."

I make my way into his small kitchen and start working on coffee while he quickly strips his bed and throws the sheets in his washer. I'm busily reaching for the mugs while shoving my phone under my ear and squishing it there with my shoulder.

The phone starts ringing and as I wait for Eli to hurry up and answer, Nic steps in behind me, placing both hands down on the counter on either side of my hips. "You have to know how sorry I am, O," he murmurs. I hear Eli answer the call but I don't respond, instead listening to what Nic has to say. "I've done a lot of shit that I'm not proud of. I've been jealous, ruthless, and downright cold. I saw you and Colton getting closer and …"

"Saw?" I grunt. "What do you mean saw?"

"I … fuck," he curses, pulling away.

I spin around, ignoring Eli's soft curse in my ear. "You have two fucking seconds to tell me what you did, and I swear to you, Nic, if you even attempt to lie to me again, I will spend every day of my life making you regret it."

He lets out a heavy sigh and his eyes drop to his hands in shame. "You're going to fucking hate me."

"Two fucking seconds," I warn.

"During Charles' wake when Kai disappeared …"

"He was stealing Charles' Rolex."

Nic shakes his head. "No, well, maybe. Who fucking knows when it comes to Kairo, but the reason he disappeared … I had him install cameras so I could keep watch over you. You'd already been raped in that fucking mansion, I wasn't going to take any chances."

"You did what?" I demand.

"I …"

"No. You've been watching me. You saw me and Colton …"

He nods and the shame radiating off him is so fucking thick that I could choke on it. He glances back up at me and the look in his eyes is crippling. "I'm so fucking sorry, O. I was so mad. I've never felt anything like it. I saw you and him first get together and I just … I snapped."

"Wait," I whisper, taking a step back as I feel a cold shiver run down my spine. "What did you do?" He shakes his head, his heart on his sleeve once again but this time, it's fucking deflated. He doesn't say the words, but he doesn't have to.

There's only one thing that happened after Colton and I were first together and it was a direct attack on him. "The DeCarlo brothers," I whisper. "We thought it was Vincent who sent his sons, but it wasn't, was it?"

Nic presses his lips into a tight line and I see the truth in his eyes, but he refuses to respond.

"FUCKING ANSWER ME," I yell. "I was in that fucking mansion. My mother was nearly caught and Maryne was fucking shot. *My friend*, Nic. They killed my friend. What if that had been me? Do not fucking tell me that you sent that hell to attack us."

His face goes white and he takes a hesitant step back from me. "I'm sorry, Ocean," he says, looking sick with himself and knowing damn well that whatever progress we had just made is now shattered into a million pieces. "The brothers owed me a favor and they paid up."

# CHAPTER 11

I sit in the Audi in Colton's dark garage, just sitting and staring at the wall in front. I can't find it within me to step out of this car and face reality.

I left Nic's place three long hours ago and have been sitting here an absolute mess since I got back. I don't even remember the drive home, all I seem to know is that Nic was supposed to be the one who protected me but he sent the DeCarlo's here. He put us in danger, he put my mom in danger, and his actions are what lead to Maryne's death.

What am I supposed to do with that information? If I tell Colton, he won't hesitate to retaliate. All my boys will be gone and if Colton is the reason that I lose them … fuck. I don't even know how I would react to that but I know for sure that things will never be the same. I don't want to lose any of them. Who am I supposed to protect here?

The shrill ring of my phone tears through the silence and I jump before scrambling to answer it. Seeing Eli's name across the screen, I slam it to my ear. "Did you know?" I demand.

"Babe…"

"Did. You. Know?"

He lets out a heavy sigh. "Yes. We didn't know at the time, but after the attack, we put the pieces together."

My heart shatters. "I can't fucking believe this. Not only are you all sitting over there and watching me fuck my boyfriend like dirty perves, but you were keeping this from me too. How could you? You were supposed to have my back."

"We do have your back, that's why we put in surveillance in the first place."

"Let me guess?" I say with a breathy scoff. "Keep me distracted in the ballroom during a fucking wake while you send Kairo upstairs to bug the whole fucking mansion. Fuck you. Fuck you all."

"O …"

"No," I snap, pushing my way out of the car and storming through the internal door into the mansion. "Where are they?"

"Babe, they're for your protection."

"Where the fuck are they, Elijah?"

I hear his grumbled cringe through the phone. I very rarely use his proper name but when I do, he knows that I'm not fucking around.

"Everywhere," he says. "Pool house, your bedroom, both the main pools, the mansion living areas, kitchens, bathrooms. Every room has been hit."

Everything sinks within me knowing just how wild I allowed myself to be with Colton yesterday. I was vulnerable and I completely gave myself to him and to think that those douchebag Widows were sitting back and watching the fucking show makes me sick. How could they do that to me?

"I want a list and I want it right fucking now. Every last one, Eli."

"Okay," he finally says. "I'll send you a list now."

I end the call without a goodbye and find myself pacing the foyer, way too on edge to even begin calming myself. I wait all of two minutes before my phone dings with an incoming text and I glance down to find Eli's text, but not only is there a text from Eli, there's about twenty from Nic.

How the hell did I miss those coming in?

I delete every single one of them. I don't need to read them because I know exactly what they're going to say. Not one of them could make up for what he did. Maryne's life is on his shoulders. He did that. The DeCarlo brothers pulled the trigger, but Nic gave the go-ahead and for that, he's just as bad. How will we ever be okay?

I scan over Eli's list and just as he had said, there's a camera in nearly every single room of the house. I start looking over the foyer and find the tiny little camera hidden in the frame of one of Charles' expensive artworks and realize that this is going to take all fucking day.

I grab the little camera and rip it off the frame before looking over it closely. These things look fucking expensive and for my sake, I hope they were. I hope they cost Nic a fucking bomb.

I mouth 'fuck you,' to the camera before dropping it to the ground and crushing it beneath my shoe, listening to the satisfying crunch as it smashes against the marble flooring.

One down, a million to go.

I get busy, going from room to room and tearing down every last one. They're tiny and hard to find. On the downstairs level, they're mostly hidden in plain sight—potted plants, photo frames, even a fucking fruit bowl. Upstairs and in rooms which don't have a 20-foot ceiling, they're generally hidden in the air conditioning vents.

I step into the private kitchen and instantly hear Colton with the boys in the adjoining den. From the sound of it, they must be chilling out with pizza and video games, so I leave them to it. It's not as though I'm in such a great mood right now anyway. I still have a job to do.

I scurry around in the kitchen and after a minute of searching, I find the stupid camera at the top of a cabinet, giving the boys a wide view of the kitchen. I clench my jaw and start climbing up onto the counter, listening as Charlie lets out a confused laugh. "Bro, what the fuck is your girl doing?"

There's a short silence as they all stop what they're doing and focus on me. "I, uhh … I've got no fucking idea. I wasn't expecting her back for hours."

Ignoring them, I stretch up onto my tippy-toes and reach the camera with a grunt before dropping it straight onto the counter and crushing it. A string of angered curses come flying out of my mouth but I continue on, moving into the living room.

"Babe?" I hear Charlie calling from the den. "What the fuck are you looking for? What was that?"

I ignore him and continue my search, finding another on the edge of the massive TV screen, a screen that I was staring at just this morning. How could I have missed this? This camera stares straight at the couch where Colton had spent the morning eating my pussy and then slowly fucking me to perfection and now all four of those fucked-up Widows have seen it.

I've never felt so fucking violated in my life.

With each camera that I tear off a wall, cabinet, or frame—my anger triples. How could they do this to me? How could they take away my privacy and claim it's for protection? Yes, I was raped in this mansion, but it happened once by a guy who is now well and truly locked up. I'm safe. They might not know that but they've been searching for Jude everywhere they go. They know he's not coming back to finish the job. The cameras should have been called off.

I make my way toward the den to find Colton standing in the doorway, watching me with curious eyes. "What are you doing, Jade?" he questions, clearly having watched me make my way from the kitchen to the living room.

I barge past him into the room and Spencer instantly hits pause on his video game to watch as I start searching the room. "What are you looking for?" he questions with a grunt.

My jaw is clenched and I sense Colton moving in closer, more than ready to grab me and force answers out of me, but I'm not having it, not until I find the stupid little thing.

I start with the TV and quickly move on until I find the camera in the top right corner of the room. "For fuck's sake," I grumble to myself, feeling the eyes of the boys heavily on my back.

I grab the small side table and drag it across the room before climbing onto it and tearing the camera off the wall. "Woah," Charlie says. "What the fuck is that?"

I jump from the table and land on the floor with a thud. I hold the camera out, more than ready to drop it on the floor and crush it just like I'd done with the others, but Colton's dominant demand stops me in my tracks. "Jade, stop," he snaps, making my head whip up. "What the fuck are you doing?"

My teeth hurt from clenching my jaw so hard yet I can't seem to stop. "Fucking cameras everywhere. Nic bugged the place, he's been watching us."

"The fuck?" he says, stepping into me and tearing the camera from my fingers as Spencer flies to his feet in alarm. Charlie just stares, unable to string together a protest of disgust.

"Where are they?" Spencer growls, his eyes heated as they flash to mine.

I see his deeper meaning. He wants to know if there's one in Charles' wine cellar and I instantly shake my head. That was the first place I looked for as I scanned over the list. I pull my phone out and open it to Eli's text before tossing it to him. "They're everywhere, every room, bathroom, living area, even the fucking pool house. But I wouldn't trust this list. They're nothing but fucking liars."

"FUCK," Colton growls, looking over the camera before dropping it to the ground and crushing it the same way I had. He glances across at Spencer. "Give me that fucking list."

My phone is tossed across the room again and Colton snatches it out of the air as simply as if he was swatting a fly. He scans over it before throwing the phone to Charlie and looking between the two boys. "You two finish down here. I'll head upstairs with Ocean."

They nod and just like that, we all clear out of the den.

With the boys' help, the house was cleared within an hour but it wasn't exactly the easiest task. Colton took over searching his sisters' and mom's room and only ended up with arguments and white lies. Luckily they all quickly left after that and Colton was able to sweep through their rooms properly.

My mood hasn't begun to calm down and sensing that, both Spencer and Charlie are quick to make excuses as to why they need to leave. They give hasty goodbyes and are out the door within mere seconds, knowing just how wicked I can be when needed.

I'm left with Colton in the kitchen as I sit upon the counter silently raging about my lack of privacy, but I can't deny the relief that pours through me knowing Nic no longer has eyes on us. Colton steps out of the secret bar behind the kitchen with a glass tumbler filled with who the hell knows what and instantly hands it over. "Here," he says with a deep grumble. "This'll help take the edge off."

I take the glass from him and look down at the clear liquid before bringing it to my lips and throwing back the whole glass. My face scrunches with the burn and I choke back on it, having absolutely no idea what I just drank.

"Woah, Jade," Colton chuckles. "You're supposed to sip it. This shit will fuck you up."

I shrug my shoulders. "Excellent. Hit me with another."

Colton ignores my comment and moves into me with a hand on either side of my thighs, caging me in on the counter. "Are you alright?"

I shake my head, feeling his closeness somehow pulling that rage out of me. "No, I'm so freaking angry. I can't understand how he could do that to me? He was supposed to be my best friend but every single step of the way, he's done something to betray my trust."

Colton's arms wrap around me and he holds me tightly to his chest. "It's okay," he murmurs. "I'm going to get a security team to come through and sweep the property properly. You won't have to worry about it anymore."

I nod into his chest, hating how much this has destroyed me. It's like the final nail in the coffin. Maybe it hurts more because seconds before that, I thought I had my friend back. We were nearly there. I was so close to starting to forgive, but the guy just keeps fucking up. How can he expect me to ever move on from this?

"So, I take it things didn't go so well in Breakers Flats?"

I pull back and meet his eyes, quickly realizing that if there's going to be a right time to tell him about Nic being behind the DeCarlo attack, that it would be now, but I find myself hesitating. If I was to tell Colton, it would be a war. He vowed that he would get revenge for the attack and if he knew that Nic was behind it all, he'd act out against him and I have absolutely no idea how far he would go.

Do I lie to the man that I'm falling in love with?

If Colton knew and hurt Nic, or Nic retaliated and hurt Colton … I don't know where that would leave me. Things would never be the same again. If I tell, I'm going to lose either one or both of them permanently and it's not a risk I can take.

I shouldn't want to protect Nic. I should be throwing him under the bus and making him pay for what he did, but I find myself holding back. Colton is my future. I know it with one hundred percent certainty, but I can't find it within myself to let go of Nic or the Widows, not yet at least.

I find myself shrugging, feeling the heaviest kind of guilt falling down on my shoulders and slowly tearing me apart from the inside. "See, that's just the thing," I tell him, deciding that I need to give him at least a little bit of truth. "It was going great. Nic and I talked things through and I thought we were just about to get back on track and find that common ground again when everything went south. We talked everything through and it was so freaking heavy but we needed it, and then I was ready to call the boys and make things right with them when Nic came with another apology and slipped up about the cameras. I just … it was the final straw."

Colton pulls me in again and I find myself staring down at the ground. I've never felt so damn pathetic. I've always made a point of being honest, and although I didn't exactly lie, I evaded the truth and to me, that's just as guilty.

"Come on," he tells me, pulling me off the counter and dragging me out of the kitchen. "I found some things while going through my sister's room that I think will cheer you up." My brows furrow as I look up at him in confusion. "It's their big plans to take you down this week at school. They're not too skilled in the art of takedowns and actually wrote this shit out like a schedule."

"Are you kidding? Everyone knows you keep that shit locked up tightly inside your head."

"Yeah," he laughs. "I never claimed they were smart."

I shake my head as he pulls me up the stairs towards Cora's bedroom and I laugh as he pushes open the door. They've only been home a week and already she's transformed her old bedroom into a Cora shrine. There are selfie pictures covering the wall, everything pink and fluffy, there's a whole wall dedicated to her jewelry with a rotating case for her diamonds. "This shit is insane," I grumble. "These girls have too much money."

"I know," he grumbles.

"Like you're one to talk. I've seen your Rolex rotisserie hiding in your closet."

A smirk pulls at his lips as he walks deeper into her room and grabs the papers off her desk. He instantly hands them over and I look down at them with a laugh. The page is titled 'Ocean Takedown' in pretty cursive writing with dot points the whole way down the sheet. "You've got to be kidding," I grumble. "Your sisters need a hobby."

Colton scoffs his agreement and drops down onto the edge of Cora's bed as I read over their ridiculous little plans, knowing damn well that I have an epic response for each and every one of them. I find myself glancing up at Colton with a small frown. "You really don't care that I'm practically at war with your sisters?"

He shakes his head. "My sisters are bitches and they're very quickly turning into my mom. They need to be knocked down a few steps and realize that they can't keep getting away with this behavior. One day, it's going to get them in big fucking trouble that money isn't going to get them out of. So, I figure it's best to learn their lesson now rather than end up in a women's prison in ten years."

"And that I'm the one who's going to teach them that lesson?"

He shrugs a shoulder. "I mean, if it's going to bring a little excitement to your life, then I have no issue with it. I won't think twice about defending you to them because they can clearly see how I feel about you and they don't respect that. I'm not close to my mom or sisters. They're bitches and I don't want anything to do with them. If they're causing you hell, then go right ahead and throw it back at them, they deserve it. Besides, once they realize that they're not going to get anything out of me, they'll fuck off to wherever the hell they've been living and we can get back to focusing on us."

I walk across the room and loop my arms around his neck. "That sounds really nice," I whisper, looking over her room. "Now, how do you think Cora would feel about me sucking her big brother's cock in her bed?"

His lips lift into an excited grin as his hands come to my waist and pull me in closer. "I think she'd absolutely hate it."

I drop down to my knees and push his knees wide as my tongue runs along my bottom lip. "Perfect."

# CHAPTER 12

I sit at the dinner table on Tuesday night, across from Mom and Colton who are busily throwing around theme ideas for next month's party and to be honest, I couldn't be less interested. Though I'm not going to lie, Colton coming here and eating dinner with us—instead of with his mom and sisters—gives me all sorts of thrills.

I love that in all this bullshit, he's stuck by my side. It means the world to me and concretes the fact that what we are building between us is real. So fucking real.

I'm starting to see myself having a real future with him when only a few short weeks ago, I'd deny the fact that I had any future at all.

Moving to Bellevue Springs is quickly becoming one of the best things I've ever done. There's a possibility that I might go to college, I'm all of a sudden saving money for a future, I have a boyfriend who cherishes and worships me as though I walk on water, and not to mention the incredible friends I've made along the way. It was certainly a bumpy start though, one that I'm more than happy to have moved on from.

Colton and I have had to do a lot of growing over the last two months, but we came out the other end so much better, stronger, and a hell of a lot happier. I wouldn't change it for the world.

"You're quiet over there," my mother says, forking another mouthful of salad between her lips.

"Oh, I, umm … yeah. Sorry, just got things on my mind."

Mom's brow shoots right up. "Oh, really?" she questions. "Usually talk of elaborate parties is enough to get your mind whirling with great ideas."

"Yeah," I say, glancing at Colton. "I mean, while the parties are freaking cool and all that, every single one of them has ended in disaster for me, so I think I'm good. I might give this next one a skip."

Mom blanches at me. "Okay, who are you and what have you done with my daughter?"

"I'm serious," I tell her, fighting against the smirk on my lips. "The black and white party ended with me throwing drinks all over Colton and the boys, the masquerade ended with me … umm," Fuck, I haven't told her about this. "Well, I think someone slipped something in my drink." She sucks in a sharp breath but I continue on. "The wake wasn't really a party but that ended with Colton kicking Nic and the Widows out and the Gatsby party ended with Nic being Nic."

Mom looks baffled for all of three seconds before she pulls herself back to today. "Okay, let's rewind a little and go back to someone slipping something in your drink. What are you talking about? This is the first I'm hearing about it."

"It's fine," I insist, averting my eyes as I struggle to meet hers. "It was handled and I slept it off, but then all the Charles stuff happened and I guess I forgot to mention it again."

"Oh, honey," she says with a heavy sigh, reaching across the table and giving my hand a firm squeeze. "I wish you would have told me about this. Perhaps Colton can get one of his security guys to go back through the surveillance tapes and find out who spiked your drink. One less predator around here, the better."

"I, uhh…"

"Of course," Colton says. "I'll have them look into it first thing in the morning."

Mom gives him a dazzling smile as though he holds all the answers to the world's problems in his hands, though if you ask me, all the answers lie deep in his pockets among the bucket loads of cash. One thing is for sure, she never gave her approval to any of my Widows like that.

We carry on with dinner and every few bites or so, mom glances up and watches me with concern all over her face. It isn't until a text comes through on her phone that the silence breaks.

Colton and I watch as she glances over the text. "Oh," she laughs, completely taken by the message as her cheeks flush the brightest shade of pink.

"Who's that?" I question, watching her with curiosity as she tries to pretend that nothing happened.

She slips her phone off the table, allowing it to drop onto her lap, knowing damn well that I'm not above swan diving across our dinner plates and wrestling the phone out of her hand. Who cares about the mess and spilled drinks. When there's information to be found, I'm going to get it one way or another.

"Mom," I warn.

She lets out a frustrated sigh, knowing me better than I know myself. "Fine," she grumbles. "It's Roman Jennings."

My mouth drops. "As in Hendrix's dad? The rich sugar daddy from the Gatsby party?"

Mom rolls her eyes. "Oh, don't pretend that you don't know. You and Hendrix have been plotting ever since you saw us dance at the party."

A grin tears across my face and I watch out of the corner of my eye as Colton conceals a smirk and shakes his head. "I don't have any idea what you're talking about."

Mom sighs and leans back in her chair, deciding to make this conversation about my little white lies rather than the actual topic of her possibly being interested in another man apart from my father. "Out with it, Ocean," Mom says.

My lips press into a tight line and I find myself sitting up a little straighter in my seat. "You know he's completely smitten by you?"

"How would you know?" she scoffs. "Have you ever met the man?"

"Well, no … but I've met Hendrix and for some weird reason, I trust her instincts on this. She said that she's never seen her dad like this before. Surely that must mean something? She thinks you'll make a great couple and I'm inclined to agree with her."

Mom fumbles over her words before stuttering out a 'no' and shaking her head. "It's way too soon. Your father only passed eight months ago. I'm not even close to thinking about dating someone, especially a man like Roman Jennings. He's so … successful. It would be very off-putting and intimidating."

Colton scoffs under his breath. "Take it from me who's looking at it from the other perspective," he says, glancing at me with a slight cringe. "No offense, of course." I roll my eyes and he glances back at mom. "Yes, he's successful. He has a great business and from where I'm sitting, it's only going to get bigger. Jennings is only a few years away from landing himself on one of the Forbes top ten under fifty lists, but just like me, he's apprehensive about women and what they want from him. Every man in my position is, but you're pure, Maria. You're not the kind of woman who would date him for a step up in the world, you're not interested in what he could give you and I think he sees that in you." His eyes slice across the table to me. "It's fucking rare and when you find it, you hold onto it with both hands. I can guarantee that if Roman thinks you're something special, he won't let you go. He'll wait until you're ready."

Mom watches Colton with tears glistening in her eyes. "I … I don't know. It's very soon after Lou died. I couldn't possibly entertain this idea. What would people think?"

"What does it matter what people think? It's not like you know anyone around here anyway, and besides, it's none of their goddamn business. If he's going to make you happy, then I say go for it."

Mom cringes and I sense her pulling away which only sends a barbed wire slicing through my chest. She deserves happiness, and as much as I loved my father, it's time she knew the truth. Otherwise, she's never going to find the strength to move on and find the happiness she really deserves.

Guilt sweeps through me and I look to Colton only to find his heavy stare already on me. Am I really going to break her heart like this and tell her the truth about dad?

Colton nods as though he can read my thoughts and I cringe a little harder. He reaches over and gives my hand a gentle squeeze. "It's time," he tells me before standing and collecting our empty plates. He looks down at mom. "As usual, thank you for dinner. It was delicious."

Mom gives him a tight smile, too overwhelmed by her own thoughts to be completely on her A-game. "Always. Thank you, sweet boy. Have a good night."

Colton places the dishes in the sink and doesn't bother with a goodbye for me, knowing damn well that I'm going to end up back in his room as soon as I'm finished here.

I wait until he's walked out before looking back at mom and feeling my stomach twist with nerves. How am I supposed to tell my mother the man who she loved for the last twenty years wasn't the man she thought he was at all? This is going to crush her, but she needs to know the truth. She needs to know that it's okay to move on.

Mom looks at me expectantly. She's no fool, Colton's hasty exit was anything but ordinary, but naturally, she's far too polite to have pointed it out while he was still in the pool house. "What's going on, Oceania?"

I cringe at hearing my full name and let out a heavy sigh. "There are some things you should know about Dad." Mom's brows take a dive and I continue on before my courage has a chance to fade away. "He's not who he always led us to believe," I explain. "I found out the other week when I went into Breakers Flats."

"What are you talking about?"

"You know how I was there during the drive-by when Kian was killed?" Mom nods and I let out a shaky breath. "Well, the reason I was there in the first place was because I found a file in Charles' office with the Widows mark on the front and all this information on dad."

"What information?" she demands, cutting me off.

"He was a Wolf, mom," I say, feeling my insides twist with guilt. "Nic and the boys knew all along. He was a wolf."

She shakes her head. "No. They're lying. Your father hated gangs. They're dangerous and only cause problems. He was in no way affiliated with them. He stayed far, far away from them. You know that."

"No," I say. "Trust me, I wish it weren't true. I wish so badly that I could tell you that he was an innocent and loving man like he always made himself out to be, but he wasn't. He wasn't just a Wolf, Mom. He was second in command and their exterminator."

Her face pales and in a flash of lightning, her hand smacks across my face with a sharp sting. I stare at her in horror, holding a hand to the side of my face and desperately trying to dull the ache. She's never hit me before and it comes just as much as a shock to her that it is to me.

"Don't you dare talk ill of your father like that," she cries, standing in a panic and looking at me in horror for not only what she's just done but for the truths I'm telling, fearing that I could be right.

I stand, brushing off the sting from her slap, knowing that the longer I hold onto my face, the more she's going to hate herself and on top of what I'm telling her, she doesn't need that too. "I swear to you, Mom. He was a killer, and apparently the best one on this side of the planet. They told me that he was ruthless, he killed for sport and not for a payday which made him the most sought after killer the Wolves and Widows had ever seen. Kian told me that he tried to recruit him all the time but he denied. He was loyal to the Wolves." I let out a sigh and look straight into her eyes, letting her see my pure devastation. "He wasn't a good man. He fooled us both."

She shakes her head, tears pouring from her eyes. "No, that's not the man I married. I would have known. If he was a Wolf, he never would have allowed those Widows to befriend you the way they did. He would have got rid of them as soon as they stepped into your life."

"I know," I tell her. "But he wanted to keep it secret. He wanted to protect us from that life and keep the target off our backs. You know my guidance counselor, Miss Davies? Her family is involved with the Wolves and when I had my meeting, she recognized my name and said that she knew my father. I didn't believe her at first but the more digging I did, the more I realized that she was right."

"That meeting was weeks ago," she says, her voice hitching up higher. "How long have you known about all of this? How long have you been keeping this from me?"

"I … I'm sorry. I just … I didn't know how to tell you. I knew it would be hard and I didn't want it to crush you like it crushed me. Please don't be mad at me."

Mom stares at me, the horrified look still etched heavily into her features. "I just …" She shakes her head, looking at me with disappointment. "I can't with you right now. I just … I can't."

With that, she turns and walks to her bedroom, closing the door behind her as my world crumbles around me.

I drop down onto the couch and lean onto my knees, allowing my head to fall forward. How could I do that to her? I should have let her go on remembering him as the man he wanted her to know.

What kind of monster am I? She'll never forgive me for hiding this, or for being the one to tell her. I lose no matter what.

What am I going to do?

I sit on the couch for at least an hour, hearing nothing but the broken sobs coming from my mother's bedroom, each and every single one of them tearing me apart. So, I do what any other loving daughter would do and I face the music.

I suck up my pain, realizing that it's nowhere near as great as hers and pick myself up off the couch. I lock up the pool house and turn off the lights before making my way into Mom's room and slipping into her bed. I wrap my arms around her and pull her into me, letting her cry out her pain while struggling to hold it together.

It's not easy seeing the woman you've looked up to all your life breaking down. She's always been so strong and has always concealed this side of her, but now that I'm grown, I'm realizing that she's not the superwoman I always saw her as, she's just a regular, fragile human being, just like the rest of us. She feels pain just as I do and tonight, I'm the reason for that pain.

I don't move an inch, holding onto her until we both fall into a fitful sleep and finally call an end to the night from hell.

# CHAPTER 13

I sit in the cafeteria, ignoring the sharp glares from Cora. At least, I think it's Cora. She's a little too far away to see the finer details of her face. It's only been a little over a week since they've been home but I'm starting to tell the slight differences between them. For example, Cora is the ring leader. She's the first to glare and the first to bite. Casey just goes along for the ride and to be perfectly honest, I think she's starting to get bored of the whole 'takedown Ocean' plotline that they've got going on. Either that or she's found someone else to keep her mind busy.

Hendrix laughs beside me as Jess continues to sulk. She's been sulking all day and from what I can gather, things didn't go so well when she tried to push a relationship on Milo. The poor girl, falling for Milo wouldn't be hard. He's so freakin' sweet and adorable. She probably thought that she'd found the one. Though, that reminds me that I should probably give him a call to discuss this after school. I've sent a few texts demanding answers but he's suspiciously ignoring them, and a guy like Milo is never far from his phone.

Hendrix turns to me, more than ready to have the word vomit come pouring out of her mouth with her thoughts on the bitch twins when the cafeteria doors slam open, making the whole student body turn to face the extremely scary looking dude with loud, shocked, and terrified gasps.

My eyes bug out of my head.

Oh, no.

Fucking Nic. What the hell does he think he's doing?

His eyes scan over the girls and for a brief moment, I consider hiding behind them, not ready to face this bullshit.

Some of the girls look with interest, more than willing to jump on the daddy issues train. Others look around for the closest exit, terrified of the massive black widow spider tattoo that creeps around the side of his neck. I fucking love that tat. I was there when he got it done and thought it was the sexiest thing I'd ever seen, hell, it still kinda is. His whole body is covered from head to toe, he's literally a work of art. Add in the few piercings and the red bandana, he looks like someone who should be locked behind bars.

I scoff to myself. Considering he's in the heart of a high school with a gun tucked in the back of his jeans, prison is exactly where he belongs. What the hell does he think he's even doing in here? If he wanted to see me so bad, he could have waited until after school. Common sense, right? Though, I never claimed that Dominic Garcia had any.

I wonder if these girls even know who he is. The tattoo kinda gives it away, but that would just lead them toward the Widows, they'd have no idea that this scary-ass mother fucker is the leader of one the most feared gangs in the country. They'd have absolutely no idea that this guy standing in their cafeteria, looking so deliciously inviting, could kill them with his bare hands. They'd have zero chills if they learned that Nic Garcia is the kind of man that nightmares are made of.

Yet, here I am still staring at him as though he holds my whole freakin' heart. I shouldn't trust him. I should be running out the exit and scrambling away until he finally leaves me alone but the fact that I'm sitting here, considering jumping off this stupid table tells me that I never learn from my mistakes.

I have Colton in my life, do I even need Nic? I should walk away. I should tell him to fuck off and never come back. Why do I have to love him like this? Why is it so hard to stop seeing him as my best friend?

A strangled moan comes from beside me and I glance down to find Drix fanning herself at the sight of the man-meat scanning the room with his dark, dangerous gaze. "Fuck me," she breathes. "Who the fuck is that? I'd let that guy bend me over every fucking tabletop in this cafeteria and destroy my whole damn life."

I clench my jaw, not about to get on board with Drix fucking Nic because that's exactly what would happen. I think I've had more than enough of knowing about Nic's sex life for now. I don't need to be hearing about how fucking awesome he is in bed every day by someone who wouldn't understand how much it would kill me. Besides, when it comes down to it, Drix couldn't handle Nic. He really would destroy her and she'd break. She needs someone with a heart too big for his own good.

Taking a breath, I jump down from the table and look back at Drix. "Trust me, you need to stay far away from this one."

I start walking toward Nic and he catches my movements immediately. His jaw clenches as I tune out the shocked gasps coming from Jess and Drix behind me. Though, if the girls at BSP haven't already figured out that this guy is here for me, then there is something wrong with them. The girls here are clean-cut and would never be seen with a guy like this, especially in public. But me? I'm different.

I walk right up to Nic, keeping as close as possible and keeping my stare heavy on his. I don't dare stop. There's no way in hell I'm about to have this bullshit conversation in front of my whole school let alone Colton's bratty twin sisters.

I step right past him, slamming my shoulder into his on the way. His jaw clenches and a soft groan comes out of him, but there's no way a hit like that would hurt Nic. His shoulders are the size of fucking trees. The groan was purely out of frustration and the fact that I made it happen swirls in my gut and makes this moment just a little more bearable. After the shit he did, he doesn't deserve for this to go smoothly, he deserves hell to rain down over him.

I step out of the cafeteria and Nic silently follows behind, knowing damn well not to say a single word until I tell him to start talking. I can't believe it was only yesterday morning that I was sitting in his apartment and we were talking everything through. I felt like we finally had everything back on track, at least almost back on track. We were making progress and our relationship had the potential to be something special again and within the space of two seconds, it was destroyed.

What he did … fuck, it's worse than lying to me about my father. He had people attack us, attack the place which is quickly becoming my home, attack Maryne. She's gone because of him. I'll never forget that he did this and our relationship will never be the same.

A direct attack on Colton is a direct attack on me, and I don't intend to sit back and let him get away with it.

I make my way out to the parking lot with him a little too close for liking. It's a risk. There's no eyes or ears out here and Nic could grab me at any time and overpower me. He could take me back to Breakers Flats and force me to hear him out, but he's smarter than that. He knows if he wants even the smallest chance of making things right between us, he needs to do things my way, and that's not something he's ever been able to do. Hell, that's clear by the way he showed up here today.

I've been ignoring his texts and calls for a reason. I don't like people forcing their timelines on me and deciding for me when I should be ready to talk things through and Nic is the worst for that. I like to sit and stew for a few days, figure out exactly what I want to say and how to say it, figure out how to make it hurt the most. This … this just feels like a trap.

I stop in the middle of the parking lot and spin around. He only just catches himself before slamming into me and the second his eyes seek out mine, his expression changes, and I see the real Nic, the one who has been plagued by guilt over what he has done.

"What the hell are you doing here?" I demand.

"You weren't answering my texts and you've silenced every fucking call that I made. You left me no fucking choice."

"There are plenty of fucking choices," I shriek, "but coming into my school, in front of my friends who know nothing about you or what you stand for is not the way. Hell, the fucking guidance counselor is a Wolf for fuck's sake. You need to leave. I don't want to see you and I don't want you coming around."

"We need to talk about this, O. Don't fucking dismiss me. There's too much bullshit between us. Too much history to just let it go like that. I won't let you do it."

"I don't give a shit what you want, Nic. You sent five fucking lunatics to attack us. Maryne was killed because of you."

"I didn't send them to fucking kill anyone. That wasn't part of the deal. We need to talk about this. You have all your wires crossed and you're just thinking whatever the fuck you want to think without giving me a chance to explain my side."

I glance down at my phone before looking back up at his pleading face. "So, talk," I demand. "You have three minutes before the bell sounds and I won't be wasting a single second more."

He swallows hard. "Come on, O. Just give me a proper chance to get this out. Let's go back to your place and we can talk properly."

I prop a hand on my hip and raise an unimpressed brow. "Like hell I'm going anywhere with you. You're fucking insane if you think I'm about to invite you back into Colton's home after the bullshit you did. Your time is ticking, so I suggest you start talking, otherwise you can fuck off," I tell him, not in the mood to be standing around in the lonely parking lot while he grovels for forgiveness.

Nic lets out a sigh and realizing that he has no other choice, he tells me what he came all this way to say. "Three years ago, Kian and I cut a deal with Vincent DeCarlo. All their bullshit ran through the Widows. Their drug runs, their dirty fucking money, the gun smuggling, everything. It kept DeCarlo looking clean on paper while my father didn't give a shit how we appeared. He was un-fucking-touchable and he knew it. When shit started going south with the cops, dad pulled back and put all that weight on me to deal with and when I wasn't prepared to take the same deal, I cut them off. Told them to find some other gang to run their bullshit through, but they needed us so we re-negotiated the terms and I tripled the premium. It's fucking risky, but I couldn't make big changes while I wasn't in power yet. If I flaked on it, the Widows would have seen me as weak so I took the deal and the DeCarlo's owed me a fucking favor."

"And an attack on Colton was what you decided to use that favor for?"

"Not exactly," he says with a cringe. "You have to understand that I wasn't dealing with you being away and moving on very well... I'm still not. I want you home where you belong."

"Oh," I scoff. "So, you want to blame this bullshit on me wanting a better life for myself?"

"No. Fuck, Ocean. Just let me get it out," Nic growls, stepping back and pacing the parking lot, trying to calm himself. "Is it too fucking hard for you to have a proper conversation without your bullshit sarcasm coming into everything?"

"Really? This is the way you want to play this right now? I've got one clue for you, Dominic. You're in the fucking dog house right now. I'll say whatever the fuck I want to say and you have no fucking choice but to deal with it, otherwise, you can fuck off. I'm not interested in wasting my time listening to your bullshit story if you're going to continue throwing bullshit attitudes back at me."

He clenches his jaw and takes a few more paces while pumping his fists. He visibly calms himself and finally turns back to me. "What I was trying to say was that I had a lot going on and I wasn't coping very well. You'd just sealed the deal with that bastard, and I saw our future slipping further away, but he shouldn't have touched you, especially so close after what happened with that fucking Carter kid."

I silently fume, hating that he brought that shit into it. "If I wasn't ready to allow a man to touch me, I wouldn't have. What happens between me and Colton is none of your damn business."

"I know that," he snaps back. "I wasn't fucking thinking. I was just so … angry. A smarter man would have saved that favor for something else, something big. The DeCarlo's have a huge pull and I could have benefited from that but as it is, I was too fucking selfish to see past my own needs."

I cross my arms over my chest and desperately try to bite my tongue. The bell will go any minute now and despite how much I want to hate him right now, I really want to hear what he has to say. "Go on," I tell him.

"Everybody knows about the bullshit between Carrington and DeCarlo. It's been going on for twenty-odd years. All I had to do was call Vincent and tell him that I wanted Colton to hurt. That's all I said, and the rest was left up to him. He fucking jumped at the opportunity and when I saw what was going on, I knew instantly how badly I fucked up. I was never going to get there in time. They ignored my fucking calls when I tried calling it off. It was their fucking show. I thought they were just going to go in there and terrorize Carrington, make him shit his pants as a way to scare him into giving up the company, but what they did … I didn't expect that at all, and that's on me.

"I should have known that they'd take it too far. Vincent's sons are … Ocean, they're fucked up, twisted bastards and you have no fucking idea how sorry I am that I sent them to you like that. I saw the way they terrorized your friends and destroyed your home. I saw you running down the hall and then trying to go back for your mom when you realized what was going on, I saw Colton do everything he could to keep you safe, and I saw the fucking terror in your eyes babe. That is all on me. I will never forgive myself for sending that to your fucking doorstep."

The bell sounds loudly through the school and I look back up at the campus, watching as the students begin moving around but I find myself rooted to the spot. "Please, O. Say something," Nic says, reaching for my hand.

I hastily pull away from his reach and take a hesitant step back. "I have to go."

"Babe, no. Just talk to me for a minute. I need to know that we're alright."

"Alright?" I cry. "We will never be alright. Maryne is dead. You sent murderers to my home because you were too fucking jealous over the fact that Colton means something to me. What kind of messed up shit is that, Nic?"

"I know it's messed up. I didn't know they were going to hurt anybody. I figured you'd be safe in a place like that."

"You figured wrong," I tell him, taking another step back. "I think you should go."

"No," he says, shaking his head. "We need to sort this out."

"It's not going to get sorted out today, Nic. I'm too upset and hurt. I'm still in shock that you could even do something like this, let alone process the hurt you caused with your misguided need to get me back. I just ... I need time. I need time away from you to clear my head and if you want any chance at all of fixing what you broke, then you're going to have to give me that."

"Babe ..."

"No, Nic. You need to go. I'm late for class and I just ... I can't do this right now. I need to think."

He takes a heavy breath and meets my eyes with regret shining so fucking brightly that it hurts. "I'm sorry, O. Please know that it wasn't my intent to hurt you, I just wanted to rattle Carrington a bit. If I knew … I never would have done it."

I nod and we hold each other's gaze for a minute too long before he reluctantly steps back. "Time," he murmurs.

I nod and he takes another step followed by another until he finally turns and walks away, leaving me a fucking mess of emotions.

# CHAPTER 14

I walk through the door of the Carrington mansion completely deflated. Today sucked, like really sucked. I went to school thinking I could forget about everything Nic had done. What a joke that was.

Sure, there were a lot of things I expected to happen today. A million phone calls, text messages, hell even the odd email or two. Never in my wildest dreams did I imagine Dominic Garcia storming through the cafeteria of Bellevue Springs Private School and forcing my hand in front of the entire student body. Then after that, I had to spend the rest of my afternoon dodging questions from Jess and Drix, trying to figure out what the hell was going on.

I wasn't ready to see him. Not in the least, but I should have known. That was stupid of me. This new version of Nic is unpredictable. He's wild and out of control. I should have known that he'd shit all over the limits I'd put in place. I'll be better prepared next time because, with Nic, there's always a next time.

I don't even know who he is anymore but one thing is for sure, the old Nic no longer exists, at least, I don't think he does. Seeing the look in his eye today told me that maybe he's still in there, buried deep, deep below the surface, but it'll take a miracle to find it. Someone needs to save him and I'm not sure I have the power to do it anymore, especially now that the Widows have completely taken over his life. He's changing by the day, by the second, constantly getting darker. He needs someone who can balance that out.

Heartache sits heavy on my shoulders as I make my way through the mansion, searching out the one person who could effortlessly put a smile on my face. I go by his office first and for the first time since taking over for his father, he's not in there.

My face scrunches up in confusion. For Colton not to be busily reading over a contract or in the middle of a business deal means that something is up.

I hope he's alright.

I start searching the mansion, starting with his bedroom and then the kitchen, because why not take a nap or stop for a treat every now and then? Not finding him, I look a little deeper, checking the living spaces and all of the meeting rooms.

Damn it. Is he even here? Maybe he headed out for the afternoon.

Giving up, I start heading out to the pool house, pulling my phone out to send him a quick text when a soft grunt comes from down the hall.

My brows furrow as I spy the entrance to the home gym.

What the fuck is he doing in there? Not once since being here has he ever worked out in the afternoon. He's a morning guy. He'd prefer to skip a good sleep-in and spend torturous hours working out in the gym, getting all sweaty, and making his body ache. Don't get me wrong, I'm all for the occasional exercise, but if I'm going to get sweaty at six in the morning, it's going to be from nasty, wild sex.

Stopping by the entrance of the gym, I peer through the open door before propping myself against the frame as my mouth begins to water. Colton hangs, shirtless, from the pull-up bar with his back to me, slowly lowering himself with a practiced control that has his strong muscles bulging to perfection.

With ease, he pulls himself back up and everything in his back squeezes, causing a waterfall of epic proportions to form in my panties. His tanned skin shines with a sheer layer of sweat and I do everything in my power not to walk in there and tear him down from the bar and screw him senseless.

After finishing his set, Colton releases the bar and drops to the ground, silently landing on the balls of his feet as though he's some sort of cat. I stare in wonder. Anyone would be fucked if Colton was sneaking up on him. He's silent and deadly, and hell, from where I'm standing, it's sexy as fuck.

He turns to grab his drink bottle and in doing so, finds me loitering in the doorway. His brow shoots up. "How long have you been there?"

"Long enough to know that I'll be sneaking into your bedroom and taking advantage of you tonight."

A cocky smirk plays on his lips and he strides toward me, his eyes growing more and more hooded by the second. His hands fall to my waist and he pulls me in flush against his ripped body. "You really think I'm the kind of guy to just lay there and allow you to take advantage of me?"

I push up onto my tippy toes and hover just in front of his face, close enough for him to close the gap but he won't dare as he waits for me to make the move. "If you know what's good for you, you will."

"Well, damn. How could I resist an offer like that?" he says, his smirk stretching wide across his face. "But for the record, if this is the way we're playing it, I want to be wined and dined first, then I'm going to need you to spank my ass, choke me a little, beg me to call you daddy, and afterward, I'd like to cuddle, you know, as the little spoon."

I scrunch my face in distaste, teasing him just as he's teasing me. "Well, shit. If I knew you were this high-maintenance, I would have stuck with Charlie."

"Fuck off," he laughs, nudging me away and walking back over to the pull-up bar. I follow and make myself comfortable on the bench so I can get the full view during this set. "Charlie really would want that shit. He'd be a clingy motherfucker and you know it."

I can't help but laugh. He's not wrong. "For the record," I tell him as he jumps to catch the bar. "I wouldn't mind a little ass-spanking and choking, but since you're apparently the bitch in this relationship, I'll have to make some changes."

Colton slowly lowers himself from the bar and I instantly get distracted by his washboard abs that lead down into his defined V that's staring right at me. My hands twitch at my side, desperate to reach out and touch.

How did I get so lucky to be able to call all of that mine?

Colton narrows his eyes at me. "Call me the fucking bitch of our relationship one more time and I'll have you down on your knees, begging for forgiveness."

"Promise you'll tie me up?"

He lets out a small huff as he effortlessly pulls himself back up. "Fuck me," he grumbles under his breath, making a show of trying to concentrate.

I get up off the bench and walk over to him, playing a very dangerous game of temptation. Will I be able to resist touching him or won't I? I lean up against the cool, metal frame, mesmerized by the slow-motion show of pull-ups happening right before my eyes. "What are you doing here? Usually, you work out in the mornings."

A grin cracks across his face. "Didn't have some chick snoring in my ear to wake me up."

I grab his water bottle and squirt water at his chest. "You're an ass. I don't snore."

He flinches from the cool water and kicks out his foot, slamming it into the water bottle and sending it flying across the gym as he laughs. "What makes you think it's you I'm talking about, Jade?"

My mouth drops and I stare at him with a blank expression. "If you've been screwing Spencer this whole time, I'm going to be pissed."

"Guilty," he says with a wink. "Don't tell him I told you though, he's very defensive of our bromance. It really is a love story."

I step into him and he releases the bar and lands right in front of me. "Tell me," I say as he places his hands to my waist. "Do you fuck him as hard as you fuck me?"

Colton dips in and brushes his lips over mine before sliding his arm around my waist. His hands travel down to my ass, giving it a firm squeeze, and grinning back at me. "Only when he begs for it."

I lose all train of thought and Colton laughs, knowing that he's got me right where he wants me. Keeping his hands on my ass, he picks me up and my legs instantly wind around his waist. "Hold on, baby," he murmurs.

I raise a brow as I thread my arms around his neck and hold on tight. "What are you doing?"

He releases me and I cling to him like a monkey as he reaches above him and jumps to catch the bar. My eyes bug out of my head while a flicker of disappointment flares through me thinking that he was about to try some kinky shit, though I guess that'll have to wait.

He pulls himself up and I gape at the way his muscles bulge but the soft groan that comes from the back of his throat has my brows shooting straight up. "Dude, I'm not that fat."

He laughs and instantly loses his grip, sending us both crashing to the floor. "Fuck," he says, unable to stop the roaring laughter as he holds onto me, making sure I'm not hurt. "I didn't mean to fall. Are you alright?"

"I'm okay but my ego is bruised."

"Your ego is just fine," he tells me, leaning back and staring at me as I sit in his lap. I meet his eyes as a seriousness comes over him. "I heard you had a visitor at school."

"Bullshit," I grunt. "How'd you hear that?"

A soft chuckle pulls at his throat "From what I can gather, Jess texted Milo to figure out who the hell he was, then Milo checked in with Spencer to ask if he knew what was going on, then Spencer asked Charlie if he'd heard from you, and then Charlie all but screamed it from the rooftops while on his way to ask me."

"So, during all this, no one actually thought to ask me?"

His brows furrow as he thinks back over the explanation he just gave me. "I guess not," he says with a shrug. "Are you okay, though? I'm assuming by the sarcastic mood you're in, it all went to shit."

"It bypassed shit and went straight to hell. It was awful, but ... I don't know. It's still Nic. I'm so mad at him but at the same time, he'll always be my best friend."

He raises a hand and brushes his fingers down my face, his eyes softening with emotion. "I know, Jade. Just give it time. As much as I want you to tell him to fuck off, I know having him in your life makes you happy, and I want that for you."

"I know," I tell him. "A weaker man would try to keep me away from him."

"I trust you, Ocean. You've never given me a reason not to."

"Thank you," I tell him. "That means a lot to me."

He nods, not needing to respond to that. "What are your plans this afternoon? Do you want me to call it quits for the day and we can fuck around or are you planning to work?"

I press my lips into a tight line. "Are you going to be offended if I say that I want to work? I'm not done sulking about what happened at school and I think the quiet time would help."

"That's fine, babe," he says, getting up and offering me his hand. I take it and he hauls me to my feet in the blink of an eye. "You do you. I've got a contract to finish looking through and should probably call the cheapskate bastard back who I hung up on this morning."

"My, oh my. And you have people out there thinking that you're some kind of CEO, businessman extraordinaire. If only they realized that you throw tantrums and hang up on your business partners when they irritate your fragile little soul."

"Fuck you," he laughs, walking across the room and grabbing his discarded water bottle. "I am a fucking CEO businessman extraordinaire, now get your ass out of here and mop my dining hall, wench."

"Careful, now," I tease, walking out of the room and smothering my smirk. "You don't want to piss off the help. Who knows what you might find in your breakfast in the morning."

I hear his soft laughter flowing out of the gym as I make my way toward the staff quarters and instantly run into Mom as she steps through the entrance. "Oh, Ocean," she says, looking anywhere but meeting my eyes. "How was school?"

I let out a soft sigh and pull her into my arms, knowing exactly what this is about. "It's okay, Mom. I'm not mad at you."

She throws her arms around me, holding me tight and burying her face into my neck. "Oh, I'm so, so sorry, my sweet baby. I don't know what came over me. I never should have hit you. My emotions were riding high and I was overwhelmed and the next thing I knew, my hand was cracking across your face. Oh, please forgive me, sweet girl. I couldn't cope knowing that you were hurting over my actions."

"Mom, it's fine. Really. I love you and I shouldn't have broken the news to you like that, but I couldn't hold onto it anymore. You needed to know and I didn't want you to hold back from being happy again."

"I know sweet girl," she says, taking my shoulders and pulling back to look me in the eye. "I appreciate that but either way, I shouldn't have laid a hand on you and I'll regret that until the day I die."

"It's okay," I whisper, giving her an encouraging smile. "I can get revenge when you're an old lady and I put you in a nursing home."

She sucks in a sharp gasp. "You wouldn't do your sweet momma wrong like that."

"Just you wait and see."

She shakes her head and goes to step around me when she stops and looks back at me. "What are you doing here? I didn't have you scheduled to work. You need to catch up on your studies so you can get into a good college."

"I know, I just had a shitty day at school and thought that I could use something to keep my mind off it."

Mom shakes her head. "Absolutely not. You're not using work as an escape. Why don't you head up to the library and pick something to read? That should take your mind off whatever awful things happened at school. You love reading and you've hardly read anything since moving here."

I press my lips into a tight line and meet her eyes. "That's not actually a bad idea."

"Good, now get out of here and go and relax, but don't take your eye off the time. You always tend to get lost in those books of yours and next thing you know, you've missed dinner and it's after three in the morning."

I laugh, knowing just how right she is. It's a sickness really.

Mom disappears and I'm left to make my way up to the library. I find the elevator and within moments, I'm stepping through to my favorite room in the house. I'm still baffled by how amazing this is. What normal people have a fully stocked library in their home? It's insane.

I quickly begin my search, desperately trying to ignore the memories of Colton devouring my pussy like a fucking king on these very shelves. It doesn't take long before I'm getting lost in the titles and covers, scanning over the blurbs and picking out a whole freaking pile that I wish I could somehow read in one night.

I narrow down my search and am just about to settle on *Jaymin Eve's* latest release when the elevator pings and the doors slide open. I freeze on the spot as Casey steps through to the library and the second she lifts her eyes from the ground, she stops and we stare at each other like deer caught in headlights.

"Umm …" I say awkwardly. "I was uhh, just leaving."

"Oh, umm … you don't have to leave on my account. I'm just

going to grab a book and go read in my room."

"Okay, sure," I say, still unable to move from my spot. "You don't mind that I'm reading your books?"

Her eyes flitter across the room as though she's trying to look busy as she searches for her book but it's pretty damn clear that she's just trying to avoid making awkward eye contact with me. "I mean, are you going to bend the pages or write notes in the margins?"

I suck in a horrified breath. "No."

"So, how do you mark your page?"

"What are you talking about?"

"If you had to put the book down to go and pee or something like that, what do you do?"

My brows furrow, trying to figure out where the hell she's going with this. "I put a bookmark in and then go pee."

Casey shrugs her shoulders. "Then I don't mind, as long as you put it back exactly where you got it from, I don't care. It took me forever to organize all of these books."

"I can imagine," I say, noting how not only are they arranged by genre, but each of those genres is also organized into alphabetical order. "You've got a pretty good system. It was really easy to find what I was looking for."

"Oh, yeah?" she questions, spying the book in my hand. "Who are you reading?"

I hold up the book to show her the cover. "*Jaymin Eve*," I say. "She's freaking amazing. Have you read her?"

Casey's face lights up like Christmas morning. "Hell yeah! Of course, I have. *Jaymin* is incredible. I love her work. I fell in love with her back in the '*Hive Trilogy*' days. That series rocked my world. Have you read *Amo Jones* or *J Bree*? I was going to start '*Hannaford Prep*' today."

"No way. I finished that series just before I came to Bellevue springs. It's so fucking dark and twisted."

"That's what I've heard," she says as her eyes widen. "Come and check this out. If you love that shit, you'll love this."

I find myself following her deeper into the library and somehow we spend the next hour going over all the books that we've fallen in love with and with each new title I list, she instantly adds it to her Amazon cart and hits buy. I gape at her, wishing I had that power with my credit card ... oh, wait. I don't even have a fucking credit card.

We sit down on the egg chairs and get comfortable while going over everything and working out the best reading orders for all the new stuff coming in. I mean, did Casey and I just become friends? I have no idea but I think I like it.

"Can I ask you something?" I question, leaning back into the egg chair and looking over at her.

"Yeah, what's up?"

"What's the deal with you guys and Colton?"

"What do you mean?"

"I don't know ... there's just this huge divide between you all and it's kinda sad. I know if you guys gave him the chance, he'd be more than happy to start building the relationship between you. I mean, I don't have sisters but I have more than enough family in the Widows and I don't know if I could survive with that kind of break between us."

Casey shrugs her shoulders and seems to wander off inside her mind before finally letting out a sigh. "I don't know. We moved away, or at least, Mom took us away when we were fourteen. Colton came with us originally but Dad came and forced him back here, and that was just it. We never saw each other and just kept growing apart. Mom never even attempted to reach out to him after that. She took it as some kind of personal attack, but he was just a kid. It wasn't his responsibility to be the parent. Mom failed there, but don't tell her I said that. She'd tear me a new asshole."

I scoff and try to smother a laugh.

Casey continues. "Colton's done a lot of growing in the last few years. I guess ... I don't know ... things just got worse from there. Everyone grew hostile and the disconnect between us just got bigger. Cora and I would speak to Colton every now and then but it wasn't anything deep just, 'Hey, how are you?' You know, that kind of stuff."

I nod and feel a heaviness come over me. "I think he'd actually like to get to know you both as adults now. I mean, I can't exactly speak for him. We haven't actually discussed it or anything, but what big brother wouldn't want his baby sisters in his life?"

She shrugs her shoulders. "I mean, I know that I miss having that same relationship that we used to have. Cora has a slightly different view on it, but I feel like she could come around. She's so bitter. She's a lot like Mom."

"No shit," I laugh. "The apple didn't fall far from that tree."

"Yeah ... about that," she says with a cringe. "I'm kinda over the fighting. I'm not exactly a grudge holder like that, so if you're down with being cool, then I am too."

I raise a brow. "Yeah?" I question. "I don't think your sister feels the same."

"No, she doesn't and she'd kill me and instantly accuse me of jumping ship, but I can see how much you mean to Colton and if I'm going to have any chance of having him in my life, then I need to get on board the Ocean train. Though, turns out it's not actually that bad. I didn't realize we would have so much in common."

"To be honest, I really thought that there wouldn't be anything under the sun that we would have in common but it's nice to know that we do."

"Exactly," she says with a beaming smile before glancing down at her book and pulling her feet up under herself. "Now shut up, I've been dying to read this series."

"Right back at ya," I grin, resting back into my egg chair with an odd smile. I can't exactly say that becoming friends with Casey Carrington was on my agenda today, but a part of me is actually kind of happy about it, unless it's a trap, of course, but something tells me it was real, and for some reason, I'm inclined to give her the benefit of the doubt.

With that in mind, I open the book to page one and lose myself in one of the best stories ever told.

# CHAPTER 15

I walk into the main house early on Tuesday morning, feeling a million times better. Maybe Mom was onto something about reading a book. I didn't exactly get through much of it after spending a good portion of my afternoon hanging out and talking books with Casey, but the little time to myself where I could get lost in another world helped to put things into perspective.

Nic fucked up and that's on him. It's in the past and while he has a long road ahead of him to earn my forgiveness, there's no point spending my time worrying and hurting over it.

It's time to worry about the more important things, like getting good grades, and being the first person on either side of my family to go to college. I can do it. I know I can.

I walk into the kitchen to find Charlie and Colton hovering over the coffee machine, very impatiently waiting for their caffeine hit by pressing every button on the machine and getting aggravated at the poor thing.

"Hey, you," I say to Charlie as I stride past him, leaning between the boys and grabbing the power cord for the coffee machine and plugging it into the wall with an amused smirk. "Where the hell have you been? I feel like I haven't seen you in ages."

Both of the boys studiously ignore the fact that neither of them was smart enough to check that the machine was plugged in and get busy actually turning it on. Charlie leans against the counter and gives me a beaming smile. "I figure since Colton here is too fucking lazy to step out of his big ass mansion these days, you could use a lift to school."

"Well, well," I say, watching Colton roll his eyes at his friend's comments. "Wouldn't that be a treat."

Colton gives me a blank stare. "You realize that there's at least thirty … no, twenty cars in the garage that I'd allow you to drive. You don't need to keep getting lifts every day."

I narrow my eyes at my irritatingly sexy boyfriend. "Why can't I drive all of them? You know, I don't think I've really gotten the feel for the Veneno. I could take that one to school."

Colton shakes his head as Charlie howls with laughter. "Over my dead fucking body. After you stole it and took it for a girls' day at the hair salon, I won't even let you breathe near it."

"That's okay," I laugh. "You've got to sleep at some point and when you do, when you least expect it, I'm going to take them all. I might invite the Widows over and we can figure out which one of your babies goes the fastest."

He shakes his head as Charlie grabs a bagel off the counter and begins slathering it with cream cheese. "Careful, Jade. Keep making threats like that and I'll have to tie you up for real."

Charlie's brows shoot up into his hairline. "Wait … why does it sound like you've done it before?" My eyes flick to Colton's wide and panicked as I recall sneaking down from the library at 1 am this morning after finally putting my book down and having him do just that. "You have, haven't you? Fuck, I didn't realize I was in the midst of two kinky fuckers. Damnnnn."

I bite down on my lip, desperately trying not to react. With a guy like Charlie, if you give him an inch, he won't just take a mile, he'll run with it until there's nothing left to take. All while keeping that cheesy as fuck grin on his devastatingly handsome face.

Colton scoffs. "Please, I've heard your stories, man. Tying a chick up and fucking her until she screams is nothing new for you. I wouldn't be surprised if you have a whole closet full of dirty little secrets."

"Well, damn, Charlie. Maybe I'm with the wrong guy."

Charlie laughs as Colton grabs me and slams me against the counter, keeping me pinned with his hard body. "Really?" he murmurs, looking at me with those mesmerizing eyes and sending the butterflies in my stomach into overdrive.

"I mean, um … what were we talking about again?"

"Yeah, that's what I thought," he tells me, easing up on my body and allowing just enough space to take my waist and lift me onto the counter. "You sit tight. I'm going to make you breakfast."

My brows shoot up as Charlie scrunches his face in distaste. "Bro, come on, don't be stupid. You can't cook for shit. Know your limits and stay there. There's no need to try and impress her with skills you don't have."

Colton ignores his friend and starts digging through the cupboards. "I didn't say anything about cooking," he says, pulling out a bowl and then showing off the wide range of cereals. He gives me a stupid grin and waves his hand in front of them. "Your wish is my command."

I roll my eyes and jump down from the counter. "Get out of the way," I tell him, barging my way into the pantry. "Let me make you guys a proper breakfast."

"Fuck yeah," Charlie grunts. "I knew there was a reason I came here."

The boys fuck around, talking about who the hell knows what, and within twenty minutes, I'm serving up the best-looking bacon and egg rolls that I've ever seen. We're just about to start digging in when I hear the familiar click of heels against marble and I prepare myself for the worst.

"Colton." Comes a shrill call from outside the kitchen. "Where are you?"

Colton's whole demeanor drops at the sound of his mother's call. "Kitchen," he grumbles, his eyes flashing to mine with an apology, knowing damn well that every time we're in a room together, it never turns out well. Though, hopefully, by now that cow has figured out that she can't beat me.

She comes striding into the kitchen, the clickity-clack of her heels already the most irritating thing I'll hear all day. She looks to her son before glancing across to Charlie and then finally at me. Her face falls. "Oh, you're here," she spits. "Is the pool house I have supplied not efficient enough that you have to come and overtake my home? Sorry, my generosity is not up to your standards."

"Mom," Colton snaps. "Lay off. You're embarrassing yourself with your shitty attitude. This is my fucking house and I'll welcome whoever the hell I want into it. Besides, Ocean has more right to be here than you do. Now, what do you want? I have shit to get done."

She rolls her eyes and reluctantly tears her glare away from me to focus on her annoyed son. "Ugh, I did not raise you like that."

"Funny," he grunts. "I don't recall you raising me at all."

She lets out an irritated huff and slams a credit card down onto the counter. "You need to put a call into your financial team. My card isn't working."

"I know."

"You know?" she questions, standing straighter as Charlie and I flick our gazes between the two like some kind of intense tennis match.

Colton looks to me for a brief second as if to tell me to pay extra special attention. "Yeah, I know. I cut you off. I'm your eighteen-year-old son, I shouldn't be responsible for funding your extravagant lifestyle."

My mouth drops and I find myself leaning in closer as Charlie does the same, not wanting to miss a single moment of this.

"Excuse me?" she shrieks. "What did you just say?"

"I think you heard me."

Oh, fuck. This is not going to go well.

"This is unacceptable behavior. You can't do this. I'm your mother. I demand you call your team and have them reinstate my access. I have a luncheon this afternoon and I can not have my card declining in front of those women, that would be mortifying. This would have never happened if your father was still here."

"Oh, you mean that man who you set alight during his own damn funeral? The man who gave you over a hundred million dollars in your divorce settlement despite the prenup and who continued paying for your lavish lifestyle even after you took off?"

"That was a part of our settlement. He had a financial obligation to me. Don't act as though he was doing me some sort of favor."

Colton scoffs. "No, of course, he wasn't doing you any sort of favors. It's not as though you've ever worked a day in your life or did anything to deserve the piles of cash that are constantly coming your way."

"How dare you speak to me like that. I put up with your father for twenty long years. I deserved every cent."

"Well, that's just the thing, Mom. Dad is gone now and I sure as hell don't have any kind of obligation to keep funding you. So, here's an idea, why don't you stand on your own two feet and support yourself for a change instead of living off other people for the rest of your life? Whatever happened to all that money anyway? Surely you didn't blow it all on extravagant trips around the world, ridiculous parties, and those male escorts you like to use so much."

A laugh bubbles up my throat as I watch her cheeks flame a raging red. "Oh, dammmmnnn, Momma Carrington. That sucks. Though, if you speak to Harrison, I'm sure he will be able to sort out some shifts for you, but beware, he'd have to clear it with the boss first."

Her jaw clenches and her stare zones in on me, and for a moment, she looks like the most dangerous woman on earth. If looks could kill, I'd be up in flames, but as it is, she's just a nasty bitch with a pathetic bite and there's not a damn thing she can do to me. "This is all your fault," she spits. "If you weren't around to poison my son's innocent mind, this never would have happened."

"Trust me, lady. Your son lost all his innocence the day his mother decided not to fight for him. By the time I sunk my claws into him, he was already as bad as they come. So, unfortunately, I can't take the credit for that work of art."

"I, uhh …" Charlie says slowly while awkwardly backing out of the room with his bacon and egg roll in his hand. "Just remembered that I need to go and stick needles in my eyes," he says, glancing back at me. "I'll meet you outside in ten if you still need that lift to school."

I nod and in a flash, he's out of here, not willing to stick around for whatever bullshit storm Laurelle is about to create. With Charlie out of the way, she's quick to throw her glare back at her son. "I want this fixed right now, Colton or so help me …"

"You'll do what?" he questions. "Take away my TV privileges? You haven't got a leg to stand on. You're getting nothing from me. Try the twins. They just got their inheritance, why don't you go mooch off them for a while. Though, they're just like you and have issues sharing so good luck getting anything out of them."

Laurelle shrieks and with a huff, she storms out of the kitchen while swiping her hand across the counter and knocking my bacon and egg roll onto the ground, smashing the expensive china in the process.

"Wow, real mature," I call after her as her heels clickity-clack faster than anything. We hear her string of curses through the whole house, making a scene wherever she goes and smashing a few vases in the process.

I turn back to Colton. "It baffles me why your dad didn't keep her around longer." Colton laughs and I walk over to him and take a bite out of his roll. "Are you alright? That couldn't have been easy."

"Actually," he grumbles. "Sticking it to her was kinda fun. I might do it again."

"Okay," I laugh. "Well, make sure that I'm around when you do. I wouldn't want to miss another show like that. Ten out of ten for the drama. You really hit the nail on the head."

Colton rolls his eyes and I help myself to another bite of his roll. "Though, speaking of you being a bad, bad boy before I showed up … what's the deal with Jude? I've kinda been avoiding that whole section of the house."

"Yeah, I've noticed," he says. "He's … surviving."

"Only just?"

He nods.

"Good. But what do we do? It's not like we can just keep him down there forever and if we let him go, we risk him telling someone."

"I know," he murmurs, keeping his voice low, not wanting to be overheard. "I'd hate to put this kind of pressure on you, but you're the one who was hurt. It's your call. Whatever you want to do."

My eyes bug out of my head. "I might be from Breakers Flats but I'm not some criminal mastermind. I don't know what to do with this shit."

"I'm not doing this to make my life easy. Trust me, if I could, I'd just do what needs to be done and take that pressure off your hands, but this justice is for you, and being the one who gets to decide his fate puts the power in your hands. He took something from you and now you have the opportunity to do the same to him."

I nod, understanding where he's coming from but really not sure how I feel about it. "Can I ask you something?"

He nods. "Of course."

"Why put him down there in the first place?" Colton's brows furrow and I clarify my question before he starts with the obvious answers. "Why put him in the wine cellar and not lock him away. I mean, the guys in prison have a shitload nicer living arrangements than he does."

Colton takes a breath and steps into me before lifting me onto the counter so that we see eye to eye. "There are a few reasons," he starts. "We have the obvious answers like for one, it was the first place that I could think of on short notice, and the fact that he was going to get his ass handed to him means that there was going to be a mess. There's plumbing down there so I could easily clean up. Reason number two, he raped you. It's as simple as that. He hurt you and that fucker deserves to suffer."

"That easy, huh?"

He nods, his lips pressing into a tight line as he bares an ugly part of his soul, hoping that it's not going to scare me away, but after everything we've been through, there's not a lot that could pull me away from him. "That easy."

I swallow, meeting his eyes. "Have you ever done something like this before?"

"No," he says. "Don't get me wrong, Jade. I'm not a good guy. I've done a shitload of stuff that I'm not proud of but keeping a fucking rapist locked in a dungeon, yeah … this is the first. I …" Colton lets out a heavy sigh and meets my eyes. "There's something you need to know about Jude, something that I'm hoping might help you to understand why I went to such lengths with this."

I watch him cautiously, feeling my anxiety beginning to spark. "What is it?" I ask, my voice a soft whisper.

"You know the other girl who he hurt? Mandy Johnstone."

I nod. "Yeah, what about her?"

"After all that bullshit with her getting hurt and Jude's parents fucking around to make it worse, she went away. Her parents claimed that they sent her to boarding school as some sort of twisted punishment for lying about what happened with Jude, even though we all knew it was fucking true. But here's the thing, I looked into the boarding schools around here and she's not enrolled at any of them. I checked with her extended family and friends, no one has heard from her. It's as though she just disappeared off the face of the earth, and my gut tells me that Jude had something to do with it. I don't know if he scared her off or if he did something worse, but I wasn't going to allow that to happen to you."

I stare at him in horror. "I … I don't even know what to say about that. You think he killed her?"

"I really don't know. I have no evidence to support that he did, just that she's missing or hiding away somewhere. Maybe she changed her name and just slipped away with the rest of the world, but what I do know is that he had something to do with that and it's about time that he got what he deserves."

I nod. "I couldn't agree more."

He leans into me and rests his forehead against mine. "Jade, I'd do fucking anything to protect you, and before you start, I know that you're perfectly capable of protecting yourself but when it comes to you, I can't help myself. I knew it the second I met you just outside this door and you gave me that hungry look as though you'd die without getting a taste. You're my fucking girl, Jade. I hate that I treated you so badly when you first arrived. It took me way too long to admit to myself that I was wrong about you, I wanted so badly to be right. I didn't want to fall for you. I always saw falling for a woman as weak, but it's not. Having you in my life has made me better despite the fucked up things I've been doing."

Warmth spreads through me and I lean into him, meeting my lips with his and kissing him deeply.

"All I want to do is make you happy, Jade."

"You do. I …"

The shrill ring of my phone cuts me off and I let out a groan as I fish it out of my bra and stare down at the screen. "Ugh, it's Charlie," I announce before lifting the phone to my ear and silently brushing my lips over Colton's again. "What do you want?"

"Coooooome ooooooon. For fuck's sake. I thought you'd be out of there just after I was."

"You said ten minutes."

"Yeah, that was twenty minutes ago."

"Fuck, really?" I pull the phone away and glance down at the screen, taking in the time. "Shit. I'm coming."

I end the call before Charlie has a chance to make a comment about my last words and Colton steps out of my way, realizing the panicked look on my face. After all, he sees it way too often to know exactly what it means. I'm fucking late. "Here," he says, shoving his roll into my hand after I've jumped down from the counter. "I'll see you after school. Try not to break any noses while you're there."

"Can't make any promises," I sing before scurrying out the door and finding Charlie very impatiently waiting, muttering about it being the last time he offers to drive my stupid ass anywhere.

# CHAPTER 16

My locker door slams closed with a bang and I pull my bag onto my back after another long day at school with way too much homework for my sanity. How am I supposed to keep up with this workload? The girls here are used to this shit, but me? Not so much. I don't think I've ever done homework in my life until I came here. It's insane.

Hendrix walks beside me as we make our way out of the school and I'm just about to tell her how I think her dad might possibly have a shot with my mom when the old beat-up shit box that's dripping oil onto the road catches my eye and everything sinks within me.

What the fuck is he doing here? He knows I can't resist his stupid face.

It's one thing for Nic to show up out of the blue, but Sebastian. I can't resist him. I love him so damn much that constantly reminding myself that I'm still furious with him is the hardest thing I've ever done.

I wonder if he's seen me already. There is a shitload of girls around here, I'm sure he could be distracted by all the potential pussy. Though, I'll have to remind him that the majority of them are under eighteen, despite them all looking like Victoria Secret supermodels.

If he's distracted, I could just slip into Drix's car and take off to avoid the whole thing. It's a win/win. Well, it's a win/win for me and Drix at least. We'd get to drive back to her place, laughing about how we avoided the sexy gangster in the beat-up car. Sebastian would clearly lose out. I bet he had to scrape the bottom of the barrel just to find the cash to fill his tank with gas. It's a long drive out here and … fuck.

Who the hell allowed me to have a guilty conscience?

I let out a heavy sigh and look towards his car and instantly meet his eyes, realizing that he would have had eyes on me the second I walked out of the gates. I had zero chance of escaping him, but the idea was fun while it lasted.

Sebastian pulls himself up onto the windowsill of his car and waves his tattooed arm at me. "Yo, babe. Get that sweet ass over here and let me take you home."

"The fuck?" Drix grunts, staring in shock. "How many of these tattooed sex slaves have you been keeping from me. Holy fuck. Look at him."

My gaze sweeps over him, trying to see what she sees. Yet to me, all I see is a brother. If you want to get all technical, then yeah, I guess you could say that he's got a rock hard body covered in stunning artwork, and the most seductive eyes I've ever seen. But to me … the idea of seeing him as anything remotely sexual is kinda disturbing.

I let out a groan and glance at Drix. "I'll see you tomorrow," I tell her.

"You better. Tomorrow I'm not holding back. I want answers on who the hell these guys are and how to get a few of my own."

I roll my eyes and find a smirk cutting across my lips while very quickly realizing that she won't let me evade her questions for much longer. She spent all day trying to get information about Nic out of me. She thought the more she asked, the more likely I'd be to break, but there are a few things she needs to learn about loyalty. Where I'm from, it's something you don't break, no matter what the circumstances.

Drix doesn't bother waiting for a reply and scurries off to her car, leaving me to face Sebastian on my own. Though, I wouldn't have it any other way. Whatever gets said here definitely needs to be done in private.

I make my way over to his car and don't miss the cautiousness in his eyes. Sebastian is always so carefree so when something is bothering him, it's as clear as day on his face. People always say that the eyes are the window to the soul and in Sebastian's case, it's absolutely true.

I stop by his driver's door and look up at him as he remains perched on the windowsill. "What are you doing here?"

He gives me a beaming smile and ignores my questions. "Thought I was going to have to drag you over here." I roll my eyes and turn away. I get all of two steps before he reels in his attitude and realizes that I'm not in the mood to play around. "No, no, no, Ocean baby. Please, let me drive you home. I came all this way just to drive you ten minutes down the road. Please don't make my trip for nothing."

"Really?" I grunt. "That's the excuse you want to go with? You realize that I don't give a shit if you walked here. That doesn't mean that I'm automatically obligated to sit on your damn shoulders as you hobble back to my pool house."

"Yeah, I know. Of course, I know that. It's just … I really miss you and I'd really, really love to drive you home."

I meet his eyes and in a flash, he gives me his award-winning puppy dog eyes and I crumble with need, so utterly desperate to have my friend back. "Fine," I groan, trying harder than ever to keep the annoyed tone in my voice. "But you better make it quick and no extra stops along the way."

Sebastian salutes me and as I start walking around to the passenger's side, he drops back through the window and makes himself comfortable. I climb in beside him and as I fasten my seat belt, I feel his heavy stare on me. "What?" I snap.

"Nothing, I just … how are you?"

I raise a brow. "How am I?" I say with a sick laugh. "My best friends all lied to me, my father was murdered, and Charles was murdered—possibly by the same guy. My father was a secret killer that sold me, I moved to a town that hated me, and now I'm possibly falling in love with a guy who has the power to destroy me. Oh, then I was raped, and nearly killed in a drive-by shooting. Not to mention all the bullshit I've had to put up with along the way like Colton's bitchy mom and sisters and the dickheads at the Academy throwing acid over me. So, you tell me how I am."

"Okaaaay," he says slowly, hitting the gas and pulling away from the curb. "So, things haven't been going so great? I mean, you've got that whole falling for Colton thing, right? That's a positive. It's not all bad."

I level a heavy glare on him and he instantly swallows whatever bullshit that was about to come flying out of his mouth. "Can we just skip over all the stupid bullshit and say what needs to be said?"

Sebastian lets out a heavy breath and as he glances across at me, I see fear in his eyes and realize that he's been working up to this moment, too afraid that I'll push him away and risk fucking it all up even more. "Okay," he finally says. "We fucked up. Each and every one of us, we fucked it all up, like royally fucked up. Every step along the way, we had an opportunity to come clean to you and we hid it in our selfish need to protect you when we should have known that not only were you strong enough to handle it, you would have been able to protect yourself better."

"I don't want to hear the same bullshit that you guys keep spouting. I don't want to hear about you as a group. Stop apologizing for them. If they want to make things right, they can come and make the effort themselves. I want to hear about your part in all of this."

He nods and presses his lips into a tight line as he pulls up at a red light. "I'm sorry, Ocean. You're my best friend, my little fucking sister and I let you down. It was a matter of either coming clean or going against the boys. We all sat down and agreed that we wouldn't say anything and then it got to the point where it had gone too far to come clean. You've got to know that we never intended on hurting you. That's the last thing I ever wanted."

"And what about the cameras. You had a million opportunities to tell me about that."

His eyes drop and he studies his steering wheel way too closely. "I kept telling myself that it was to protect you, a way that we could watch out for you. I wasn't on board at first and then that fucker put his hands on you and I climbed on board pretty fucking fast after that."

"So, not one of you gave a shit about violating my privacy?"

"Of course we did, O. It felt so fucking wrong and when I realized that the threat from the Jude kid was gone, I wanted it out. I was planning on coming down here and stripping the place myself and then things got serious between you and Colton and that's when everything took a turn. I didn't realize what Nic had done at first but when I figured it out … fuck, babe. I'm so fucking sorry."

I glance over at him, watching as he navigates through the streets with his heart on his sleeve. Tears begin welling in my eyes and I instantly hate myself for it. "You were a brother to me, Sebastian. You and Nic. We've always been the closet and all I see is a list of betrayals that just keeps getting longer and longer. Do you have any idea how bad that hurts?"

"I know."

"Imagine if I did that to you."

I watch as the guy that I've always seen as larger than life gets smaller and smaller, completely deflated until he finally pulls over on the side of the road. I stare at him, wondering what the hell he's doing when his hand flies across the car and he unclips my seatbelt. I'm pulled up onto his lap before I even know what's going on and then his arms curl tightly around me and my head is crushed into his strong chest. "I'm so fucking sorry, Ocean. If I knew it would end with you hating me like this, I never would have done it. I would have gone against Nic and done what was right. If I could take it all back … fuck. I love you so goddamn much. Please don't end this. I need you in my life."

Fuck, that's some big words he's saying there. Big words with big fucking consequences. Saying that he'd go against Nic's wishes just to make things right means he'd turn his back on them for me, and that's a shitload of weight right there.

My tears fall heavier. Sebastian has always been the softie of our group but he's always been so strong. I've never seen him break down like this, never seen him so damn vulnerable and it shatters every last piece of me. "I don't hate you, Sebastian," I murmur over the lump in my throat. "I'm just hurt. What you guys did … it hurt. It really fucking hurt."

"Tell me what you need, O. Tell me how to make it right."

I shake my head. "I don't know," I whisper. "I just want my friend back. I want to be able to trust you again. I miss you so much."

His arms tighten around me and he holds me so damn tight that it hurts. "I'm right here, baby. I swear, anything you need, it's yours."

I suck in a deep breath before slowly letting it out and trying to calm my wild emotions. We sit on the side of the road for twenty minutes, just sitting in each other's arms until the pieces of my soul finally start gluing themselves back together.

I wipe my eyes on his shirt and pull back, meeting his soft, careful stare. "Do you want to stay for dinner? We can make tacos."

A wide beaming smile spreads across his face and I watch as the weight visibly lifts off his shoulders. He presses a rough kiss to my forehead and all but shakes me with joy. "Fuck yeah," he exclaims, practically tossing me back over to my side and hitting the gas before I have a chance to right myself in my seat. "Let's get you home."

We get back to the Carrington mansion in record time and I laugh at how out of place his car looks in this driveway. He barrels out of the car and instead of going through the house, I take him around the side, not wanting to risk him bumping into Colton. I only just got him back and despite Colton declaring that he's good with the boys, there's definitely still bad blood between them, especially now after the whole camera bullshit.

Dropping down onto the couch in the pool house, Sebastian fills me in on everything that's been going on back home and giving me any updates on my boys. I didn't ask for them, but deep down he knew that I needed to know every last detail.

The hours tick by and before I know it, it's time to make dinner and just as I knew he would, Sebastian gets up to help. He drops his phone down on the counter to free up his hands and within moments, he's by my side, screwing everything up.

His phone dings on the counter and both our gazes drop to read over the incoming text from Nic and my brows instantly shoot up in curiosity.

**Nic - Antony DeCarlo just got charged alongside his brother on drug charges and manufacturing. The fucker is going away for a long time. Lorenzo must have squealed. keep your eyes out. If he cut a deal, we could be next.**

"No shit," Sebastian laughs.

"What?" I question, pretending to have absolutely no idea what's going on as though I didn't just read over his private text.

"Fuck me," he says, still stunned. "You know the DeCarlo brothers? They're the fuckers who came in here and shot up this place. You know, after Nic …"

"I know the ones," I snap.

"Yeah, well one of them got arrested a few days ago and now another brother did. I highly doubt Lorenzo squealed. They have to be going down some other way. Either way, they're both fucked."

A smile pulls at my lips, knowing damn well that this was Colton's doing. There's no if, what's, or buts about it. Colton is a fucking genius and I have absolutely no idea how he's pulling it off. I don't think it really matters though, all that matters is that these fuckwits are going away, just as they deserve.

"Shouldn't you be concerned?" I question. "Nic told me that you guys have deals with them."

"Yeah, they won't say anything. Nic is being too paranoid. Without us, their side businesses can't operate and with two of the brothers being locked up, it'd be too risky to start making changes now. We're good."

"Clearly the cops are good too if they've got two brothers. What's to stop them from digging a little deeper and getting you guys too?"

He scrunches up his face as he starts dicing the tomatoes. "Nah, that won't happen."

"How can you be so sure?"

"Because we have too many cops on our payroll, judges, lawyers. You name it, we've got it. The Widows don't operate by running scared, we're prepared for this shit."

Relief filters through me. I want nothing more for the DeCarlo family to go down in a blaze of fire but I don't want my boys getting caught up in it, despite how angry I might be with them. If time is going to be done for the Widows, it's going to be dealt by me.

With that said, we focus on getting everything ready for dinner, and just as I'm serving up, Colton and Mom come barreling through the door, continuing their discussion from the other night about this month's party arrangements.

They both stop in their tracks when they find Sebastian taking over the kitchen. I suck in a breath and hold it, not sure how this is going to go down. Mom's eyes flick to mine and I give her a small nod, letting her know that everything is good and within seconds, a welcoming smile spreads across her face. "Oh, Sebastian. How lovely it is to see you again."

She strides towards him and he pulls her in for a warm hug as

Colton's eyes remain locked on mine. "Are you good?" he questions, not giving a damn that Sebastian can overhear our conversation.

I give him a smile and a nod. "Yeah," I say, knowing he can sense the joy radiating out of me at having my friend back. "Better than good."

He nods and walks deeper into the pool house before stopping by Sebastian and holding out a hand, ready to officially introduce himself. "I guess it's time we clear the air," he says. "I'm Colton."

Sebastian takes his hand and gives it a firm shake. "Sebastian."

And just like that, everything is fine in the world.

We sit and have dinner and I watch in amazement as the boys talk and get to know one another, closing the massive gap between my two worlds. Hell, they even seem to get along and agree on a few things.

Dinner goes by all too soon and before I know it, I'm crushed into Sebastian's arms before he drops down into his car and takes off with a promise to stop by as soon as he can.

Colton stands by my side and instantly curls a hand around my waist. "I haven't seen you this happy in a while."

I curl into his hold, looking and meeting his hazel eyes. "Thank you for welcoming him in," I murmur, pushing up onto my toes and brushing a kiss over his lips. "That meant the world to me."

Colton smiles down at me and shrugs his shoulder. "To be honest, I really wanted to hate him, but he's actually not a bad guy. A little rough around the edges though."

I can't help but laugh, feeling my eyes shining with happiness. "He's so freaking rough around the edges."

Colton pulls me along. "Come on," he tells me. "It's getting cold out here. I don't want you getting sick."

"Yes, sir," I laugh, allowing him to drag me along.

"I heard a rumor about you today," he says, making me roll my eyes. I think I've been the center of enough rumors to last me a lifetime. What could possibly be going around about me now? "Maybe you could clear it up for me because I'm kinda confused."

Frustration takes over me but it's not nearly enough to sour my fantastic mood. "Go on," I say as we start climbing the millions of steps to the front door.

"Why does Casey seem to think you and her are best friends now?"

"Oh," I laugh, looking up at him. "About that. There's something you need to know …"

# CHAPTER 17

I sit out by the pool on a beautiful, sunny, Saturday afternoon with Drix by my side and Casey on the other. Jess floats in the pool on a massive blow-up lounger while Harrison glares at us from the staff kitchen, busily making more cocktails than he's ever made in his life.

Who knew if I just said please he'd be more than happy to help out? Though, that was after attempting to make our own and making a mess of the kitchen instead. It could also have something to do with the fact that Casey, Drix, and Jess are here, but either way, I'm winning today.

Who knew it could get so good? I have Colton, Sebastian, a bunch of incredible girlfriends and I'm living the life. You know, if you pretend there isn't a rapist locked up in the dungeon, and what's better, these people don't give a shit that I'm practically broke with no idea what I want to do with my life. They like me for me and that's all that matters. Well, at least I think Casey does. The jury is still out on her but for now, she's cool to chill.

After explaining the growing friendship between me and Casey to Colton, he gave it a thumbs up and told me that she's a lot more like him than his mother or sister, but also warned me to watch out because she can have a mean streak when she doesn't get her way, but don't we all? Maybe it's a chick thing.

"WHYYYYYYY?" Jess whines from the pool sipping on the straw of her fifth cocktail as I re-adjust the strings of my black triangle bikini. "Who just ghosts a girl like that? Milo can go and suck my dick. I want him back. He was so good and caring and nice, and I swear, no one has ever eaten my pussy quite so delicately."

My face scrunches up. Hearing about Milo's sex life isn't exactly something I want to hear about, especially if it's coming from Jess. It's one thing to listen to Milo's confusion about the topic, but to hear the actual details. Nope, hard pass.

Hendrix laughs, more than familiar with Jess' topic of conversations. "What did I tell you, girl? The only way to get over a guy is by getting under another, or on top. Whatever floats your boat."

"But no one can do it like he did."

"Like who did?" Comes a too chirpy voice from the back door.

Our heads whip around to find Spencer, Charlie, and Milo striding through the door, grinning at us as though they just walked in on a scene out of their wildest dreams.

"YOU," Jess shrieks from the pool, pointing at Milo and rolling in her floating lounger to glare at him. "You ruined me for other dick." Milo's eyes bug out and as Jess attempts to scold him a little more, she slips straight off the edge of her lounger and straight into the pool with a screechy "Oh, fuck."

The boys howl with laughter but I don't miss the slight twinge of guilt dancing in Milo's bright eyes.

As Jess flounders around in the pool, desperately attempting to save what's left of her cocktail, the boys walk over and join us. Spencer drops down at the end of Drix's sunbed, Milo all but overtakes mine while Charlie claims Jess' vacated sunbed as his own.

"What's going on?" Spencer asks, leaning back on his hands as Milo eyes my cocktail.

"Not much," Drix says, bringing her glass to her lips and searching for the straw with her tongue. "We're just chilling. Soaking up some rays."

"Mind if we join?" Charlie questions, looking across at Drix and raking his eyes over her toned body. "Fucking around with you girls seems a little more exciting than playing video games in Spencer's den all day."

Drix laughs and grins back at him. "Mi casa es su casa."

"The fuck?" comes Colton's booming amused grunt from behind us as Casey scoffs. He walks up behind me and places his warm hands over my shoulders, gently squeezing. "When did your bitch ass move in? As far as I'm aware, this casa is still very much mine."

Drix shrugs her shoulders. "Sorry, big guy. You have the best pool in Bellevue Springs and a butler dude who makes the best cocktails I've ever tasted. Good luck getting me out of here. You might as well admit that I live here now. It'll be easier for us all."

I tilt my head back and look up at Colton, meeting his warm, loving eyes. "She has a point," I laugh. "With the way Harrison is practically pouring the cocktails straight down her throat, you can expect her things in one of your many guest bedrooms by the end of the day."

He dips down low and brushes his lips over mine. "No way in hell. It's bad enough having your stubborn ass taking over around here. I couldn't handle two of you."

"Actually," I tease with a whisper, seductively running my tongue over my bottom lip. "I think you could handle two of us remarkably." His brow raises and he gives me a questioning look, making me choke on my cocktail and realize that I'm all talk. "Don't even think about it," I laugh. "I don't share very well."

A grin cracks across his face. "Good," he states. "Neither do I."

Jess finally emerges from the pool, dripping wet with her empty glass. She meets Colton's eyes. "Sorry, I uh … kinda spilled my cocktail in there. I'm pretty sure there's a whole fruit platter at the bottom of your pool now."

Colton shakes his head, more amused by the streaks of mascara making their way down her cheeks and making her look like some kind of drowned rat. "It's fine," he laughs. "Enrique will be in tomorrow. He can deal with it then."

She lets out a sigh of relief before striding over to the sunbed that Charlie is currently laying back on. She reaches down, dripping water all over him, and in one quick pull, tears her pool towel out from under him.

"Woah," he laughs, throwing himself to his feet and having to adjust everything. "A simple please would have been nice."

Jess scoffs as the rest of us watch the show. She drops back down on her sunbed, quickly and effectively stealing her spot back. "I'm done using manners with you boys. What does it get us? We all get screwed over in the end."

Milo cringes and I search out his eyes, knowing damn well that was a stab at him, but he shrugs it off, intent to enjoy the sunny afternoon.

Harrison comes out with more drinks and as Drix and I compete over who can throw it back faster, Charlie fiddles around with his phone and connects his playlist to the sound system. Before we know it, music is pumping through the massive property and we're all vibing and having a good time.

Charlie walks over to the opposite side of the pool and drags back a few more sunbeds so we're not all squished on the same ones and as he turns back to face us, I get a proper glimpse at his shirt, but more importantly the letters across his chest.

DYWMTCOAEYPTYCOMF

A grin tears across my face as he catches my eyes, realizing that I know exactly what it means. A booming laugh tears out of him as everyone else just watches us with confused stares.

"What did I miss?" Hendrix questions, looking over Charlie

through narrowed eyes. "Is it his shirt? What does it mean?"

I shake my head. "If you don't know, you're too innocent."

"Bullshit," she says as Colton chuckles to himself behind me, clearly having figured it out. "You know I'm not innocent. Tell me, fuckers."

Casey laughs beside me, her eyes going wide as she puts her cocktail down, terrified of spilling it all over herself as she laughs hysterically. "Oh shit, I just got it."

"What?" Colton snaps. "The fuck do you mean you just got it? You're sixteen. You're a fucking baby."

"Fucker, I'm seventeen," she says. "But don't stress yourself out worrying about me. The whole innocent ship sailed a loooong time ago."

His eyes bug out of his head as his hands tighten on my shoulders. "What? How long ago? With who?"

Casey cringes and glances around the small ground. "I mean, a while," she says with a guilty laugh. "It was with that friend of yours, Jude, before we left. Where is he anyway? All you guys used to be glued to the hip."

"Tell me you're lying," Colton begs as we all stare at her in shock. "You were hardly fourteen when you left."

"Yeah," she says with an embarrassed smirk. "What can I say? I wanted to get it over and done with and he was always creeping around. Besides, you were a jerk back then so I figured two birds, one stone."

"I .... I ... fuck, Casey. I don't even know what to say to you right now."

She places a hand to her heart. "I always thought you'd be proud. I grew up just like my big brother," she teases. "It's not a big deal. I know I'm not supposed to throw my twin under the bus like this but it's nothing compared to her. Don't get me wrong, I love her and all but that girl is a bit of a whore if you ask me. I think she's screwed half of the East coast by now. She's made way too many bad decisions."

Colton shakes his head in disbelief. "You, me, and Cora are going to have a little chat this weekend. I don't care if I have to get chains to keep both of your legs closed. You're not fucking up your lives by getting pregnant this young."

She gives him a blank stare. "Who are you and what have you done with my brother?"

"I'm serious, Casey. Your days of whoring around are over, especially with guys like Jude. Hold out until you find a guy you love."

Casey leans back in her sunbed and crosses her arms over her chest, dropping her curious gaze to me. "Is that what you did? Waited until you found someone you were in love with?"

My whole world stops.

She didn't just say that.

I freeze just as Colton goes still behind me. "I, umm ... uhh, I ..."

"What's wrong?" She laughs as Spencer and Charlie watch on with shit-eating grins. "Oh, I see. You haven't told her that yet. My bad."

"Okaaaaay," I say awkwardly, getting up and grabbing another cocktail while looking anywhere but at Colton. We're not ready for that. Not even in the slightest. We might feel it, but there's no way those words are ready to be spoken out loud. Just … no. "I think it's time for another drink."

"Good idea," Colton grumbles, walking over and snatching a beer off the table before striding back and dropping down onto my sunbed. I keep my distance, the unspoken emotions between us too strong to deal with.

Colton zones me out and focuses very intently on Charlie while ignoring his sister as though she's not even there. I butt into Spencer and Hendrix's conversation, but truth be told, I haven't heard a single word that's been said.

I lean on the back of Drix's sunbed—just as Colton had done to mine earlier—and I find myself staring at him, watching his movements, and the way his eyes light up when he laughs with his friends. I take note of the small things, like how he unknowingly scratches his nail over the label on his beer bottle, and how every few minutes, he looks back to make sure I'm still here and doing alright.

He really does love me. At least, I think he does. It feels too real for him not to.

"Hey," Drix says, snapping in my face. "Earth to Ocean. Where the hell are you? I've been having a full conversation with you and you haven't heard a word I've been saying."

My gaze sweeps down to her and I laugh. "Sorry, I'm a little distracted."

"Yeah, no shit," she grumbles. "You could be watching that guy take a shit and you'd still be mesmerized."

My face scrunches in disgust. "Please don't put that image in my head. We're too new. We couldn't withstand that."

"Bullshit," Spencer says. "You two could withstand anything."

I meet his eyes and I see his deep honesty and while a statement like that generally wouldn't mean too much, for me and Colton, it means the world, especially considering the kind of shit we've already fought our way through. I mean, if he's willing to still remain by my side after watching me nearly murder a man, then I'd dare say that we're in it for the long haul.

"Anyway," Drix cuts in. "What I was saying was that I think we should set our parents up on a blind date. You know, maybe not even a date, just a 'chance' encounter."

I look out at the pool and really think about it. "You know, I don't think that's such a bad idea. She's still really hurting over Dad, but that might just be the little spark she needs to get back out there. They'd totally be cute together."

"Who's getting together?" Charlie questions from the other side of our group, raising his chin and making a point of being far too nosey for his own good.

I grin back at him while he eyes Drix beside me. "You and Drix," I tell him, watching as his brows shoot straight up.

Drix sucks in a strangled gasp beside me but it cuts off as Charlie focuses his heavy stare on her. His eyes drop over her body, hungrily taking it in and making a point of liking what he sees. His voice lowers, deeper than I've ever heard it before. "I'm down if you are."

Drix squirms beside me and clenches her thighs while roaming her eyes over every inch of his skin, just as he had done to her. She shrugs a shoulder, acting impartial while every ounce of her body is screaming with desperation. "Yeah, I guess I'm down."

Charlie grins and leans back onto his hands, watching her like she's his last meal that's going to be savored with every last bite being thoroughly enjoyed. Her cheeks flush and she lifts her cocktail to her lips, needing something to keep herself busy so that she doesn't bound across the pool and throw herself at him.

Charlie laughs but their moment is cut short by Jess attempting to climb onto Milo's lap. "Please, baby. Just give me one more chance. I promise I won't try and push a relationship. We can just keep hanging out like we've been doing. Maybe the feelings will grow with time or … I don't know. Did I do something wrong? Just help me understand. I don't want to lose you."

Panic slices across Milo's face as he attempts to push her off him but she's had too much to drink and has clearly lost all sense of what's socially acceptable. She keeps trying, refusing to be pushed away.

Milo's panicked gaze flashes to me with a universal sign for help and I rise to my feet, taking a step towards them and placing myself right beside Colton. "Jess, come on. Maybe now isn't the time. Why don't you guys meet up tomorrow in private and you can talk there without an audience?"

"No," she snaps. "I'm sick of not having any answers. I need to know what I did to fuck up because it's driving me insane. One minute we're good and the next thing I know, he's pulling away. I just need … I don't even know what I need but I know I need it."

Colton raises his hand to my waist and I find myself clutching onto it as Milo meets my eyes. My heart breaks for him seeing the uneasiness building within him. He's lost and doesn't know how to play this and then all of a sudden, defeat claims him.

"Jess, get off me," he says, giving her a slightly harder shove than necessary and flying to his feet. He stares down at her in a panic and the words come rushing out of him before he gets the chance to stop himself. "I'm gay. I don't fucking like you. I like dudes. I always have. You and I were just some twisted experiment."

Oh, fuck.

Shocked gasps sound around the group as Jess stares up at him with wide eyes and then as if realizing what the fuck he just said, his eyes go wide with fear and I see the exact second he decides to run.

"Milo stop," I demand, throwing myself in front of him. I reach out and grab hold of him, refusing to let him run. He's been hiding in the closet for too long. It's finally time that he embraces who he is. "Don't run from this. Stand up and face it. There's nothing for you to be scared of—not in front of these guys. They'll have your back just like I do."

His eyes flash over my head to the group sitting behind me and he instantly starts shaking his head. "I can't," he says. "If word got out ..."

"It won't," I promise him. "You know these guys. They're the good kind."

"I ..." he lets out a heavy sigh and squeezes my hand. "You really think so?"

"Well, you've kinda already said it so there's really no going back now. Just own what you said and be your true self, and then maybe you can take Jess aside and apologize for that bullshit because if you don't, you and I are going to have words, that was mean."

His hands begin to shake as the nerves spread throughout him. "Okay," he finally says. "You're right. I can't keep this bottled up anymore." He pulls me aside and I turn to face the group, keeping myself right beside him and not allowing him the chance to back down. He's strong enough. He can do this.

The look on his face is terrifying. The self-doubt and fear of the unknown shining so fucking bright it nearly cripples me, but he raises his chin and takes a hesitant step towards them.

Milo glances around our small group, watching the way they all sit up straighter in dead silence waiting to hear what he's about to say, all except Jess who looks nothing short of broken. "So, I, uhh … didn't mean to just blurt it out like that but, yeah …" He looks back to Jess with his heart on his sleeve. "I'm really sorry Jess. I think you're one of the most beautiful women I've ever had the pleasure of getting to know, but I'm gay. I've always been gay, and that night at the party, I was trying to cover it up. People had been whispering about me for weeks, assuming they knew but didn't have the proof, and when you kissed me …"

"You used me."

Milo's gaze drops to the ground. "Yeah, I did," he whispers, "and I'm so fucking ashamed about that, but then things kept happening between us and for a short minute, I thought maybe I was bi because, girl, damn … you knew what you were doing. You're a fucking rocket in the sack and that tongue. Fuck, baby. You're a man's dream come true."

"Just not yours."

Milo shakes his head as Colton's questioning gaze meets my eyes, realizing that I knew this all along and didn't say a word.

Jess lets out a heavy sigh as her eyes begin to fill with tears. Drix scurries over and squishes herself beside Jess, holding her tight, just as a best friend should. She looks up at Milo with a fierce stare. "That's really low of you, Milo. I get that you weren't ready to come out and tell people yet. This world isn't exactly accepting of gay people, but using her like that … it's fucking wrong."

"I know," he says, "Which is exactly why I cut things off with her. She doesn't deserve that and I could see that she was starting to have real feelings for me. I couldn't morally let it go on. I've been so far locked in the closet that the thought of coming out has made me physically sick, and believe me when I say that in this world, it's safer to pretend to be straight than to be who I really am."

Jess looks down at her lap. "It's fine," she whispers. "I should have known. No straight man has the right to be that manscaped. You're practically a work of art down there."

"Hey," Charlie snaps, throwing himself to his feet. "There's nothing wrong with a bit of manscaping. I'll have you know that my junk looks like a fucking treat."

Drix raises her chin. "Prove it."

Charlie's brow arches as his hands fall to the front of his shorts and within the blink of an eye, his dick is out and gently waving around, showing off every inch of manscaped skin.

"Fuck me," Colton groans, standing up and looking anywhere but at Charlie's dick. He walks over to Milo and pulls him in for a tight hug. He claps him on the back and a warm smile spreads across my face. "You're all good, man. Your secret is safe with me. That couldn't have been easy."

Milo pulls back and gives him a grateful nod. "Thanks."

"I got to say, I feel a shitload better about the bullshit with you dating my girl before I got to her now. It finally makes sense why you didn't put up a fight when I stole her away."

Milo laughs. "Yeah, I wasn't about to stand between that shit. I have a feeling you would have taken me out if I kept her from you."

Colton's eyes flash down to mine and sparkle with mirth. "You're damn right."

Spencer moves in next and gives Milo a hug and within seconds, everyone is surrounding him—even Jess—and promising that not a word will be said until he's ready to share it with the rest of the world.

# CHAPTER 18

I roll Colton's sweatpants over at my hips, keeping them in place so they quit falling down to my ankles. I have no idea what happened to mine after our fuck-fest last weekend, but they're gone. Like, gone gone, not just hiding in the laundry somewhere, but freaking gone. I was too preoccupied with the mind-blowing dick I was getting to realize that when he tore them off me, they must have been thrown or shredded or … I don't fucking know. Either way, I need a new pair because Colton's just won't do. My hips are far too small to pull this off for much longer.

I lean over the counter as the party rages around me. I don't know how our little poolside chill session turned into a huge party but somehow it did and I wouldn't have it any other way.

After Milo finally came out of his closet—well, halfway out—the mood accelerated and everyone was ready to party. Though that could have had a little something to do with the cocktails we were sucking down way too fast for our own good.

Charlie made one call and nearly the whole senior class from Bellevue Springs Academy was here and when Drix did the same, the sausage fest suddenly had an equal share of buns to go around.

Charlie and Drix haven't stopped flirting with each other since I put the idea in their heads and now that I see it, I like it. The two of them would be perfect together. Charlie needs a strong girl like Drix to even out his bullshit. Hell, he just needs someone who could put up with him, and Drix is perfect for that. Not to mention, they're both sexy as fuck. They're a perfect match.

There's nothing better than sitting back and watching two people come together and now that the idea is in my head, I'm intent on making it work between them. Charlie and Drix together would be like a sonic boom. Fucking perfect.

I lean over the kitchen counter, watching the party around us. When all the girls from BSP showed up, Cora came wandering out of her bedroom as though the party was her idea in the first place and after rolling my eyes for the hundredth time, I gave up caring. Casey can deal with her, she's not my problem.

I pick at the grapes on the counter, watching Milo as he dances across the party. I've never seen him so energetic before and that's saying a lot when it comes to Milo. He's always the life of the party but now, it's like Milo on crack. A massive weight has fallen off his shoulders and while he's still keeping his secret from the rest of the world, around our friends, he can finally be himself and nothing will ever make me so fucking happy.

The lights are dimmed and the vibe in the room is enough to have me forgetting all the shit going on in my life. Nic who? Widows who? Except for Sebastian, of course. He somehow managed to weasel his way back in. Even though I'll always question if I can trust anything he says to me, I'm glad to have him back in my life where he belongs.

My hips sway against the counter as I get lost in the music. Two warm hands claim my waist and their familiarity has me pressing my ass back and rubbing against the front of Colton's pants. I feel his cock hardening against my ass as his fingers tighten on my waist.

He pulls me in until my back is flush against his wide chest and dips his head until I feel his breath tickling the sensitive skin of my neck. "Do you have any idea how fucking good you look?" he murmurs into my ear as his hand curls around the front of my bare stomach, lowering into the front of my sweatpants.

My eyes roll into the back of my head and I encourage his touch by grinding my ass against his hard cock. "We shouldn't," I murmur, my voice far too breathy for my own good but with the loud music and the partiers oblivious to anything going on around them, I'm all good.

His lips press down on my neck and as his tongue brushes against my skin, his hand dips lower until I feel his fingers at my clit. I suck in a desperate groan. "Just tell me to stop, Jade, and I will."

Stop? Fuck no. That'd be a tragedy.

We stay right where we are, knowing damn well that someone would have to walk around this side of the counter to see what we're doing. That's a risk I'm more than willing to take. After all, the lights have been dimmed and the main part of the party is hovering out around the pool. We should be good to fuck around for as long as we want, but I can't deny that the risk of being caught has me wetter than I've ever been before.

I reach behind me as he pushes two thick fingers into me and drives me in-fucking-sane. My hand slips into the front of his pants and my fingers curl around his thick, veiny cock. I pump my hand up and down, rubbing my thumb over that sweet bead of moisture at his tip, wanting nothing more than to drop down to my knees and suck him dry right here for the world to see.

Actually … it's not a bad idea at all.

I turn in his arms and the movement forces his hand out of my pants. Colton meets my eyes and confusion shadows his beautiful face until I lick my lips and lower myself down to the ground between him and the counter, spreading my knees wide just to tease him.

Colton props his hands against the counter and to anyone looking his way, all they'd see is Colton standing in the kitchen, watching over his party. They'd have absolutely no idea that I was here about to help myself to the best meal I'll ever taste.

His eyes flame with need as I loosen his shorts and pull them down just enough to free his cock. It bounces out in front of my face and I bite down on my lip, loving how fucking perfect it is.

I take him in my mouth, still needing to use both hands to take exactly what I want, sucking up and down while exploring every inch of him with my tongue. I feel him at the back of my throat and I push myself further, truly believing with every ounce of my heart that Colton Carrington deserves the best there is.

Colton's hand drops from the counter and he buries it into the back of my hair, telling me that he's close but before I can taste him on my tongue, he tears himself out of my mouth. In a flash, he grabs me around the waist and barges his way through to the private bar hidden in the kitchen.

The door is slammed behind us and before my feet have a chance to hit the ground, I'm bent over the bar and he tears my sweatpants down my legs. His hand slaps across my ass and then his warm mouth is on my pussy, his tongue lapping up my arousal.

"YES," I scream out, needing so much more.

I feel him groan against me as he strokes his cock, desperately needing that release and after bringing me close to the edge, he stands up and buries himself deep within me in one hard thrust.

"Fuck, Jade," he says through a clenched jaw, slamming into me over and over again.

"More," I cry out. "I need more."

He gives me exactly what I'm begging for, building me up until we both come hard and fast on the bar.

"Holy shit, Jade," he murmurs, breathless, bending over me to find my lips. He kisses me deeply with his cock still buried in my pussy, right where I like it. Only when we've both regained enough energy does he pull himself out of me and release me from his kiss.

I clean myself up and after straightening my bikini top and watching Colton put himself back inside his shorts, we emerge from the private bar with grins far too big not to be obvious.

As we walk back into the kitchen, we find Spencer making his way toward us from the living space with a grim look on his face. We both watch him as he makes his way over to us, stealing a grape off the counter and popping it into his mouth before finally reaching us.

"What's up?" Colton asks, slapping his arm around my waist and holding me tight.

Spencer moves in right beside us and looks out at the party, making sure no one is in hearing range or watching us over here. "Nothing," he finally says. "I just checked on Jude. He looked like shit."

A low, chilling voice comes from behind us. "The fuck are you talking about?"

We all whip around to find Charlie standing right there, hearing every fucking word Spencer just said. My eyes go big as my heart starts beating wildly in my chest.

"Charlie," Colton starts, a low warning tone in his voice.

Charlie steps into us and focuses all his attention on Colton, seeing him as the ring-leader here. "Don't fucking bullshit me," he says through a clenched jaw. "Where the fuck is Jude?"

Colton lets out a heavy sigh and looks to Spencer before finally glancing back at Charlie and releasing a broken sigh. "He's in my father's wine cellar."

Charlie shakes his head. "You're keeping one of your fucking brothers locked up? You're all fucking dead to me." Within seconds, he spins on his heel and starts stalking out of the kitchen.

"Fuck," I curse under my breath before taking off after him with both Colton and Spencer keeping right on my ass. We break out into the hall to find Charlie heading straight for the wine cellar. "Charlie, wait. You don't understand."

Charlie forges ahead, his anger getting the best of him. "Come on, bro," Spencer says. "Give us a fucking chance to explain."

Just as he reaches the wine cellar door, Charlie spins around, fixing a sick glare on each of us. "What the fuck is this? I've been asking for fucking weeks where the hell he went and you've all been fucking lying to me. Has he been down here the whole fucking time?"

Colton sighs and nods and within a split second, Charlie's fist swings out and slams hard against Colton's jaw. I suck in a sharp breath and throw myself in front of Colton. "Calm the fuck down," I demand, giving Charlie a hard shove and forcing him back from Colton. "You have no fucking idea what's going on. Just give us a chance to explain."

"A chance to explain?" he scoffs. "You've had weeks to explain where he is. How many times did I bring it up?" He glances back at Spencer. "How many fucking times did I ask if you'd heard from him?"

"I know," Spencer growls. "But it's not my fucking story to tell."

"Then whose is it?"

Spencer looks down at me and Charlie's heavy glare follows right along. He steps into me, clenching his jaw and the hatred in his eyes puts me on edge. I've never seen this side of Charlie. He's always been sweet, loving, and kind, but right now, he's anything but. "What did you do?"

Colton reaches around me and pushes Charlie back a step. "Back the fuck off, man. Don't talk to her like that."

Charlie scoffs. "This chick came in and divided us from the beginning and now she's fucking gone as far as to have you two fuckers keeping shit from me? You have Jude locked in a fucking dungeon. We don't do that, we never have. What is so fucking bad that you didn't trust me? What could he have done to you?"

Tears grow in my eyes but I won't allow Charlie to keep going like this. He has to know and right now, I don't give a shit if it means that he'll look at me differently. His words are hurting and if my truth hurts him right the fuck back, then so be it.

I step into him, slamming my hands against his shoulders and forcing him back with a strength I didn't know I possessed. I slam him against the wall, right beside the wine cellar door. "That friend of yours, that brother, raped me. He spiked my drink, tore my fucking dress off my body, and as I cried for help, he fucked me like I was his to destroy. That's why that motherfucker is locked in a fucking dungeon, and the look you're giving me right now, that's why I didn't say a goddamn thing."

Colton's hand finds my waist and he pulls me back a step, knowing I need a moment to calm down. "No," Charlie says. "I know him. He wouldn't do that."

Spencer scoffs. "Come on, man. You can't be that fucking naive. He raped that girl two years ago and she fucking disappeared."

"He didn't. He gave me his word."

"Charlie, come on. You always want to see the best in people but he fucking lied to you. He hurt that girl and now she's gone. He's admitted it time and time again, and now he did the same to Ocean and I won't let him get away with it."

Charlie continues shaking his head as his horrified gaze comes back to mine. "Surely you saw the signs," I whisper, hating that I have to open this old scar but the blank expression on his broken face has me going on. "He hated me from the beginning. He came into my room on my first night here and tried something, then the Black Widows beat him up. He cornered me on Colton's boat to try again, he cornered me in the school pool. It was only a matter of time before he finally got to me, and the night of the Masquerade party, he did. He broke me, Charlie. He hurt me and I'm sorry that this was kept from you but I couldn't bear the thought of you looking at me like I was used goods. You have such a sweet innocence about you and I love that because when I'm around you, I feel it. Your goodness is contagious and I needed it so damn bad. I couldn't risk it."

His gaze sweeps past Colton and Spencer before coming back to mine. "You told them."

I shake my head. "I didn't. Colton found me while Jude was … you know. I didn't tell either of them."

Charlie glances up at Colton. "You saw it."

Colton silently nods, not packing on any more details for Charlie to have to work through later. They hold each other's stare for a moment longer than necessary and the hurt spilling out of Charlie is enough to have me feeling like the world's worst friend. He trusted us and we lied to him. We kept a secret that would change the way he looked at us and just like that, we became just as bad as the Widows.

Who am I becoming? I don't like this dishonest, murderous version of myself that I'm turning into. I've always prided myself on being a loyal person but that's not who I am at all. I'm weak. I'm a liar.

Charlie looks toward Spencer and with a heavy breath, he moves over to the wine cellar and peels the door open. He looks back at the three of us and knowing exactly what he's about to walk in to see, a single tear tracks down my cheek and splashes against my black bikini top.

Charlie tears his gaze away and disappears into the wine cellar, closing the door behind him and I swallow back fear, not knowing what's going to come from this. Is he going to free him? Give him help? Or is he going to find that same darkness in his soul that I found? Who knows, maybe it'll completely take over him and he'll take all his hurt and frustration out on Jude just like I did. Maybe he'll go too far or maybe it'll have him throwing up. Charlie is a sweet guy. He wasn't cut out for torture and murder and now we've exposed him to this ugliness.

Charlie will never be the same again.

"Come on," Colton finally says, pulling on my arm. "We need to give him his space. He's hurting right now and he hates that he didn't know you were going through that, but our methods of dealing with it … he won't accept that easily. It might take some time, but he'll come around."

I let Colton pull me along and I find myself staring at the shiny marble beneath my feet. "Are you sure?"

"Yeah," Spencer says, stepping into my other side. "He'll be alright."

I nod, not convinced by either of them in the least, especially as they don't believe the words themselves. All I know is that this could be a game-changer. Charlie is either with us or against us and right now, I have no idea which way he's going to go.

# CHAPTER 19

Four days down and not a word from Charlie.

My heart aches for him. He hasn't come around in the mornings before school, he hasn't texted stupid memes, he hasn't even sent a sexually suggestive text message.

He's hurting and that's on us.

We should have been upfront with him. He spent weeks worried about his friend, completely in the dark, and not knowing what happened to him. The boys should have been honest with Charlie about the girl Jude hurt two years ago and I should have been honest about him hurting me now.

What kind of friends are we?

I walk from my last class and meet Drix and Jess by their lockers while giving fake smiles to everyone who demands my attention. I'm not in the mood today. Sunday was easy to pretend that nothing was wrong, but the days after that just sucked.

Colton had gone down to see Jude after Charlie had left to get some kind of indication of what had gone down in there. From the way Charlie left him, I'd dare say that our secret is safe. Charlie isn't the violent type though—no matter how much he talks it up—and that kind of shit would have left a scar.

I dart across the hallway and grab my stuff out of my locker before slamming the door closed with a sigh. I really hate this. I've been against my boys for weeks now and that doesn't hurt nearly as much as knowing that Charlie is hurting. Maybe it's because, with my boys, I was the one who was wronged, but with Charlie, I'm the one doing the hurting.

I have to find a way to make it up to him. This isn't fair to him. He shouldn't have been left in the dark, just as Colton shouldn't have left me in the dark with the same damn thing.

Why can't things be simple for a week or two? I just need a break from all the constant bullshit. I need to go away and forget everything that's been going on. I don't know, maybe Colton will sweep me away to a deserted beach resort and show me the time of my life where I can pretend the rest of the world doesn't exist.

Damn it. I can't even suggest that to him because he will and then I'll be stuck on a beach wishing I was back home so I can handle my shit and stop running away like a little bitch.

I make my way back over to the girls when my phone buzzes in my bra. I fish it out of its little hiding spot that it lives in during school hours and glance down at the screen to find a text from Milo.

**Milo - You need a ride home today? I need to be somewhere but can swing by and get you first.**

**Ocean - Nah, don't worry. I can find my own way home.**

**Milo - Cool, thanks. Call me tonight. I've got to spill some tea.**

I roll my eyes at my phone while hashing out a response. Milo's idea of spilling the tea is gushing over the boys at school and telling me all about what he saw in the locker room. Last time it was a full breakdown on how some kid got his dick pierced and was showing it off at every chance he got which then went into me convincing Milo that he really didn't need to get one himself.

**Ocean - Okay, but it better be worth it!**

**Milo - It is.**

I look up at Drix and am just about to ask her to drive my ass home when I find the words crumbling and disappearing in my throat. "You good?" she asks, seeing the weird look on my face.

"Oh, umm, yeah. I'm fine. I have to go. I'll see you guys tomorrow."

"Yeah, no problem," she says. "Do you need a ride?"

"Nah, I'm good. I think I'm going to walk."

Her face scrunches up in distaste. "You're fucking with me, right?"

"No," I laugh. "I could really use the walk to clear my head. It's been a shitty few days."

"Yeah, I've noticed," she says, leaning back against her locker.

"What's going on with you guys? Charlie's been super quiet. I thought he was into me but he practically ghosted me."

"Nah, he's just going through some things. Maybe he could use the distraction. Why don't you go and chill with him this afternoon? He could use a friend or two."

Drix presses her lips into a tight line while thinking it over. "Maybe. I don't know. I'll think about it."

"Okay," I say, adjusting my things in my arms and getting comfortable for my walk home. "I'll see you guys tomorrow."

Jess gives me a small smile and focuses back down at her phone in her hands. She's still hurting after finding out about Milo's love of dick but at the same time, she understands it. It doesn't change that she's been really quiet though. She'll move past it eventually and realize that having Milo around as one of the girls is a million times better than having him there as one of the guys.

"Kay," Drix grumbles, giving me an odd look. "Call me if you change your mind and I'll come and grab you."

"Thanks," I say before turning my back and walking out of the school. I step out into the afternoon sun and take a deep breath. I rarely get time to myself and even though I hate my reasons for needing this time, I can't deny that the peace and quiet is one of the sweetest things I've ever experienced.

Realizing that it's going to be a very long walk if I keep overthinking everything, I try my best to zone out and focus on the good times, focus on Colton, and the way I've been making some incredible new friends. I focus on Mom and her need to find happiness, hell I even spare a thought for Nic and try to forget the shitty things he's done while remembering his apology and his need to always keep me protected.

It's been just over a week since I went into Breakers Flats and spent the morning with him. The time we had together was incredible before it all went to shit. I finally felt like I was finding something important to me, something that I'd lost along the way. I was going to have it all. Turns out I was fooled.

I get halfway home when my legs start giving out and I cut through the mall before shooting out the back. The first half of my walk was good but turns out that's all I needed to clear my head and now I'm stuck having to walk the rest of the way back.

I could call Colton or Hendrix but by the time they actually get here, it'd be quicker just to walk.

I make my way out through the back of the mall parking lot and am just about to cross the road when a noise up ahead draws my attention. I glance up to find a guy leaning against a brick wall. He's not paying attention to me but my stomach twists, telling me that he's more than aware that I'm here.

Why the hell did I have to walk out through the back of the mall? That was fucking stupid. Nic has always drilled into me to always stay on the main roads whenever I have to walk somewhere. Never take shortcuts.

Trusting my gut, I cut across the road and walk to the other side only to find the prick following me across, this time his eyes focused heavily on me.

Fuck.

Why the hell did I have to insist on hiding Nic's gun away in my underwear drawer? I should be carrying it everywhere in this fucked-up town.

I pick up my pace and get a good grip on my math textbook, preparing to launch it at the fucker when another guy appears at the other end of the walkway and starts heading toward me. My heart starts racing. I'm in fucking trouble here.

They couldn't know each other, could they? Is this a trap?

The guy in front of me is covered from head to toe in tattoos, and not the sexy kind, but the kind that makes my skin crawl. My palms grow sweaty as I remain extremely aware of both the men, constantly watching the guy in front while keeping my peripheral vision on the guy behind, especially as he starts picking up his pace.

Going against my better judgment, I slow down, trying to avoid getting closer to the guy in front.

I'm fucked.

What do they want?

I glance around in a panic. I've already had my innocence stolen from me, I'm not about to let it happen again. There's an alleyway across the road and right now, it's my only chance of getting away. If I can run across and somehow lose them, I'll be alright.

These guys don't look like they're from around here, they look more like the kind of guys from back home, the kind that you'd never want to be alone with. In fact, they look a lot like my boys—deadly, cold, and vicious.

The gap between us gets smaller and I stop in the center, flicking my gaze between the two. They nod at one another as they bear down on me, making it clear that I've fallen right into their trap, but I'm not a fucking quitter. I'm not about to roll over and allow them to have their wicked way with me.

I'm better than that. I have to fight this.

I drop everything in my arms and run.

I dart across the road faster than I've ever moved in my life, running straight for the alleyway. I've never been down here before and I have absolutely no idea what's at the other end but I have to hope that there's salvation. I can't have this happen again. I won't survive it a second time.

My feet pound against the road and I hear the two guys instantly take off after me, their feet moving like lightning. Panic surges through me as I become extremely aware of every step I take, desperate not to fall or stumble knowing that one tiny little fuck up could end me.

I glance back over my shoulder to find one of the guys with a gun in his hand and an involuntary scream tears from deep within me.

I remember the words Nic always taught me—if you can't fight back, run. Run as fast as you fucking can. A slow target is a dead target.

Repeating his mantra over and over again, I race up the pathway and slam my hand against the brick wall to fling myself around the corner faster. I dive into the alleyway but don't dare stop as their footsteps grow louder, closer.

Glancing up ahead and trying to figure out my next step, I come to a screeching halt, finding three men already there, waiting for me at the end of the alleyway.

"Fuck," I breathe, glancing around in a panic, desperate for some kind of escape. I start backing up as they move toward me and for some reason, I find it impossible to tear my eyes off them, particularly the older man standing in the center. He has an air about him, something that screams danger.

He's in a suit and the way he holds his shoulders and oozes importance tells me to keep my fucking mouth shut.

The two men behind me finally catch up and I feel the gun at my back, forcing me to walk forward and meet the men in the middle.

My eyes flick around, desperately searching to figure out who's the weakest link, which one would I be able to take down, which one could I fool?

The suited man takes a step forward. "I wouldn't, Oceania Munroe," he warns, shocking me as he uses my full name, though I hardly hear him over the deafening pulsing in my ears as my blood pumps wildly through my body with fear.

"Who are you?" I demand, far too bravely for how I feel inside as I try to look over them in a new light. They clearly know me and I too easily just fell into their trap. These fuckers have been watching me, waiting for me.

He steps in closer and scans over my face, looking for something but I have no idea what. "I think the real question here is who the hell are you?"

I slam my hands against him, forcing him a step away from me, his closeness way too disturbing for my own liking.

The gun at my back moves to my skull. "Don't fucking tempt me," the guy murmurs at my back, his hot breath hitting the side of my face. "I've been waiting for my fucking chance to take out Dominic Garcia's girl."

Fuck. They're Wolves.

I'm in more trouble than I could ever have known.

"Easy, Snake," the suited guy demands, his sharp, deadly glare shooting up over my shoulder to the armed man at my back. "Hurt her and you'll spend the next week in the cell."

The gun instantly eases off the back of my head as a low, rumbly growl sounds behind me. "Yes, boss."

"Boss?" I question, my eyes going wide as I stare at the man standing way too close. I suck in a sharp breath. No, this can't be happening. "You're Mikhail Russo."

His eyes sparkle with danger and in the blink of an eye, he seems to grow a million feet taller. "Ahh, so you know who I am."

I swallow back fear, doing everything in my power not to let on just how fucking terrified I am. "What do you want with me?"

He licks his lips and shivers travel right down my spine, turning my blood freezing cold. "I've been watching you, pup," he says in a chilling tone. "You've been a very naughty girl spending so much time with those Widows. Anyone would think that you're a traitor to your family."

"Family?" I scoff. "What's that supposed to mean?"

"You're a Wolf, girl, and have been since the day you were born."

"No," I say, shaking my head and scrunching my face in distaste. "'I'm no Wolf and I sure as hell am no Widow, but I know where my loyalties lie. I don't want anything to do with your stupid gang."

A hand shoots out and slaps hard across my face, leaving a stinging ache in its wake. "Watch your mouth," Russo spits. "The Wolves are your family whether you like it or not. Out of respect for your father, I've kept my distance, but I'm not a very patient man. With Dominic Garcia now leading the Black Widows, it's time for you to come home. You could be of great use to me."

I laugh at him. "You think I'm about to come and sit by your side in your shitty little clubhouse and tell you everything I know on Nic and the Widows. Yeah, fucking right."

"Careful," he says, stepping into me and forcing me back a step, only to stumble over the gunman's boot and fall into the brick wall of the alleyway. "Keep talking like that and my men may get the impression that you're a traitor to who you are, to your father, and your family."

Fuck. Being labeled a traitor by anyone is never a good sign, even if they're not your people. That's practically begging for a bullet through my temple, but at the same time, I won't turn on the boys—they're my family.

"I am not a Wolf," I tell him, raising my chin in defiance. "And I sure as hell won't be giving up Nic to you. I'd sooner die."

His men step closer and I become completely surrounded by Wolves. "Let me at her," one of them snaps. "She's not loyal. She'll only stab us in the back and cause problems. Just end her now before it gets out of hand."

Russo places his hand against the guy's chest and he instantly retreats, like some kind of lap dog. The two share a look and Russo's little Wolf goes white. Apparently speaking out of turn is a big no-no and threatening to take out the girl that the boss man clearly has plans for is an even bigger mistake.

Russo looks back at me and somehow the leer he gives me is a million times worse than anything I've ever experienced. It's darker than my soul during those moments with Jude, it's more lethal than Nic with a blade, and fuck, it's a shitload worse than any damage my father could have ever done. He's the real definition of a monster. The shit my boys bring to the table is just child's play. This right here is the big leagues and I'm in over my head.

"Listen here, pup," he says, folding his hands together and drawing my attention to a chunky, black ring on his left hand that has an engraving of a Wolf. He slips it off his finger and hands it to one of his men. "Whether you like it or not, you belong to me. You're a Wolf and you're going to be in my ranks. You are loyal to me."

I swallow my protests, being smart enough to know when to keep my damn mouth shut, only when he looks to the tattooed man who'd chased after me and led me into this fucked-up trap, his next words have screams of terror tearing from my throat. "Turn her around."

In a flash, the tattooed man grabs me and spins me around. I'm slammed back against the brick wall with both of my wrists locked in his tight grip behind my back. My face is pressed hard against the rough wall and I feel the brick slicing through my soft skin.

I fight against his hold, fearing the absolute worst. "LET ME GO," I scream, desperately trying to free my hands and kick out against his vice-like hold.

I hear a strange sound, one that's familiar but one that I can't quite place. I try to peer around to see what's going on, but the tattooed man holds me tighter. He steps right into me and I feel his horrid warmth against my back. "This is going to hurt just a little."

My breath comes in sharp, terrified gasps as another guy steps into me and bunches up my hair until the back of my neck is completely on display. "NO," I scream. "NIC IS GOING TO FUCKING KILL YOU FOR THIS, JUST LIKE HE KILLED THOSE SCUM LOSERS WHO SHOT KIAN."

Laughter sounds at my back and just as Russo takes a step closer, that odd familiar sound suddenly clicks and my blood runs cold.

It's a fucking blow torch.

He's going to brand me like cattle.

I scream louder, absolutely terrified for what comes next when a rough hand presses down over my mouth, muffling my cries. Russo steps in right behind me and the tattooed man moves out of his way but doesn't dare let up on his hold.

I hardly have a chance to fight before a searing, sharp sting burns into the back of my neck. My skin blisters and bubbles under the ring and I clench my eyes as my teeth bite down hard against the hand on my mouth.

I howl in agony and feel myself becoming light-headed. My knees give out and just like that, the five men step back from me and I crumble into a mess on the dirty ground.

Tears stream down my cheeks, dropping into my lap. My head remains against the brick wall being the only thing that's keeping me up. There's an odd rusty taste in my mouth and as my senses begin to come back to me, I realize that the first man I had seen in the street is clutching his hand with blood pouring between his fingers.

Realizing it's his blood I taste, my stomach churns and I throw up the contents of my stomach right into my lap and all over the ground before me. Having absolutely no energy to do anything about it, I just sit here weeping, knowing damn well that this isn't the last I'll see of these men.

Sobs begin tearing from my throat and as Russo looks down at me in disgust and leans in, I try my best to reel it in. "This isn't over, pup. Like I said, I'm not a very patient man, but I respected your father and I respect his wishes. He didn't want you brought into this life until you were eighteen. Fucking stupid if you ask me, but lucky for you, I'm going to allow you to see out your senior year, and then you'll be coming home right where you belong."

I shake my head but the movement sends a searing bolt of agony shooting through me. "Be smart, girl," he warns in a chilling tone. "I'm watching you. You're branded with my mark and that means that you will never escape me. If you run, I will find you and you won't like the consequences, so I suggest that you come with a fucking smile on that pretty face."

I go to look up at him but by the time I find the energy to raise my chin and fight the pain at the back of my neck, all I see are five retreating forms, escaping the alleyway in their need to get out of here before someone comes looking.

I keep my eyes locked on them and not once do they look back.

They hit the end of the alley and finally disappear from view but I'm not fooled. I know they still have eyes on me. Either way, it's enough to allow me to finally take a proper breath.

The pain in my neck is next fucking level but the relief is too great to pay attention to it right now. All I know is that I have to get out of here.

Finding the energy that I just don't have, I dig into my bra and find my phone before pressing a few buttons and holding it to my ear as my hands shake, still rattled by fear.

"O?" his concerned voice comes streaming down the line, making the tears spring from my eyes once again.

"Please," I sob, my voice barely audible. "Please, I need you to come and get me."

# CHAPTER 20

Forty-eight minutes is all it takes for Nic's car to come screeching to a halt at the top of the alleyway. Car doors are thrown open and within seconds, their feet are pounding against the pavement, the echoes bouncing off the walls in the narrow space.

"Baby," Nic rushes out, dropping to his knees and searching over me from head to toe as Sebastian watches on with wide, horrified eyes. "What happened? Who did this?"

Nic reaches for me and a strangled squeal tears out of my throat, the vibrations from my voice box aching against my sore throat. I flinch away and instantly regret the movement. "Don't touch me."

His hands fly away from me and for a brief moment, he just stares in silence, completely horrified by what he's seeing. I've never allowed the boys to see me in pain, but truth be told, I've never experienced anything like this around any of them before.

Sebastian crouches down to see my face and the anguish in his eyes is enough to cripple me. "Ocean, please," he begs. "I know you're hurting but we need to know what happened. We need to make it better."

I meet his haunted stare and everything inside of me breaks.

Painful sobs tear up my throat and I try my best to swallow them down while struggling to breathe past the massive lump in my throat. "Mikhail Russo," I say, looking across from Sebastian to meet Nic's eyes. "He wants me in their ranks to take Dad's place."

Nic flies to his feet and turns away, running his hands through his hair. "FUCK," he roars, his voice traveling right through to the other end of the alleyway. He spins back around to look down at me and there's nothing but guilt shining in his eyes. "I'm so fucking sorry, O. This is all on me. This is retaliation. He thinks he can get to me through you."

"Well, it fucking worked." I nod and cringe at the burning pain at the back of my neck. "He marked me," I say, feeling more ashamed than I have the right to feel.

"The fuck?" Sebastian grunts as understanding dawns on Nic's face, knowing all too well what the fuck I'm talking about. After all, he stood behind three Wolves not that long ago and paid specific attention to their necks, he would have seen their mark, the same one that now has a permanent residence at the back of my neck.

Nic drops down beside me, his face so fucking white he looks ready to pass out. "Please," he says, cautiously reaching for me. "I need to see it. I need to make sure you're okay."

I pull back from his touch, in far too much pain to have him poking and prodding me but realizing that if I don't have someone pay attention to it and get some first aid, I could end up with a severe infection. I let out a shaky breath and nod. "Just ... go slowly," I whisper, fearing my voice will break and show just how miserable I feel. "It fucking burns."

He nods and ever so gently brushes my hair back from my neck. Strands have dried into the wound and he has no choice but to pull them away, making me groan in pain as shivers run through my body. "Fuck," he breathes as Sebastian moves in beside him and crouches down to get a good look.

"We have to get her out of this dirty alleyway or she'll end up with an infection."

"Yeah," he says, raking his eyes from my head all the way down to my toes. His lips press into a hard line and the grimace on his face tells me that I'm not going to like what he's about to say. "O, I need to get you out of these clothes, and then we're going to get you out of here."

I glance down, almost having forgotten that I'd thrown up all over myself. "Okay," I finally whisper, hating how weak I must appear to them.

Sebastian moves around to block me from sight from anyone who happens to walk by as Nic takes my hand and helps me to my feet. I start unbuttoning my blouse as Nic pulls his hoodie over his head and wedges it between his legs.

He helps me get my shirt off and just as I knew he would, he doesn't stare or rake his eyes over my body like other men would do in his position, and right now, despite the fact that he's already seen me in my naked glory a million times over, I appreciate his respect.

Not wasting time and desperately just wanting to get home and off the dirty streets, I start tugging on my skirt. Nic brings his hoodie over my head and carefully settles it into place as my skirt drops to the ground.

The fabric of Nic's hoodie falls to my knees and the boys instantly take my hands and pull them over their wide shoulders before helping me out of the alleyway. My stained uniform is left in a crumpled mess on the ground and despite the scolding I'll receive from Mom, I can't help but be grateful for the memories and evidence of this bullshit being left behind, you know, apart from the Wolves brand mark burning into the back of my neck.

Nic's hand curls into mine and I can't help but wonder if it's the need of having me close or if he's just trying to be a gentleman by helping the damsel in distress. The old Nic would have just scooped me up and carried me out of the alley but the fact that he's allowing me to at least attempt to help myself tells me that he's growing. He's taking a step back and allowing me to dictate what I want and although I'll never say it out loud, he and I both know that I'm grateful. I need to feel this control and having the boys swoop in and tell me how it's going to go isn't going to help with that.

For Nic, this is a massive step in the right direction. It's a silent message between us telling me that he's giving me space to finally start making my own decisions and not try to step in and shit all over it.

Maybe he's finally starting to accept that I'm moving on.

I instantly shake the thought from my head. Now isn't the time to start decoding Nic's actions. I could be here for years trying to figure out his motives. It's not worth the time or the pain.

Sebastian slips out from under my arm and hurries in front of us. The car door is pulled open and just as we reach it, Nic adjusts his hold on me and all but puts me inside the car. He grabs the seatbelt and starts reaching across me to buckle it, but I take the clip out of his hands, more than capable of managing on my own.

After getting it fastened, I look up and meet Nic's eyes to find him watching me intently. "I'm going to fucking kill him," he promises me.

I nod, knowing damn well that the correct response is to tell him not to, to tell him to back off and leave it be. The war between the Wolves and the Widows is already at boiling point and this just tipped Nic over the edge and upped the stakes in the game. He won't stop for anything, for anyone. When Nic is intent to do something, he keeps at it until the job is done.

Mikhail Russo will die for touching me and that's all there is to it

"I know," I finally whisper, feeling a pang of guilt that doesn't sit right with me. Why should I feel guilty for knowing this man is going to die? He was my father's leader, an evil, toxic man who has ordered more kills than I could ever imagine—kills that my father undoubtedly carried out. I should be happy, I should be jumping for fucking joy, yet I just feel cold inside.

Is this what I'm becoming? An emotionless monster? Someone who is okay with death? Maybe I'm just becoming immune to its horrors.

Nic lets out a heavy sigh, probably already putting his plan into place yet for some reason, he remains hovered in the open car door staring at me. His eyes harden and in an instant, I know exactly what he's looking for but I can't give it to him, not yet.

I shake my head ever so gently, holding back the cringe that desperately wants to tear out of me. "Not yet, Nic," I murmur as Sebastian pretends that he can't hear a damn thing that's being said. "I'm still so mad at you. I just need some time."

Heartbreak settles over his features but in a blink of an eye, the hard Nic is back. "Okay," he finally says, straightening up and closing the door. He takes a step back and starts to make his way around to the driver's side, but I hear his grumbled murmur through the open window. "Let's get you back to your new family."

I keep my gaze settled out the window as Nic puts the car into gear and takes off down the road, being careful to avoid any bumps. He takes a corner and the momentum from the turn has pain shooting through my burn. I suck in a sharp breath through my teeth, trying my best not to show my pain but failing miserably.

A hand falls to my shoulder and squeezes and I latch onto it with desperation, curling my fingers through Sebastian's and appreciating every ounce of his comfort.

Every gasp, cry, and groan has Nic pushing his car faster and faster, desperate to get me off the bumpy road and into the safety of the pool house where he can help take the pain away. By the time we reach Colton's street, his careful driving is all but forgotten as he turns into a mad man, driven by emotions.

We reach the gate and I hastily tell him the code and watch as frustration claims him when it slowly peels back. The gate has hardly opened the whole way before Nic shoots past it and races down the drive, narrowly avoiding knocking off his side mirror.

He doesn't stop where normal people stop, but drives around the side of the mansion, over Charles' manicured lawns and only just avoiding taking out archways that Enrique, the gardener, has spent years molding.

His car pulls up right outside the pool house and I look across at Nic as he swings his door wide. "Door to door service, huh?"

"I might have a habit of making shitty decisions but you can never claim that I wasn't thorough and didn't look after you."

I roll my eyes as he smirks to himself and climbs out of his car. Sebastian appears at my door and opens it wide before offering me his hand. I take it gingerly and as he helps me out of Nic's car, the back door of the mega-mansion swings wide, slamming against the wall with such a loud bang that both of the boys flinch for their guns.

Cora stands at the door, staring at me with distaste. "What the fuck do you think you're doing?" she demands. "You just ruined my father's gardens."

Nic steadies his gaze on her and as if only now just realizing who it is standing at my sides, her eyes go wide with fear, remembering damn well what happened at Charles' wake. "You got a fucking issue," Nic growls. "You can take it up with me."

Cora swallows back her fear as her face grows so pale that I fear she's about to pass out, but as if remembering who she is, she stands tall and gives an award-winning huff. "I'm calling the cops to have you arrested for trespassing."

Nic steps closer and I watch with delight as she shrinks away from him. "Go ahead and call them. Tell them that Dominic Garcia is standing on your property and you want me carted away. Watch how fast they shit their pants and tell you to deal with our own fucking problems."

Her jaw clenches. "My brother is going to hear about this."

Nic takes another step and her chest starts rising and falling in rapid movements. "You threatening me, girl?" he demands, snapping his arm out and curling his fingers around her throat. He presses her up against the open back door and leans into her. "Go and get him. Your brother and I have a little unfinished business."

Shit. I'd almost forgotten about the last time the boys actually saw each other. They beat the living shit out of one another and made everything so much worse. Neither of them technically won that fight and while Colton can let it go, Nic sees it as a score that needs to be settled.

Cora's eyes flick to mine, silently begging me for help but I let it go. Nic would never hurt her unless she was to make a physical move against me. Our petty bullshit isn't exactly something Nic is going to bother himself with, especially knowing that I can more than handle a few school house rumors myself.

I raise a brow and prop my hip against Nic's car, making a point that Cora is on her own here. If she's stupid enough to provoke the leader of the Breakers Flats Black Widows, then that's on her.

She slowly turns her gaze back to Nic and after a long, drawn-out pause, Nic smirks and then finally releases his grip on her. "Run along, princess," he says. "Go and get that brother of yours."

Cora's eyes flick around our small group and being smart enough to know when to call it quits, she turns on her heel and scurries away like someone just lit a fire under her ass.

Nic turns to me with a proud grin. "Was that really necessary?" I demand, raising a brow and crossing my arms over my chest.

The hard ridges of his face begin to soften and his eyes sparkle with laughter. "Fuck yeah. Do you have any idea how much fun it is making that bitch squirm?"

I roll my eyes and peel myself off the side of Nic's car. "Come on," I tell him, turning towards the pool house. "Get me fixed up and then feed me. I'm starving."

With the reminder of why we're all here, a seriousness comes over him and he strides toward me, placing his hand at my lower back and leading me into the pool house as Sebastian grabs the doors.

Nic gets me set up on a stool while Sebastian disappears into my room. He comes out a minute later with my hair clip and gets busy curling my hair into a high bun and clipping it up so they can see what they're dealing with.

"Why am I so surprised by your hair skills?" I ask Sebastian as Nic finds the first aid kit and places it on the counter beside me. He starts rifling through and finding everything he needs as Sebastian leans against the counter on my other side, smirking at my question.

"Trust me," he says. "It's in a guy's best interest to learn how to put a woman's hair up, especially so he can wrap his hand around it and tear her sweet head back while her ass is up in the air."

"Okaaaaaay," I drag out. "I shouldn't have ask—OH, HOLY FUCK," I screech, cutting myself off as Nic presses a cold, wet compress to the back of my neck.

"O, I have—"

The door slams open and rattles against its frame as Colton barges into the pool house. "THE FUCK IS GOING ON IN HERE?" he demands, staring down Nic and Sebastian before his eyes come flying back to mine. "Get the fuck away from her."

"It's okay," I insist. "They're not hurting me. I mean, it does fucking hurt but they're helping. I promise."

"Helping?" he questions, walking deeper into the pool house and ignoring the boys' presence, hating the pain that flashes across my face. "Helping with what? What's going on, Jade?"

Nic scoffs from behind me and I resist slamming my elbow back into his ribs. "I ... shit," I look away, unable to meet his eyes as I feel shame for being so weak ripping through me. "I was walking home from school and ran into a few ... *friends*."

"Ocean," Nic warns, not liking me discussing gang-related business with outsiders, but who the fuck is he to tell me what I can and can not say?

I shoot an icy glare toward Nic. "After the bullshit lies and secrets you kept from me, you're really in no position to be telling me to keep my mouth shut. Unlike you, I don't keep secrets from the person I'm sharing my life with."

Sebastian looks away, again pretending that he doesn't hear a damn thing that's going on while Nic clenches his jaw. He stares at me for a long moment and then finally looks back at my neck and presses the cold compress against my burn again.

I suck in another sharp breath that has Colton at my side in a heartbeat. "Ocean, what's going on?" he demands, raking his eyes over the first aid kit on the counter and the small cuts and bruises on my face from when Russo's men pressed me up against the brick wall. "Who the fuck touched you?"

I slide my hand across the counter and latch onto his and he takes it instantly. I don't miss the way Sebastian and Nic eye our hold and see the clear need we have for one another. "Mikhail Russo," I whisper. "He's the leader of the West Side Wolves in Blaxlands Grove."

"The gang your dad was a part of? The one who shot up ..." his gaze sweeps up to Nic and I nod, knowing he's referring to the night Kian was murdered and everything changed.

"Yeah, that's them," I confirm. "Russo had his men corner me on the street today and lead me into an alley where Russo was waiting for me. He said that he wants me in his ranks to take Dad's spot. He seems to think that he has some kind of claim over me because my father was part of their bullshit family. He didn't like it when I turned him down and he didn't like it more when I mentioned that I'm loyal to Nic. He says he'll be watching me until the end of high school and then

I'm his." I turn to face the brooding guy behind me as Colton's hand tightens in mine. "He wants me to get to you. He thinks I'm going to give up everything I know about you guys."

Nic scoffs. "That'll never happen."

"Never."

"Jade," Colton says, drawing my attention back to him. "What happened?"

I look down at our joined hand. "He had me branded like fucking cattle."

"What?"

I nod and turn my head, indicating to the back of my neck. His brows furrow and he steps around me, getting dangerously close to Nic but more than willing to take the risk for me. He sucks in a gasp and despite not being able to see him, I feel the rage burning out of him.

Sebastian watches the two over my shoulder, his eyes flicking between them as Colton looks up at Nic. "I want in. Whatever the fuck you have planned for these bastards, I'm in."

Nic laughs. "No fucking way. You're a little rich kid with deep pockets. That's all you're fucking good for."

"Nic," I warn, swiveling in my chair to see them better. "You don't know what the fuck you're talking about. Trust me, you want him on your side."

Nic narrows his gaze at me, able to tell when I'm holding back. "What's that supposed to mean?"

I glance at Colton and he gives me a small nod, knowing exactly what it is that I need to say. "Colton is the reason that the fucking DeCarlo brothers are getting picked off one by one. He's the one righting—"

I cut myself off before I have the chance to admit in front of Colton that Nic is the reason Maryne is gone but from the look on Nic's face, he understands exactly what I was about to say—he's the one righting your wrongs.

He looks across at Colton with a curious gaze. "You have that kind of pull?"

"I can guarantee that I have a bigger fucking pull than you could even dream about."

Nic takes a deep breath and turns back to me. He doesn't confirm whether Colton will be included in his little revenge plan or not, but he doesn't need to. We all know he will, and if he isn't, Colton is more than capable of stepping in and taking the job right off Nic's tainted hands.

"Come on," Nic says, pushing me back around on the chair. "Let me get you cleaned up."

Half an hour later, I stand outside the pool house with Colton by my side and the boys standing at Nic's car and while I'm still so pissed with Nic about everything that's gone down, I can't help but feel grateful for his help today.

He looks back at me as he opens his car door. "From now on, you don't go anywhere without that gun, got it? It's non-negotiable."

I nod, not prepared to fight him on this. "Yeah, I got it."

"Good. Now, keep that neck clean. I'll come back in a few days to check on you."

"You don't need to do that, Nic. I'll call if I need anything."

Sebastian groans. "Don't start this bullshit, babe. We'll come back either way and you know it."

I roll my eyes and watch as the two Widows drop down into Nic's car and disappear around the corner of the Carrington mansion. As I watch them go, I quickly realize that every time I watch them drive away, the sting hurts just a little less.

"Are you okay?" Colton murmurs, curling his arm around my waist and pulling me into his warm chest, right where I belong.

"I, umm … I don't know. I'm still processing."

"How can I make it better?"

I shrug my shoulders and tip my head up to brush my lips over his. "Cheap Chinese takeout and a movie night on your big ass couch will go a long way to helping me forget that a gang leader wants to drag me into an insane gang war and use me as his personal rat."

"Okay," he promises, slipping his hand down to cup my ass. I feel his smile against my lips. "Anything you want, Jade, is yours."

# CHAPTER 21

The bandage sits heavy at the back of my neck and I'm more aware of it than anything I've ever been aware of before. It's a constant reminder of what went down, a reminder of my future, of what's going to happen.

Every slight move I make, every soft brush of my hair, every tiny little thing has my stomach turning. I've never felt pain like this. My skin burns and I feel as though I'm in a constant sweat which is just another reminder that my whole future has been taken away.

I didn't sleep one bit, despite the boys' reassurances that they'll take care of it. Somehow, I feel it's an impossible task. Especially when it comes to a man like Mikhail Russo. What he wants, he gets. It's that simple and it's not humanly possible to have someone watching over me every second of my life. Eventually, a back is going to be turned and when that happens, I'll be snatched away like the last pair of black pumps during a half-off sale.

Colton stayed with me all night, holding me as I dreamt of being branded over and over again. I felt the hot sting of Russo's ring pressing against my skin, I could feel the powerful burn, smell my flesh singe while being held down with no way out. My dreams were so realistic. It was as though I was living it over and over again every time I closed my eyes.

I walk out of the Carrington mansion and start making my way down the sixty-six steps.

It's been a long morning. Getting dressed and doing my hair was an absolute pain. I've never noticed just how many times I touch the back of my neck. I had to come clean to Mom and let her know what happened so she's been fussing over me, wanting to make sure that I'm alright. She helped me redress it after my shower this morning and I'm sure she'll be there waiting with a new bandage in hand when I get back this afternoon.

The news of what happened nearly killed her. It's one thing to learn her husband was a killer in a gang, but to learn that her daughter is only a few short months away from being dragged into that same world couldn't have been easy.

I don't know what I'm going to do. I trust Nic, the boys, and Colton to come through. I won't be joining the Wolves despite their mark on my neck, but there's always the chance that something can go wrong.

I want to go to college and have a normal life. I'll never get that if Russo gets his hands on me again. I can't let it happen. I can't fall down that hole. I'll never make it out.

The thought seeps out of my mind as I get to the bottom of the stairs to find Milo very impatiently waiting for me. "Heard of a phone?" he calls through the window. "You didn't answer my call last night. I told you I had tea to spill."

I cringe, remembering the exact moment he told me he was going to call. "I'm sorry," I say, walking around the front of his car to the passenger side. I drop down into his car and get comfortable. "It completely slipped my mind. I had a bit going on yesterday."

"What could possibly be more important than me?" he questions, hitting the gas and speeding down the drive. His momentum has me falling back against the chair of his Aston Martin and a low groan comes tearing out of me.

"Hey," he snaps, ignoring the question that just flew out of his mouth. "That better not have been a stab at my driving. I'm a fucking badass bitch behind the wheel. Keep your shitty groans to yourself."

"It's not your shitty driving I'm groaning about, dumbass," I say, adjusting myself in the seat. "I had a little … *accident* yesterday."

His brows furrow as he slows his car to a comfortable speed so that he can stare at me without being the cause of another little accident. "What kind of accident are you talking about?" he asks, scanning his eyes over my body and stopping at the big white bandage peeking through my hair. "What the fuck is that? What happened?"

Milo reaches to grab my bandage and I slap his hand away before he can do any damage. "Don't touch it. It's a bandage, you moron. Who just grabs at bandages?" I grunt before getting on with my explanation. "I had a run-in with some dickhead gang members after school yesterday and—"

"What?" he squeaks, his eyes bugging out of his head as he cuts me off before I can get any further with my recap. "Your boys did this to you?"

A strangled grunt comes tearing out of my mouth and I gape at him in horror. "The hell? No. My boys would never do this. It was the Wolves."

"The who?"

I stare at him blankly. "Where the hell have you been? What do you mean 'the who?'"

"I mean what I mean, now stop pussyfooting around the topic and tell me what in the sweet hell happened to you yesterday."

I groan and settle into my seat, having to adjust myself again. "I cut through the back of the mall on my way home and was cornered by the leader of the West Side Wolves, Mikhail Russo with four of his douchebag henchmen. They're the gang my father belonged to and they wanted to make a point that I belong to them."

"They what?" he breathes, unable to believe what he's hearing.

I press my lips into a tight line and finish my explanation. "They branded me with their mark using a ring and a blow torch. I have a third-degree burn at the back of my neck that will eventually heal in the shape of a wolf. They fucking held me down and claimed me like a prize then promised they'd be watching me."

Milo pulls off to the side of the road and brings his car to a stop before looking at me with wide, teary eyes. "I'm so sorry," he says with his heart on his sleeve, looking guilty as shit. "I was supposed to drop you home but I bailed for a fucking dick appointment. I left you vulnerable and you got hurt. I should have been there. I should have stuck to my word and driven you home like I said I would."

I reach out and take his hand from his lap. "It's not your fault, Milo. Russo said he'd been watching me for a while so whether it happened yesterday or a week from now, he would have eventually got to me. There's nothing neither of us could have done to avoid it. It was inevitable."

"I don't like it."

"I know," I murmur. "I don't like it either but it is what it is. It's done now so can we please try and forget about it? It's bad enough that I'm dreaming about it. I don't want to be talking about it too."

"Of course," he says, checking his side mirror and pulling back out onto the road. "You're really having a shitty time since moving here."

"Tell me about it," I grumble. "But if I was back home, I can guarantee that they would have gotten to me sooner."

"I guess," he says with a hint of cluelessness seeping out of his tone as he shrugs a shoulder. "I always figured that your Widows were the worst there is and that no one would be stupid enough to make a move against them."

"To me, they're at the top of the game, but to the Wolves, Nic is just a kid. Now that his dad is gone and changes are being made, they're taking the opportunity to remind Nic just how fucking bad they can be."

"Shit, Ocean. It's like it's some kind of gang war."

My voice drops to a low grunt. "Gang war is exactly what it is."

"Well … shit. I don't know what to tell you, but you know you can always come to me if you feel like they're watching you. I can hide you at my place and no one would ever know. I've got a pretty big closet that's good for hiding in."

"No shit," I laugh. "Your closet would be pretty squishy with you already in it."

"Shut up," he laughs. "It's not like I'm completely in it. I have one foot out."

"You have your big toe out and that's it."

Milo rolls his eyes and just like that, the heaviness of yesterday begins seeping away and I laugh at his ridiculousness. He's been such an amazing friend since the second I showed up here. I don't know what I'd have done without him. Shit, I probably would have had to be besties with Charlie and who knows how that would have turned out.

Charlie. Charlie. Charlie. Sweet Charlie.

It's only been a few days that he's not been talking to me and I really hate it. He should come around soon, I hope. The boys said he just needed some time but I fear that things will never be the same between us. He's going to look at me differently now. I'm no longer the edgy new girl who he wanted to bring home to Mommy and Daddy, I'm now the girl with issues, the girl who's been broken and abused. I'm dirty, touched, dark, and now destined to spend the rest of my days as a gang girl.

I try to put it to the back of my mind. There's no use worrying myself over it today. He'll come around just as the boys said he would and I need to be patient, otherwise, I'm just panicking for no good reason when I already have so much going on. Charlie is out of my hands and I just have to hope that he decides that I'm valuable enough to have in his life.

Milo pulls up at my school a short moment later and before I have a chance to push my way out of his Aston Martin, he reaches over and takes my hand. "You're going to be okay, Ocean," he promises me. "Whatever you need, you know all you have to do is ask. With me, Colton, Charlie, and Spencer at your back. No one will touch you. You're safe with us. I don't want you feeling as though you're not when you're here."

I flip my hand over and give his a squeeze. "Thanks, Milo. I know. I do feel safe with you guys and believe me, I'd do just about anything to avoid running into those guys again. Nic and the Widows are just as bad, but they're on my side. These guys ... they're bad news and I know you want to help any way you can, but I'd never drag you guys into this world. It's not safe for guys like you."

"Guys like me?" he questions, his brows furrowed.

"Yeah, guys with their pockets filled with cash," I explain, realizing he thinks I'm talking about his sexual orientation. "You'd be steam-rolled until you had nothing left but the shirt on your back. All of you would and I can't let that happen."

"I ..."

"No," I cut him off, leaning in and pressing a kiss to his cheek. "Just be the guy I run to when the world turns to shit. Don't try to be a hero. I couldn't bear the thought of you getting hurt. The Widows are their own army. They'll take care of it. They'll make sure I'm safe. You just need to worry about my sanity. Okay?"

His lips press into a hard line and the irritated stare he gives me is more than enough confirmation that he's not happy about a damn word that I just said. But I'm not backing down on this. The gang world is no place for a guy like Milo. Hell, it's no place for any of the guys from Bellevue Springs. They'd be torn apart and drained of every last cent and I can't imagine what bastards like that would do with that kind of money. they'd be unstoppable and I won't allow that to happen. I can't have that on my conscience.

Milo finally lets out a deep breath and releases his grip on my hand. "We're not done with this conversation," he says.

I roll my eyes knowing damn well that this conversation is so done that it's already a distant memory. "I'll see you after school, okay? Don't do anything stupid."

A cheesy as fuck grin stretches across his face and his eyes instantly sparkle with excitement. "Trust me, I'm going to be doing all sorts of stupid things today."

My brows furrow as I take in his hidden message but I don't quite understand it. I hear the sound of my school bell ringing in the distance and I'm forced to throw myself out of his car, leaving his comment as something to decode later. "I'll see you later," I call over my shoulder, shutting the door and then taking off.

I hear Milo's car speed off behind me and I cringe. If I'm late for school, that means that he's really late. I race down to my locker and grab the things I need before slipping into my homeroom just as my teacher is closing the door.

She gives me an unimpressed glare and I hurry past her, trying my best to avoid eye contact. As I settle into my seat and give a few smiles to the girls wanting my attention, a thought occurs to me. Milo said something about spilling the tea and the whole car ride to school, absolutely no tea got spilled. I wonder if it had anything to do with his comment before I got out of the car.

Glancing up at the teacher to find her attention immersed in the papers on her desk, I quickly dive into my bra and pull my phone out. I hide it under my desk and I glance down at it, knowing that Milo would be just pulling up to school now.

**Ocean - You didn't spill any tea.**

**Milo - Because it was the Ocean show this morning. Ocean this, Ocean that. Does anyone else even exist in your world?**

I roll my eyes and decided to play along.

**Ocean - Nope. No room for anyone else when I shine so brightly.**

**Ocean -Also, you're a bitch!**

**Milo - Ha. Ha.**

**Ocean - Spill the tea already! What's been going on? Did someone get caught sucking off Dean Simmons? I bet it was you, wasn't it? God, you're such a dirty little whore!**

**Milo - Bitch, do you want the tea or not?**

I laugh to myself and quickly flick my eyes to the teacher, making sure I haven't been sprung using my phone.

**Ocean - Fine.**

I wait an agonizing three minutes before his text finally comes through and when it does, I realize that he had to really scrounge up the balls to actually hit send on this one.

**Milo - I may have let my gay flag fly yesterday and fucked a guy under the bleachers while the rest of the school did a fire drill.**

My eyes bug out of my head and I throw myself to my feet. "THE FUCK?" I screech before snapping my head up and coming face to face with my teacher then instantly regret it as the pain shoots through the back of my neck. "Oh, umm … sorry," I say with a cringe, trying my hardest not to grab hold of my bandage to try and relieve the pain. "I just realized that I left my English essay on my desk at home."

Her glare somehow becomes sharper before she lets out a heavy sigh and it's clear as day that she doesn't believe a word I say, but she's not prepared to put up a fight. "Go to the student office and request to put in a call to have it delivered."

I nod and grab my things before darting out of the classroom, knowing damn well that my English essay isn't due until next week but she doesn't need to know that. I take off down the hall before slipping into an empty classroom.

I perch myself against one of the desks and pull my phone back out, wishing I could call him and demand answers but knowing that I can't because he's in school.

**Ocean - UMMMM…. WHAT??????? That's not spilling the fucking tea. That's giving me a goddamn drop. SPILL THE FUCKING TEA, MILO!!!! WHO'D YOU FUCK????**

**Milo - …..**

**Ocean - No. Don't you dare do this to me.**

**Milo - I'm sorry. I can't say. He's not … I don't know. Saying will cause problems and it's still new. I gave him my word and I really don't want to fuck this up. I kinda like this guy but I promise, as soon as I can tell you, I will.**

A loud, frustrated groan tears from deep within me, and I sound like a toddler throwing a tantrum. I wonder if I could hold him down and force it out of him, but that fucker would just overpower me and with my neck hurting so bad, I'd get absolutely nowhere.

Damn it!

**Ocean - I hate you.**

**Milo - Fucking love you too, bitch.**

Realizing that for Milo to not even budge on the topic means that he truly must like this guy, I let it go. He'll tell me when he's ready and until then, I just have to be patient. I don't want to be the reason to screw up something good. Who knows, maybe Milo just found the love of his life, or maybe he just found the guy who's going to break his heart for the first time. Either way, it's not my business to be getting involved.

Though I guess that means that the Jess and Milo show is well and truly over now. She came to terms with it after Milo finally came out to our small group but she still hurts. She was really falling for him and I kinda hate myself for allowing it to happen.

The bell rings, indicating the start of the first period, so I slip my phone away and trudge out of the empty classroom, not wanting to be caught in here.

I hurry out into the hall and have to really think about my schedule. I've been going here for a few weeks now but remembering my class schedule really hasn't been a strong trait of mine.

I start wandering the halls and glance around at the students busily making their way past. I find Drix coming toward me with her brows furrowed. "Where the hell are you going?" she questions, giving me a strange look. "We have Biology."

Oh. Whoops.

Her arm loops through mine and her momentum has me spinning on the spot. She pulls me along and I have to skip a step to catch up with her long strides. "Where have you been all morning?" she questions. "I've been waiting for you."

Recognizing the excited tone in her voice, I raise a brow. "Why? What's happened?"

"Nothing yet," she grumbles. "But my dad was asking about your mom again."

"Really?" I say as a sly grin stretches across my face.

"Uh-huh."

Her eyes sparkle and as a similar grin stretches across her pretty face, all my plans begin coming together. "Are you thinking what I'm thinking?"

"I fucking hope so," she laughs.

"Good," I say, knowing all too well that it's about time my mom finds her own kind of happiness. After all, she's just spent twenty years with a man who lied to her. She may have loved him, and despite him being my father, she deserves better. "Let's set them up."

# CHAPTER 22

I sit on the kitchen counter with Casey across from me and Colton's hands gently at the back of my neck. He insisted on checking my burn despite Mom only checking it an hour ago. He's so over-protective and I kinda love it. The second Milo delivered me home from school, Colton was there, asking me how it went today and checking that I hadn't accidentally hurt myself or run into any trouble.

He was only seconds from asking to check the burn when Mom came tearing in with a new bandage and cream, insisting that I sit my ass down and redress it. I have a feeling this is going to be my life for the next few days. I'd hate to see what it's like if I was to seriously injure myself. Colton would probably hire a full-time nurse just to follow me around. I mean, they know I'm more than capable of taking care of myself, right?

Colton gently presses a new bandage on after declaring that it looked much better today, something he'd heard my mother say only a short hour ago, but I guess nothing is really true until you've seen it with your own eyes.

Colton presses a kiss to my lips before stepping away and heading toward his private bar. "Do you want anything to drink?" he questions, pausing at the door.

I scrunch up my face, thinking over my options but instantly get distracted by the way his loose tank gapes at the front and every inch of his fine, strong, and chiseled chest is put on display. He had no meetings today so he didn't bother putting a suit on and damnnn, it looks good on him.

A knowing grin tears across his too handsome face. "Jade," he says, his voice low and warning. "Concentrate."

"Oh, umm, right … I'll have—"

"I'll take a vodka sunrise, thanks," Casey says from her position across the kitchen, lowering the book that she's had her face glued in since she got home from school this afternoon.

Colton gapes at her. "No fucking way. You're sixteen."

Casey groans as I bite my tongue about the fact that he happily stood by over the weekend as she poured cocktail after cocktail down her throat. "For the millionth time, I'm seventeen and what does it matter? Ocean is only seventeen, and it's not as though you're any better. You're only eighteen yourself."

"I—" His face falls as he cuts himself off, realizing that she has a very good point. "Fine," he finally says as though he's her parent giving her permission to make bad decisions. "But only one drink. I don't want Mom riding my ass for letting you have a drink. She'll probably try to sue me."

Casey scoffs out a laugh, all of us knowing that while his comment was a small jab, it wasn't far from the truth. I wouldn't put that kind of shit past her. She's a bitch like that, and I don't doubt that she'd do some pretty stupid things to get her hands on someone else's cash.

"What about you?" he questions, looking back at me.

I shrug a shoulder, not really caring that much. "I'll have what she's having," I say, keeping it easy and knowing all too well that the simpler I keep my order, the quicker he'll be back with his hands on my body.

Colton nods and pushes through to the private bar, keeping the door open so he can be a part of the conversation as he pours us some drinks.

I look up at Casey, studying the front of her book. "What are you reading?"

She peers up at me, her eyes all I see of her delicate face but the way they scrunch and the tops of her cheeks press up into them, I'm more than aware of the big ass grin taking over her face. "Oh, girl. This one is fucking good. It's—"

The familiar buzz of the front gate sounds, cutting off Casey's explanation as we both flick our gazes toward the small monitor behind me. My bows pinch. "Who's that?" I ask, feeling a slight familiarity as I take in the guy waiting by the gates.

There's a pissed-off scowl over his face and I try to think back to the many meetings I've seen Colton sitting through. The guy is older, but I don't think he's one of Colton's business partners. I've seen them all, but this guy is … different. There's something darker about him. Something dangerous that puts my nerves on edge.

The guy leans out of his expensive car and hits the buzzer again, holding it down so the loud buzz vibrates through the whole mansion, demanding our attention.

"Who the fuck is that?" Colton demands, coming out of the bar with no drinks in hand, walking straight over to the small monitor with an annoyed frown marring his perfect face. He grabs the monitor and spins it around so he can get a good look at the screen. "Fuck," he curses, hitting accept on the gates so they peel open. "It's Vincent DeCarlo."

"Then why the hell did you let him in?" I demand as Casey sucks in a sharp breath, recognizing the name.

I watch in horror as Colton crosses the kitchen and presses his hand down on the scanner to unlock the little safe which holds all of the keys to his many cars. Only as the drawers full of keys pops out, he lifts it and curls his fingers around the sexiest, sleek gun I've ever seen.

"What the hell?" Casey demands, looking at her big brother with a gun, most likely the first time ever seeing a sight like that. While I've never exactly seen Colton with one myself, having guns around isn't exactly something new.

I spy the monitor and watch as Vincent's car shoots through and starts racing down the long drive.

Colton looks at his sister. "Get upstairs. Find Mom and Cora and take them to the panic room." She nods and rushes away without another word as Colton looks at me. "Where's your mom?"

"Pool house."

"Good. She'll be okay there."

He starts making his way to the front door and as he disappears from the room, I find myself flying off the counter and following behind. "What are you going to do?" I question, panicking and not wanting him to do what I think it is he's going to do.

He clenches his jaw and keeps walking, crossing the staff quarters and finding Harrison. "Get all the staff out of here. DeCarlo is on his way. You have thirty seconds tops."

Harrison's eyes go wide and although there's nothing he wants more than to see Vincent go down for taking Maryne away from him, he has a job to do and he won't risk any of the staff in the process. We don't need a repeat of what happened here a few short weeks ago. This time, we have our wits about us.

Harrison nods and within seconds, he's pressing an alarm that sounds throughout the house. The staff instantly fall in line and start racing toward Harrison, waiting on instructions. Once Colton sees his people are being taken care of, he moves ahead. This time he doesn't stop on his way to the front door.

"Colton," I say, attempting to get his attention but his stubborn nature has him intent to ignore me, knowing damn well that I'm about to try and stop him. "What are you doing? You could get hurt."

He wordlessly reaches down and takes my hand, trying to ease my worry yet he doesn't say a damn word, just keeps moving ahead until we reach the front door.

He tears it open and pulls me out before hitting the lock on the back of the door and closing it, making it harder for anyone to get back through it. He starts racing down the stairs, pulling me along with him, intent to get this bullshit as far from his home and family as possible.

Vincent's car appears racing down the drive, and by the time we reach the bottom step, Vincent is skidding to a halt, leaving two thick rubber lines on the immaculate drive.

Vincent pours out of his expensive sports car and barrels toward me and Colton. My hand is instantly released and Colton forces me back a step, keeping me away from Vincent's reach but the way Vincent stares down Colton, it's as though I'm not even here.

Vincent shoots his arms out, aiming for Colton's neck but Colton evades him like some kind of MMA pro. In seconds, he has Vincent pinned to the side of his stupid car, his sleek gun pressed under his chin, exactly how his son had done to Maryne. I stare in surprise. I didn't know Colton was capable of that and damn, it's a massive turn on.

"Release me," Vincent spits, knowing damn well that Colton won't hesitate to pull the trigger, especially after the shit storm his sons rained down on this property.

Colton laughs. "Release you?" he questions. "Now why the fuck would I go and do something so stupid?" The gun presses harder against his chin, forcing Vincent's head up so that his eyes meet Colton's. "You sent your sons to terrorize my home, my family. A woman who was the only motherly figure in my life was brutally murdered by Marco. I should kill you right fucking now."

Vincent pushes against Colton, trying to get him away, but he doesn't budge. "You don't have the balls."

"Don't I?" he questions with a sick smirk, showing me just how badly he wishes to do it. The gun flinches and Vincent jumps in fear, his eyes going wide as he realizes that his brain was nearly smeared all over his ridiculous car.

"You have a lot of nerve showing up here."

"I know you're behind it. You're the one putting my sons in prison."

"Oh," Colton laughs. "Did you think that was supposed to be some sort of secret? I told you clear as fucking day, your sons came into my home and I was going to make them pay one by fucking one, leaving you for last." Colton leans into him, trailing the gun around Vincent's face like some kind of sick killer. "But don't you worry, I have something extra special planned for you."

"You won't get away with this."

"But I already am. In fact," he grins. "Maybe you should check in with your youngest tonight. I think you'll find he's about to get himself in a little bit of trouble."

Vincent pushes at Colton's chest again, harder this time but still there's no movement. He's like a solid brick wall, impenetrable and it's the sexiest thing I've ever seen. "What did you do?" Vincent spits, the threat of his son's impending doom enough to have him forgetting the gun that's now jammed against his temple.

"Who me?" Colton questions. "I didn't do a damn thing. Now, Alejandro, he's been a very naughty boy but you know all about it, don't you?"

Vincent struggles against Colton's hold but doesn't get anywhere, proving just how strong Colton really is. "He didn't do anything."

"I think the dead, drugged hooker in his hotel room would say differently."

"He didn't do it. Leave Alejandro out of this. He's a good boy."

"Is he?" he questions. "So, which one is it? Is he a good boy or a murderer? Talk him up all you want but he was there that day, waving his fucking gun around my staffs' faces. He's fucking guilty. He killed that hooker and you helped him cover it. You know it, I know it, and now the whole fucking world will know it. You and your boys are done. There's nowhere you can go where I won't get you. You fucked with the wrong person."

Vincent's jaw clenches before his gaze flashes to me. He disregards me as though I'm trash before looking back at Colton. "You better watch yourself, boy. I'm not the only one with secrets. Someone like you doesn't get where you are without them and I guarantee that I will find them and when I do, you're going the fuck down."

Colton smiles wickedly and steps in nice and close, sending chills sweeping through my body with how damn turned on I am right now. "I'll let you in on a little secret," he says, making Vincent's jaw clench even harder. "I don't have any. You're mistaking me for my father. But you have my blessing. Go ahead and waste what little time you have left trying to take me down because it won't work. I'm un-fucking-touchable."

"No one is untouchable," he snaps.

"I made a promise that I'd leave you till last. I want to watch as everything important to you is taken away. I already have three of your moronic sons. I'd really love to watch you lose the other two, but pulling this trigger right here, right now is very fucking tempting."

"You think I care if you end me? That's where you have me wrong. Fucking pull the trigger if you want to. It doesn't mean shit."

A booming laugh tears from deep within Colton's stomach. "You see, that would be too fucking easy. When I come for you—which I will—I will have already destroyed you and you'll be on your fucking knees begging for me to end it, begging for me to take out your pathetic existence, and just when you can't take it anymore, I'm going to put a bullet right through the top of your spine, paralyzing you so that every fucking day for the rest of your life, you're going to wish you were dead. You'll be a fucking vegetable, unable to wipe your own fucking ass, completely dependant on the people around you. But that's just the thing, you won't have anyone around you because all five of your good for nothing sons will be locked up. They're going to die behind bars. They're going to rot, and once the last of them are gone, the DeCarlo name will cease to exist."

Vincent looks up at Colton who towers over him and fear begins seeping into his eyes knowing damn well that Colton has the resources to come through on every tiny promise that he's made.

BANG!

I jump as a bullet slams into the polished concrete of the driveway, sending broken fragments showering around us. I throw my hands up, masking myself from the sharp pieces while listening as they ricochet against Vicent's car.

Colton's gun remains pointed down at the ground and as I look down, I find the bullet an inch away from Vincent's foot.

The bastard jumps in fear and Colton steps away from him. "I suggest you get the fuck off my property before I show you what else this gun can do."

Vincent looks up in hesitation but decided to use his brain instead, diving back into his car. He hits the gas and takes off like a rocket, and as we watch his car disappear down the drive, I hold my hand out. "Gun," I demand.

Colton's brows furrow but he hands it over without hesitation and watches as I raise the gun and concentrate with everything I have.

I pull the trigger and the gun rings out loudly, making me flinch, but I don't dare move as I hear the loud POP of the bullet hitting Vincent's rear tire.

Colton howls with laughter as his car swerves, the back tires swinging around and hitting the manicured lawn. Vincent works hard to right his car, but in doing that, tears up the grass in a big way.

"Fuck, sorry. I didn't think that through," I say, watching as Vincent finally disappears.

Colton's hand falls on top of mine and he takes the gun off me before I can shoot at anything else. "It's more than alright," he tells me. "Knowing that he's going to have to pull that piece of shit over on the side of the road and wait hours for anyone to come and help him is worth it. Besides, Enrique is a fucking pro when it comes to fixing the lawn. He'll have it fixed in no time, along with the mess that Nic made the other day."

I smile up at him as he puts his arm over my shoulder and leads us back to the stairs of the mansion. "How the hell did you learn to shoot like that?"

"You don't grow up in Breakers Flats and not learn a thing or two about shooting," I explain. "And … I also had Kairo who thinks spending hours in a shooting range is fun."

"No shit."

"Mmhmm. So, you better be careful, Carrington."

"Look who's talking," he says. "I don't see you running after hearing how fucked up my plan is."

I look up and meet his hazel eyes. "To be honest, your plan kinda turned me on."

His brow arches as his eyes begin to sparkle with excitement. "If I didn't have to go and release my sisters and Mom from the panic room, I'd be fucking you right here on these steps."

A low groan pulls from deep within me and if I didn't have to go and explain what the hell was going on to my mother, I'd be stripping off my clothes right now and begging him to do it.

"I'll tell you what," he says. "Why don't you hold onto that thought and I'll meet you back in the formal dining room in fifteen?"

"Dining room?"

"Every time I see that fucking big ass table, all I can think about is laying you over it and spreading those perfect legs. Baby, I'm going to eat your sweet pussy until you're drenched and screaming my name and there's not a damn thing you can do to convince me otherwise."

I grin up at him. "Only if you promise to bend me over the table and fuck me until I'm seeing stars afterward."

"You've got yourself a deal, Jade."

I grin up at him as we reach the top of the stairs. Colton unlocks the door and as he releases his hold on me and starts walking toward the grand staircase that leads up to the panic room, he stops and turns back to me with lust in his eyes. "You know what?" he murmurs, his voice low and filled with need. "Make it ten."

"You got it."

With that, he skips up the stairs two at a time and I find myself walking through the mansion. I know I should be looking for mom but I find myself standing in front of Charles' wine cellar door instead.

I must be insane to be standing here right now but for some reason, my hand latches onto the handle and I push the door open wide. I step into the darkness then watch as the sensor lights come to light, filling the room with a clinical brightness.

I make my way down the few steep steps and head through the rows of wine bottles until I finally find it.

The door that holds Colton's biggest secret.

I guess it's my biggest secret now too. It's all of ours—me, Colton, Spencer, and now Charlie.

Maybe I'm a glutton for punishment or maybe seeing Colton face his demons so epically gave me what little encouragement I needed to finally end this. Hell, maybe it has a little something to do with the empowerment I felt after firing that gun at the douchebag's car. Either way, I'm here now and I won't ever be here again.

This ends tonight.

From now on, Jude Carter will not reside rent-free in my mind. He does not win, I do.

I pull the heavy metal lock and hear that same loud BANG that I'd heard the first time I walked in here. I slowly push open the door, still kinda terrified of what I might find inside, despite knowing exactly what it is.

The smell hits me first and it's clear that this trash has been living in his own filth, too fucking scum to bother getting up and using the fucking toilet like the rest of the human population.

Dried blood lines the room and I have no doubt that it's adding toward the stench but I try to see through it and put it to the back of my mind. I'm here for one job and one job only.

Jude sits in the corner of the room, his hands still bound with heavy chains. He looks up at me, squinting against the light that floods the room. "Come to finish the job?" he questions.

I ignore him, knowing that I need to keep my control. If I allow him to get inside my mind, I'm going to lose myself and without Colton here to stop me, I don't think I'll have the strength to walk out of here with my soul still attached.

"I've come to tell you that this is it. You don't own me anymore.

You don't consume me, you don't scare me. You don't hold that kind of power, not anymore. You thought you won by touching me, by taking what wasn't yours, but you didn't. You're hardly even a blip on the radar and all you managed to do was fuck yourself in the ass."

"Quit lying to yourself," he grumbles, not putting any energy into fighting because he knows that I've won and there is no longer a point of even trying.

"You're scum, Carter. You always will be, always have been and in fact, I'm fucking thrilled because had you not decided to do what you did, I never would have had the opportunity to destroy you."

"You can't destroy me," he scoffs. "No one can."

I smile sweetly. "You see, that's where you're wrong," I tell him, slipping my phone out of my back pocket. "I can do just that."

I press a few buttons and hold the phone up against my ear, keeping my eyes on Jude as I listen to the phone ring.

"O, what's wrong? Are you okay?"

"Nic," I say, watching as Jude's eyes widen in horror, knowing exactly who the Widows are. "We found Jude. He's locked in the back part of Charles' wine cellar."

Jude shakes his head. "No," he panics. "Don't do that."

"I'm getting the boys now," Nic says. "We'll handle it."

"NO," Jude yells in fear, rattling against his chains and desperately trying to get to his feet.

I smile at Jude while letting out a deep breath. "I know you will," I tell Nic before ending the call and turning on my heel. I walk out of the dungeon and slam the door with a loud BANG knowing damn well that I will never have to see Jude Carter again.

278

# CHAPTER 23

"How did this even happen?" Mom demands, standing in the full-length mirror of my bedroom while sliding my borrowed earrings into place.

I stand behind her in the mirror, watching as she gets ready for the ballet that she was so lucky to win tickets to, despite not entering a competition for it. In fact, there was no competition at all.

I grin wickedly. This plan is flawless.

Mom has always talked about going to the ballet but it's one of those things that we've never been able to afford. Hendrix however, just happens to own box seats in the theatre and her father just so happens to be going.

It's a match made in heaven. Or at least, a match made during high school biology.

Mom has been questioning it all week. I came to her on Tuesday after school, racing in like a fire had been lit under my ass telling her how I'd entered a competition on her behalf and that I'd just got the email to confirm that we'd won. Hendrix and I even spent our lunch period creating a fake email address to send the announcement from because we're smart like that.

I've then slowly started coughing through the week, hinting that I'm coming down with something and just spent the last hour standing on the couch and getting my head as close to the air vents as possible. I cranked the heat right up and twenty minutes ago, mom walked in to find me snuggled in bed with a high 'fever.'

Thinking that I was sick, she insisted that we stay at home and it took me ten minutes to convince her that she should still go and have fun without me. Besides, what am I going to do at the ballet? Sounds fancy and all but I'd fall asleep during the opening dance and end up embarrassing her. She'd never forgive me and she knows it.

Which brings us to now.

"You look amazing," I tell her, scanning my gaze up and down her champagne gown. "You're going to have the best time. Why don't you treat yourself to a nice dinner afterward?"

"By myself?" she scoffs. "I hardly think so."

"Okay," I say with a shrug, not wanting to push the topic because I know damn well that dinner is exactly where she's going to end up and hopefully, I'll catch her sneaking in through the pool house doors during the early hours of the morning. "It was just a suggestion."

She harumphs but lets it go as she takes a step back to take a proper look at herself. Her make up is done perfectly, keeping it light and natural while her hair falls in soft dark curls around her shoulders. Any man would be lucky to have her.

She watches herself for a short moment and I wonder what could possibly be going through her head. Stuff like this isn't normal for us, it's something like a fairytale, and knowing that she's going to run into her prince charming tonight just makes it so much better.

I might have to sleep in Colton's room tonight because she's bound to have a few things to say to me once she realizes that she's been set up, but hopefully, she won't allow that to ruin her night. She's going to have an amazing time complete with butterflies, champagne, and a handsome man who thinks the world of her.

"Okay," she finally says. "Get your butt back in bed. I'll make sure Colton knows to come and check on you. Maybe he could order you some chicken soup to help your throat."

"Sounds good," I tell her, slinking back to my bed and making a show of climbing back in and dropping down onto my pillow. Mom turns back to the mirror. "Are you sure I look alright?"

"You look killer in that dress. Everyone who sees you is going to either want to be you or be with you. Own it, Mom. You deserve a night off."

She bounces her shoulders nervously before letting out a strained breath. "Okay," she says, turning back to me and walking over. She pulls the blankets up high like she used to do when I was a kid before pressing a kiss to my forehead. "Don't you dare move from this bed, okay? Text me if you need anything and I'll come right home."

I roll my eyes and agree anyway, knowing she's bound to stay home if I was to give even the slightest hint that I'd not text if I was in trouble. "I will," I tell her. "Now go before your Uber cracks the shits and leaves."

Mom presses another kiss to my forehead before giving me an excited smile. I watch as she practically skips out of sight. When I hear the sound of the pool house door closing behind her, I finally throw the blankets off. It was like a sauna under there after my time spent in front of the heat vents. I need a freezing cold shower just to stop sweating.

I hurry around our little home and check out the front window to make sure she's well and truly gone before rushing back into my bedroom and grabbing my phone off my bedside table.

"IT WORKED," I cheer as Drix answers the call. "She's on her way."

"Bullshit. Really?" she laughs far too excited for her own good. "HELL YES! We should be criminal masterminds. What's our next plan? Should we hit up Tiffanys or start slow with a bank?"

"Are you insane?" I laugh. "First off, you probably have more diamonds in your bedroom than Tiffanys has on site and a bank? Are you trying to get us arrested? You're too pretty for jail but I'm sure we could gang up and I could make you my bitch so no one else steals you away."

Drix lets out a sarcastic sigh. "I'm so glad I have such a great friend."

"Yeah," I laugh. "You're so lucky."

"Speaking of being lucky," she says in a strange tone. "I, uhh … actually wanted to talk to you about something."

My brows pinch as I drop down on the couch. "Yeah, what's up?"

There's a slight pause, almost as though she's trying to work out how to string her sentence together. "I, um … well, you can totally tell me if you're weird about this and I'll back off, but you know on Monday you said that I should go and chill with Charlie?"

"Yeah?" I say slowly, wondering where this is going.

"I kinda did and we've been hanging out quite a bit now and well, I know you two used to have a thing and if you're weird about it, I'll totally stop hanging out with him." There's another short pause before I hear her suck in a breath through her teeth and just before I can tell her to spit it out, the words come out in a rushed, panicked whisper. "But you should know that I kinda slept with him last night."

My eyes bug out of my head as I throw myself to my feet. "FUCK, YEAH! Are you guys together now? Tell me you're a thing?"

"What?" she breathes, her tone a million times lighter as though telling me that news caused the weight of the world to fall from her shoulders. "You're not upset or anything?"

"No. God, no. Why would I be upset? Charlie is an amazing guy and yeah, he kinda hates me right now but I still consider him one of my best friends and if he really likes you and you feel the same, then I have nothing but love for you two together. I have Colton now and he's … well, he's everything I could ever want—"

"Are you in love with him?"

"I, uhh … umm …"

Shit.

"Oh, god," she laughs. "You totally are. You're in love with Mr. Money Bags."

"Shut up," I tell her. "I am not, I'm just … fuck. Okay, maybe I am. I haven't really had a chance to sit down and define it yet."

A loud, booming belly laugh tears out of her and I have to pull the phone away from my ear to avoid her laughter bursting my eardrum. "Girl, there's no defining it. You either feel it or you don't and I can tell by the way you look at him that you totally feel it, and the same goes for him. Colton Carrington is head over heels for you, Ocean."

"How did this go from finding out how the hell you ended up with Charlie between your legs to my love life?"

"I … I really don't know actually," she says with a soft, breathy laugh. "We were just hanging out and then one thing led to another and before I knew it, I had my ass up in the air and he was giving it to me harder than anyone's ever done before. It was …"

"Yeah," I laugh. "Trust me, I know how good it was. Charlie has a certain set of skills that can make even the toughest criminal blush."

"Right?" she breathes, the smile in her tone infectious.

"So, what's the deal then? Are you two getting together or are you still figuring it out?"

"I don't actually know," she tells me. "I think we're something but we could also be nothing. It's complicated. It's that weird in-between stage … I think. The last I heard he was still crushing on you pretty hard."

"Nah, that was ages ago. He's over that. I've not been getting those creepy 'I want to see you naked again' vibes from him anymore. He knows that me and Colton are solid and he wouldn't stand in the way of that."

"Are you sure?"

"Yeah, of course. Look, Charlie is a lot of things but he's no liar. Go and talk to him and he'll be straight up with you and I can guarantee that he'll tell you exactly what you're wanting to know. What's not to love about you, Drix? You're freaking awesome."

"So, what? Just go over there and ask him and be like 'Hey, I know we fucked and all, but do you want to do it again exclusively?'"

"Umm … yeah? What have you got to lose?"

"Yeah, but what if—hold on," she says, cutting off what she was about to say. "Someone's at the door."

I wait patiently as she goes to check who's knocking on her door when her voice comes grumbling through the phone. "Well, well, speak of the devil and he shall appear."

"Wait," I say, listening intently. "Is that Charlie? Did he come to claim your ass?"

"Who are you talking to?" I hear softly, but the low, rumbly flirty tone of Charlie's is unmistakable.

Drix's guilty laugh comes through the phone. "I, uhh … got to go."

"He's so into you," I boom. "Nail that bastard down and remember, once you've licked him, that means he's yours."

"You're fucking gross, and for the record, I more than licked him."

"Look who's gross now," I laugh. "Enjoy your fuck fest."

I end the call and instead of climbing back into bed like a good little girl, I slip my phone into my back pocket and break out of the pool house.

I get halfway to the back door of the mansion when I find Colton walking out with what looks like an envelope in his hand. "Oh, hey," he says, not having expected to find me out here. "Is your mom gone?"

"Uh-huh."

"And?" he says with a grin, knowing damn well what Drix and I had planned.

"It worked like a charm."

He meets me in the middle and wraps his arms around my waist, the envelope rubbing against the bare skin of my back. "Of course it did," he says proudly. "Because you and Drix are forces to be reckoned with."

"And don't you forget it," I laugh.

He rolls his eyes and gently presses a kiss to my lips. "I'd hate to see what evil plot you two come up with if a guy was to break either of your hearts."

"Do it," I dare him. "We've already worked out every last detail and trust me, I don't think you'll come out the other end alive."

"I don't doubt that, but you have nothing to worry about. I'm not about to go breaking your heart."

"You better not be," I tell him, raising my head to meet his hazel eyes. "Were you coming to find me?"

"Sure was," he says, pulling out of my arms and holding out the envelope. I take it from him with drawn brows. "This came for you."

"What is it?" I ask, scanning over it to see my name printed on the front. I don't think I've ever received a letter in my life. The only things that we ever used to find in our mailbox were bills, overdue notices, and an eviction notice. Though, the letter I got from Tommy Peters in first grade telling me he thought I was cute doesn't really count … or does it?

"How am I supposed to know?" Colton says, his voice thick with sarcasm. "Why don't you open it up and find out?"

I roll my eyes and flip the envelope over and stamped across the back is the return sender details together with the logo of The University of Bellevue Springs.

I suck in a breath and find myself holding the letter out as far as it can go, almost as though it's diseased. "What are you doing?" Colton grumbles, looking at me as though I just boarded the train to crazy town.

"It's from the college," I say, knowing damn well that he would have already seen that and was just waiting to see my reaction. My nerves bubble up in my stomach as I ignore Colton's presence beside me, unable to stop looking at the letter. This tiny slip of paper determines what I'll be doing for the next few years. Assuming Russo and the Wolves don't get their filthy paws on me again. "What do I do?"

Colton chokes back a laugh and holds a straight face. "Um … read it?"

I roll my eyes. He's such a boy, but despite that, he's right. There's no use standing out here, staring at it. I need to figure out what it says and start planning my future.

Taking a shaky breath, I slip my finger under the lip of the envelope and tear through it, hoping that I'm not accidentally destroying what's hidden inside.

I get it open and my hands instantly begin shaking. I can hardly see the paper, it's so bad. Flipping it over, I unfold it and the dread begins flooding me. If this was an acceptance letter, wouldn't it be a thicker envelope? More papers with course details and all that kind of shit? Just one lone piece of paper seems a bit ... bad.

Shit.

I'm just about to start looking over it when a thought occurs. This is a huge moment for me and maybe I should be waiting for Mom, but then, do I have the strength to hold back? The curiosity of leaving it lay open on the table would kill me.

No. Sorry, Mom. I love her and all but I can't wait. This is too big.

Colton steps right into my side and starts reading over my shoulder as I begin scanning the letter, my breath coming in short, sharp pants.

*Dear Miss Oceania Munroe,*

*It is our pleasure to congratulate you on your acceptance to The University of Bellevue Springs...*

A high-pitched squeal wails out of me and I jump up and down, clutching the paper so freaking hard that it crumples between my hands. "HOLY SHIT," I squeak. "I GOT INTO A FUCKING COLLEGE

WITHOUT SUCKING SOMEONE'S DICK."

Colton grabs me and pulls me up off the ground, sharing in the joy as he spins me around. "I fucking knew you would do it, babe," he says, crushing his lips to mine. "Now, let me take you somewhere to celebrate."

# CHAPTER 24

I sit across the table from Colton in one of the fanciest restaurants that Bellevue Springs has to offer and I've never felt so out of place. It's not my kind of restaurant. The meal costs more than I could make in a week but damn it, it's so good. It's certainly no Chuck E Cheese or Chili's though.

My acceptance letter sits on the table between us and I find myself reading over it for the millionth time, only my mood isn't soaring anymore. My whole world fell apart as soon as I finished reading the opening sentence and got further into the details of what it means to be a college student.

Finance.

"Jade, come on," Colton says, reaching across the table and taking my hand. "I don't know what you're freaking out about. I've got you. If you want to go to college, then I'll sort it out. Why are you worrying about this so much?"

"I'm not taking your money, Colton," I say, looking up to meet his eyes while wondering how the hell Mom and I are going to make this work. The fee structure is insane and I already know without even trying that I'm not exactly the greatest candidate for a student loan. "You're my boyfriend, not my sugar daddy. I've already let you get away with paying for my school fees. It's not about to happen again. I can take care of myself. I'll find a way."

"Babe, come on," he groans. "Do you have any idea how frustrating it is knowing that you're going to sit here and panic over paying it when I could have the tuition transferred and paid by the time we've finished dinner?"

"Gee, thanks for rubbing my nose in it."

"That's not what I'm doing and you know it. I don't want to see you going through that kind of torture when I could take it away for you."

I shake my head. "No, I'm sorry, but no. I'm not tying myself to you financially. Mom and I will talk about it tomorrow and see what we can come up with."

Colton falls back into his chair and stares blankly at me. "You're serious about this? You're really going to let a little stubbornness and your need to feel independent potentially stop you from attending college?"

"Dead serious," I tell him, "I'm going whether I can pay for it or not so don't worry about that. My independence is important to me and I'll come out the other end with it still intact, but if I find out that you've gone behind my back and paid my fees, hell will rain down on you, Mr. Carrington."

He sighs and from the guilty expression that cuts across his face, it's clear that was exactly what he had intended to do. "Fine," he groans while rolling his eyes at my stubborn nature. "If this is how you really want to do it then you have options, a few actually."

I raise my brow and lean in, paying close attention while equally shocked that he's actually entertaining the idea of me doing this on my own. "Like?" I question, ready to hang off his every word.

"There are all sorts of things," he says. "Student loans, financial aid, grants. You could apply for a scholarship and if you really want to be independent about it, I could *loan* you the money."

I shake my head at his last suggestion but feel my mind whirling with possibilities. "I doubt I'll be accepted for student loans or any of the financial aid."

"Don't write it off too soon," he tells me. "You work and your mom works, you shouldn't have any problems getting financial aid. Not to mention, my dad was good friends with the dean of UBS. So, if all else fails, I could put in a good word and see if he'll consider you for a payment plan."

"Really?" I question, my eyes going wide as my hope slowly begins to resurface.

"Yeah, Jade. I can see how much you want this. You've set your boundaries and as much as I hate that I can't help you with this, I respect that. So, I'm going to do everything else in my power to make this happen for you."

His words send my heart racing with warmth and as my blood circulates throughout my body, that warmth spreads until I'm completely overwhelmed by his love.

I reach across the table and find his hand already waiting. He gives it a gentle squeeze and just like that, I fall a little bit harder. Maybe Drix was onto something. Maybe I'm already there. The thought of completely giving myself to someone again scares the shit out of me but more and more, I'm starting to trust that he's not going to break me.

We finish our dinner and before we know it, we're standing out the front of the restaurant, waiting for the valet to return his Veneno.

"Let me get this straight," I say, folding into his side. "You'll let random valets drive your car, but you won't let me even breathe near the steering wheel?"

Colton presses his lips into a tight line and I see the string of responses flying through his mind while he tries to decipher the right thing to say. "Well, umm … fuck," he cringes. "I guess you're right."

"Damn straight I am."

"Do you want to drive home?"

My eyes bug out of my head. I was expecting a lot of things out of this conversation but certainly not that. "Are you insane?" I shriek, stepping away from him only so I can stare at him properly. "I can't drive that. What if I … I don't know, what if I break it?"

"Are you planning on breaking it?"

"No," I scoff. "I'm an incredible driver."

His Veneno appears from around the corner and as it inches toward us, Colton raises a brow as his lips lift into a wicked grin, the challenge clear in his eyes. "Then what are you so scared about?"

My mouth drops. "Scared? I'm not scared."

"Good," he says as the Veneno stops right in front of us. The valet pours out of it with a satisfied smile on his face while Colton walks around and holds the driver's door open for me. "What are you waiting for?"

Fuck yes.

I fly toward him, making sure to brush a kiss over his unsuspecting lips as I pass. I drop down into the Veneno and instantly adjust the seat while feeling the purring rumble of the smooth engine beneath me.

This is going to be good.

"Hurry up and get your ass in or I'm taking off without you," I warn, watching him step back only to start salivating over the way the automatic suicide doors begin to close.

Colton makes his way around to the passenger side and I find myself smirking at the sight. He isn't the kind of guy to sit shotgun. He likes to be in control so not sitting behind the steering wheel is a big gesture and I appreciate it more than he could possibly know.

Once he's in, I prepare to get myself going when my phone chimes from my bag. I start digging through and laugh as I find a text from Mom.

**Mom - I know what you two did. Ask Hendrix to come over**

**in the morning. I need to have a little chat with the two of you.**

Oh, shit.

**Ocean - I don't know what you're talking about …**

**Mom - You're a rotten liar but I can't deny that I'm having a fabulous time.**

**Mom - Thank you. Love you. I hope you're feeling better.**

**Ocean - Don't worry about me. I'm miraculously feeling much better!**

**Mom - I should have known!**

With that, I slip my phone back into my bag and dump it on Colton's lap before finally hitting the gas and sending us roaring down the street.

Every nerve inside my body wakes and I feel more alive than ever before. I press harder on the gas and it's as though the car reads my every thought. It was made for me. The way it reacts to my touch, my feel. It's everything a car should be and judging by the way Colton watches me with a dark sparkle in his eye, he's enjoying the ride almost as much as I am.

I'm in heaven.

"Was that your mom checking in?" he questions as I take a corner so damn smooth that I almost come in my pants.

"Yeah," I laugh. "She figured out that we set her up and was demanding a private audience with me and Drix in the morning. I have a feeling we're about to get our asses handed to us, but it's so worth it. She said she's having a fabulous time."

Colton laughs. "Do you think she'll actually hit it off with Roman?

I haven't dealt with him too much but he's an alright guy."

"I hope so. From what I've heard he's been infatuated by her since the gatsby party and she deserves a man who's going to put her up on a pedestal as if the sun shines out of her ass. I want her to be happy."

"You know," he says, thoughtful. "I don't think I've ever met someone so selfless before."

"Who? My mom?"

"No, moron," he laughs. "You. You would do absolutely anything to make your mother happy. I love that about you."

My eyes flick toward him before slowly scanning back to the dark road ahead. "There's that word again."

I don't see his smirk but from his tone, I know it's there. "Uh-huh," he grumbles, not speaking any further on the topic. "But speaking of people getting together. I think Spencer is seeing someone."

"What?" I grunt, flicking my gaze back to him again to see him deep in thought. "Why do you say that? Did he mention someone?"

He presses his lips into a tight line and softly shakes his head. "No, not exactly but he's been MIA this week and when I asked him about it, he was really shady. Judging from the past, he's only ever like that when there's a girl."

"No shit, really?"

"Yeah, I'm going to get him drunk after the business dinner tomorrow night. He tends to get a bit loose when he's had too much to drink."

A smile tears across my face at the thought of getting Spencer fucked up. I don't think I've ever seen him like that, he's always so put together. He's like Colton in that way, in fact, while we're at it, I might encourage Colton to let loose as well. Now that would be a fun night.

I store my plan away for safekeeping and find myself glancing at him again. "What kind of business dinner is it that has Spencer coming over?"

"It's all the partners. It's some stupid tradition that my father put in place. Every few months or so, all the partners come together with their families and share a meal."

I raise a brow. "All the partners?" I question. "That's Charlie's dad and Milo's, right? So, they'll be there?"

He nods. "Along with the rest of their families."

"So, what you're saying is that Charlie won't be able to avoid us tomorrow night?"

A grin tears across Colton's face. "Why the hell do you think I didn't cancel that shit? I'm not exactly known as the guy to enjoy business dinners."

I roll my eyes but find myself laughing. "The level of bullshit you'd happily sit through just to get the tiniest thing in return astounds me."

A wide grin spreads across his face and not a second later, his hand presses down on my thigh, slowly riding up until it's only a breath away from my promised land.

"If you want your car back in once piece, I'd highly suggest that your hand stops moving right the fuck now."

His tone drops low and the rasp in it has me relaxing into Colton's touch. "Or what?" he murmurs, moving his hand just that slight bit more and grabbing what's his to take. He cups me over my pants and

I find myself grinding against his hand, wondering how the hell he manages to set my body on fire so damn quickly.

I keep my focus on the road, terrified of actually hurting this precious car but I don't dare stop him as his hand begins to rub over me. "I should have let you drive this ages ago. Do you have any idea how fucking sexy you are driving my car?"

A low groan pulls from deep within me, hearing his words wrap around me but the mood is quickly cut off by the shrill ring of my phone. Colton lets out a frustrated groan and grabs my bag from where he dumped it at his feet. He digs through it and pulls out my phone.

"Ugh, it's Nic," he says. "That motherfucker is such a cock-blocker. Does he have a fucking camera in my car too?"

I laugh as I glance at the phone but a seriousness comes over me. Nic has been giving me my space since showing up at the school. He hasn't tried to call me like he usually does and for some reason, I feel compelled to answer it.

"Can you put it on speaker?"

"Fine," he groans. "But as soon as you're done talking to him, you're all mine. All fucking night."

"Deal."

With that, Colon hits accept on Nic's call and his voice instantly sails through the Veneno. "O."

"What's up?"

"What are you doing? Turn on the news."

"Can't," I say, flicking my gaze to Colton. "I'm driving. What's going on?"

"Well pull the fuck over and bring it up on your phone. Trust me, you don't want to miss this. I fucking know you, O. You're going to be pissed if you find out through someone else."

My brows furrow and I instantly realize what the hell this is about. My eyes go wide. "Thanks," I say, grabbing the phone off Colton and ending the call. I drop my phone into my lap and hastily dart to the side of the road, bringing this magical beast to a startling stop.

"What the fuck is going on?" Colton questions, watching me in a panic.

I grab my phone and instantly bring up the news before turning the media volume right up. Colton leans over and together we watch as a reporter appears on the screen.

The wind brushes through her hair as she holds the microphone to her face with the Bellevue Springs Police Station right behind her. "Jude Carter, son of the wealthy business tycoon, Francis Carter, was arrested today at the Bellevue Springs Police Department, following his confession to multiple counts of rape and the murder of 16-year-old Mandy Johnstone."

I suck in a deep breath and my eyes go wide, all while Colton sits beside me in confusion, thinking that Jude is still safely locked in his little dungeon. I guess I may have forgotten to tell him something.

The reporter goes on as the screen cuts to earlier footage of Jude showing up at the precinct and handing himself over. Next comes footage of his parents arriving with their many lawyers and the press going nuts with cameras. "Tonight, Bellevue Springs police are scouring bushland for the remains of Miss Johnstone who was reported missing by her parents nearly two years ago. Mr. Carter has not released any other names at this time. Police are urging the young lady to step forward to make a statement. More on this breaking news soon."

The story cuts out and I remain staring at my phone as though it's going to magically continue telling me every little detail.

"Ummmm … what the fuck?" Colton grunts, looking up at me in surprise. "Did you know about this?"

"Kinda," I say with a cringe. "I was done. You said I could handle it however I wanted to handle it and all I wanted was to move on and be happy. With him in the wine cellar, it was always sitting on my mind so I called Nic and had him handle it. I figured he'd just put a bullet between his eyes but I think Nic knew that the guilt would eat at me so they must have had him hand himself over."

"Fuck me," Colton says with an impressed smirk. He rubs his hand over his face. "They must have done a fucking number on him to get him to voluntarily walk in there and admit to what he did."

"Well, what can I say?" I grin. "The Widows certainly have a few impressive … skills."

"I can imagine," he says, still a little in shock. He shakes his head and a faraway look enters his hazel eyes. "He really did kill that girl."

"Yeah, sounds like it," I whisper, reaching over and taking his hand, hating the guilt that spreads across his handsome features. He links his fingers with mine. "There's nothing you could have done, Colton. You couldn't have known that he was going to hurt that girl again. You were only a kid yourself."

His features fall and I have a feeling that a few lousy words from me isn't going to do the trick this time. This is just one of those things that are going to sit heavy on his heart until the day he takes his final breath.

"Come on," he finally says, squeezing my hand and lifting his chin toward the road. "Let's get home. There's bound to be a mountain of press waiting outside the gates wanting a statement from me."

"Okay," I say, releasing his hand. "But as soon as you're done with that, you're all mine."

A soft smile lifts the corner of his lips. "Deal."

# CHAPTER 25

om's heavy glare settles on me as she passes by the massive dining table that seats at least a hundred business partners and their families. It's freaking huge but all that matters right now is not breaking and smiling at my mother.

Just the smallest little grin from me will have her storming through the room and removing me from the table by my ear before dragging me back to the pool house to curse me out. With the business dinner being a lot bigger than we anticipated, Mom has spent the whole day preparing and hasn't had a chance to tell me and Drix exactly what she thought of our sneaky little plan, but whatever she has to say about it, it doesn't matter.

There have been at least twenty times today when I've caught her smiling to herself. It's almost as though she's floating. I don't think I've ever seen her like this. It's like she's a teenage girl again, experiencing the attention of a boy for the very first time. Her cheeks have been flushed all day and if there were music playing, I'm sure she'd be dancing around as though she stepped right out of a musical.

I absolutely love it. Her happiness is contagious. Hell, she can come and yell at me all she wants because, in the end, it will always be worth it. Unless Roman turns out to be some psychotic serial killer, only then will I admit that I might have been wrong.

Mom disappears through the service entrance with her arms full of plates and guilt soars through me. Under any other circumstances, I'd be out there helping her but instead, I'm sitting at the table as a guest while my mother slaves away. It's wrong.

I insisted on helping but Colton wanted me with him while Mom also insisted that she was fine. She has a whole kitchen full of staff helping her with about twenty hired waitresses. I'd probably just be in the way but I can't help the guilt that fills me. Maybe one of these days I might even get used to it. Who knows? With Roman digging his claws in and making her all shades of happy, she might be the one to have waitresses serving her one of these days.

The table is filled with bodies and I can't help but scan my way around. The Bryant family is here, sitting just across the table, while Charlie does everything in his power not to look directly at us.

Milo sits with his parents just down from them, making rude

gestures to me and Colton while Spencer sits with his father who I don't think I've actually met. Judging by everyone else's parents, I don't really care to get to know him either.

Laurelle and the twins are sitting on Colton's other side as though they belong there. I was surprised to see a few more familiar faces. There are a few girls from school, and I recognize two guys that I used to go to BSA with. Though two faces that are noticeably not here are Jude's parents and seeing as though their son's charges are the topic of conversation, I'd dare say they were smart to stay away. Jude's actions have the potential to destroy his father in the business world and I'm kinda excited to watch it all play out.

The business center of Bellevue Springs really is a small world. Everybody knows everybody and I have no idea why I seem so surprised by it. Maybe this is how Colton, Spencer, Charlie, and Jude became friends in the first place. They would have all been forced together at all of these functions since they were kids. It would make sense, and it'd make even more sense why Charles was so adamant to help Jude hide his rape charges the first time. His actions would have come down on his father which in turn, would have reflected poorly on Charles.

We get halfway through dinner when Laurelle stands beside Colton and slips out from behind her seat. The conversation is flowing but I find myself watching her like a hawk. As she walks around the table, her fingers brush across the shoulders of every man still seated. A few of the wives pick up on her subtle touches and glare as she passes by them.

Laurelle steps between a couple and dives headfirst into their conversation, touching the man as often as she can while his wife stares on in shock. The husband eats up her attention like a lion starved of food.

I elbow Colton and his head whips around to face me. "What the hell is your mother doing?"

Colton scans the room and I see the second he finds her shamelessly flirting with a married man. His lips lift in a disgusted scowl as embarrassment washes over him. "Fuck me," he says under his breath. "I guess she's trying to find a new husband seeing as though I cut her off."

"You really have to get rid of her."

"I know," he says with a heavy sigh. "If I wasn't just starting to build a relationship with Casey again, I'd have kicked her out already."

I glance around him to where Casey and Cora are seated, finding both of them staring at their mother with matching looks of horror. "Can't Casey just stay?"

He shakes his head. "She's always welcome to stay but she won't. Cora would go with Mom and Casey wouldn't separate from Cora like that. I don't know, maybe it's a twin bond thing."

"Then what—ugh," I grumble, cutting myself off as I watch Laurelle slip the man her number before moving onto the next guy. A fight breaks out between the husband and wife, and suddenly, the whole table is watching the show while the wife calls out Laurelle for being a slimy hooker.

All eyes dart to Colton, waiting for him to put a stop to the catastrophe but he sits back and watches as his mother is publicly called out on her bad behavior, and I have to admit, I can't fault him.

Laurelle laughs it off as though the wife is being dramatic which only infuriates her more. The woman rises from her seat and in a flash grabs her champagne flute and saturates Laurelle's white Prada dress.

My eyes flash across to Milo who looks back at me with an amused smirk, knowing damn well what's running through my mind right now. Cora looks to her brother. "Are you going to do something about this?" she demands.

Colton laughs and shakes his head. He rubs his hand over his face, masking the grin that cuts across his delicious lips. "Nah, I don't think I will."

"Colton," Cora snaps in horror.

"What? She's a grown-ass woman. If she wants to go whoring herself out, then let her be. She's only tarnishing her own name and destroying her reputation. You're more than welcome to step in though but I'd be careful which side you want to show your support for, especially in front of all these people. Once you show your hand in this world, it's impossible to go back."

With that, Cora rests back into her chair, leaving her mother to clean up her own damn mess. Every eye at the table watches as Laurelle shrieks at her ruined dress, some laughing, while others are equally as horrified.

Laurelle turns to face her son at the other end of the long table. "Remove her at once," she yells, demanding his attention as the whole room falls to silence, waiting to see what will happen.

I bite down on my lip to stop from saying anything but turns out I don't need to because Colton has it handled like a fucking pro. "Harrison," he calls, gaining his trusted butler's attention. "Get Mrs. Rodgers a new glass of champagne. It seems hers has spilled."

Harrison nods, trying his hardest to hide his smirk. "Right away, Mr. Carrington."

He scurries off and Mrs. Rodgers gracefully sinks back into her seat with her husband by her side. She nods gratefully at Colton while Mr. Rodgers does the same, but judging from the harsh line set in his lips, he knows he's going to get hell from his wife when they're in the privacy of their own home.

Laurelle stares at her son in shock, though truth be told, I'm almost certain she's faking it. She knew there was a good chance that he wouldn't have her back so I don't know why she's acting so surprised when he didn't. "Excuse me?" she calls from the other end of the table, insisting to continue this 'I'm your mother and you must respect me' charade. "Did you not see what that woman did to me?"

"I did," he says, grabbing his glass tumbler and taking a sip of his drink. "But I also saw you shamelessly trying to steal what was hers. Mrs. Rodgers had every right to put you in your place. Now," he continues, gesturing around the table at his guests. "Unless any of the available men at this table are actually interested in allowing a gold-digger such as yourself into their wallets to take everything you can get your thieving hands on, I suggest you hurry off and clean yourself up. That champagne certainly looks as though it might stain."

Laurelle's eyes go wide as gasps are heard around the table. She silently scolds her son but the Laurelle show is over and she knows it. She starts storming toward the door when I clear my throat and steal her attention. "I'd recommend a warm hand wash on that dress. I can write out a step by step process to follow if you'd like."

Her jaw clenches and if looks could kill, I'd be dead on the spot. She harrumphs and clenches her jaw before storming toward the door once again, only on her way out, she passes Harrison and flips his tray of champagne flutes, sending liquid gold all over the room.

The wait staff rushes in to clear the mess while Colton stands and faces his guests. "I apologize about that," he says, taking charge like a fucking boss. "How about we open some of my father's vintage whiskey."

The men in the room cheer as Colton glances to Harrison who nods and scurries off once again.

Colton settles back into his seat beside me and I look at him as though he's some kind of stranger. The way he takes charge like that is so damn impressive. I know working for his father's business was never what he really wanted but there's no denying that he's the best this world will ever see.

"What?" he grins, knowing exactly what's going through my mind.

I shake my head. "Nothing," I whisper. "You're just pretty freaking incredible." He rolls his eyes and I lean into his side. "Are you okay? I don't think I've ever seen a woman like that throw a tantrum."

A loud booming laugh tears from deep within as Colton's hand falls to my thigh under the table. He squeezes my leg and his eyes instantly sparkle with happiness. "Stick with me, Jade, and you'll see this shit more than you could ever care for."

"I don't know about that," I laugh. "I could watch your mother being drenched in champagne every day of the week and never get tired of it."

Colton shakes his head, his eyes dancing around in amusement. The mess is quickly cleaned up and before we know it, the dinner plates are being taken away and the conversation begins to flow again.

Desert is brought out and I glance up, looking at Charlie. He's slouched back in his chair and I've never seen someone look so miserable. Before I even know what I'm doing, I grab my uneaten dinner roll from the small fancy plate before me and launch the fucker across the table.

"Hey, Hot Sauce."

The dinner roll lands right in Charlie's lap and his head snaps up, along with it one hell of a nasty glare. The dinner roll is launched back at me with a speed I'm not ready for. I try to catch it and groan as it slams against my chest.

Charlie's eyes bug out of his head as he sits up in horror. "Fuck, sorry," he rushes out as I rub a hand over my chest and pull it away only to find a big red mark.

I burst out laughing and catch a few curious glances from the people around me as I look back at Charlie. "No, I'm sorry," I tell him. "Please stop hating me. I can't take your miserable pouting anymore."

He scrunches up his face, probably hating that we're having this conversation with a hundred ears all listening in. "Fine," he finally grumbles. "You're forgiven, but keep something like that from me again ..."

Charlie lets his response dangle in the air between us and I nod. "I know," I tell him. "You'll make me watch anime porn on repeat until my eyes bleed."

"Damn straight," he says, a small smile slowly beginning to spread across his boyishly handsome face. His mood instantly lightens and just like that, everything feels right in the world. Well, mostly. There's always some shit going on in Bellevue Springs, but right this very minute, everything feels just right.

Milo looks between me and Charlie and calls across the table. "What were you two fighting about anyway?"

Spencer laughs and catches Milo's eyes. "Trust me, you're better off not knowing."

Milo laughs and I watch as he stares at Spencer. His cheeks flush and it's almost as though he's got a bit of a crush on the guy. I roll my eyes and am just about to file it away in the 'things to tease Milo about later' category when I glance back at Spencer to find that same longing.

What the actual fuck?

The two of them continue staring, locked in each other's gaze as though some kind of secret messages are passing between them. I recognize the look in Milo's eyes. It's as though he wants to see Spencer naked, but the look in Spencer's eyes is the one I get from Colton, the one that says 'I've already seen you naked and damn it, I want to see it again.'

No. This can't be what I think it is. Milo spilled the tea and said he was screwing one of the guys at school who is deep in the closet while Colton said just last night that he thought Spencer was seeing someone.

I wonder if … yeah. It has to be.

I look between the two, feeling as though I'm bursting from the seams. My knees bounce and I bite my lip, desperate to talk about it but knowing damn well that right here and right now is certainly not the place, especially now that my bouncing knees have caught Colton's attention.

I catch Milo's eyes and as he watches me, I flick my gaze between the new couple. His eyes go wide and within seconds, Spencer catches on to what the hell I've just worked out. His eyes go bigger than Milo's and the horror is confirmation enough.

I fly to my feet, unable to control my excitement. "I freaking knew it."

Without thinking, Spencer barrels out of his chair and scrambles across the table, sending cutlery and drinks flying in every possible direction. All eyes turn our way but before I can say another word, Spencer falls into me, slamming his hand over my mouth as we go tumbling to the ground.

His arm curls around the back of my head, protecting me as we go crashing to the ground. "What the fuck, Spence?" Colton roars staring down at us in shock.

Milo comes running around, grabbing my hand and hauling me up but before I can get properly to my feet, Spencer is there, grabbing me around the waist and throwing me over his shoulder. "Just need your girl for a few minutes," he says as he starts heading for the door.

Spencer and Milo practically storm through the mansion until they step through to one of the many private rooms. I get put on my feet and I can hardly stand still as the door closes behind us.

They face me down with their secret sitting heavily between us and just as Spencer takes a breath, the door opens with Colton and Charlie forcing their way in.

"What the fuck was that?" Colton asks. "What's going on and why the fuck did you just destroy my dinner table?"

"It's nothing," Spencer says, looking as though he's about to be sick.

"Nothing?" Charlie scoffs. "I'm not about to let you fuckers keep me locked in the dark again. What the fuck is going on? Be fucking real with me for once."

"FUCK," Spencer roars, glancing at Milo as he begins pacing the small room. "I, um… fuck. I don't know how to tell you guys this." My legs start bouncing, desperately wishing he would hurry up and spit the words out so I can start celebrating with them. Spencer takes another slow breath and glances everywhere except for Charlie and Colton. "I, uhh … sorta started seeing someone."

Colton harumphs with pride as he looks to me, bouncing his brows as though he's a fucking genius for guessing it last night. "Told you."

"Yeah, you did," I grin, knowing there's so much more to the story.

Colton focuses on Spencer, forcing him to look his way. "You made a scene at my business dinner because you're seeing someone?"

"Well, that's just the thing … it's really not what you think."

"What's that supposed to mean?"

"Well, umm …" he stutters, looking back at Milo. "You know last week when we were chilling around the pool and Milo and Jess had that fight and he kinda came out of the closet?"

"No shit. You're dating Jess?" Charlie beams, his brows shooting up in excitement. "We can all triple date. I'm kinda working on Drix."

"I …" he shakes his head, his hands pumping nervously at his sides. "No, that's not what I was going to say. I'm not dating Jess, I'm actually dating … Milo."

The boys stop and stare in shock. "You're … what?" Colton says, his mouth dropping in shock as Charlie just stares, still repeating Spencer's last words over and over in his head, making sure he heard them correctly.

Milo steps into Spencer's side for support but they don't dare touch, not until they know the boys have fully wrapped their heads around it. "Umm… yeah," Spencer says. "After Milo came out last week and seeing how open you guys were to it, it kinda gave me the courage to seek him out and you know, we got to talking and … he's an alright guy."

Milo scoffs. "I'm a little more than alright."

Spencer smirks at his comment but keeps his eyes on his best friends. Charlie licks his lips that seem to have gone completely dry while his jaw was on the ground. "I mean, don't get me wrong here. If you're into dudes, then that's cool, I'm just a little confused because I was certain that you were into chicks."

Spencer shrugs his shoulder. "Eh," he says. "They're hot as fuck and all that, but I'm really not that interested."

I raise a brow. "Is that why you so subtly suggested we skip the whole dating thing and get married on my first day at BSA?"

Spencer laughs to himself. "Yeah," he says. "I wasn't interested in fucking you, no offense. I thought you might have been Charles' illegitimate kid at first and if I was right, you would have had some serious coin coming your way. Figured, I'd lock you down early."

"The fuck?" Colton laughs.

"Hey," Spencer argues. "If it was anyone but her, you would have tried the same thing."

Colton shakes his head and comes to stand right by my side as if to claim me as his own, but in this room, it's really not necessary. "So," I say, looking up at Milo and Spencer. "You two are a thing now?"

They look at each other and Milo cringes. "I … I think so?"

Spencer shrugs his shoulders. "It's still new," he says, glancing back at us. "But if you don't mind, I don't want anyone to know. Not yet at least."

I crash into them, throwing my arms around the two big idiots. "You know I love you guys, right?"

"Yeah, yeah," Spencer grumbles, desperately trying to peel me off him but in the blink of an eye, Colton and Charlie are there, pulling him back in and sandwiching me between the four guys.

"You've got my word, bro," Colton says, holding his friend tight. "I've got your back."

# CHAPTER 26

I hitch up my sweatpants while trying to make my way around the living area, cleaning up after the boys as they sit around talking all sorts of shit. "Babe, come on," Colton groans. "Just sit your sweet ass down and take a break."

"I can't," I tell him, dodging away from him to avoid being caught in his clutches for the third time this morning. "If I get denied for a student loan or financial aid, then I need to be able to pay for college somehow."

"Loan?" Charlie questions, sounding shocked by the word. "Shit, that's a word we don't hear much around here."

"Forgive me, oh wealthy one, for my pockets are not lined with gold."

Charlie cringes. "Sorry, Ocean. I didn't mean that as a stab toward you. It just threw me a bit. I guess it just really points out the differences between your world and ours."

"No shit," I tell him, walking around to his side of the massive couch and scooping up his forgotten plate. "Though, I figured the fact that I have to pick up after you slobs was already proof enough of that."

Charlie shrugs his shoulder. "I guess," he says. "But I kinda forget about all of that. You're just part of the furniture now. I see you as one of us. I forget that things aren't so easy for you."

"Trust me, I certainly haven't."

Spencer gets up and takes his own plate back to the kitchen to be washed and calls over his shoulder. "Why are you applying for loans anyway? You realize that you're dating Colton Fucking Carrington right? He could blink toward the school and have your tuition paid. Why are you putting yourself through all of that?"

I groan and can't help but notice the cocky smirk lifting on Colton's lips. "Did you really have to go there?"

Colton laughs, looking over at Spencer in the kitchen. "Say it a little louder for the people in the back," he says, his eyes sparkling with attitude. "Better yet, just say it again for Ocean until she decides to stop being a stubborn princess and lets me take care of it."

"We've talked about this," I grumble, cutting past the back of the couch and gently knocking the back of his head with my elbow. "And the answer is still no."

"Babe," he groans, putting his hand to his head and falling back on the couch as though my rejection physically wounds him.

I hold back a laugh as I walk up into the kitchen and dump all their crap on the counter before turning on my heel and stalking right back. "I told you, I want my independence. It's important to me that I earn everything that I have. I don't accept handouts, especially from my boyfriend. It'll make me feel cheap."

I stride past Colton and his arms shoot out, locking around my waist before he pulls me down on the couch. "I'm not letting you go until you agree."

I lean into him, hovering my lips just above his and teasing him with the promise of what they can do. I roll my tongue over my bottom lip and let out the softest groan, one that only he could hear. His eyes trail my tongue's movement, heating with an intense need. "Then I'm not sucking your cock until you agree."

His lips pull into a wicked grin and the low groan that tears out of him is the most rewarding sound I'll ever hear. "Baby, that one is going to hurt you just as much as it'll hurt me."

"You mean like how allowing you to pay for my schooling is going to hurt me just as much as my fist is going to hurt you."

"Fuck, I love it when you speak like a lady."

I pull back and look down into his eyes. "I mean it," I tell him. "I want to pay for it myself, even if it takes me years."

His fingers tighten on my waist, holding me to him. "Do you have any idea how hard that's going to be for me to watch?"

I nod, knowing damn well but I also know that he's more than strong enough to bear it. "You'll be fine," I whisper, dropping back down and pressing a soft kiss upon his warm lips. "I trust that you'll respect what I want."

He lets out a huff. "Fine, but just so you know, I'm probably going to bring this up about a million more times."

"I know, you have some serious self-control issues to work on."

He rolls his eyes before looking at me thoughtfully. "I mean, if you really want to pay for college, I'm sure I could come up with a few things to help you earn a few extra dollars."

I groan and pull myself up off his wide chest. "I'm not your personal hooker, Carrington."

"Who's not a personal hooker?" Milo says, walking into the living area as I make myself comfortable beside Colton. Milo strides over to the couch and drops down beside Spencer then leans into him, and presses the smallest kiss to his lips, not ready to flaunt their new relationship.

A soft chuckle escapes Charlie's lips. "Ocean was just saying that she wants to be a hooker to earn some extra cash."

I launch a cushion across the room and it smacks Charlie right in his unsuspecting face. "Take that back," I demand.

"Why?" Milo questions, a sparkle hitting his eye, the only hint that I've just become the target of their taunts. "It's true. You were just telling me yesterday all the things you wanted to try with Colton. Why not make a little coin while you're at it. You gotta hustle, girl."

Colton's brow instantly arches as his eyes flick to mine. "What kind of shit is he talking about?" he questions, his eyes becoming hooded with excitement. "You know there's nothing I wouldn't do to make you scream. Just say the word, Jade."

"Really?" I question with wide eyes, looking at him as though he holds me in his very hands. "Because Drix told me that Charlie let her shove a dildo up his ass and he loved it so … you know. If you really want to try it, I guess we could."

Charlie flies to his feet as Colton's face falls in horror, not exactly pleased with this turn of events. "The fuck did she say that I did?" Charlie demands, more than ready to start defending his honor.

"It's okay, Charlie," Milo says, knowing damn well that I'm teasing. "No need to be defensive. No one here is judging, ass play is fun." He turns to Colton. "I think it's great you guys are keeping your sex life adventurous and exciting. Take my word for it, and I'm sure Ocean's too, but it's worth it. Use plenty of lube though. You don't want nothing going through the backdoor dry."

Colton's face goes white as he turns to look back at me. "Please, baby. You know I'd do it if you really, *really* wanted me to, but tell me that you're fucking with me," he swallows past a lump in his throat. "I'm really going to have to work myself up to that."

I can't help but laugh. This incredible man before me is always so put together, so strong, and ready to face down the world but with me standing in his way, he'd happily shove a dildo up his ass just to make me happy.

Fuck. Maybe I do love him. What other man would do that for me?

"It's okay," I laugh. "I'm more than happy to live the rest of my life without witnessing you putting a dildo up your ass, but I have to admit, Milo has a point. Ass play is nothing to frown upon." His brow raises, more than into the conversation again.

"Ewwwww," Casey says from the door with her mother and bitchy twin sister following her through with bags upon bags of shopping dangling from their fingers. "Please tell me that I didn't just hear that."

Colton laughs, sitting up on the couch. "You better fucking believe it."

Casey scrunches up her face and I laugh it off as I peel myself off the couch and start getting back to work, except I should have known it wouldn't be that easy. "What have I told you about wearing your uniform?" Laurelle spits at me.

"And what have I told you?" I throw back at her. "The second Colton asks me to put a uniform on, I'd happily do it. Until then, screw you."

She steps forward, preparing to hit me because she sure as hell hasn't learned any new moves.

"MOTHER," Colton's deep roar tears through the living room. "Lay one fucking hand on her and the world will know that you spent over six million dollars on male escorts."

The boys behind us laugh in shock as Casey and Cora's mouths drop in disgust. "You wouldn't," she seethes toward her son.

"Fucking try me."

Laurelle strides past me as though I've completely been forgotten. She walks down the three steps into the sunken living room and steps in front of her son, her six-inch heels putting her nearly eye to eye with him. "It's about time you and I have a little talk."

"Yeah, I think so," Colton says. "It's about time that you pack up your shit and get the fuck out of my house. I'm done with your bullshit games. You come in here and insult my girlfriend every chance you get, you willingly allowed Melissa Carter into my home—knowing damn well that her son is a rapist—and then you completely embarrass the Carrington name in front of every investor and partner of Carrington Incorporated by throwing yourself at my CFO. I'm done and so are you. I'm not fucking stupid, Mom. After you lit my father's casket on fire, your motives became pretty fucking clear and I'm not going to stand back and allow you to try to bring down Carrington Incorporated. Dad worked too fucking hard and so have I."

"Your father was a monster. How could you take his side?"

"I'm not taking his side. I'm making my own goddamn side. My father *was* a monster, but you're turning out just like him and you're doing the same to Cora. At least Casey has some sort of spine and can stand on her own."

Cora sucks in a broken gasp and for the slightest second, I feel bad for her, but the glare that comes straight after pulls me back in line. She steps up beside her mother. "You're a real prick, you know that? How dare you say that about me."

"How could I not?" he throws back at her. "Have you looked at yourself in a mirror recently? You're a spoiled brat. I've been watching you, Cora and you haven't got a redeeming quality about yourself. You're materialistic and the way you're going now, you're going to end up married to a rich businessman on his deathbed with your mother still dipping into your pockets, both of you absolutely broke."

"You're not going to get away with this," Laurelle hisses as the rest of us watch on like it's an award-winning daytime drama.

"I already have, mother. Harrison was given the order to start collecting your stuff this morning. Your Uber will be here in an hour to take you back to the airport."

"Uber?" she shrieks in horror. "Airport? I don't ride in Ubers and I sure as hell don't fly on commercial airplanes. I have my own car and my own jet but they will not be needed because I won't be going anywhere."

"No," Colton corrects. "I own your car and I own the jet which your access was cut to the second you embarrassed Carrington Incorporated last night. Now, you have an hour to pack the rest of your things, after that, you'll be considered trespassing and I'll have no other option but to call the police and have you escorted off the premises, and for the record," he says, walking back toward the couch for his mic drop moment. "I have a press meeting scheduled in an hour. It'd be a real shame if they were to witness you being taken out of here in cuffs."

Laurelle's face drops. "You can't. I'm your mother."

"Exactly. You're my mother which is why I've allowed this to go on for so long. You weren't welcome when you showed up a few weeks ago, and you're not welcome now."

Colton drops down onto the couch and the room remains silent, all eyes on Laurelle, waiting and watching to see her next move. Except, with the pressure of an audience, she finally cracks. She stomps her foot against the marble floor like a toddler and within the blink of an eye, she turns on her heel and stalks out of the room. "You will not get away with this, Colton. Mark my words, you will pay."

"Holy fuck," Spencer howls, roaring with laughter as Milo sits beside him with his jaw hanging wide.

A slow smile begins pulling at my lips but it falls away as a soft sniffle sounds behind me. The room falls to silence once again as we find the twins standing awkwardly in the kitchen, staring at their big brother.

Silent tears track down Casey's face as Cora stands there dumbfounded. Casey glances around, not strong enough to meet her brother's eyes. "Does that mean us too?" she asks in a soft tone.

Colton watches them for a second, figuring out his next move. His gaze sweeps to me before falling back to the guys, unsure how he wants to play this. "I don't know," he tells them honestly. "Do you want to be here?"

Casey instantly nods while Cora holds back, not ready to give in to her brother, especially after the way he just tore her apart. Perhaps being away from her mother and living with Colton is what she needs to gain a little perspective. Hell, it sure worked for me.

Casey's eyes go wide, her bottom lip quivering. "Please don't make me go. I like it here. I actually have friends here who don't care that my daddy gave me a bank account."

"Mom's going to fight you on it," he warns.

She nods vigorously. "I can handle Mom."

Cora scoffs at Casey's confidence and Colton turns his sharp glare on her, making her shrink under his stare. "And what about you?"

She pauses, looking up at her brother as though she's trying to find the courage to actually speak. "Did you really mean what you said? You think that lowly of me?"

"I'm not here to parent you, Cora, I'm not going to sugarcoat it. Yes, I think you're a spoiled brat with a shitty attitude and my first instinct is to send you back with Mom. I don't want your fucking drama."

She looks away, and for the first time I see a true emotion come out of her. "I don't want to go," she whispers so low that I have to strain to hear her.

Colton takes a step back, crossing his arms over his wide chest and studying his sisters. "Okay," he finally says. "You can stay, but there are conditions."

"Like?" Cora questions cautiously.

"Take one guess."

Her eyes flick to me before going back to Colton. "No, don't make me do it."

"Then don't stay," he says simply. "Ocean is my girlfriend and I plan on keeping her around for a long fucking time and if you can't get on board with that then you can fuck off to whoever the fuck knows where with mom. I'm not having your hostility in my house. If you're here, you're chill. Make things right with her. I don't give a shit if you're besties or not, but there won't be bad blood between you. Got it?"

Cora looks back to me while Casey appears to be shitting herself, knowing her fate lies in the hands of her bratty twin sister. Cora slides her gaze back to her brother before letting out a sigh. "Fine," she says. "I'll clear the air."

"All the bullshit ends," he says.

"Yes."

"Or else, Cora. You'll be out before you even know what's happening. Got it?"

"Yeah, yeah. I got it. Anything else, oh wise one?"

"Your attitude fucking stinks," he tells her. "If you're here, I want you to be an active member of this household. You're not just coming home, sleeping, and then leaving. You're going to help plan the parties, clean up after yourself, and be a pleasant person to be around. Those are my rules."

Cora and Casey look between themselves and I see the clear begging in Casey's eyes, desperately wanting this to work out. "Okay," Cora says. "I'll make an effort around the house."

Colton looks at Casey expectantly.

"Yep, me too. I'm all in," she tells him.

Colton finally sighs and drops his arms from across his chest. "Fine," he says. "You can stay but you're dealing with the storm Mom cooks up over it. I want nothing to do with it."

Casey runs full steam ahead, bolting into his chest and wrapping her arms tightly around him. "You won't regret it," she tells him on the verge of tears. "Thank you. Thank you. Thank you."

Colton laughs and for just a brief second, he squeezes his sister, overwhelmed with joy to finally have her back in his life. As for Cora, that's a work in progress.

# CHAPTER 27

## Colton

What the fuck am I doing here?

I should turn and walk away but the second Harrison stepped into my office and told me that Marco DeCarlo was back in the city, I had no choice. I had to make this right.

Mom was gone after raining down hell over me and the twins. Realizing that they didn't want anything to do with her didn't sit well and naturally, she blamed that bullshit on me, but just as the girls promised, they stepped up and handled their shit. And just as I promised, I stepped up and handled mine.

After an hour of screaming through my home, I had her escorted from the premises with cuffs tightly bound around her wrists and cops at her back. The press was in full force and all afternoon, footage of Mom has been splashed across every news outlet in the country.

I'm not usually one to allow my family bullshit to get out like that, but taking down that woman needed to be done with the eyes of the world on her. She's too good at hiding behind her precious reputation, but fuck it. I blew that shit right out of the water today and now the world will know exactly who she is. Her reputation be damned. She's nothing but a gold-digging bitch anyways. What kind of woman blows through that much cash and then goes after her children's? I didn't think it was physically possible but Laurelle Carrington has been proving me wrong since the day I was born.

Crouching by the window of the shitty warehouse that Marco DeCarlo has been calling home for the last two years, I grip the gun that's been waiting in the waistband of my jeans. My finger runs over the trigger, feeling the power it holds.

This motherfucker is finished.

Memories of Maryne begging for her life filter through my mind. Harrison desperately trying to protect her, Ocean standing beside me terrified, Maryne on the ground being dragged from the wine cellar by her hair.

The gun forced under her chin.

That haunting echo of the gunshot.

The blood.

Ocean's scream.

Maryne would have been so fucking scared and I just stood there, unable to do a fucking thing, but that ends now. Marco will not get away with this. Tonight, he is going to learn that coming into my home and threatening my people, was the biggest fucking mistake he ever made.

Gripping the gun, I spy Marco in his cramped kitchen. His back is to me and despite the dog barking in the distance, warning him that I'm here, he's too fucking engrossed in the cheap whore he's hired for the night.

She sits up on the counter with her legs spread wide as Marco slams into her with a force that couldn't be comfortable. I don't doubt that he's hurting her but because he's paid for her, he thinks that she's his to do with as he likes.

Her pained groans sound through the warehouse walls and has my jaw clenching, even more determined to finish him. It's pretty fucking obvious that he's hurting her, but he couldn't care less.

I wonder if she knew what she was getting herself into when she showed up here tonight.

Marco DeCarlo is fucking scum. He has zero respect for anyone but himself, but I guess after tonight, that won't matter because I won't be leaving this shitty warehouse until it's done.

I just know that Ocean is going to find out about this. With her connections to the Black Widows, she'll know what I've done before the night is out and she's going to hate me for it.

I stopped her from taking revenge on Jude and ending his life knowing the guilt that would have sat on her chest until her dying days.

She's too good, too pure, but me? I've been a fucking goner since the day I was born. There's nothing good left. The only good I have comes from Ocean. She makes me a better person, she makes me want to be her everything.

She won't forgive me for this. She thinks I'm stronger, she thinks I have self-control, she thinks I'm different from the guys she grew up with but she's wrong. I'm just like them. The things I've done … fuck, I'm not proud of myself, but I'm my father's son. If only she knew who I really was, she'd hate me.

I've seen the way she pulled away from Nic when she saw him end another man's life and it would kill me if she did the same to me. She's too fucking precious. I want her with me all the time. She thinks she's this big badass bitch who can face down anything, but truth be told, she's like a little puppy with a nasty bite. She needs to be protected at all costs because girls like her are fucking rare.

I never intended for her to find Jude in that cellar but she did, and every day I fear that the darkness I brought down on her is too much for her soul to bear. She's surprising me though. I don't think I gave her enough credit. She's fucking stronger than I ever thought.

Maybe that's why I pushed her away so hard at the start. It's almost as though deep down, I knew she was going to destroy me. She was going to get inside my world and tear it apart from the inside out. I think on some level, I knew that she'd discover all of my secrets, and damn it, I'm so fucking bewitched by her, that if she decided to take me down, I'd go willingly.

The question is; what's she going to do with my secrets once she finds them out? Surely she knows me well enough to know that I'd never hurt her. I'm not a bad guy, I just handle the shit that others are too fucking scared to touch.

I guess tonight, I'll finally have my answers.

Taking a breath, I unhook the open padlock from the chained backdoor and gently drop it into the overgrown grass. I'm never going to get a chance like this again. It's too good. Too easy.

Fuck, I must sound like her father. I don't enjoy death, but there's no mistaking the power that taking a life gives you. It's a rush and for that slight moment, I'm untouchable. I don't chase that feeling though, not like Ocean's old man did. Hell, not like her precious Widows still do.

I kill out of necessity. I kill because it's the right thing to do. I should have fucking killed Jude, but he was handled. I'm just glad I got the chance to tell him exactly what I thought of him. He's going to spend the rest of his life behind bars and that's the outcome that Ocean needed, whether she comes forward or not.

I push the door open and cringe at the soft squeal of the metal hinges. I pause in the darkness, listening out for Marco but he's too engrossed in his whore's raw pussy to notice that his life is only minutes away from ending. I guess he's lucky to be dying with his dick wet. If only Maryne was offered the same generosity to die doing something she loved.

Confident that my presence hasn't been made known, I sneak in through the back door, leaving it open for a quick getaway. There's nothing worse than having a nosey neighbor peering through the window after hearing a gunshot and accidentally getting your dumbass locked in the house. After spending twelve hours hiding in an attic, I very quickly learned from that mistake.

I creep through Marco's home, looking over the way he lives. He's twenty-six and living in a run-down warehouse. He's a fucking slob. There's shit all over the place. Old takeout containers, probably from when he was in town last, dirty clothes, and not to mention the state of the bathroom. I'm doing him a fucking favor here.

I walk through to the kitchen and find my mark. His back is still to me while his paid pussy is digging her nails into his back but not for the same reasons that Ocean digs hers into mine. This chick is in pain and it's about time I put her out of her misery.

Marco grunts in pleasure. "Yeah, you fucking like that, don't you, you dirty little slut."

I hold back a gag. I've never understood men calling their women dirty sluts. Have a little class. If you treat a woman well, she'll do the same for you. It's simple math.

I walk up behind them and as I grow nearer, I raise the gun to the back of Marco's head. The woman sees it within a split second of warning and her eyes go big before a squeal tears out of her.

The barrel of the gun presses against the back of his head and he freezes with his hands in the air. The girl instantly pulls back from him with a pained groan, watching me with wide eyes. "Go," I tell her.

She doesn't hesitate and sprints out the door, leaving her clothes behind.

"That was a fucking mistake," Marco spits, not bothering to turn around. He would have hundreds of enemies all wanting to stand where I stand right now. Not turning around to see who's at his back is a mistake, but making any kind of move would also be a mistake. I guess it doesn't matter. Either way, he's going to end up dead.

"Turn around."

He takes his time but does as he's told, assuming the man at his back is too fucking pussy to pull the trigger.

As he meets my eyes, his lips twist into an amused grin. "If it isn't Carrington Jr." he laughs. "I'll give you two seconds to get out of here. Trust me, you're not going to like the repercussions of coming onto my turf."

"Just like you're not going to like the repercussions of coming onto mine. Tell me, how're your brothers doing? I trust they're becoming well acquainted with their new housing situation."

His face falls as if only just realizing who's responsible for putting his scumbag brothers behind bars. To be honest, I'm a bit disappointed in him. His father dearest had worked it out in no time. I guess there's a communication issue between the family. I had originally planned the same fate for Marco, but in his case it was a little different. It would have been as easy as handing over my home security footage to the cops, showing the moment he ended Maryne's life but I found myself holding onto it.

I think I always knew I'd end up here but I had to try to be better, for Ocean's sake. She deserves someone good. I guess I'm not him.

The twins were occupied, the boys had gone home, and Milo was keeping Ocean busy with the latest gossip on the guys from BSA. It was too easy to just slip out the doors. Hell, I'm sure I'll even be able to slip back in without anyone blinking a damn eye.

Marco spits, keeping his gaze locked straight ahead. "You're going to fucking die for that."

I jam the gun under his chin, stepping into him and watching as the force of the gun pushes his chin up. "You see, that's where you're wrong. How are you going to tell them when you're already dead? But don't you worry, I have plans for them too."

Marco's jaw clenches, finally realizing just how much trouble he's in. "I should have fucking shot you when I had the chance."

"Yeah," I laugh. "You should have. It's funny how the tables have turned, isn't it?"

"You won't get away with this."

"That's just the thing, Marco. I already have. Now get on your fucking knees so I can end you just like you ended Maryne."

Marco tries to pull away from the barrel of my gun but I keep on him, not giving him anything to work with. "Who the fuck is Maryne?"

My fist slams up into ribs, winding him. He buckles over and as he goes, I kick his feet out from under him, dropping his dead ass to the dirty as fuck floor. "Don't speak her fucking name," I growl, jamming the gun under his chin once again. "Tell me, how did you picture you were going to die? I bet you never pictured your brains being painted all over your shitty little kitchen for your father to find."

"Fuck you."

I twist my wrist back and forth, playing with the barrel under his chin, making him hyper-aware of it. "Any last words?"

His eyes sharpen with hatred and I laugh at his pain. "Go to hell," he spits, knowing damn well that I'll never spare him, not in a million years.

My lips twist into a sick grin as my finger touches down on the trigger, hovering there as I prepare to take exactly what Maryne deserves.

I meet Marco's eyes, showing him the devil who lives inside of me. My voice lowers with a deadly promise as a satisfying, sick laugh tears out of me. "I'll see you there."

BANG!

# CHAPTER 28

I lay across my bed on Sunday night, staring up at Milo as he crashes down on my bed. "So, were you ever going to tell me how you ended up screwing Spencer under the bleachers? Actually no, go from before that. Tell me how you guys ended up getting close in the first place. I just can't wrap my head around it. You realize this is Spencer, right? Like mousy brown-haired, blue-eyed, looks like a good boy but is actually the devil with a wicked jawline Spencer?"

"Yes," he laughs. "I know who he is and as if you can deny that he's one of the most attractive guys you've ever laid your eyes on?"

"I mean, yeah, he totally is and don't get me wrong here, I'm completely aboard the Spencer train to pound town, but I thought you didn't like him? You always made out like he was a bit of a douche."

"I did," he clarifies. "He's always been the biggest douche but after getting to know him and stripping away that shield that he always has up, he's actually a really cool guy. I think we could actually have something real going on."

My brows fly up. "No shit?"

"Yeah," he laughs. "I think he liked to hide behind his attitude so no one got in and saw the real him. He's just like me. He's been terrified of being himself because of how unaccepted guys like us are around here."

"But hasn't he always been a bit of a slut?"

"With chicks? Not really. There's a lot of rumors about him with girls but they're just that. Rumors. He said that he's been with one chick and has never been softer in his life— and that was the turning point for him. That's when he realized that he was definitely gay and he's been hiding it ever since."

My heart breaks for the guy. All this time, he's been hiding himself away, terrified of what the world would think of him. "I should have known. My gaydar must be off. I knew straight away when I met you that we batted for the same team, but I had absolutely no idea with Spence. If I'd only worked it out sooner, he could have been himself with me instead of feeling the need to hide."

"Don't beat yourself up about it," he tells me, grabbing my leg and giving it a gentle squeeze. "He had us all fooled. Not even I worked it out."

I let out a heavy sigh and squished my pillow under my head. "So tell me all about it. How did you end up with your knickers around your ankles under the bleachers?" I look back at Milo with a smirk crossing my lips. "He's the top, isn't he?"

Milo laughs but the blush that spreads across his cheeks confirms what I already know. "Do you want to hear the story or not?"

"Yes," I groan, rolling over so I can see the full effect of all of his facial expressions as he recaps his story.

His face instantly brightens and a cheesy as fuck smile tears across his boyish face. "Well, like he said last night after I came out to the guys last week, we got to talking and—"

"Stop," I demand, cutting him off. "You've already skipped crucial details. Who initiated the talking? Who came to who?"

Milo rolls his eyes and grabs the pillow from behind his back. I instantly get smacked over the head. "I'm seriously so close to telling you to come up with your own damn story and calling it quits."

"Fine, okay," I laugh. "I'll shut up, but don't skip out on the details."

He rolls his eyes again but thankfully gets on with the story, this time giving me the information I want to know. "Okay, so that night, Spencer showed up at my door after the party and he looked like he was going to be sick and then just blurted it out like word vomit. Almost as though his secret had been eating him up inside and was forcing its way out of his mouth. But once the words were out, he was like a whole new version of himself. He was freed from his own torture and fuck, babe. It really suits him."

A fond smile sets itself over Milo's face and I find myself smiling right back. "You really do care about him, don't you?"

"Yeah, I think I do. I mean, it's weird. This time last week, I would have laughed at the thought of me and Spencer hitting it off, but so much has changed. It's insane."

"You're telling me. I was wracking my mind trying to figure out who the guy you were screwing behind the bleachers was for days and the answer was right under my nose the whole time? You know, I can honestly tell you that Spencer never entered my mind."

"I know," he laughs, "Which is why I told you about it in the first place. I knew that tiny snippet of information was going to drive you insane."

"You're such a bitch."

"I know," he grins. "Anyway, so he came over that night, and the more we talked, the closer we seemed to get. I didn't even realize it until we were practically on top of each other. It's almost like our bodies were drawing us together. We talked all night and before I knew it, the sun was up and he was shocked that we'd stayed up like that. He went to leave and I don't even know what possessed me to do it but I just grabbed him and kissed him."

"Wait," I say, wide-eyed. "You kissed him?"

"Yeah," he laughs. "I was shocked too. I'm all talk and no game. I didn't even know I had it in me to make the first move like that."

"Well, shit. What did he do?"

"He pulled back and we both just kinda stared at each other in shock and then without warning, he kissed me back and since then … well, you know."

"No way," I laugh. "That's insane. You guys literally just figured everything out in the space of a day while Colton and I were tiptoeing around the topic for months."

"That's true. You two were giving me whiplash for ages, but now that everything has calmed down, you guys can just focus on being together and being happy."

My mind instantly takes me to all the bullshit with Nic and the Wolves which then reminds me of the goddamn bandage at the back of my neck. "Well, nearly everything has calmed," I remind him.

"Yeah," he says with a heavy sigh. "Were you ever planning on going down to the police station and making a statement about you being Jude's other rape victim?"

"I mean … yeah, may—"

My bedroom door swings open with a bang and my mother gapes at me in horror. "Excuse me?" she breathes, staring at me as though I'm some kind of stranger.

My eyes go wide and Milo looks at me as though he's about to be sick. "Mom, I …"

"What did he just say?" she demands, not taking her eyes from mine for even a second.

I sit up on the bed, feeling my heart begin to break as she realizes that I've kept this massive secret from her. "I …" I shake my head, not able to get the words freed from my throat, but nonetheless, I keep trying. "I … I…"

Milo peels himself off the bed from beside me and gives me a heavy stare. "I'm going to go and give you guys some space to talk," he murmurs, not making any sudden movements as the tension in the air continues to rise. "I'll see you tomorrow, yeah? Call me if you need me."

I try to swallow over the lump in my throat and give Milo a small nod as he slips past my mom. He gives her a gentle kiss on her cheek. "I'm sorry you had to find out like that," he whispers before moving past and slipping out of the pool house.

I'm left with my mother staring at me with her heart shattering into a million tiny pieces. Not just for the fact that her baby girl was hurt and abused, but because I kept it from her. I kept one of the biggest secrets and I can only imagine the kinds of things that would be going through her mind. Betrayal, heartache, devastation. She probably fears that I don't think I could tell her something like that. She's probably busy trying to convince herself that she's failed as a mother when in reality, I just didn't want her to feel the same hurt that I did. I wanted to spare her. She has such an innocent heart and I desperately wanted to keep it that way but all I've done was made it a million times worse.

A single tear streaks down her face and I see the very moment she breaks. "I'm your mom," she whispers, her voice shaky and broken. "How could you not tell me?"

My own shame and fear come up and cripples me as the tears spring freely from my eyes for what I went through, what I've neglected to deal with, and for the fact that I've just betrayed my mother's trust and broken her heart.

She deserved so much better than that.

She deserved the peace of mind to have been able to sit with me the morning after, holding me and telling me it was all going to be alright. She deserved the chance to be angry, the chance to go after Jude for hurting her child. She deserved it all and I took that away from her. Instead of being truthful and remembering that she's so damn strong and can take on the world, I hid it away. I lied and for that, I'll never forgive myself.

She raised me better than that.

How many times am I going to be the reason for her heartache?

I wipe the tears on the back of my arm and swallow over the growing lump, making it nearly impossible to breathe. "I'm sorry," I cry, feeling the weight of the world drop down over me. "I should have—"

"Yeah," she says, ever so slightly nodding her head. "You should have."

And just like that, her already falling tears shoot from her eyes like a waterfall, completely devastated and crushed. Unable to even face me, she walks away without another word, taking every little piece of hope along with her.

I listen for the soft click of her bedroom door and hear as she collapses into her bed and cries into her pillow, knowing all too well that her tears are filled with guilt for not having paid enough attention and the self-doubt for being too busy with work.

The need to go in there and comfort her rocks through me but I just can't. I can't face her knowing that I betrayed her trust. She counted on me to always be honest with her and I held back something so big, something that changed my world and turned me into this dark person that I've become. She could have saved me from that, she could have made it all better and I robbed her of that chance.

My eyes begin to sting with the constant tears but I can't make them stop.

I need to go to her and I don't doubt that she's feeling that same need with me, but neither of us is making the move, neither of us strong enough to face what we've neglected.

My phone chimes on my bedside table and I reach for it while wiping my tears on the back of my sleeve, feeling the ache of my raw skin as I drag the material across it.

I unlock my phone and read over the words, feeling my soul somehow shatter even more.

**Nic - I guess your boy isn't as clean-cut as he's been making himself out to be. Marco DeCarlo was just found dead in his kitchen. One bullet through the chin, just like your friend. Maybe that bastard has a pair of balls after all.**

No.

# CHAPTER 29

I don't remember the walk from the pool house to the Carrington mansion but one second I'm sitting in my bed, reading over Nic's text for the fifth time, hoping that my sore eyes are deceiving me and the next thing I know, I'm searching through Colton's mansion, desperately seeking him out.

I know he didn't just kill a man. He couldn't have. That's not who we are. Sure, we did some fucked-up things and the whole Jude situation was fifty shades of messed up, but Colton was there when I was about to slaughter Jude and he stopped me. Colton saved me from myself, saved me from endless amounts of guilt because that's not who we are.

We're better than that.

We're not cold-blooded murderers but the evidence pointing toward Colton is just too much to deny. He was coming after each of the DeCarlo brothers, he vowed that much and then promised to go after Vincent.

He said that he was putting them in prison. He said nothing about putting them in the ground.

Colton couldn't have done this. Please, someone, tell me that this is some kind of horrible coincidence. Colton isn't a killer. He's an amazing guy with a big heart. He's the guy that I've maybe fallen in love with. I couldn't have fallen for another killer. I just can't. That can't be my life.

I only just escaped guys like Nic who think the world revolves around them and the bullets in their guns. Colton isn't like that. I know him. I refuse to believe it. He's cold and calculating, but he's no murderer.

Although, I never imagined that he'd be the kind of guy to lock a rapist in a cramped little dungeon and use him as his personal punching bag, just waiting for him to slowly rot and die. Then again, I never thought I had it in me to slit a man's throat but standing in that dungeon with Jude on his knees, I would have done it without hesitation.

Maybe Colton is a monster. Maybe this is all some sort of act and he's just like Nic. Just like the Widows and everything I was trying to escape.

What's he going to do when he realizes that I know his little secret? Will he lock me up? Will all the tables turn on me and I'll suddenly become the victim?

I should have listened to Nic in the first place. He's never liked Colton. Maybe someone like Nic can sense that darkness in another. Maybe he knew I've been walking into a trap this whole time.

I always knew Colton was going to break me. I just never expected it to be like this. I thought he was good. I thought he was the light that I've always been missing.

My feet take me flying through the mansion. I peer into every room, desperate to find him, desperate for answers, knowing this must be some sick misunderstanding. He couldn't have done it. Sure, finding Marco dead isn't surprising, but Colton being the one to shoot him?

I just … fuck. He'd totally do it if it meant avenging Maryne.

I throw open his office door and scan the room before quickly moving on. Where the fuck is he? I fly past the internal garage door and look inside. His Veneno is here and I can guarantee that means he is too.

My mind is a mess of torturous thoughts, each one of them trying to convince me to give him a chance. I should hear him out, at least listen to him plead his case before I let him have it. He can't be a killer. He can't be like Nic. It's one of the reasons that I've allowed myself to get so close. I can't keep falling into this trap. Sure, I knew he was dark. Locking Jude up was proof of that, but he's supposed to be the good one. He's supposed to be the one with his head screwed on properly. I'm the mess in this relationship—not him.

Maybe I'm being too hard on him. After all, I nearly killed a guy myself, but he was the one bringing me back. He was the voice of reason, so if he did this, if he ended DeCarlo's life, does that make him a liar or just a hypocrite?

After checking all the places he could be on the lower level, I race up the stairs taking them two at a time. I go straight for his bedroom. It's the only place he'd be up here.

The unknown kills me. I need answers. I need to know who I've been allowing myself to fall in love with. Without knocking, I throw his door open and find his room empty, only his bathroom door is slightly ajar. I don't even think, my feet just take me there.

I slam my hand against the door and it instantly swings open.

I come to a screeching stop finding Colton standing before me. His hands are braced against the counter with his head dipped low, only the second the door slams against the expensive tiles, his sharp gaze snaps up.

I take in his reflection in the mirror, the panic that's outweighed by the blood splattered across his face. I search his eyes for a brief moment, unable to determine what emotions are pulsing far too quickly through my veins.

My gaze follows the line of his body, hoping to whoever exists above that this is all some kind of fucked up mistake. I scan over his face, down his bare chest until I'm following the line of his strong arm to the counter where a black gun lies forgotten beside him.

I suck in a sharp gasp, shaking my head as the horror pulses through me. "No," I whisper, begging for it to not be true.

Colton straightens up, not taking his eyes off mine through the mirror. I instantly back up, taking note of his blood-stained shirt laying on the bathroom floor.

He's a murderer. A cold-blooded murderer.

"Jade," he murmurs cautiously, slowly turning around to face me while raising his hand to prove some fucked up point that he's not going to hurt me.

I take another step back.

"Jade, please," he begs, stepping with me. "You need to hear me out."

"You did it," I whisper, terrified. Not terrified of him, but terrified of what he's capable of doing. Is this the first time or has he done this before? "You killed him."

Colton seeks out my wild, wide eyes and cautiously nods, attempting to step closer. "I did," he admits, not prepared to keep a damn thing from me. His face breaks and for the first time, I see the agony beneath the surface. "I had too. I couldn't let him live. Not after what he did."

I shake my head, feeling as though I'm staring at some kind of stranger. I back up another step, my heart racing in my chest. When I almost killed Jude, I was a mess. I couldn't eat, I couldn't breathe. I had to scrub his blood from my hands as soon as I could but Colton just stands here, perfectly fine and more worried about explaining himself.

If this was the first time …

Everything shatters inside of me and not in the way it did when I found out that Nic was cheating. Not in the way it did when I discovered who my father really was, not even when I found out that my Widows betrayed my trust. No, this is something much deeper. This is the kind of shatter that a girl will never recover from.

Tears begin forming in my eyes as I stare at a man who I'm starting to realize that I don't know at all, a man who I thought I was falling in love with. Is it even possible to fall in love with a stranger?

A single tear falls down my cheek and splashes against my collar bone. "You're a murderer," I whisper, the lump in my throat making it nearly impossible to breathe. "You … you killed a man. You told me you were going to put them behind bars."

"I'm sorry," he says, hesitantly taking another step. "Please stop looking at me like that, Jade. I'm still me."

I shake my head, feeling the panic continue to rise. My hand falls down over my mouth, desperately trying to mask my pain. "How can I be in love with a killer? I … I can't love you like this."

His face falls as his head drops in shame, looking down at his blood-stained hands. A heavy, broken sigh pulls from deep within him and as he speaks, it's as though every sound that comes out of his mouth is laced with pain. "Please, baby. No, don't run. I'm still me. I've been dying to hear those words on your lips but I can't have it like this. I can't have the only time you tell me you love me followed by that." He takes another step and I back up again, feeling the backs of my legs hit his bed. "Ocean please. Give me a chance, I'll explain it all just …"

He reaches for me and I flinch away. "Don't touch me," I screech. "You're just like Nic, just like the Widows. My father. The Wolves. Your father. The whole reason I happily left Breakers Flats was to give myself a new life. I can't do this again. I can't keep surrounding myself with death."

"Ocean, baby …"

Another perfectly round tear falls from my eye and joins the other rolling down my chest. "I can't do this," I tell him, feeling the last piece of my soul crumble. My hands weave into my hair and I fist my hands into it, unable to control the overwhelming emotions. "I just … I need some time to think, time to process. You took it too far. That's not what we do."

Colton finally closes the gap between us and throws his hands around me, dragging me into his chest. "Please, Ocean," he begs, holding me tightly with the hands that just took a man's life. "Just stay. We can sort it out. I swear, I'll tell you whatever you want to know. I don't want to lose you. I can't lose you. You're fucking everything to me."

I slam my hands against his chest and push hard, forcing him off me and hating the pain that ricochets off me. "Don't touch me," I cry, darting away from him and far out of his reach. "I can't. You *killed* a man, Colton. You're a murderer." I step toward the door, watching as the small fragment of hope in his eyes grows duller by the second. "I just … I can't. I'm sorry, Colton. I have to go."

With that, I step out of his room and dart for the fucking stairs, running as the tears cascade down my cheeks.

My mother hates me and now this. When it rains, it fucking pours.

I drag my arm over my already sore eyes as the loud sobs begin. I hit the bottom step and fly across the foyer, needing to be out of this house. Needing the air, and needing clarity. My shoes thump against the marble floor making my every step echo through the massive foyer but the sounds are drowned out by my cries.

I reach the door and just as I tear it open, I look back to find Colton standing at the top of the stairs watching me go with his heart in his hands, completely and utterly shattered. I've never seen him look like that and I want nothing more than to run into his arms and tell him that it's all going to be okay, but it's not. I don't know how I'll ever be okay with this. Why didn't he hand him over to the cops like he promised? Why did he have to ruin us like that?

I don't hesitate a second longer and throw myself out of the big front door and the second the cool night air hits my face, I crumble.

My knees give out from under me and I fall to the hard ground with my face dropping into my hands as I cry for everything I've lost tonight. My mother is hurting from my betrayal and now Colton is someone that I have to forget.

I always knew he was going to hurt me but I never knew it was going to be like this. I never knew it would hurt so bad.

I hear the familiar sound of the security camera turning to face me and I pick myself up off the ground, knowing that he's watching me. Always watching me.

Refusing to be the pathetic girl who can't pull herself together, I start walking down the steps, unsure where the hell I'm going or where I'll end up. All I know is that I can't be here.

I make it to the end of the long drive, not doubting for one second that Colton has painfully watched every step I've taken.

I slip through the large gates and only then do I finally pull out my phone and bring it to my ear. "Milo," I say after the third ring. "I need your help."

# CHAPTER 30

I stand in the living room of Nic's tiny apartment staring at the four Widows as Milo hovers awkwardly beside me. "Umm," he grumbles, looking at the four boys and then slicing his gaze back at me. "Are you good here?"

"Yeah," I tell him. "Go before your car gets stolen and stripped for parts."

His eyes bug out of his head. "Fuck, are you serious?"

Nic raises a brow, watching Milo through narrowed eyes, wondering just how much he knows. "Yeah, I watched you pull up and park that sweet ride right on the street. Big fucking mistake. I can guarantee that my guys are already putting in calls and working out a plan to lift it."

"Shit," Milo groans stepping toward the door as I roll my eyes knowing damn well that Nic's boys wouldn't dream of lifting Milo's Aston Martin while he's one of Nic's guests. The guys down on the street watched me step out of it. They wouldn't be that stupid.

Milo reaches for the door handle before turning back and meeting my eyes. "So … I'm assuming you don't need a ride to school tomorrow?"

I shake my head. "Nope."

"Are you…" he starts before dropping his eyes and showing just how much he's hurting. "Do you know when you're coming back?"

I press my lips into a tight line and take the two steps to the door. I pull Milo in for a tight hug and hold him close. "Thanks for driving me. I know that's not exactly what you had planned for your Sunday night," I tell him. "I'll call you tomorrow once I've had a chance to sleep on it and think a bit."

"Okay," he says, squeezing me back. "Do you want me to tell your mom where you are?"

I shake my head. "Don't bother. She would already know."

"Okay, girl," he says, glancing up over my head and spying the four boys who haven't stopped watching us, two of which I haven't spoken to in weeks. His gaze drops to mine. "I'll see you later. Call if you need anything."

"Alright, love you," I say, taking hold of the door and watching as he walks out, taking my final connection to that life with him. As he disappears down the hallway, I gently close the cheap wooden door and lean into it, resting my forehead against it and contemplating my next move.

Coming here wasn't exactly a huge priority, but it's a place I know that I can always come to, no matter what bullshit is going on between us. This place is my home, my real home.

I hear someone move from the couch and I don't dare turn around to see who it is. I'm not ready to face them yet. In a perfect world, I would have made them all suffer for a few more weeks or at least until Kai and Eli showed up on my doorstep begging for forgiveness. But being here right now in this small living room, I have no choice but to hear them out.

A hand falls to my waist and before I know it, I'm pulled away from the door and slammed against Nic's hard chest. I breathe him in, finding comfort in his familiarity. And within seconds, emotions from my day and the emptiness from walking out on Colton come up and hit me like a freight train, bringing on another round of tears. "It's okay, O. Cry it out," he murmurs. "Take all the time you need. We're not going anywhere."

The tears come on faster and realizing that the flood gates have been opened wide, he scoops me up and takes me over to the couch. I curl into him just as I've done a million times before and the boys quietly talk among themselves as I struggle to pull myself back together.

Sebastian's hand finds mine and he gives it a warm squeeze. "You're in love with him, aren't you?"

I feel Nic tense beneath me but I have absolutely nothing to hide from these guys, and fuck it, it's about time Nic realized just how serious things are between me and Colton … assuming there still is a me and Colton.

I lift my head off Nic's chest and meet Sebastian's eyes. I'd never spoken the words out loud until tonight and I hate the way that I said them, but on some level, despite the manner in which I told him, I'm glad he knows.

"Yeah," I finally say. "I am."

I feel something inside of Nic break as he holds me, maybe that last piece of hope that he's always been holding onto. I don't know what it is but I feel it in the way he holds me. I never once told him that I was in love with him, even when we were together. Sure, I told all the boys that I loved them, but there's a big difference between having love for someone and seeing them as the other half of your world. Colton is that for me and right now, I hate that I feel this way.

Sebastian gives me a sad smile. "If he's really the one for you, you'll figure out a way to move past this."

I shake my head. "I don't know if I can. He killed a man. He's a cold-blooded murderer."

"So are we," Nic grumbles, the vibrations from his chest loud against my ear.

"It's different," I tell him. "You guys have never hidden who you are. You've always been upfront with me, well … mostly. I knew you were Widows the day we met and you never allowed me to think that you were clean. I knew you had killed people and you never let me stray from that knowledge. Hell, you even protected me from it

… until you didn't," I say, recalling the night I watched Nic slice a blade across the throats of the men responsible for killing his father. "Colton hid it. He wasn't going to tell me. He had absolutely no intention of telling me. All this time, he could have said something or told me what he was … does. I thought he was a good guy."

"He is a good guy," Sebastian argues.

I shrug my shoulders. "What does that say about me? I only ever fall for toxic men who don't even flinch at the thought of taking a life."

Nic's hand rubs down my back. "It means that you're stronger than the rest. You were built to handle more than what those other bitches could. Any other woman would have run straight to the cops after witnessing what you saw me do, but you didn't. Even while hating me, you were loyal, just as you're loyal to Colton. We're the weak ones, Ocean. You're the kind of woman we need to keep us from drowning."

Eli grunts a sound of agreement but that's all I hear from him, knowing I need a few minutes to calm down before I focus on the two who have stubbornly refused to apologize over the last few weeks, claiming that they're trying to give me space.

Realizing that I'm not going to comment on his declaration, Nic pulls back and meets my eyes. "What else is going on?" he questions, narrowing his eyes at me. "It has to be more than finding out your boyfriend is just like the rest of us. It's not as though finding out someone is a killer is something you've never experienced before. There has to be something more."

My eyes drop, hating how he's still able to read me so well. "Mom overheard that I was Jude's other victim and it broke her. She's not talking to me. I betrayed her trust by keeping it from her."

"Fuck," Nic breathes, pulling me tight again. "She'll be alright. I can't exactly speak for her, but she's probably more angry at herself than at you. Just give her a moment to process it all and once you come out the other end, you'll have an even stronger bond."

"I don't know," I whisper. "She's still hurting over the Dad being a Wolf bomb I dropped the other week. It seems like every time we're in a room together, I say something that tears her apart."

"Well, luckily you don't have any more secrets to tell her."

"It's not like I've been particularly open about what I saw you do in your warehouse and what Colton did to Marco. Should I take this as turning a new leaf and start being honest?"

"Nope," he says, his lips pulling into an amused grin. "You can go right ahead and keep those little details to yourself."

"That's what I thought," I say, pulling out of his arms and drying the remaining tears off my face, feeling as though I have some level of control over myself despite the pain that continues spearing through my chest.

I'd do anything to feel Colton's lips on mine just one more time.

"So," Nic goes on. "What did you tell Milo?"

I look back at him, realizing this is his way of trying to figure out just how much Milo knows but he doesn't need to worry. Milo understands that there are things in my life that I need to keep to myself. "Nothing," I finally say. "I told him that I'd had a fight with

Colton and just needed some breathing room. He was there when Mom found out about Jude, so he already knew about that."

Nic nods, his only response a slight grunt of approval.

I slip off his lap and fold down between Nic and Sebastian on the couch, only I'm sitting on my phone and have to dig it out of my pocket. I glance down to find three unread texts from Colton and my heart instantly starts racing out of control again.

I slide my thumb over the screen, unlocking it, then opening the texts while holding my breath. Sure, I'm used to having screaming matches with Colton, and I'm more than used to putting him in his place, but this was different and I have no idea how either of us will handle it.

**Colton - Where are you?**

**Colton - Please, Jade. Just let me know that you're safe.**

**Colton - Are you with Nic?**

A throat clears from across the room and my gaze sweeps up to find Eli's guilty eyes on mine. "How long are you going to make him sweat it?" he asks cautiously, not wanting to set me off as he slowly begins his shitty way of sliding back into my life.

A sharp glare comes shooting out of me and settles on the turd who's perched on the armrest beside his equally turdy friend. "As long as I need to," I say, really trying to reign in my inner bitch who had her claws sharpened for this very moment. "But you'd know all about that, wouldn't you? It's been a while since you came round? I was expecting you to come groveling for forgiveness weeks ago."

Eli shrugs his shoulders. "What can I say? I know the way you work, Ocean. You needed time to cool down before I came to you with an apology. Sebastian and Nic forced it on you and I knew you wouldn't stand for another one of us doing that, so I've been very impatiently waiting. But surely you know how sorry I am. I hate that you're hurt and I hate that you no longer trust me. I'd do anything to fix that.

I watch him for a second longer before turning my gaze on Kai. "And what about you?" I ask, watching the way he stares at me through narrowed eyes.

His brow arches and I see the reasons that have been flying through his mind since our falling out all ready to be thrown at me headfirst. "I haven't been around to kiss your ass because I'm not fucking sorry," he says blatantly. "Look, O, I'm going to be real with you because it seems that all these other motherfuckers don't have the balls. Am I sorry that you had a shitty father? Hell yes, I am. Am I sorry that you were dealt a messed up hand and had all this awful shit happen to you? Yes. Am I sorry about the way you found out? Fuck yeah. But am I sorry that I kept the truth from you and allowed you the chance to have a real relationship with your father before he was killed? Something that none of us ever got the chance to have? No. Am I sorry helping Nic put surveillance in the house you were raped in? No."

I raise a brow, silently watching him as he continues. "There is not a damn thing that I wouldn't do to protect you and your innocence, even if it means having you hate me for it. I'm sorry that you got hurt and that the way it was dealt with made you lose trust in me, but

I'm not fucking sorry for doing the things I did that kept you safe and happy."

I keep my gaze locked on Kai and feel the emotions well up inside of me. He was brutally honest and I can't deny that what he said made me feel somewhat cherished. He said what he had to say without bullshitting his way through it like the others had. He was real with me and I appreciate that despite the way he admitted to not being sorry for half the shit he did. I understand it though and for that, I'm grateful.

I rise out of my spot beside Sebastian and Nic and cut across the small living room before dropping down onto Kai's lap and folding into his open arms. "Thank you," I whisper. "I still hate that I was left out in the dark for so many years but I understand it and I'm beginning to believe that if the tables were turned, I probably would have done the same thing for you guys."

Kai nods and presses a soft kiss to my temple which is just about all the affection that he can handle. After saying what needed to be said, he instantly starts pulling away. Kai has the emotional capacity of a brick wall and sometimes, I absolutely love that about him.

Realizing that Kai is finished with me, Eli locks his firm grip around my upper arm and starts dragging me into his lap. "Get over here and love me," he demands.

Just for the sake of it, I make him work for it, pulling away and squirming out of his grasp. I'm pretty sure that I almost kick Kairo in the balls at one stage and end up dropping like a bag of potatoes to the hard ground. Eli comes down on top of me, squishing me beneath his large frame while laughing in my ear. "Can't get away now, can you?"

I jam my fingers into his ribs, laughing as I try to free myself.

"Dude," Nic's grunt comes over the sound of our howling snorts of laughter. "She was fucking raped. Ease up."

When I say that this kid flew up off me like gravity doesn't exist …

Eli stares down at me, horrified by his actions but I shrug it off as Sebastian offers me his hand and pulls me up off the ground like I weigh nothing at all. I walk straight into Eli's arms and finally allow him the chance to feel at ease. "You know I love you," he murmurs into my hair.

"I know," I murmur, glancing up at the other guys while I speak. "But if any of you fuckers ever cross me again, there's going to be blood."

Sebastian winks while Kairo just smirks, probably thinking that he's too fucking fast for me to get to him like that, and he'd be right, but it wouldn't stop me from trying. Nic just stares, raising a curious brow. "So, does this mean you don't hate me anymore?" he questions, knowing damn well that the role he played during all this was a shitload worse than the rest of the guys.

I shrug my shoulders. "I don't hate you, Nic. I could never hate you and for the most part, I've started to move on. I don't like holding in all that anger toward you, but learning that you're the reason the DeCarlo's came down on us in the first place … well, that still hurts."

He nods, satisfied with my answer, but I know it's not the end.

Nic won't rest until everything has gone back to how it used to be. He's just that kind of guy, but like Kai, he won't offer any apologies that he doesn't mean.

Eli finally releases me and when he does, I look around at my four guys while feeling a broken piece of my soul finally come back to me. My world might be in the middle of falling apart, but with my boys back on my side, I can finally breathe a little easier.

They all watch me, waiting to see what my next move will be and being more than ready to put all the shit to bed, I let out a sigh and cross the small apartment into the kitchen. "Alright, I'm starving. What's for dinner?"

Just like that, the boys fall in around me and after pulling out all the ingredients to start cooking, Nic pauses, looking down at the counter. "Fuck this," he grumbles, putting everything back again and pulling out his phone. "I'm ordering pizza."

Sebastian sighs with relief and I can't deny that I kinda like the idea too. "So," I say, meeting the boys' stares as I pull myself up onto the counter with Nic's murmured conversation in the background, ordering all my favorite toppings. "Which one of you guys allowed Carmen Fucking Saunders to weasel her way back into Nic's bed?"

Guilty expressions stare back at me, each of them fumbling for the right thing to say and just like that, everything goes back to how it was always meant to be.

# CHAPTER 31

Hours turn into days and before I know it, it's Wednesday night and I've been taking over Nic's small apartment for nearly three days. I'm not going to lie, having this time to build up my relationship with the boys again has been nice.

I really hate being away from them for so long, but these few days have put everything into perspective for me and because of that, I've learned more about myself than I've ever learned before.

I am one hundred percent in love with Colton Carrington and the more time I spend away from him, the clearer it becomes. I've learned that the things a normal person wouldn't be okay with are things that have become far too normal in my life, and I've learned that no matter what, I will always have someone in my corner.

The past three days have been nice while also filled with all sorts of heartache. I miss my mom and not having her there at the end of the day to unload all my problems on has been hard. I've talked briefly with her and while we've technically both admitted that things were handled in a really shitty way, it's still not the same as sitting down and talking it all through. In the end, I know Mom and I will always be okay. She's my mom and no matter what, I love her just as she loves me. I'm pretty sure I could tell her that I'm going to replace my father and become the world's most feared killer and she'd still love me.

What really sucks though is not having Colton and feeling his fingers brush over my skin as he passes behind me, or having his sweet little nothings whispered in my ear, his touch, his kiss, his everything.

I hate that I miss him so damn much. He's been blowing up my phone to the point that I blocked his number. Then he started hitting me up on my Facebook messenger, then my other social media accounts, and finally, he went with a good old fashioned email that read—

*To: Oceania Munroe*
*From: Colton Carrington*
*Subject: Unblock me, Jade!*

*Stop fucking playing with me. Un-fucking-block me so I can hear your sweet voice bitching me out, then get your stubborn ass home so I can fuck you until the mattress breaks.*

*I didn't almost agree to shove a fucking dildo up my ass for you to walk away now. You know me, Jade. You've always known what I was capable of. I know the company you keep and despite how they chose to live their lives, you're okay with that. Deep down, you know you're okay with this too. You're not pissed about what I did, you're fucking furious that I didn't tell you about it.*

*I'm not a patient man, Jade. I want you home so we can talk this through and then I want to eat your pussy like a Thanksgiving turkey.*

*I know you're not angry anymore. You're just fucking stubborn and making me sweat it, but that's okay, two can play that game.*

*I'll be waiting for you, Ocean.*

I think I read over his ridiculous email twenty times before finally shoving my phone back into my pocket. He's a dumbass if he thinks I'm just going to roll over and forget about this. He killed someone. He took a life and didn't even bat an eyelash about it.

Am I okay with that? Truth be told; I don't fucking know.

Colton might be onto something. I'm okay with what Nic and the boys do. I've known for years that they're killers and it's never pushed me away, so why am I giving Colton such a hard time for the same thing? Maybe I've been holding him on some kind of pedestal, thinking he was better than that, but that's not fair. No one should be put on a pedestal as it only makes expectations that are impossible to reach.

Is that what I've been doing to Colton? He deserves better than that. He also deserves a girl who isn't going to block him every time he tries to reach out to make things right.

Shit. I fucked up.

I was an emotional wreck from dealing with Mom's hurt and instead of handling it like a normal person, I turned my back and ran.

What must he think? I kept walking away from him, too afraid to let him touch me but he would never hurt me and I know that with absolute certainty.

I let out a heavy breath and finish putting the dishes away. It's time to go home.

The bathroom door opens and I turn around to face Nic as he pulls his shirt down over his body. I meet his eyes and give him a tight smile and in an instant, he knows. "No," he says, shaking his head. "You're not leaving yet. I only just got you back."

"Nic," I sigh. "Bellevue Springs is my home now. It's where I go to school, where my mom is, my friends, it's where Colton is. I can't just sit back here and pretend that I'm not neglecting all of that, and besides, after the bullshit that went down between me and Mom, it's about time that I go back there and make it right."

"I thought you and your mom sorted things out?"

"We did," I tell him. "But it's not the same as sitting down and talking it all though. She just found out that her baby was raped and hasn't had a chance to squish me in her arms yet. I know that's got to be killing her."

"Babe," he says, walking around to the kitchen and standing right before me. "Just stay a little while longer. You can get that chick from school to email you the work you missed and I don't know … Facetime with your mom or something. Just don't go yet. It's already halfway through the week. You might as well stay until the weekend and then I'll drive you back."

"Nic … no. I need to go home."

Nic steps into me, forcing me back against the counter. He braces his hands on either side, caging me in with his body. "Babe, come on. I just got you back."

I look up and meet his eyes, knowing that I have to break his heart, only he doesn't give me a chance when he takes my waist and lifts me onto the counter. He steps in between my legs and drops his hands to my thighs. "Haven't things been nice the last few days? It's been like old times, like the old you and me before everything got fucked up."

"I know," I whisper. "It's been nice, but it's not the same …"

"Just … wait. Wait here for two seconds."

Nic takes off like a bat out of hell and I hear him fumbling around in his room, digging through drawers. He comes back less than thirty seconds later with a strange look on his face; a weird mix between nervous, excited, and shit-scared.

"What's going on?" I question, studying him through a narrowed gaze as he makes his way back into the kitchen. "What did you get?"

"Listen," he says, coming right back to where he was before. "You're not going to like this but I need you to hear me out, okay? Just wait until I've said what I have to say before even thinking about cutting me off."

"Nic," I warn, not liking where this is going. "What's going on?"

He clenches his jaw and all the blood rushes out of his face as he takes my hand out of my lap. He flips it over until he's looking down at my palm and then drops a silver ring into it.

My stomach clenches as my eyes bug out of my head. I look up at Nic, terrified. "What is this?" I demand, dropping my gaze back to the offending item in my hand, wondering just how far I could throw this fucking thing. "Nic, fucking speak now. What the hell is in my hand right now?"

He looks sick as he watches me. "You said that you'd hear me out."

"I didn't agree to shit," I remind him, holding the ring between my fingers and raising it to his eye level. "Now start explaining what the fuck this is."

Nic takes a shaky breath and places his hands on my thighs before finding his balls. "I think we should get married."

"WHAT THE ACTUAL FUCK, DOMINIC? On what fucking planet is that a good idea?"

"You're my girl, O. You've always been my girl and you've been denying us for so damn long now, but you know it in your heart. You know we're going to end up together so why are we bothering with all this in between bullshit? Let's just skip ahead to the finish line."

I bark out a sharp laugh because surely, this must be some twisted joke. I bet the guys are hiding out in the apartment with a hidden camera, ready to tell me that I'm being pranked. There's literally no other logical explanation for this other than Nic has finally gone insane.

"Okay, sure. If skipping ahead to the finish line is what you really want, then let's go ahead and skip to the finish line of this conversation." I slam the silver ring down on the counter beside me, feeling more annoyed than I have the right to feel. Who does he think he is throwing this shit in my face? "You and I are not happening. I'm not about to marry you and I'm not about to let you talk me into it. I'm seventeen. This is insane. I swore to you that I was never going to be with you after you fucked Carmen Saunders on this very counter. You broke my heart, Nic and that was the biggest mistake you ever made because now I've gone and given mine to someone else."

"That's bullshit," he roars, grabbing the ring and shoving it back in my hand, never being one to handle being told no. "How can you deny this? You're not in love with that rich prick. You just think you are because he can offer you a fucking glamorous lifestyle. You're acting like a fucking barbie bitch. You need to remember who you are and where you belong."

My hand slaps out across his face, the sound of the sharp sting echoing through his small apartment. I push him back and jump down from the counter, glaring up at him with venom in my eyes. "I know exactly who the fuck I am and after all this time, I thought that you'd have figured it out as well. I'm not your little whore that you can mold into the perfect gang wife and I'm never going to be that person. Sure, a year ago the thought of being with you was thrilling, dangerous, and exciting, but it's not anymore. I've moved on. I know my worth and it's not visiting some dead beat husband in prison every second week, finding some other women's underwear under my bed, or sitting by your bedside after being shot for the hundredth time. I'm not doing that to myself. I deserve better. I deserve a guy who looks at me as though I'm all that exists in his world, a guy who values me and makes me his priority, and a guy who's not afraid to sit the fuck down and let me be the ruler of my own damn life."

"What?" he scoffs. "And you think Carrington is that guy?"

"I fucking know he is," I spit. "He's never once hurt me, he's never once dragged me down three flights of stairs out of pure jealousy. He's stood back and let me make my own fucking mistakes and then stood by my side, helping build me back up once I realized where I went wrong. He doesn't hold me back, telling me I belong somewhere I don't. He doesn't try to guilt me into loving him, and he sure as hell doesn't keep me from trying to better myself."

"You don't know what the fuck you're talking about. I've been there for you since day one."

"No, Nic. You've lied to me since day one. You've kept secrets, made me believe what you've fabricated me to believe. That's not a healthy relationship. You and me together are toxic and I won't do that to myself, not anymore. I'm sorry, Nic, but there's no way in hell that I would ever marry you, not after everything that's gone down between us."

I turn on my heel and stalk back to his bedroom, taking his stupid little ring with me. He comes tearing down the hall after me. "Don't fucking walk away from me," he yells. "We're not done with this conversation."

"Ha," I scoff. "This conversation was done before it even started. There's nothing more to say. Surely you had to have known what my answer was going to be? How could you ever think that I'd want that? How many times have I told you that I wanted out of Breakers Flats? How many times have I told you that I wanted more for myself?

College? A home of my own? A proper life where I don't have to be worried about drive-by shootings and gang violence?"

"What do you want from me?" he demands. "I'm not leaving the Widows for you. That's not an option."

"Fuck, Nic. Did I say that I wanted you to leave the Widows? When, over the last six months have I ever given you the impression that I wanted more from you than just friendship? I don't want to be with you. I don't give a shit that you're the leader of the fucking Widows because it doesn't affect my life. It has nothing to do with who I am or where I want to go. And for the record, why would I want to be with someone who wouldn't even consider leaving that life for me? The Widows are your priority, not me, and that says it all."

I walk around the side of his bed and tear open his bedside drawer before dropping the ring into it and slamming it closed harder than it's ever been slammed in its life, only as the little table rocks from the force something detaches from the back and I hear the familiar sound of a blade clattering against the cheap wooden floorboards.

My brows furrow as Nic goes impossibly still.

What the fuck was that?

Anger courses through my body and I practically throw his bedside table out of the way and what stares back at me has my stomach sinking with dread.

An old dagger with intricate carvings, the exact same one that not eight months ago was protruding from my father's chest, only to then be stabbed through the back of Charles Carrington, ending both of their lives.

I suck in a sharp gasp, my body instantly shaking with fear as I find it impossible to look away from the blade that has wreaked so much havoc in my life.

Nic takes a step and I instantly back up.

"Ocean," he says, his voice low with a warning, coaxing me not to run. "Let me explain."

I look up at him, meeting the guilty expression on his face. "What the fuck is that?" I demand, my voice shaking as I feel a kind of terror that I've never experienced before. "Why do you have that knife?"

He clenches his jaw and swallows hard, looking as though he's working extra fucking hard to figure out what the hell he's about to say to me.

"FUCKING ANSWER ME, DOMINIC. WHY THE FUCK DO YOU HAVE THAT?"

Nic raises both his hands, similar to the way Colton had done on Sunday night, only there's something so much different here, something darker. I trusted that Colton wouldn't hurt me, trusted that he was only showing me that he wanted to explain himself, but the way Nic looks at me with his hands raised is more like he's trying to convince himself of the same damn thing.

I back up another step, putting myself closer to the door and further away from Nic. "Ocean," he starts. "Just listen to me. I had no choice …"

"No choice? Had no choice about what? How did you get that knife? It was locked in Colton's safe."

Nic clenches his jaw again. "You have to understand. I couldn't let him have it."

Tears begin to well in my eyes. "You did it, didn't you? You killed my father and then came to me, standing in my fucking home and holding me while I sobbed, vowing that you'd find whoever did it."

Nic doesn't respond, just stares at me with that same guilt building in his eyes.

The tears fall as I stand in his bedroom doorway, feeling as though I'm staring at a complete stranger. My hands shake and my chest rises with short rapid breaths, struggling to feel anything. Numbness shoots through me to the point of pain and I want nothing more than to run out the fucking door and never look back but I know that if I don't stay and find the answers I need, I'll never get them. "Answer me, Nic. Tell me it wasn't you," I cry. "Tell me that you didn't come into my home and stab my father through the chest and then leave him there to die."

His jaw clenches and then finally he dips his head. "I'm so fucking sorry," he murmurs, his voice filled with self-hate and guilt. "You have to believe me that I didn't want to do it. I had no choice. It was either me or Kian and I know my father would have made him suffer. He would have taken pleasure in killing your father."

I shake my head. "No. Kian promised me that the Black Widows had nothing to do with killing my dad. He ... he told me—"

"He lied."

"No ... I."

Nic drops down to the edge of his bed and looks up at me with eyes so filled with pain and regret. "It was just after your father had officially sold you to Carrington. Even though your father thought the transaction was done, Carrington wasn't. He paid my father to take Lou's life. Dad was testing me, seeing if I had it in me to get the job done. I had to. It was either him or me so I did it."

I shake my head, staring at him in disgust. "I hate you," I whisper, feeling the tears rushing down my face and dropping onto my borrowed shirt. I take a step back, more than ready to leave when his voice has me pulling up and looking back at him.

"Stop, Ocean. There's more." His head falls and he looks at the ground. "The morning after you were attacked by Carter, I was at your place."

I nod. "You sat with me through the night."

He swallows hard. "I ran into Charles that night and he told me to stay away from you. He knew that I was the one who had taken out his job and didn't want it coming back to him. He saw me as a loose end and threatened to hurt you if I didn't comply, so I did what any other man would have done in my situation and fucking killed him too, but don't be fooled, I made that one hurt."

I swallow past the lump in my throat and just as he stands and steps toward me, ready to start pleading his case, my phone rings in my jeans pocket. Desperately needing to hold Nic back, I hastily pull the phone out and hit accept on the private number then bring it to my ear.

"What?" I breathe, unable to take my eyes off Nic.

"Ocean," Colton's panicked tone comes rushing through the phone. "It's Milo. He's been hurt. You need to come home."

# CHAPTER 32

I race through the door of Bellevue Springs Private hospital in a panic, unsure of where I'm even going but just knowing that I have to get to him.

"Jade," I hear Colton's panicked tone call through the Emergency Room. My head whips toward him and I race into his open arms. "Shhhh, baby," he soothes. "Don't cry. He's going to be alright."

I squish my face into his chest and wipe my eyes across his shirt, watching as it comes back wet. I didn't even know I was still crying.

I ran out the door of Nic's apartment with him racing after me. The tears streamed down my face and haven't stopped, even now. Perhaps they never will. I didn't realize it was possible to cry this much, but then, I've never quite felt pain like this.

Dominic Garcia killed my father.

He murdered the man who used to kiss my knees when I fell off my bike.

He murdered the man who used to yell at me for taking too long in the shower.

He murdered the man who held me when my heart broke for the very first time.

Yes, my father wasn't a great man. He was a stone-cold killer for the West Side Wolves, but he was still the man who raised and loved me. He was my daddy. He was the first man I ever loved. Did he deserve to die? Probably. But did he deserve to die by Nic's hand? No. Not in a million fucking years.

How could Nic do that to me? He knew how much I loved my father. He knew how I looked up to him and saw him as the one man who was always going to be there for me through thick and thin. Nic stole that happiness from me. He stole my father's life and then had the nerve to stand over me as I sobbed into his chest, rubbing his palm up and down my back and promising me that he was going to make it right.

Dominic Garcia is a liar and a murderer and from now on, I am done.

The question is; do the boys know about this? They already proved that they're capable of lying to me without hesitation, but did they lie about this too? Did they also make empty promises about finding my father's killers and ending his life or do they not know?

No, I refuse to believe it. They wouldn't do that to me.

"Hey," Colton says, taking my shoulders and pulling me back to see my face, looking relieved that I'm even allowing him to touch me after the last time he saw me. "What's going on? Are you okay?"

I wipe my eyes again, feeling like an absolute wreck. I shake my head and as I meet his eyes, everything inside of me crumbles. How am I supposed to tell him that Nic is the reason his father is dead?

I just … I can't. At least not right this very minute. I'm here for Milo and after I've made sure that he's alright, then Colton and I can talk. We have a lot to discuss. I've made the mistake of being loyal to Nic once before when I didn't tell Colton about the part that Nic played in the DeCarlos attack—but that loyalty is gone. I won't be holding back this time. I need to right these wrongs.

I take hold of his hand and lace my fingers through his. "Just … no. I'm not but we can talk about it later," I say over the lump in my throat. "How's Milo? What happened to him?"

Colton watches me for a long moment, trying to figure out if he's going to push the topic when finally giving in and trusting my judgment. "We don't really know yet," he murmurs, making me realize that we're standing in a room full of our friends and Milo's family. "Spencer went by his place and found him out back. He was beaten and barely breathing."

"By who?" I demand, searching his eyes for some kind of answers.

"I don't know," he says, anger flashing in his hazel eyes, telling me just how much he's come to care for Milo over the last few months. "He's still in surgery. He had a few broken bones that needed to be set and a collapsed lung. We're hoping that once he comes out of this, he'll be able to tell us who did it and if it was random or a planned attack."

"Planned attack?" I question. "Who would do that to him? Milo is—" I cut myself off, knowing exactly what kind of person would attack Milo. He was targeted because he's gay, because he has the strength to love who he wants to love.

Colton meets my eyes, understanding exactly what it is that I've just worked out, and nods, silently telling me that whoever did this will have hell coming his way. "Come on," he tells me, pulling on my hand and leading me toward a row of chairs.

Colton drops down between Charlie and Spencer and he pulls me into his lap. I curl into him and meet Spencer's eyes. He looks completely broken and I find myself reaching out to him. "How long has he been in surgery?"

Spencer shakes his head and lights up the screen on his phone, looking at the time. "I ... I don't know," he says, appearing too lost to try and work it out.

"Two hours," Charlie murmurs from Colton's other side. "At least, just coming up to it. Google tells me it could take anywhere up to six hours but add all his other injuries and he could be in there for a while."

I let out a heavy sigh, more than prepared to sit here for as long as it takes.

The room falls into silence, everyone caught inside their own thoughts. Colton doesn't move an inch, always keeping me in his arms as I silently cry while begging for my friend to be alright.

The only reason Milo was so scared to come out to the world was because of this very reason. He was terrified of what it would mean for him, terrified of the horrendous people who would want to hurt him, terrified of the rejection he'd get from his family and friends.

It's a feeling no one would ever understand unless you've walked a mile in his shoes. I can't even imagine the fear of being who you are, fearing falling in love with someone, and being judged because that person has the same body parts as you.

Don't we live in the twenty-first century? Why is homophobia still a thing? How can people still be so cruel?

The minutes turn into hours and then finally an exhausted doctor comes striding through the doors. "Rinaldi," he calls, glancing around the massive room.

We all sit up straighter, watching with wide eyes as Milo's parents rise from their chairs and go to meet with the doctor. Their conversation is hushed for privacy but I can read the relief all over Milo's mother's face.

The doctor squeezes her shoulder and with a warm smile, walks away. I watch as Milo's parents turn to each other and fold themselves into one another's arms, their relief the loudest silence in the room.

They soon pull away from each other and make their way over to our small group. We all stand, waiting to hear exactly what they have to say.

Milo's father gives us all a strained smile. "Milo is doing okay," he finally says, glancing around to each of us. "The doctor says that he had some extensive injuries and needs to remain in the ICU for a few hours for observation. His surgery went well and they're expecting a full recovery, however it will be a long road. He is just coming off the anesthesia so he'll be sleeping for another few hours."

Milo's mother takes over. "We're going to go and sit with him while he wakes. You're all welcome to stay and wait or you can go home and come back later."

"We'll stay," Spencer announces. "Can you let him know that we're here once he wakes?"

Mrs. Rinaldi reaches out and squeezes his shoulder. "Of course, sweet boy," she says. "I know he's really going to appreciate that you all stayed, so thank you for that."

All three of the boys nod and with that, Milo's parents disappear through the big double doors of the hospital, leaving us all to settle back into our seats and wait the long agonizing hours before we finally get to check on him.

The exhaustion of my wild emotions has me falling into a fitful sleep on Colton's shoulder, which is only possible due to the safety net he gives me with his arms wrapped tightly around me.

I'm woken three hours later to Colton's soft murmuring, telling me that it's time to go and see Milo. I peel myself off his shoulder, feeling as though I could still sleep for another ten hours. I've never felt so emotionally drained like this, but right now, there are more important things that I need to do.

I climb off Colton's lap and he gets up behind me, slipping his hand back into mine as the four of us start making our way to the big double doors his parents had only disappeared through a few hours ago.

We walk down the hallway, studying the numbers on the door until Spencer stops in front of room 482. He steps into it and lightly raps on the door before pushing it open and peeking inside the room, either checking that this is the right room and if it is, that he's good for visitors.

After a moment that seems to last forever, Spencer pushes the door wider and we all trail in behind him. The room is filled with clinical light and has that clean hospital smell that reminds me of death, but I put it to the back of my mind the second I lay my eyes on my best friend.

He looks like death.

I've never seen Milo so down.

He gives us all a small smile that doesn't hit his eyes and as we finish pouring into the room, his parents walk out, giving us space to check on our friend.

Spencer awkwardly hovers by his side, staring over his new boyfriend in horror while Charlie hovers in the back, not as close as the rest of us. Colton stands by my side as I walk right up to Milo and look over his injuries.

His eye is black and nearly swollen shut while his usually beautiful face is covered in dark bruising of the deepest blues and blacks. His arm is in a cast and his neck scraped. The rest of his body is covered with blankets but I don't doubt that it's just as bad under there.

I gently lift his hand into mine, fighting back the tears. "Who did this?" I whisper, not sure if he can handle anything louder.

He groans at the slight movement in his hand but doesn't try to pull away from my touch. "I …" he starts then gently shakes his head. "I don't know, but they called me a fag."

Everything inside of me shatters as he confirms exactly what we thought it was. Colton moves in a little closer to my side. "We're going to catch the bastard," he promises. "He won't get away with it."

"Two," he grumbles. "Two guys. They made jokes about double-teaming me."

Spencer growls, curling his hands into fists before dropping down to his knees beside Milo's bed to be as close as physically possible. "I'm going to fucking kill them," he declares, looking right into Milo's eyes.

Milo nods but the movement has him cringing in pain. "Don't try to move," I say, all but diving on him to get him to lay still. "It'll get better soon. How are you feeling? Do you need more pain meds?"

"I'm fine," he grunts, his usual chirpiness a thing of the past. He looks to Colton and then to Charlie. "There's security footage of that section of the property. My parents haven't thought of it yet, but you could beat them to it before they find it and discover the reason why I was attacked."

Charlie nods and quickly glances at Colton, knowing he'd be able to somehow get access to those tapes. "We'll handle it."

With that, the boys start to leave but Milo stops them as he looks up at Spencer. "You should go with them."

"What? No. I'm staying right here."

Milo cringes as he shakes his head. "Go," he insists. "You're not going to be able to think until this is handled. Go find the fuckers who did this, settle the score, and then come back to me. I'll be fine with Ocean until then. They weren't wearing anything to cover their faces so you should find them pretty fucking fast."

Spencer glances at me and it's almost like a warning that if I was to even leave this room while he's not here that I'll be suffering the same consequences as the fuckers who hurt him in the first place. "I swear," I tell him. "I won't leave this room. Not even to pee."

Spencer glances back at Milo with a heavy sigh. "If anything happens, if you need anything…"

"I know," Milo groans. "I'll call. Just go and handle this."

Spencer glances back at us and very quickly drops down to Milo and brushes the softest kiss over his lips before walking out the door with Charlie and Colton behind him.

"Now, you," Milo says, forcing my attention right back to him. "Get that fucking chair and drag it over here. You've been gone for three days and I want to know everything that's been going on."

I do as I'm told and as I'm dragging the chair over, I meet his eyes. "Everything?" I question. "Because I'm not sure that you can handle everything at the moment."

"Shit," he says. "Is it that bad?"

"Fucking worse than bad."

"How is it that those fucking idiots keep fucking everything up? What the fuck did they do this time?"

"Only one of them," I warn him with a heavy sigh, feeling the raw emotions of the last twenty-four hours creeping up on me. I settle into the chair beside his bed and prepare to tell him every last thing that has gone down over the past day. "You'll never guess what fucking moron decided it'd be a good idea to propose."

His one good eye goes wide and just like that, we fall into conversation without a single detail being spared until the boys finally return, each of them with bruised and bloodied knuckles, promising that justice has been served.

# CHAPTER 33

I walk out of Milo's hospital room with Colton, feeling a million times better now knowing that Milo is going to be alright. He has a long recovery ahead of him, but the second the boys returned with the news that his attackers were left hardly breathing, his spirits brightened right up.

He hadn't quite hit the usual level of Milo-ness that he generally functions at, but by the end of our visit, I could see him slowly beginning to return. Plus, the nurse came in and hit him with some pretty strong drugs so that could definitely have something to do with it.

Milo is generally a happy guy with high spirits so long as he holds onto that and doesn't let this attack bring him down, he should be able to heal a lot quicker. There's nothing better for a healing body than a healthy mind and with me and the boys at his side, he's going to be alright.

Though, the fact that he told me where to find his porn stash, glitter, and sex toys, and then gave me the password for his computer to wipe his browsing history says a lot. His dramatic flair was back and that told me everything I needed to know. Milo is going to be back to bugging me as often as he can in no time.

We stayed in his room all through the night and it wasn't until the early hours of this morning that the nurses finally got sick of us and kicked us out, insisting that Milo needed to rest—despite his objections. But she was right, the door hadn't even closed behind us before Milo passed out.

Colton and I step into the elevator to take us down to the parking garage and as the doors lock us into the confined space together, our issues suddenly become very loud.

Colton hits the button to send us down and as the elevator starts moving, he crowds me into the wall, blocking me with his hands on either side, keeping me trapped. "I missed you," he murmurs, raising his chin and brushing his lips over mine. "You walked out on me."

I nod. "You lied to me," I whisper. "You let me believe that Marco was going behind bars just like his brothers."

"To be fair," he says. "When I said that, I thought that was what was going to happen. It wasn't until Sunday afternoon that I heard he was back in town. I couldn't miss the opportunity to make it right. He killed Maryne, I couldn't just let it go."

I nod again and press my hand against his chest, feeling the rapid beat of his heart beneath his shirt. "I got your email."

"I know," he grumbles with a cocky smirk. "I got a notification that it was read only thirty seconds after hitting send. You never replied though."

"You didn't deserve a reply."

His eyes heat, realizing that I'm just being stubborn and loving that we're able to talk about this without it turning into something so much more. "You're not scared of me," he comments, referring to the way I backed away from him in his bedroom.

I take his hand and curl it into a fist, looking down at his bruised knuckles. I press my lips to them, loving that he'd go to such lengths for Milo while also hating that he's hurt. "You were right," I tell him. "I'm not afraid of you or what you did. I've been around the Widows for far too long that I feel somewhat immune to that darkness. I guess it just came as a shock that you had that in you. I'd filed you away as one of the good guys and then you made me go and undo all my paperwork."

"I am still a good guy," he insists. "I don't kill for sport."

"I know," I whisper as we hit the bottom ground and hear the familiar ding of the elevator before the doors slide open.

Colton steps back from me, keeping his eyes on mine as he tugs me away from the elevator wall. Together we walk out of the elevator and I can't help but rub my thumb over his sore knuckles. "Tell me that you're coming home with me," he questions, stopping in the middle of the nearly deserted parking lot and meeting my eyes.

"I …" I let out a breath, not having thought about it since before Nic's ridiculous proposal. "I'm not entirely sure yet," I tell him with all honesty. "I can't get past this feeling that you're just like the rest of the guys I know. You kept this part of yourself hidden from me. Especially after everything we went through with Jude in the wine cellar. If you were going to come clean about it, that would have been the time."

"I know," he says, dropping his forehead to mine. "I should have told you when we were sitting in the shower after you nearly took out Jude. I've thought about that moment nearly every fucking day but it's not something that you just tell someone."

"I would have been able to handle it."

"I know that now," he tells me, squeezing my hands. "Just please, Ocean. Come home with me. We can work this out. I don't want to lose you over this."

My heart breaks as I meet his eyes, seeing the raw desperation within him. "I … I feel like I need to think about this for a minute. Too much has happened. I can't even think clearly right now. After everything that just went down with Nic. I just need—"

Colton cuts me off as he drops to his knees before me. "I'm so fucking in love with you, Jade. Please, baby, come home with me so we can sort this out. I need you in my life, but I'll get it if you want to leave. I won't hold it against you, but it'll fucking hurt."

I look down at him on his knees, begging me to stay and the raw emotions begin to rise within me until they're completely overwhelming me. A lump forms in my throat and I step into him, desperately needing to be closer. "You love me?" I whisper, feeling my voice break as he says the very words I've wondered about since the day he sat at my mother's dinner table and admitted that he didn't love me … yet.

"I do," he says, the desperation shining brightly in his eyes. "I love you so fucking much that it hurts. I've hated being away from you these last few days. I need you in my life. I don't know how you did it but you weaseled your way in and now I can't fucking breathe without you."

I fight the tears that well in my eyes as I curl my hand around the back of his neck. "I love you too," I whisper, meeting his eyes and letting him see just how much I mean it.

A smile tears across his face. "I know," he says with the slightest amusement. "You blurted it out on Sunday while you were screaming at me."

"Shut up," I laugh just moments before he grabs me and brings my lips down to his.

Fucking home.

I kiss him deeply, feeling all the hurt from the last few days finally dissolve into nothing and allowing my aching chest to finally begin mending.

His fingers lace through mine and I pull him up, never wanting to see my man begging on his knees again. As he stands, his arm twines around my waist and he pulls me off my feet, refusing to break our kiss.

"Put her down," comes a pissed off growl from across the parking lot.

My back stiffens, recognizing that voice from anywhere.

Colton's hands tighten on my waist and he pulls away from me, lowering me to the ground as his head snaps around to find the threat.

Nic stands across the lot and I find him leaning up against Colton's Veneno with his finger through the finger grip of his gun, spinning it in circles like a fucking idiot. Did nobody teach this guy gun safety? If he wants to accidentally shoot his balls off then that's one sure way to make it happen.

"What are you doing here?" I demand, looking at the man who killed my father in distaste. Colton instantly picks up on my tone and I'm sure that he's reminded of the state I was in when I first arrived at the hospital and is currently putting the puzzle pieces together. Sensing my unease, Colton discreetly puts himself in front of me.

"You and I haven't finished our conversation."

"Yeah," I scoff. "We're more than finished. In fact, I'm pretty certain that there won't be a damn thing left for us to ever discuss."

Nic's face drops and anger flashes in his eyes. "Don't fucking say shit that you don't mean. You're a lot of things, O, but you're not a fucking liar."

"Sorry," I laugh. "I must have learned that trait from you."

His eyes narrow, pushing off Colton's car and striding toward us. Colton moves with him, always keeping himself between me and Nic's gun, and from the look on Nic's face, he's more than aware of what's going on.

He stops a few feet from us and glares at Colton. "Do you mind fucking off now? I'm trying to have a conversation with my girl."

"You see, that's just the thing. She's *my* girl and judging from the way she's shrinking away from you, she doesn't want a damn thing to do with you."

The gun spins around his finger again, making me more nervous than I should ever have to be around a man who claims to love me. For fuck's sake, it was less than twelve hours ago that he was trying to convince me to marry him, and now he shows up here with a fucking gun?

Where are the boys? They should have a leash on their fearless leader.

"Get out of here, Nic," I say, continuing on from Colton's statement, not denying it in the least. "I'll talk to you when you're not trying to intimidate me with your fucking gun."

"What? This?" he laughs, holding up the gun and making a show of studying the barrel then looking over the revolver and making a point to show that it's fully loaded. "This ain't for you, baby."

I read him like a fucking book and reach for Colton, pulling him back a step before putting myself in front of him. Nic might be a fucking cold murderer, but he'd never risk shooting Colton with me standing so damn close … at least, I think. Apparently, I really don't know him half as well as I thought I did. Hell, he admitted himself that he killed Charles so he wouldn't share his little secret. What's to stop him from doing the same to me? What's he going to do if he thinks that I've told Colton? I can't have these two at war, though if Colton knew everything that Nic had done, he'd have already been dead.

Colton takes my waist and leans into me. "You have two fucking seconds to get your sweet ass behind me before I put you there."

"Not a fucking chance, Carrington," I tell him. "Now shut the fuck up and let me handle my business."

Colton groans and I feel the rumble from his chest vibrate against my back, but he knows better than to try to change my mind. Besides, if he thought there was any way in hell that Nic would ever try to shoot me, I'd already be out of here. Clearly, he doesn't know what I know, otherwise this night would have turned out very differently. I won't be holding back though. If Nic wants to go there, then fuck it, we'll go there, and I won't just air a bit of his dirty laundry, I'll tip out the whole fucking basket and watch it scatter all over the floor.

All this time I thought Kian was the bad one. It turns out that Nic is just as bad. I guess the saying, like father like son, has never been so true. The apple really doesn't fall far from the tree. Charles and Colton are proof of that. I just hope that Colton fell a little further than what Nic did.

No wonder Kian was so willing to have Nic as his replacement. He molded him just the way he wanted. He's a manipulator, a murderer, and my biggest mistake.

I keep my gaze locked on Nic as he spins the chamber, making me sick with that familiar clicking. Nic used to do it all the time. It was like some kind of sick habit. Some people drum their fingernails against tables, others like to whistle, Nic plays with guns. In hindsight, I should have picked up on the signs.

"Nic," I say in a calming tone, trying to get this situation under control. "What are you doing here?"

"I'm going to need you to get in my car. You're coming home with me and we're sorting this shit out once and for all."

Colton scoffs under his breath as I raise a brow, knowing damn well that is never going to happen, not after he showed his fucking crazy and then went ahead and proved that he could never be trusted again. Hell, at this point, if I were to go anywhere with him, I'd probably be gagged and bound before someone found me lying in a ditch.

"You know that's not going to happen," I tell him, wondering if maybe Kian accidentally dropped him on the head as a baby because there's no way in hell that this shit is normal.

Nic takes a step toward us, lifting his lips into a wicked smirk. "I thought that's what you were going to say."

If Colton wasn't behind me, I'd be backing up right now but his presence makes me braver which in all honestly is pretty fucking stupid. Here's an idea, let's play a game of provoking the crazy man with a gun.

"Do the boys know you're here?"

"I'm their fucking leader. They don't need to know shit about where I am."

Colton's hand tightens on my waist, preparing to pull me out of the way if need be. My hand hovers over his, needing his touch more than anything, needing his comfort and support. "Why don't you give them a call? Let them know what you're doing right now."

Nic laughs. "Ahh, baby. You know that ain't ever going to happen."

"Nic," I say, a little more forceful. "This is ridiculous. Put your fucking gun away and go home. No matter what you say or do, I'm not leaving with you, not after what you did. I'm with Colton and he's taking me home so I can sort shit out with my mom. You need to forget about me, Nic. I'm not coming back."

"No," he says, shaking his head, the hurt blazing out of his eyes. "I'm not giving up on this. You belong with us. You belong back home, not with this rich prick."

"Listen to yourself. You fucking proposed to me after I told you that I was in love with another man," I cry, listening as Colton grunts in surprise from behind me, his answering scoff more than enough response to gather his thoughts on the topic. "You don't love me, Nic. You just don't want anyone else to have me. Can't you see how wrong that is? You're fucking sick. You need help, like professional help."

He shakes his head. "You don't know what the fuck you're talking about."

Colton steps out from behind me, having heard more than enough. "Give it up, man. She's done. She told you to fucking leave now go before—"

"Before what?" Nic demands, throwing his arm up and pointing the barrel of his gun right between Colton's eyes.

A loud gasp comes tearing out of me and I throw myself in front of Colton as Nic rushes forward, knowing that one tiny little word from Colton's mouth right now would have him buried ten feet under. Killing a guy like Colton isn't something that's going to get swept under a rug, especially if I have something to do with it. "Shoot him and I swear to you Nic, you will never see me again and that's a fucking promise."

Nic tightens his jaw. "Step out of the fucking way, Oceania."

"Nic," I spit. "Put your fucking gun down right the fuck now."

"You and I both know where your loyalties lie. Step aside so I can end this."

I laugh, pressing my back against Colton's chest. "You know, that's funny. Had you said that to me yesterday, I would have questioned myself, but after finding out what you did, you're right, I now know exactly where my loyalties lie."

"What the fuck is that supposed to mean?"

I nudge myself back against Colton while keeping my eyes locked on Nic, proving once and for all that there's no going back. Knowing that once these words come out of my mouth, that's it for me and Nic. He will never trust me again and after this, I'll be a loose end that needs to be sorted out. I just hope my boys will still have my back even though I no longer have their leader's.

"You know what I found last night," I say to Colton, keeping my gaze trained heavily on Nic.

His eyes widen just a fraction, realizing just how damn serious I am. "Don't do it," he warns me, stepping forward and pressing the gun right against my temple, testing me.

"What did you find?" Colton questions, his voice low and careful.

I stare into Nic's eyes, watching as the betrayal registers in his mind and I play the most dangerous game I'll ever play in my life; I call his bluff. "I found a silver dagger, the exact one from your safe in your office, strapped to the back of his bedside table like a trophy because Nic killed my father ... and then he killed yours."

Colton's hand flinches on my waist but with Nic's gun pressing against my temple and my betrayal thick in the air, he doesn't dare make a move despite wanting nothing more than to kill him with his bare fucking hands.

Nic leans into me and I feel his lips against my skin as my heart races with fear, silently begging for him to spare me. He pauses and I feel his breath rush past my ear before his deadly whisper finally hits me. "You're fucking dead to me, Oceania Munroe. You better watch your back because I will not forget this."

His gun flinches at my temple and my world freezes but not a second later, the gun is gone and Nic's back is to me, walking out of my life for the very last time.

# CHAPTER 34

On the drive back to the Carrington mansion, we sit in silence, both of us completely lost in our thoughts as our hands rest on my thigh, linked just as they were always supposed to be.

My hands shake and I'm thankful that Colton doesn't mention it despite the fact that I know he feels it. He always feels it. He's so in tune with my body, it's insane. Instead, he just squeezes my hand, letting me know that he's here and giving me everything I need.

My mind spins as I try to come to terms with what the fuck just happened.

It's really over between me and Nic and not just the romantic stuff but the whole relationship. My crew no longer exists. It's just me with a few guy friends who may or may not have my back from time to time. I wonder what they will say when they find out what's been going down.

They'd want to take my side but their vow to the Widows prevents that and I don't want to see any of them getting hurt from turning their back on Nic.

I still can't believe he did it. I haven't really had a chance to process everything since first finding out. It's been one thing after another but here in the silence of Colton's Veneno, it's all beginning to sink in.

Nic hates me and considers me a traitor now. I honestly don't know how to feel about that. For so long, Nic and the boys were all I knew. Had I still been living in Breakers Flats and didn't have the family of friends that I have now, I would have crumbled. That news would have broken me. I don't know how I would have gone on, but as I turn to look at Colton, I realize that there's still something that I need to come clean about—even if telling him this might just see him walk away too.

"Are you okay?" he questions, quickly glancing at me as he feels my stare on his stoic face.

I let out a soft breath and drop my eyes to our hands, unable to meet his hazel eyes. "I fucked up," I whisper, feeling the words struggle to come out.

"I know," he says, giving my hands a gentle squeeze. "We both did. I shouldn't have hidden that part of my life from you. I don't want secrets between us, but we're moving past it. You'll see, it was a learning curve. We'll come out the other end stronger. Unbreakable."

"No," I say, softly shaking my head. "That's not what I'm talking about, but you're right. There shouldn't be any secrets between us but I've been keeping one from you and it's been making me sick."

His brows dip and he cuts his sharp gaze away from the road for just a second, just enough time to take in the nerves radiating out of me. "What's going on, Jade?"

Fear rattles me like never before. It's one thing risking Nic walking away from me, but to lose Colton? I couldn't handle that. "Please don't hate me."

"Babe, you're really starting to make me worry."

I suck in a deep breath, mentally preparing myself for the worst while knowing that for us to truly move forward, we need to do so with a clean slate. "You know the cameras that Nic had Kairo install in your house?"

I pause and watch as he swallows hard, his Adam's apple bobbing up and down. "What about them?"

Shame takes over me as I realize just how badly I fucked up. I didn't come clean to Colton about this because I was loyal to Nic. I always had his back despite the many wrongs he'd made against me, but I should have told Colton about this. I should have told him the full story instead of the many half-truths that came out of my mouth.

Had I told him, maybe Colton would have taken the fight to Nic, and maybe I would have saved him from taking Marco's life despite how much the bastard deserved it. Maybe Colton would have still killed him anyway. After all, Marco wasn't told to terrorize the staff and he sure as hell wasn't asked to shove his gun under Maryne's chin and pull the trigger.

"Do you remember the day I went to Nic's place to clear the air, the day I found out about the cameras?"

"Yes."

"There was more to the story. More that I didn't come clean to you about when I should have."

"What are you talking about, Jade?" he questions, his voice a little more demanding now that I'm dancing around the topic.

I take a calming breath and will myself the strength to possibly destroy the one good thing I have going for myself. "That day I found out that Nic had seen you and me together for the first time in your room," I drop my gaze while trying to figure out the best way to continue. "It had made him angry and he wanted to make us hurt like he was," I say, unsure why I'm still trying to defend him during all of this. I should just spit it out and tell him what's going on. He deserves to know. Rip it off like a bandaid. "Nic was the one who called Vincent and had his sons show up at your house."

Colton swerves off the side of the road, slamming his foot down on the brakes. His car skids, the back tires flying out to the side and forcing Colton to hastily correct himself. "The fuck did you just say?" he demands, whipping his gaze to me the second the Veneno comes to a complete stop.

My heart breaks at my betrayal. He deserved so much better than that. "I'm sorry," I whisper. "I should have told you the second that I found out but you would have retaliated and I couldn't have you in a war against the Widows. I just … I couldn't. He would have tried to kill you and I couldn't have that. I couldn't be the reason that he came after you."

Colton slams his hand down on the steering wheel so damn hard that I expect the airbag to come bursting out into his chest. His hands curl around the steering wheel, turning his knuckles a bright white. "Nic sent the DeCarlo brothers to my home?" he confirms. "Nic is responsible for all of that shit?"

I nod. "He is. However, he just told them to come and scare us a bit. He told me that he watched the whole thing and when he saw what they were doing, he tried to call it off but they wouldn't respond. They were determined to cause as much hell as they possibly could."

"And you believe a fucking word that bastard says? He killed both of our fucking dads and had the nerve to stand in front of us as though he didn't do a goddamn thing. He came into my home, he stood by your side for months, every day lying to you, betraying your trust. I'm fucking sorry, Jade, but I won't let him get away with this. Dominic Fucking Garcia is going down and I don't care if I have to stand against every fucking Black Widow to make it happen."

"Colton," I breathe. "You can't. You don't know what you're getting into. These guys … they're not just kids who grew up in a bad neighborhood, they're killers. They love it and they won't stop until you're gone. You can't declare war against them. It won't end pretty."

"I won't be declaring shit," he tells me, clearly pissed off with me but the fact that he hasn't thrown me out speaks volumes. Maybe he really is serious about making this work. Maybe he is prepared to look over my shortcomings and take me as I am—flaws and all. "I'm going to hit him where it fucking hurts and he'll never see me coming."

My hand flinches in his, the thought of Nic getting hurt still tearing at my soul but it's a feeling that I'm going to have to get used to because I won't try to stop him. I trust Colton and if this is how he wants to deal with this, then I'm standing by his side through thick and thin. Nic has wronged me one too many times.

"What about the others?" he asks. "Were they in on this?"

I shake my head. "No. They found out only after the fact and handled Nic themselves."

"I don't give a shit if they handled Nic. No one takes my revenge from me."

I nod, understanding his pain as clear as day. There's something a person just has to do themselves, something that a stand-in just won't cut it for. "You haven't thrown me out of your car yet," I note, biting down on my bottom lip as I look up and meet his eyes.

"Don't get me wrong, Jade. I'm fucking furious with you. You should have told me the second you found out, but I understand why you didn't and I can't fault you for that, but if you ever keep something like that from me again, you and I are going to have problems."

"I won't," I whisper. "You have my word."

Colton nods, reaching across the car and taking my hand. He pulls it up to his lips and brushes a gentle kiss over my hand. "I only just got you back, Jade, and watching you walk away isn't something I'm willing to see again. I wasn't kidding before, I fucking love you and I'm all in. You and me until the end, even if it means we have to tear each other to shreds just to get there."

My lips pull into a twisted grin, watching as the change of topic has the anger slowly fading out of him. "Just for the record," I tell him. "If it came to tearing each other to shreds, I'd definitely win."

"Are you really sure about that?" he questions, checking his mirrors and pulling back out onto the road to take us home. "I'm pretty fucking certain that I'd let you win just so I could see that proud grin on your face when you think you've finally outdone me."

"No one ever lets me win."

"Really?" he laughs. "All those times I would walk away at the beginning, do you really think that was because I couldn't handle you or because I wanted you to fall in love with the idea of being able to beat me."

My brows pinch. "And why the hell would you do that?"

"Because when you think you already have a win in the bag, you let your guard down, and then taking it out from under you is so much more satisfying."

My mouth drops as a shocked gasp sails out of me. "No, you wouldn't do that."

He looks across at me, his eyes sparkling with laughter. "Wouldn't I?"

My mouth drops, realizing that he one hundred percent would. "You little bitch. Fuck you. I was so proud of myself for being able to take down the egotistical bastard making my life a living hell."

He laughs. "I know. Watching the little house kitten thinking she could take on a fucking lion was pretty entertaining so thank you for that."

I roll my eyes and glare out my side window. "Word of warning, Carrington. Those who underestimate the little house kitten usually end up with scars."

"In that case," he murmurs, keeping his eyes on the road. "Let's hope that Dominic Garcia underestimates you."

We return to the Carrington mansion and I can't help but feel happy to be here. I feel a million times lighter despite the hell that's going on in my life. Milo is having a shit time but I know he's going to be alright. I still have absolutely no idea how this bullshit is going to go down with Nic and the Widows, but I know it's going to be bad.

Despite all of that, I'm happy. I feel as though I've removed all the toxicity from my life. Questions finally have answers and while there's still so much to work through, I can finally start to discover who I really am.

Jude is gone and no longer someone that I have to fear. Nic is on his way out and the fuckers who burned their mark on the back of my neck will be handled when the time comes. As for now, I have Colton, a shitload of new friends—who wouldn't dream of stabbing me in my back—and as always, I have my mom.

Speaking of …

Colton brings his car to a stop out front of his flawless mansion and I don't waste a second opening the door and running around to the stairs. I just spent the last few minutes of the car ride home explaining exactly what had gone down between me and Mom and now that I'm home, I can't possibly go another second without making this right.

Colton can hardly keep up with me as I race up the stairs and before I know it, I'm barging through the door, feeling a million times better knowing that there's no chance in hell that I could run into Laurelle. I race through the mansion, aiming for the staff quarters when I hear the familiar sound of the vacuum coming from down the hallway.

I hurry after it, knowing damn well that there's only one person in this mansion who would have the nerve to use the vacuum and make all that noise while the Carrington's are still in the house.

I step through to the private kitchen and find Mom in the sunken living room, vacuuming the most expensive rug that I've ever had the pleasure of sinking my toes into. As she turns around, she finds me flying toward her, only having the slightest chance to brace herself and throw her arms out.

I slam into her chest and her arms wrap around me, tears instantly forming in both of our eyes. "Oh, my sweet, sweet girl," she cries into my shoulder as I do exactly the same to hers while she shuts off the vacuum with her foot. "I'm so sorry. I handled it wrong. I should have been there for you. I failed you. I want you to feel as though you can come to me about everything and the one time you need your mommy the most, you couldn't. I should never have made you feel that way. I swear to you, my sweet angel, I will never make you feel like that again."

"No," I say, wiping my tears against her shirt. "I should have been honest with you. I didn't want to hurt you. You were so happy here and I didn't want to be the reason that you started worrying. You'd already been through so much with losing Dad. I couldn't bear the thought of adding to that pain. I know how you worry and I feared that you would regret the decision to come here when in reality, this is the best thing that has ever happened to us."

"Oh, honey. When will you realize that I'm the parent in this relationship? You don't need to always be strong for me. You went through something traumatic and I wasn't there for you when you needed me and I will always bear that on my soul, but I promise you, you always have been and always will be my number one priority. I will be better. From now on, you will never feel that you can't come to me. I just wish I'd have been there for you. I would have just sat there with you and we would have cried until the pain went away."

"I know," I whisper. "I hated keeping it from you. I was so ashamed. I felt like I had failed you with every single life lesson you've ever taught me. I allowed myself to be vulnerable and because of that, I got hurt."

"No, no. You didn't do anything wrong. That awful boy took advantage of you. He hurt you. You were victimized and attacked. You did nothing wrong but try to be comfortable in your home. You are not at fault. Do you understand me? You are the most beautiful, bravest, strongest, courageous, intelligent, and loving human being I have ever had the pleasure of knowing, and don't you ever forget that." she tells me, holding me impossibly tighter.

My eyes close as I sink into her hold, taking every ounce of love she has on offer. "I love you," I whisper.

"I love you too my sweet baby girl."

I pull back and meet her eyes that are so similar to mine. "We're turning over a new leaf," I tell her. "From now on, there are no secrets between us. Straight up honesty."

"I agree," she says, taking both of my hands.

"In that case," I say, letting out a shaky breath. "Why don't you sit down? There are a few things I've discovered over the past twenty-four hours, things that we really need to talk about."

# CHAPTER 35

**M**om takes a seat on the couch just as Colton walks into the room. He takes one look at us and the grim look in my eyes and spins on his heel, only to stalk right back out again. I can't blame him. This isn't exactly a place I want to be either.

How am I supposed to tell my mother that the man I brought into our lives is responsible for killing her husband?

I take a shaky breath and mom reaches for my hand, giving it a gentle squeeze. "What is it, honey? Do you need me to come down to the police station with you to give your statement?"

"Oh," I say, slightly taken by surprise. "No, I uhh … well, actually yeah. That would be good, but that's not what I needed to talk to you about."

Her brow raises, knowing it must be something serious after I went to the added effort of asking her to sit down. "What else could there possibly be to talk to me about?"

"It's about Dad," I warn.

Her brows fly straight back up. "What about him?"

"More about who killed him."

Mom's body freezes and she stares at me with fear. "You know?" she questions, her hands beginning to shake. "You know who did it?"

A single tear falls from my eye and I try to find the strength to continue, knowing that she deserves the absolute truth. I can't hide this from her. He was her husband and this isn't just hiding little details from her, this is life and death.

I meet her eyes and feel the heartache creeping up my chest but I push it back down, intent to get this out. "It was Dominic, Mom. I found the dagger in his room last night. He killed Dad and then he killed Charles Carrington to keep it quiet."

Mom pulls back, sucking in a gasp and staring at me as though I'm telling some sick, twisted joke. "Dominic?" she questions in horror. "No, Ocean. That's not funny. Who told you to say that?"

"I really, really wish I was joking," I tell her. "He betrayed us. He killed my dad and he's not even sorry about it. He stood in our living room and promised me that he would find whoever did it, but he was lying. It was him."

Tears begin to well in her eyes as it starts to sink in. "Nic did it? The boy I've always treated as a son? The boy who I welcomed into my home?"

I drop my gaze, too ashamed to meet her eyes. "I'm sorry. He told me last night because he was backed in a corner and couldn't lie his way out. This is all my fault. I brought Nic into our lives and ..." A strangled cry cuts me off as the emotions come up with the force of a freight train, completely pulling me under until I'm drowning under its weight. "If I knew ... if I'd have just ..."

"No, no, no, honey," Mom says, throwing her arms around me and crushing me into her chest. "How could you have known? You did nothing wrong. You discovered the truth and you came to me right away."

She rocks me back and forth like she used to do when I was a kid and we sit there for nearly an hour, lost in our tortured thoughts.

Only when her tears have finally dried, does she ask about the finer details and I tell her everything I know, hating that I have to be the one to break this news to her. If the cops cared about people like us, they would have found this out months ago and this could have been a wound that was already beginning to heal, but it seems more like one that continues to get torn wide open time and time again.

After talking it through and Mom calling it quits for the day, she settles in the pool house with a bottle of Charles' most expensive wine, suddenly not giving a shit about the man that she used to see as charming, especially after learning that I was bought and that's the only reason why we ended up here.

As all the truths came spilling out of my mouth, the weight of their ugliness lifted off my shoulders until I finally felt like I could breathe.

I find myself in Colton's shower, turning the heat right up and allowing the hot water to wash away the pain of the last few days. Colton's words in the parking garage went a long way to helping heal what was broken inside of me, but they won't do anything to take away the sting of Nic's betrayal.

I wash my hair and scrub my body clean as though I'm somehow able to cleanse myself of all of the bullshit.

Nothing will take it away, nothing except time. The sooner I accept that the sooner I'll be able to move on. I just have to figure out how I'm going to get by without having Nic in my life. It's one thing hating him for lying and knowing that deep down I'll eventually forgive him, but this is the end of the chapter for the Nic and Ocean love affair. We're officially done. I'm closing the book. There is not a damn thing that Nic could say or do that will make any of this okay.

The minutes tick by and I find myself staring at the expensive marble tiles of the shower wall before realizing that my whole body is beginning to prune. I step out of the shower and pull the white towel around my body, soaking in its warmth and admiring its soft brush as it drapes over my skin. I'll never get used to how amazing these towels are. I would have loved to have this kind of luxury growing up, but on the other hand, if I had become accustomed to this as a child, I wouldn't consider it so damn special now.

It's the little things, I guess.

I fold the towel around my body and stand in front of the mirror brushing through my long hair. My eyes grow heavy and despite it being the middle of the day, the emotional roller coaster of the last twenty-four hours has me more than ready to call it a day. I could seriously get in bed right now and not wake until this time next week.

With my hair still damp from my shower, I twist it up into a bun before stepping out of the bathroom and into Colton's bedroom. I find his eyes already on me, studying the natural curves of my body and I can't help but make my way over to him.

I missed him more than I could ever admit. I've never known pain like that before and it just proves how right this is. I was meant to be here with him and no matter what, I feel like all roads would have led right back to him.

Colton is my guy, my man, and my heart. I don't know how it took me so damn long to realize it. I felt the connection right from the very start but I was confused about what it meant. Not anymore. I've never been so certain.

I stand before him, staring down at his hooded eyes as they rake over my body. His hand is propped behind his head, showing off the strong bicep, bulging from his arm. He's so deliciously perfect.

I haven't felt his touch in so long. I guess catching some z's can wait just a little while longer. After all, it wouldn't be right for me not to prove to him just how much I've been missing him.

I reach for the top of my towel and with a quick flick of my fingers, the world's softest material falls in a heap at my feet. The low, needy growl that rumbles through Colton's chest is all the satisfaction a woman could ever need and has me stepping out of the towel and climbing into his lap.

I straddle his waist, feeling him already hardening beneath me as his warm hand falls to my hip. His fingers spread, claiming as much skin as possible and sending goosebumps flying across my body.

My nipples instantly begin to harden, already begging for his attention.

Colton reaches up, scanning his soft gaze over my face with awe shining brightly in his eyes. I don't think anyone has ever looked at me this way. It sends butterflies soaring as my heart explodes with love.

His fingers play in my hair until the bun comes undone and my hair spirals down over my back, landing in soft curls over my shoulders. "Mmmm," he groans, his lips so damn soft as they curve into a satisfied smile. "That's better."

I brush my hair back over my shoulder wondering how that could possibly be better. My hair is heavy as hell and there's no way that it just dropped from the bun like a shampoo commercial. I can guarantee it would have dropped down more like a sack of shit, but if he liked it, then I'm cool with that.

I rock my hips back and forth, grinding against him and feeling his hard length right where I need it as his heated gaze roams over my body. His hand slides up my side, leaving a wake of shivers spreading over my skin.

I need so much more.

Colton sits up and instantly takes my lips in his, kissing me deeply but not even touching the surface of giving me what I need.

I reach down over his wide back and scrunch his shirt up in my hands before pulling it over his head and finally feeling his bare skin against mine. I never want to fight with him again, but if it means getting this in return, I'll scream and walk out every day of the week.

His fingertips trail down my skin like the softest silk and I crave their touch, their power, and domination. They skim over my hip and I muffle a gasp at the sweet tickle but it's gone before I really have a chance to register it.

His fingers drop down between my legs and my eyes instantly roll in my head as he finds exactly what he's looking for. His fingers rub intoxicating circles over my clit, pulling a groan from deep within my chest.

My hand weaves into his hair, keeping him close, and just when I thought I couldn't take it anymore, two thick fingers slide deep within.

"Holy fuck, Colton," I moan against his lips as his fingers explore everything I have on offer.

"That's right, Jade."

Fuck, I love those words on his lips.

I tip my head back and he doesn't miss a single opportunity, dropping his lips to my neck and instantly hitting the sweet spot under my ear. Everything clenches deep within me and I can't wait a second longer. My hand dives down between us and slips inside the front of his sweatpants, desperate to feel his velvety skin.

He's rock hard and I don't waste a second curling my fist around his impressive length. I pull him out of his sweatpants and put that monster on full display. My mouth instantly waters. All the pleasure I could give him … damn. I want it so bad.

My body is set alight and his lips trail down to my breasts and he sucks my pert nipple into his warm mouth, electricity burns throughout my body.

I can't wait.

There will be plenty of time for all the other stuff later. I need to feel him inside me. I need to take all his pleasure and I need to scream his name, only then once our bodies are thoroughly exhausted will I start all over again, this time with his heavy cock in my mouth and my tongue working up and down his length, tasting everything he has on offer.

My thumb circles over his tip and I don't waste a second, raising up on my knees. Reading my body, Colton reluctantly pulls his hand away as I line him up with my entrance. I bite down on my bottom lip and then ever so slowly, I sink down onto him, feeling inch by inch as he completely fills me.

I groan low and in response, his cock twitches, sending fire burning within me. "Fuck, Jade," he groans, his eyes hooded as he takes my waist. "I need you to start moving."

My arms hook over his shoulders and I drop my face into the crook of his neck, nowhere near ready to move as I soak up the feel of him seated deep within me. My lips begin moving over the sensitive skin of his neck and only then do I allow us the slightest bit of relief.

I rock my hips, feeling him move within me like the most sensual massage. I hardly even moved but just that slight feel of his cock slipping within me holds all the fucking power in the world.

It's intoxicating and I need it all.

Not holding back, I rock my hips again, feeling my clit grind down against him. I do it again, and again, and again.

My eyes clench and as his hands slide around and take hold of my ass, giving it a firm, encouraging squeeze, I can't hold back any longer. I pick up my pace and fuck my man the way he deserves to be fucked. I give my all, taking everything while giving it all right back.

Colton groans, his hand continually roaming over my skin while his lips find mine with an intense urgency. Our bodies grow sweaty but we're not stopping. Nothing will hold us back from getting exactly what we're looking for, what we're craving, and desperately needing.

His hands find mine, lacing our fingers and giving a tight squeeze. He curls our joined hands around my waist and raises his ever so slightly, using his momentum to flip me onto my back. He hovers over me, somehow managing to do it without once slipping out of me.

He picks up my rhythm without skipping a beat, only in this position, he's somehow able to push so much deeper that I practically feel him in the back of my throat. His lips come down on mine and he worships my body like I'm the goddess of all things pure.

"Fuck, I love you," he murmurs against my lips, sending my heart into overdrive. Those words are so sweet on his lips, so full of passion, fire, and honesty. I can feel his love pulsing through my veins, and I know I will never get enough.

"I love you too," I whisper before capturing his lips and kissing him deeply.

He sinks into me, grinding against me as he moves in and out, making me hyper-aware of the places deep within my body that I didn't even know I had. My body quickly burns with his touch and the familiar pull of my orgasm begins to build within me. "I'm going to come," I pant.

Colton grins against my lips, loving the knowledge that the way he worships my body has me coming so completely undone. "Fuck yeah, baby. I want to hear you scream my name."

He instantly picks up his pace and I throw my head back, unable to handle the intensity but I stay along for the ride, knowing that when I come, I'm going to do so much more than just scream his name.

It builds higher and higher, and as he grunts holding out, I know that it's going to be absolutely mind-blowing. He thrusts deep into me one more time and I cry out as my orgasm finally tears through me, so intense and full of power. I clench down on him and scream his name as my nails dig into his strong muscles.

He doesn't stop moving as my pussy pulses around him, squeezing as tight as humanly possible. I feel him come hard, spurting his warm seed into me, and only once I've finished riding out my orgasm does he still within me, dropping down and gently brushing his lips over mine. "I will never get tired of you."

I lift my chin and brush my lips over his again. "I'm counting on that," I tell him, feeling his love burning brightly within me, completely encompassing my heart and holding it hostage.

His body drops down on top of mine while keeping himself propped up as to not squish me beneath his impressive size. "You're amazing," he whispers. "I don't ever want to be without you again."

"Me too," I murmur, my lips stretching wide across my face. "But we need to work on your email skills. Even in writing, you're an egotistic, demanding asshat."

Colton laughs. "Tell me that you wouldn't have done the same after being blocked from everything, which by the way, I'd appreciate it if you unblocked me now, thot."

My mouth drops open. "You did not just call me a thot."

He laughs and flinches within me, his cock still hard and ready for more. His eyes sparkle with mirth and as that familiar, teasing grin twists across his face, I know that it's on. "What are you going to do about it?"

Well, well … if that's the game he wants to play, then that's the game he's going to get.

# CHAPTER 36

I wake in the early hours of Friday morning to the sound of my phone's familiar buzz somewhere in Colton's room. I pull myself out of his arms and prop myself up onto my elbow, feeling the welcoming, raw burn from my lady bits. It was a big day with Colton yesterday and it was hours before we finally dropped into bed and crashed.

Usually, that wouldn't be an issue but after the exhaustion of the day that I'm probably going to refer to as hell day, I probably could have used those extra few hours of sleep. I don't regret it though, being back here in his arms just feels so right. I should never have walked out the way that I did. It's as though I didn't have a hold of my emotions at the moment. Everything is setting me off, every small conversation has me in tears, every normal reaction is intensified.

We skipped right over dinner and it shows in the way that my stomach instantly grumbles but it feels far too early to even consider getting out of bed and making myself breakfast. Especially when I have this warm bed right here with Colton's welcoming arms wrapping around me. Who could resist?

My phone dings again and my head whips around in the dark room, searching it out. In the thirty seconds that I've been awake, I'd already forgotten the reason that I woke in the first place.

I drag myself out of bed, hating the feeling of the cool night air brushing against my skin as I slip out from beneath the warm blankets. Colton groans, feeling around the bed. "Where are you going?" he grumbles in a sleep-filled tone, opening one eye and watching as I traipse across his room.

"I'm just grabbing my phone," I say on a yawn, scooping the offending item up from the floor, just where I left it when I came upstairs after talking to Mom and instantly pulled my clothes off in favor of a scalding hot shower. My phone had been in the back pocket of my jeans and that's exactly where it stayed.

With my phone in hand, I trudge back to bed and slip in the blankets beside Colton where he instantly falls back into a deep sleep, more than content having me in his arms. I curl into his side and as I unlock the screen of my phone, my eyes begin squinting against the harsh light. There's nothing quite like staring at a phone in a dark room. It's one of the worst feelings, it's right up there with stepping on a lone lego.

My eyes slowly adjust to the brightness and as I look over my notifications, I find that my phone must have been going insane all night. There are missed calls and texts from all the boys sure enough having heard of my betrayal against Nic but I can guarantee that they haven't heard the full story. Milo has been checking in, bored in his small hospital room, and even the girls have been wondering if I'm back, but what woke me was the familiar sound of incoming emails.

I hardly ever get emails unless it's bullshit spam and promotional stuff that I accidentally signed up for while trying to win a competition, so the fact that I heard that same ping at least four times had my curiosity peaking. Who would even be emailing me now anyway? That's insane. I don't think I've even given my email address out to anyone. I'm pretty sure that the last email I got, that wasn't Colton demanding I unblock him and wasn't from Bed, Bath, and Beyond's latest catalog, was when Colton's account sent out a notification that I'd gotten a pay rise, and even then, I haven't actually read it. It still sits in my inbox waiting for me to do something with it.

I press on the little email icon and open the app to find the usual mess that is otherwise known as my inbox. There are four new emails, all from unknown senders but the subject titles more than have my attention. These are my student loan applications. I applied to as many as I could that fit my criteria and staring at them now, my stomach sinks.

Why would all four applications come back at the same time? That doesn't seem normal.

My tongue pokes out and rolls over my suddenly very dry lips as my thumb hovers over the first email, absolutely terrified of reading what's inside.

If this isn't what I need it to say … I'm fucked. What am I going to do? I have to get this. I can't be that girl who doesn't go to college and doesn't get my life together. Going back to Breakers Flats isn't an option for me, especially now. I need to make something of myself. I need to make myself, my mom, and my father proud. Besides, my only other option is to have Mikhail Russo come and claim me as his own. I'm sure that would make my father ecstatic.

Letting out a sigh, I remember that I like to brag about having balls of steel and I suck up the courage to figure out if I'm doomed or not.

I click on the first email and my world stops.

*Your application for a student loan has been rejected.*

Fuck.

I fly through the emails, checking over the other three, my body freezing with the panic pulsing through my veins.

*Your application for a student loan has been rejected.*

*Your application for a student loan has been rejected.*

*Your application for a student loan has been rejected.*

No. No, no, no. This can't be happening. How did I get rejected? I fit the criteria for every application. I ticked all the little boxes as I went. I shouldn't have been denied. I should be reading over four congratulatory emails and trying to figure out which option was the best to accept.

This isn't right.

What am I supposed to do? I need college. It's the only road in my mind that takes me to where I want to go. I refuse to be some girl who lives off her boyfriend's generosity for the rest of my life. I have to make my own way in the world. I just have to. Not affording college isn't an option.

Tears well in my eyes and slowly roll down my cheek as I read over the emails again and again. What am I going to do? Colton said that if this didn't work, he could always talk to the dean. Apparently, he owed Charles a favor. Maybe we could work out some kind of payment plan but I doubt that I'll ever make the kind of money to quickly pay off student fees. Mom will insist on helping but I don't want to do that to her. She should be focusing on rebuilding everything we lost after Dad died, not spending her hard-earned money on me. That's not fair, and despite the way she insists on doing it, I won't let that happen.

Feeling my tears dropping off the side of my face and splashing against Colton's arms, I slip out of bed, not wanting to wake and alert him. I'm not ready to share this news with him yet. I need a few hours to process and only then when I've finally let it sink in will I have that conversation with him. Besides, I know how it's going to go and I don't think I have the strength to deny his offer right now.

I grab the throw blanket off the end of Colton's bed and wrap it around myself before slipping out of his bedroom. It's just past five-thirty in the morning and I'm sure he'll be waking up soon for his usual morning workout and when that happens, I don't want him to see the devastation on my face. I feel like every time he looks at me lately, that's all he sees. It's just one hit after another and I don't know how much more I can take.

I trudge through the quiet mansion and take myself up to the private living area that Colton had shown me the night of the Gatsby party. I open the massive windows and drop down on the wide couch, pulling the throw blanket tighter around my body as I look out at the impressive property.

My phone rests in my hand, feeling heavier than it ever should have the right to feel. I try to calm my wild emotions but find it near impossible. I never used to be like this. This isn't me. I've always had control of my emotions. I've always been able to reel them in and put a lid on it, except I just can't anymore. I've been a mess.

I try to go over my options with a clear mind and realize that they're not great. I could try to pay as I go to get through the first semester without running out of cash, or I could ask Colton for help.

Fuck. These options suck harder than a prostitute attending a private party for the Bellevue Springs elite.

I remain curled up on the couch, just staring out the window until the early morning sun is peeking through and hitting me right in the eyes. I glance down at my phone and realize that I've been sitting here for nearly two hours.

My bladder is screaming at me and after waking up to find I'm not in his bed, I'm sure Colton would be worried, though it's not like he's blown up my phone yet.

I pull myself off the couch but as I go, a cramp tears through my lower stomach and I groan in pain, instantly dropping back down onto the couch. Either my bladder is really, really full, and is now angry with me or I'm finally getting my period.

I've suffered from PCOS and have had irregular periods since I first hit puberty and to be completely honest, it freaking sucks. Other women have it so much worse than me and it completely affects their lives. Me, I just have to put up with not knowing when my period will come. Sometimes it's right on schedule and will be there every month, other times, I could go for six months without it. It's been a solid three months since my last one but I'm really not surprised. I'm sure all the stress and bullshit I've been through lately also has something to do with that.

The cramp finally eases and I try getting up again, this time being able to find my feet without any added drama and I thank my body for complying for once.

Dropping the blanket onto the couch, I make my way into the closest bathroom and quickly glance around. I haven't been in this one before. It's actually kinda nice in here, though definitely on the larger side of things. I really don't get why Charles insisted on building a house with so many bedrooms and bathrooms. There's no way he could ever have had a use for it all. I also don't understand the need for having more bathrooms in a house than bedrooms. That just boggles my mind.

Being the nosey bitch that I am, I find myself peeking in the cupboards and roll my eyes at how it's fully stocked. There are shampoos, conditioners, body washes. I mean, who is actually going to use this stuff? I don't think anyone else has actually stepped foot into this bathroom since before Charles was killed by my supposedly best friend.

I open the drawer next and find more menstrual supplies than any woman could ever need and I search through the options, you know … just in case. There's nothing worse than having your period come up and surprise you, only to find yourself not prepared.

As I search through all the products and stare at a diva cup in horror, my fingers brush over a box that has my world coming to a standstill.

Pregnancy tests.

My brow arches. If I'm going to be technical, then yes, it's a possibility—but it's on the lower end. Having PCOS makes it difficult for me to get pregnant anyway so the chances are slim, yet for some reason, I find myself picking up the box.

Colton and I have been having unprotected sex which in itself is fucking stupid, but it couldn't hurt to take the test anyway. In the grand scheme of things, I guess it's better to know than to leave it. What's one wasted test? Besides, I know those cramps all too well. It's definitely my period coming and judging by how bad it hurt, it's going to be a nasty one.

I take the box, as well as all my other supplies over to the toilet with me and sit my ass down. The cool porcelain stings my ass for the slightest moment as it gets accustomed to the chill. Desperate to pee, I tear the box apart and quickly glance over the test. I've seen chicks do this in movies all the time. You just hold it down there, pee on it, and wait, right? It couldn't be that hard.

Feeling confident that I'm overthinking things, I get it over and done with before finishing up on the toilet. I find myself glancing at the bidet that almost seems to be staring at me, enticing me to climb aboard and ride the bidet train.

I mean … I have two minutes to wait before I can check the test results. I wonder if I was to hit the right spot, if it'd be worth it …

Nah, that's insane. What am I thinking?

"Sorry," I mutter to the bidet, pulling my underwear back up my legs and starting to feel the nerves creeping through my bloodstream as the pregnancy test seems to draw every ounce of my attention. "Not today, buddy."

What is it about pregnancy tests that make you feel so damn sick? The waiting kills me. I've only ever had to do one before and that was with Nic. I knew for certain that I wasn't but he wanted me to check anyway. Even then, I hate the waiting. The what-ifs are always a killer.

I pace the bathroom, walking around and around in circles, trying not to look while failing at every turn.

The seconds tick by painfully slow and then finally I allow the anticipation to subside as I take hold of the test and flip it over. My hands shake with nerves.

Please, please, please be negative.

I glance down and scan over the results, my heart racing with fear until my whole world stops.

Fuck. This isn't good.

# CHAPTER 37

Oh, no, no, no, no, no.

Pregnant? I can not be pregnant.

Colton is going to have a heart attack and Mom is going to whoop my ass. How could we have been so stupid? Unprotected sex?

FUCK.

What were we thinking?

How am I supposed to tell him that I went and got myself knocked up? From the very start, he would accuse me of being just like the other girls who come around here looking for their meal ticket and wanting just this to claim a piece of the Carrington fortune.

Fuck going to college now. I guess that was all an epic waste of my time.

I see it happen all the time to girls. They get pregnant and scared, wondering how the hell they're going to survive but it's one of those things where you always think 'no, that wouldn't happen to me.'

What am I going to do? I'm only seventeen. I haven't even had a chance to live yet. I know Colton will support me but he's always going to wonder if I did it on purpose, always assuming that I was trying to lock him down. He's going to hate me.

"Holy fuck," I groan, pacing the bathroom once again with the test in my hand. I glance down at it and double-check the instructions. Maybe I read it wrong. There has to be some kind of mistake.

I can't be pregnant. I have too much to do. Too much is at stake.

I drop back down onto the toilet seat and tear at the test in my hand. My whole life is going to change. I'm not ready to be someone's mother. I'm not even ready to be responsible for myself.

Panic surges within me and before I know it, it's nearly eight in the morning and I've spent far too long pacing the bathroom. I have to go and figure this out. I have to talk to Colton. He'll know what to do.

I grab my phone and tuck the test safely into my hand before rushing out of the bathroom, leaving Colton's blanket right on the couch. I can come back for it later.

I race down to Colton's room and as I push through the door, I find him stepping out of the bathroom with the steam from the shower blowing out behind him, making him look like some kind of exotic God. He stands before me with only a towel wrapped around his narrow waist and drops of water slowly trailing down his muscled body.

My mouth instantly waters.

Shit. No wonder I so willingly jumped him without protection. This is how I ended up in this situation in the first place.

"There you are," he says, giving me a warm smile that hits his eyes in just the right way, leaving them sparking with warmth. "I was starting to worry. Where did you disappear to?"

I gape at him for a moment, my mind too distracted by the test in my hand to be capable of forming a proper response. He steps toward me and I find myself hiding the test behind my back, unsure why I didn't just come right out and tell him. "I, umm … couldn't sleep," I tell him. "I was just chilling upstairs."

His brows pinch together as he walks over to me and snakes his hands around my waist. He pulls me against him, the fresh smell from his shower overwhelming me with need. "You should have told me," he grumbles, dipping his face into my neck and kissing me there. "I'm sure I could have found something for us to do."

"I'm sure you could have," I say with a laugh that sounds fake coming out of my mouth. "But no, you need your rest. It was a big day for you yesterday too and now you need to get dressed and start your day."

"Get dressed?" he questions. "In all the time I've known you, not once have you told me to get dressed. In fact, I was starting to think that perhaps you preferred me with no clothes at all."

I roll my eyes, this time the laugh so much more real. "You're an idiot, Carrington," I tell him. "But you'd be right. I do prefer you without any clothes but if you drop that towel right now, neither of us is going anywhere today and I kinda need to go out this morning."

"Out?" he questions. "Where to? It's Friday morning. You have school starting in just over an hour."

"I know," I say with a cringe. "I umm … just have to go and see someone."

His brows furrow as he raises his chin, knowing damn well that I'm being shady. "Do you want me to come?"

I shake my head. "No, that's fine. You already missed work yesterday. I'll be fine."

"Do you need a car?" he questions, choosing to trust me rather than continuing to question me, knowing I'll be back with answers when I'm ready.

"Is that okay?"

"Yeah," he says slowly, releasing his hold on me and walking toward his closet before getting busy picking out today's business attire. "You can take the Audi. It was serviced over the weekend so it should drive like a dream."

I give him a small smile and nod, feeling as though not speaking up right now is somehow lying to him. Hell, I don't even know where I'm planning on going. All I know is that I just need to get out and give myself a chance to think. "Thanks," I tell him with a soft murmur. "I'll be back as soon as I can."

"I know," he says, finally choosing a suit that would make him look like any woman's wet dream. He walks out of his closet and leans against the door frame, keeping his eyes trained heavily on mine. "Is everything okay?"

I walk into his arms and raise my chin. My lips brush over his and I give him a tight smile. "Honestly," I tell him, needing to keep him optimistic. "I don't know. But I'm going to work it out and when I do, you'll be the first to know."

"You're worrying me, Jade. If something is going on, let me help you."

"I will," I promise. "I just need to wrap my head around it and understand what's going on first."

Colton's lips drop to mine and he presses the softest kiss to my mouth. His voice drops to a low whisper that instantly wraps around me. "Are you sure?" he questions. "You look kinda freaked out."

"Yeah," I whisper. "I'm okay."

"Alright then. Don't be gone for too long."

With that, Colton kisses me once again and as he releases me to start getting ready for his day, I slip out of his room and dash down to the pool house, feeling the test still resting so heavily in my hands.

I barge into the pool house and narrowly avoid running into Mom who thankfully overslept and doesn't have a minute to stop and chat. She hurries out the door while calling over her shoulder that she left breakfast out for me.

I call out a brief thank you as the door slams behind her, knowing that I'm more than likely to skip eating this morning. I don't think I can stomach it right now, but then, if I truly am pregnant, maybe eating and looking after this unborn baby is in my best interest.

Shit. There's going to be so much that I'm going to have to do to get ready for this, but what's worse is telling my mother that at only thirty-six she's going to be a grandmother. She's going to kill me.

I quickly dress in my school uniform, knowing there's a good chance that I won't even make it to school today but hey, I need to be optimistic. This might be my last chance at getting an education.

After getting ready and eating a small bite of breakfast, I quickly check in with Milo and make sure that he's doing alright. I have no idea where I'm going today but had he said that he was having a shitty time, I would have been there in a heartbeat. I can only imagine what he would have to say about the little situation that I've just gotten me and Colton into.

Letting out a sigh, I head out of the pool house and walk back to the mansion. I find the keys on the kitchen counter waiting for me and it instantly brings a smile to my face. He is so damn thoughtful. How could I have ever thought that he was anything like Nic? Sure, he has some pretty dark secrets, but he's also the most incredible guy I have ever known.

Making my way into the garage, I find the Audi and can't help but take a shaky breath. Expensive cars and mansions are going to be my child's life. He or she will never know the heartache and struggle of living day to day without food or electricity and while that's the most I could ever ask for my child, it also scares the hell out of me. Am I doomed to raise an entitled heir or heiress who doesn't understand me?

I am in way over my head here.

Diapers. Breastfeeding. Crying.

Can I handle that?

I start the engine and just as I knew it would, it purrs to life beneath me, reminding me just how good Colton has it. I press the button for the garage door and it instantly raises, opening up to the long driveway ahead and leaving me with endless options.

I hit the gas and before I know it, I'm flying up the road with absolutely no plan.

I just drive. Using the time to clear my mind but two hours later, I'm still just as lost while standing in front of a hardwood door.

I take a breath, wondering what the hell I'm even doing here and knock.

A minute passes and then finally, I hear the sound of the door handle jiggle. I should run. I should take my ass back home and go to school. I'm not ready to face this.

The door peels open and all too soon, a scowling Elijah is standing in front of me, opening my view up to the small apartment he shares with his older brother, but I don't look past him as judging by the scowl that rests over his face, he sees me as the enemy.

"What are you doing here?" he demands, adjusting his position in the doorway to make it clear that I'm not welcome, but I don't miss the twinge of regret that flashes in his eyes as he takes that harsh tone with me.

"Give it a rest, Eli. Nic clearly didn't tell you the full story because if he did, you'd be on your knees begging me not to hand him in."

His brows furrow as he leans a little closer. "What the fuck are you talking about?" he questions, glancing up and down the hallway to make sure none of his neighbors can overhear. "What did he do?"

I shake my head. "I'm not here to talk about Nic, Eli. I need your help."

He takes my hand and gives me a hard tug, pulling me into his small apartment, the very same place that I've spent countless nights sleeping on the couch, the very same place that I lost my virginity all those years ago. "Why?" he demands, always the first to jump to my rescue and instantly trusting my word that there's so much more to the story than what Nic would have shared. "What do you need?"

I swallow hard, glancing up and meeting his concerned stare, knowing that no matter what, I'll always be able to trust him. I hold up the positive pregnancy test. "I fucked up."

# CHAPTER 38

My hands shake as I lay back on the flimsy protective paper that lies against the doctor's table. My knees are up and my underwear has been tossed carelessly on the ground. Why did I listen to Eli? I should have gone with my gut instinct to keep ignoring the problem. Maybe I could have made it the whole way through the pregnancy before actually admitting that something was going on.

Colton wouldn't notice. He's a guy, they hardly ever notice that kind of stuff.

"Would you just calm down?" Eli demands, standing up near my head and holding both of my hands in just one of his. "You're going to be fine."

"How do you know that?"

"Trust me, O. This isn't my first visit to this particular doctor's office."

"Bullshit," I gasp, wide-eyed as we wait for the doctor to come back to complete the dating ultrasound after confirming that I was definitely up the duff. "You knocked someone up?"

A laugh bubbles up his throat as a sick grin twists across his face. "Two someone's," he confirms, looking guilty as shit. "Scariest fucking days of my life."

"You're lying."

"I swear," he says. "Why do you think the doctor has been scowling at me since the second we walked in here?" he points to my stomach. "He thinks this is another one of my messes."

"It doesn't help that you told him you were the father."

Eli shrugs his shoulder. "They wouldn't have let me in if I was just some dude you picked up off the street. Though, I'm still kinda wondering how I ended up here in the first place. Sebastian would have been better at this."

"I know," I say, "But you owed me. You didn't think you were going to get away with making me check out your diseased infected dick without any consequences, did you?"

Eli groans low and lets out a heavy sigh. "I was wondering when that bullshit was going to come back and bite me on the ass."

"Well, today is your lucky day."

The doctor walks back in and we both shut the hell up as my nerves skyrocket. I don't exactly know what a dating ultrasound consists of but from the position he's got me in with my knees open and a blanket draped over my knees, covering the goodies, it can't be good.

"Alright, Oceania," he says, powering up the ultrasound machine and pressing a few buttons. "We're going to do an internal ultrasound to measure the fetus and find just how far along in your pregnancy you are. Now, what that means is," he says, picking up a long, narrow wand that looks very suspicious, "That I'm going to insert this into your vagina which—"

"What?" I question, wide-eyed, gripping onto Eli's hand as though it's my only lifeline. "You're going to stick that where?"

"There's no need to fret. There will be a slight pressure and only mild discomfort. For the most part, you won't even know it's there."

Wait. I'm only seventeen. Is this even legal without a parent or guardian by my side? Though, I guess he's a doctor and it's not as though he's going to be fucking me with the thing … just inserting. But in the long run, I'm going to have to get used to my lady bits being overtaken for the next nine months.

Eli squeezes my hand. "I've seen it done before," he tells me. "There's nothing to worry about."

I glare up at him as the doctor puts the wand back down and pulls on a pair of latex gloves. "You get an opinion when you grow a vagina," I tell Eli, watching the doctor out of the corner of my eye and taking in the way that he takes the wand again and begins squeezing something onto the end of it, something that looks suspiciously like lube.

The doctor looks back at me. "This will help me measure the baby and make sure that everything is looking healthy in your womb."

Well shit. This just got serious.

"Okay," I nod, knowing there's no need to be nervous but feeling it anyway.

The doctor doesn't hesitate and pushes the ultrasound wand inside of me and I can't help the slight gasp that comes bubbling out of me. "Geez," Eli grumbles. "You didn't sound that excited when it was me going in there."

I squeeze his hand as tight as humanly possible, knowing damn well that it's got to hurt. "Shut up, otherwise I'm going to take the damn thing and shove it up your ass so you know exactly what it feels like."

"Noted," he says. "Shutting up now."

The doctor grunts as a sign telling us to shut the fuck up and concentrate on what's going on. He moves the wand around and just as he promised, I feel pressure but nothing uncomfortable.

I see the small little blob on the monitor and assume that's the baby, then get a little more certain when the doctor starts taking measurements.

Holy shit. That's my baby. That's a miniature version of Colton inside of me and for some reason, just a bit of the fear begins to fall away. This is real. It's actually happening and it's time that I get on board and make sure this baby has every chance possible to grow healthy and strong, just like his or her daddy.

It takes a little while but eventually, the doctor pulls the wand out of me and asks Eli to leave the room to give me a chance to get dressed.

I'm going to be a mommy.

Fuck. I'm going to be someone's mother.

I'm only seventeen. This is insane. I didn't even picture myself having kids at thirty.

They both walk out and I jump down from the table to make myself decent again, having to clean myself up. I pull my pants back on and then take a seat, calling Eli and letting him know that I'm good for him to come back.

He does just that and explains that the doctor had gone to print out my results. A nervous silence falls through the room as we wait for the doctor to come back. Every few minutes Eli softly murmurs that I'm going to be okay, and even goes as far as offering to be my baby daddy if Colton was to run.

The doctor shows his face again and I take a deep breath. It's time to get this over and done with so I can go home and work out how I'm going to break the news to Colton.

"Alright," he says, handing me a small picture of the baby, one that I still struggle to make out. "Everything looked really good. Your baby is developing just as expected for seven weeks."

Seven weeks?

Eli grins beside me, proud of the news while the doctor continues. "I'm going to need to see you regularly throughout your pregnancy, so on your way out, make sure to book another appointment for next month to check your progress."

My mouth hangs open as I nod.

"Do you have any questions?"

I just stare at him.

Seven weeks.

"Okaaay," Eli says slowly, taking my hand and trying to pull me up. "Let's get out of here so you can go home and tell Carrington the good news."

I gape at Eli, still struggling to understand what the doctor just told me as I mentally do the math. Seven weeks ago, Colton and I had nearly slept together, but we didn't. We were interrupted when his father was found dead on his office desk. We were so close, but that only leaves one option, an option that I just can't fathom.

"Seven weeks," I breathe. "Colton and I haven't been screwing for seven weeks."

Realization dawns on his face. "What are you saying, Ocean?"

I swallow hard, beginning to panic. "Seven weeks ago was the masquerade party. The night that Jude …"

Realization dawns on his face and he instantly begins shaking his head. "No, it couldn't be his. I was told he didn't finish. The bastard didn't fucking come in you. Your fucking rapist isn't the father of this baby." Eli shifts his gaze around to the doctor who sits there with his brows raised. "Is it possible? Could she be pregnant to a guy who didn't finish?"

The doctor presses his lips into a hard line, sensing this is a hard topic. "Yes, unfortunately, it's possible. There is a slim chance that a woman can get pregnant when pre-ejaculation occurs. I've seen it happen many times."

I shake my head, looking to Eli in panic. "I can't ... I can't have Jude's baby."

"I know," Eli says, pulling me up beside him and holding me close. "It's okay. We're going to figure this out. You'll be okay."

The doctor hands over some pamphlets and Eli reluctantly takes them. "There are options," he tells me. "Have a read over these and give it a few days to really think about what you want to do. You don't want to make any drastic decisions."

I nod and thank him and within seconds, Eli has whisked me out of the doctor's office. He takes me out to the Audi and doesn't takes his eyes from me, getting in the driver's side and patiently waiting for me to make my way around and get in. "You don't have to do this," he tells me. "Just say the word and I'll book the appointment."

I shake my head. "I ... I don't know. I need to think about this. It's a baby, not leftover dinner that you either put away in the fridge or just throw out. I can't ... I need to go home. I need to talk to Colton."

"Are you sure?" he questions.

I nod, knowing that's where I need to be.

"Alright," he tells me, hitting the gas. We get back to his apartment and he jumps out of the Audi then waits as I get back in the driver's seat. "Drive carefully, okay," he tells me. "You've got a lot on your mind and the last thing you want is to be getting in an accident."

"I know," I tell him. "Thanks for coming with me."

"Wouldn't have it any other way," he says.

I give him a tight smile, trying to forget the fact that I'm currently holding my rapist's baby inside of me. "Please don't tell the guys. I'll do it when I'm ready."

"You have my word."

With that, I hit the gas and take off up the road.

I'm having Jude's baby.

How can this happen?

Tears form in my eyes and desperation takes over me. I need to get home. I need to talk to Colton and figure out what the hell I'm going to do. The pamphlets sit beside me on the passenger's seat and I can't help but rake my eyes over them.

There are options but I don't know if I have it in me to go down that route.

What am I supposed to do? Have Colton raise a baby that isn't his? No, I can't ask that of him. I can't ask anything of him.

I need to handle this myself.

Taking a deep breath, I turn the Audi around and within the space of three minutes, I bring the car to a stop, feeling the desperation completely overtake me.

Tears flow from my eyes and as I get out of the car, I realize just how fucking stupid this is but I can't stop myself. I have to do this. I can't keep bringing Colton into my problems. He has enough of his own for now.

I step up in front of a heavy metal door and bang my fists against it three times, silently willing myself to stop crying. I hear the familiar sound of a heavy metal lock sliding out of place and chills run down my spine at how similar it sounded to when I unlocked Jude's dungeon.

The door pulls open and an expectant Mikhail Russo stands before me, watching me through narrowed eyes with his wolves at his back. If he's surprised to see me, he doesn't show it. "What do you want, girl?"

I look up at him, hating that I'm here. "I need your help."

His eyes somehow narrow further and as he steps out of the doorway and into my personal space, I do everything in my power to keep myself from shrinking back. "Understand this, pup. If you walk through my door, you're mine. You accept your position in this family." His hand comes up and brushes past the still healing burn at the back of my neck. "You live by this mark. You are loyal to me. Loyal to your family. Is that clear?"

The weight of his words sits heavy against my chest. Giving him my loyalty is the final nail in the coffin. I won't just be dead to Nic, I'll be the enemy, and that includes Sebastian, Eli, and Kai.

Fuck. They're going to hate me.

Can I do that to them?

I meet Russo's stare and raise my chin. "I'm all in."

# **<u>Rejects Paradise Series Playlist</u>**

Game of Survival - Ruelle
I'm Gonna Show You Crazy - Bebe Rexha
Nightmare - Halsey
Never Tear Us Apart - Bishop Briggs
Bird Set Free - Sia
Helium - Sia
Dusk Till Dawn - Zayn feat Sia
Heaven - Julia Michaels
Graveyard - Halsey
Bad Bitch - Bebe Rexha
Love Drug - G-Easy feat Halsey
Hurricane - Tommee Profitt
Unloveable - Delacey
Power - Isak Danielson
Cruel Intentions - Delacey feat G-Easy
Not Afraid Anymore - Halsey
Unstoppable - Sia
Monsters - Tommee Profitt
Can't Help Falling In Love - Tommee Profitt
Angel Cry - G-Easy feat Devon Baldwin
Bad At Love - Halsey
Creep - G-Easy feat Ashley Benson
In The End - Tommee Profitt
Wicked Game - Daisy Gray
Haunted - Beyonce
Gasoline - Halsey
I Feel Like I'm Drowning - Two Feet
Twisted - Two Feet
Wild Horses - Bishop Briggs
The Fire - Bishop Briggs
Killer - Vallerie Broussard

Thanks for reading!

If you enjoyed reading this book as much as I enjoyed writing it, please consider leavinge a review.

www.amazon.com/dp/B08DN3TBWN

For more information on Rejects Paradise, find me on Facebook or Instagram –

www.facebook.com/SheridanAnneAuthor

www.instagram.com/Sheridan.Anne.Author

# Other Series by Sheridan Anne

www.amazon.com/Sheridan-Anne/e/B079TLXN6K

### Young Adult / New Adult - Romance

The Broken Hill High Series (5 Book Series + Novella)

Haven Falls (7 Book Series + Novella)

Broken Hill Boys (5 Book Novella Series)

Aston Creek High (4 Book Series)

Rejects Paradise (4 Book Series)

### New Adult Romance

Kings of Denver (4 Book Series)

Denver Royalty (3 Book Series)

Rebels Advocate (4 Book Series)

### Urban Fantasy - Pen name: Cassidy Summers

Slayer Academy (3 Book Series)

www.ingramcontent.com/pod-product-compliance
Lightning Source LLC
Chambersburg PA
CBHW030948190726
48285CB00004BB/1279